Frederick George Kenyon

Poems

From a Papyrus in the British Museum

Frederick George Kenyon

Poems

From a Papyrus in the British Museum

ISBN/EAN: 9783337401078

Printed in Europe, USA, Canada, Australia, Japan

Cover: Foto ©Andreas Hilbeck / pixelio.de

More available books at **www.hansebooks.com**

THE POEMS

OF

BACCHYLIDES

FROM A PAPYRUS IN THE BRITISH MUSEUM

EDITED BY

FREDERIC G. KENYON, M.A., D.Litt.

HON. PH.D. IN THE UNIVERSITY OF HALLE
ASSISTANT IN THE DEPARTMENT OF MANUSCRIPTS, BRITISH MUSEUM

PRINTED BY ORDER OF THE TRUSTEES OF THE BRITISH MUSEUM

SOLD AT THE MUSEUM

AND BY LONGMANS AND CO., 39 PATERNOSTER ROW
B. QUARITCH, 15 PICCADILLY; ASHER AND CO., 13 BEDFORD STREET, COVENT GARDEN
KEGAN PAUL, TRENCH, TRÜBNER AND CO., CHARING CROSS ROAD
ALSO BY HENRY FROWDE, OXFORD UNIVERSITY PRESS WAREHOUSE, AMEN CORNER

1897

PREFACE

THE poems of Bacchylides, now for the first time published from the unique papyrus in the British Museum (Pap. DCCXXXIII), have been arranged, transcribed, and edited by Mr. F. G. Kenyon, Assistant in this Department.

An Autotype Facsimile of the whole MS. is published in a separate volume.

EDWARD SCOTT,
Keeper of MSS.

BRITISH MUSEUM,
November 18, 1897.

INTRODUCTION

—··—

IN the list of those whom the Alexandrian critics reckoned as the nine lyric poets of Greece, the **Bacchylides.** last name is that of Bacchylides. He stands last, as youngest in order of time, not necessarily as the least in merit, and until now we have had no means to form any estimate of his genius. His work, like that of all the lyric poets except Pindar, and like all Pindar's except his epinikian odes, had perished, and was known only in chance quotations, of which only two were of any substantial length. Now the fortune which presides over the discoveries made among the sands of Egypt, and which has hitherto given us, for its novelties and special prizes, not the greatest masters of Greek literature, but Hyperides, and Herodas, and a historical work of Aristotle, has given us a papyrus manuscript containing some twenty of the poems of Bacchylides, more or less complete ; and his name may once more be reckoned among those of the authors whose works are alive and form part of the literary possessions of the modern world.

Of the life of Bacchylides little has been recorded [1].

[1] See (in addition to the standard histories of Greek literature) Neue, *Bacchylidis Cei Fragmenta* (Berlin, 1822), Della Giovanna, *Bacchilide* (Turin, 1888), and Michelangeli, *Della Vita di Bacchilide* (Messina, 1897).

He was a native of the island of Ceos, as ancient
writers record [1] and as his own works testify [2],
His nationality. and of the town of Iulis [3]. His father's
name is given variously as Medon, Milon, and
Midilus [4], while his grandfather, who is said to have been
himself an athlete, bore the same name as the poet [5]. On
his father's side he thus had a tradition of athletic distinction, while on his mother's he was connected with
poetry, since his mother was a sister of Simonides, who
was likewise a native of Iulis [6]. It would appear that he
claimed Homeric ancestry, and a connexion with the
Pylians of Messenia ; for in one of his poems (XI. 118–
123, according to the most probable reading of the passage)
he states that his ancestors, after sacking Troy, set up
a shrine to Artemis in the territory of Metapontum, a
city which claimed foundation by a colony of Nestor's
Pylians.

The dates of his birth and death are unknown, but he is
habitually spoken of as a contemporary of
His date. Pindar (circ. 518–438 B.C.), both being junior
to Simonides (circ. 556–468 B.C.), though their periods of
literary activity overlapped. His works add no certain
chronological data, the only poems which admit of precise
determination being those which coincide in subject with
some of the odes of Pindar. The general impression left
by them, however, is that Bacchylides was the younger of
the two and the later to enter the field of poetry. Pindar's

---

[1] Strabo X. 5, 6, Suidas s. v.

[2] See Odes II. 14, III. 98, in the present collection, and frag. 71
(Bergk 48).

[3] Strabo, Suidas, ll. cc.

[4] Suidas, l.c., an epigram published in Boeckh's *Pindar*, vol. II, p. xxxi,
and *Etym. Mag.*, s.v. Μείδυλος.

[5] Suidas, l.c.   [6] Strabo, l.c.

activity begins with the twenty-second Pythiad (=498 B.C.), but there is nothing in the odes of Bacchylides which appears to go back to so early a date. Of the poems to which precise dates can be assigned (III, IV, V, XIII), the earliest (XIII) must have been written before 480 B.C., but not very long before (probably 483 or 485), and the latest (III) in 468 B.C. The poems connected with Athens (X, XVII, XVIII, XIX) would appear, in the case of the last three at least, to have been written subsequent to the Persian wars; for, though there is no direct allusion to these or any other political events, the tone in which Athens is addressed seems to imply that she had already attained that eminent position which was due to the battle of Salamis and the formation of the confederacy of Delos. The other poems afford no clue to their dates, but their literary style suggests a stage in lyric composition later than that of Pindar. The form of the ode is more conventional. The myths are introduced mechanically, with little attempt to connect them with the subject of the ode. In some cases they appear to have no special appropriateness, but to be introduced merely at the poet's pleasure. There is no originality of structure ; the poet's art is shown in graceful expression, in craftsmanship rather than in invention. It is perhaps dangerous to add that in some passages there would almost seem to be imitations of Pindar, since it is only when the chronological sequence of the poets has been determined that it is possible to say which is the imitator. In this case, however, the presumption is already in favour of the conclusion to which the consideration of the stronger originality and more marked individuality of Pindar would naturally lead us ; and if there be actual imitation at all, it is fairly safe to conclude that it is on the part of Bacchylides.

Taking wide margins, therefore, the poetical activity
of Bacchylides would seem to have ranged between 490
(perhaps too high a limit) and 460 B.C.[1] Of
his life very little is known, the principal concrete fact on record being his visit to the court
of Hieron[2], which probably took place in 476 B.C., on the
occasion of the performance of his fifth ode, the first and
most elaborate of his tributes to the ruler of Syracuse. In
this visit he was probably the companion of his uncle
Simonides and of Pindar, though it cannot be concluded
with absolute certainty that, because all three poets are
said to have been guests at Hieron's court, they were all
there at the same moment. It is, however, independently
probable that Pindar was present during the performance
of his first Olympian, which was on the same occasion as
that of the fifth ode of Bacchylides.

Visit to Syracuse.

The ancient commentators repeatedly refer to an acute
rivalry between Pindar on the one hand and
Simonides and Bacchylides on the other,
dwelling especially on such passages as *Ol.* II.
95–97, *Pyth.* II. 52–56, *Nem.* III. 82[3]. It is not out of
accordance with the impression which Pindar's poetry
gives us of his genius, to suppose that he was conscious
of his own superiority and impatient of criticism and mis-
appreciation ; but there is no adequate ground for regarding
him as constantly filled with envy and jealousy against any

Supposed rivalry with Pindar.

---

[1] Of the ancient chronologists, Eusebius attaches the name of Bacchylides
to Ol. 78 (468 B.C.), and the *Chron. Pasch.* to Ol. 74 (484 B.C.). Syncellus, it
is true, gives his name under Ol. 88 (428 B.C.), in agreement with a second
notice in Eusebius (Ol. 87 = 432 B.C.) ; but these dates can be ignored as
impossible.

[2] Aelian, *Var. Hist.* IV. 15.

[3] Mr. Bury (*Nemean Odes of Pindar*, p. 126) sees another allusion to
Bacchylides in *Nem.* VII. 105, conceiving that the term μαψυλάκας, the
scansion of which is identical with that of Βακχυλίδης, is aimed at him.

particular rival. The accusation is precisely one of those pieces of malicious gossip with which the names of great men are constantly associated, having just sufficient basis in truth to give them vitality, though the fragment of truth has been distorted and exaggerated. Certainly the poems of Bacchylides lend no support to the idea of enmity, or even ill-feeling, on the part of the younger poet. On the contrary, in the poem which appears to have been composed in direct rivalry with Pindar (Ode V), he goes out of his way to introduce with praise the name of another Boeotian poet, Hesiod, in a manner which suggests the thought that he intended to pay a graceful compliment to his own contemporary. For the rest, there is no allusion to any competitor, and the general tone of the poems indicates an equable and quiet character.

The only other detail in the life of Bacchylides which has been preserved to us is the fact that he was banished from Ceos and lived in the **Banishment from Ceos.** Peloponnese[1]. Neither the cause nor the date of this exile is recorded. The former was presumably connected with politics, as in most similar cases, and it may fairly be supposed that Bacchylides, whose profession brought him into contact with rich and powerful patrons, was associated with the aristocratical party; but he makes no allusion to such matters in his poetry (in I. 21 ff. he emphatically praises a middle station in life), and it is not in the least likely that he was an ardent partisan. With regard to the date, it was evidently later than 476 B.C.,

---

[1] Plutarch, *de Exilio*, 14. Della Giovanna (op. cit. p. 4) is wrong in quoting this passage as including Bacchylides among those who left their native countries voluntarily. On the contrary, his name occurs in the same list as Thucydides, Xenophon, and Timaeus, among persons expelled from their countries (τῶν πατρίδων ἐκπεσόντες) and reference is made to those who expelled them (τῶν ἐκβαλόντων καὶ καταστασιασάντων).

when he describes himself as sending his poem to Hieron ἀπὸ ζαθέας νάσου (V. 10); but no more fixed point seems to be derivable from the poems. The four poems (I, II, VI, VII) which celebrate Cean victories may be presumed to have been written before his exile[1]; and the same may be said of X, in which (according to a probable restoration of l. 10) he describes himself as 'the clear-voiced island bee,' and of XVII, which was performed by a Cean chorus (l. 130). It would be pressing the point too far to argue that Ode III, written in 468 B.C., necessarily belongs to the period before his exile because he there describes himself as 'the Cean nightingale'; a man does not cease to claim his nationality because he has been expelled from his country by an opposing political faction.

His residence in the Peloponnese has not left much mark **Residence in the Peloponnese.** upon his poetry. The only poems which can be directly connected with the Peloponnese are an epinikian ode in honour of a native of Phlius, and a hymn or dithyramb entitled 'Idas,' which is stated to have been written for the Lacedaemonians. Of the remaining poems, four appear to have been written for Athenians or in some intimate connexion with Athens, three for Hieron of Syracuse, two for Aeginetans (showing that Pindar had not quite a monopoly of the poetic patronage of that island), one for a Metapontine, one for a Thessalian, and one for an athlete whose nationality is unknown; while two poems which are not epinikian contain no indication of the patron for whom they were composed, beyond the Dorian character of their heroes, which may suggest a connexion with the Peloponnese, but cannot be pressed very far.

---

[1] As also the ode referred to in Bergk's frag. 58, where he is said to have celebrated his native city, Iulis.

The scholiasts on Pindar state that Hieron preferred the poems of Bacchylides to those of Pindar; but it may be doubted whether this is more than a deduction of the scholiasts themselves from the phrases in which, as they suppose, Pindar expresses his scorn of the pretensions of his rival. **Ancient estimate of his poetry.** Pindar wrote four odes for Hieron, Bacchylides three; and if the Cean poet had the last word, being commissioned to celebrate Hieron's Olympian victory in 468 B.C., it has to be recorded on the other side that, on the next occasion after the rivalry of the bards in 476 B.C. (Pindar *Ol.* I, Bacch. V) when a victory had to be commemorated, the most important part in the celebration was assigned to Pindar, and only a short ode invited from Bacchylides (Pindar *Pyth.* I, Bacch. IV). So much is clear, however, that Bacchylides continued in favour with his royal patron, whose estimate, though possibly not that of an expert critic, may yet be taken to represent the judgement of a competent literary amateur, which may reasonably have been shared by a considerable section of public opinion generally. His inclusion in the list of the nine lyric poets of Greece shows that he held a position of some eminence in the eyes of the later critics of Alexandria, though the comparative scarcity of quotations from his works would tend to show that he was less popular than Simonides, even allowing for the greater fertility of the elder poet. A well-known passage in the treatise *de Sublimitate* shows that, in the opinion of a very competent critic (whose judgement in the case of another recently discovered author, Hyperides, has been confirmed by modern taste), he was not to be compared with Pindar in genius, but was smooth, equable, and pleasing, neither rising so high as his great contemporary, nor falling so low. The same passage, however, implies that popular estimation gave him a higher rank than the critic was prepared to allow. Like Hyperides, he was easy and attractive to the reader ; and like him he continued to hold a high, if not quite foremost, position in the esteem of the Alexandrian and Byzantine students of ancient Greek literature.

How long he continued to be read is a matter of some uncertainty. Didymus, at the close of the first century B.C., wrote a commentary upon him. Quotations from his writings are found in Strabo and Dionysius of Halicarnassus (first century B. C.), Plutarch (first century), Apollonius, Zenobius, Hephaestion, and Aulus Gellius (second century), more plentifully in Clement of Alexandria and Athenaeus (third century). In the fourth century we have, besides quotations in Himerius and Servius, the express statement of Ammianus Marcellinus that the emperor Julian was fond of reading him [1]; and by far the largest harvest of fragments is derived from the collections of Stobaeus, who cannot be placed earlier than the end of the fifth century. To Stobaeus, in fact, are due no less than forty-four lines out of the 107 which (according to the arrangement of Bergk) had survived previous to the discovery of the manuscript now published, including the longest single quotation of all, the twelve-line fragment upon peace. It is therefore clear that up to about the year 500 the poems of Bacchylides were extant, whether complete or not we cannot tell, but at any rate in some substantial and coherent form. Further than this we cannot go with certainty. Two epigrams are included in the *Anthologia Palatina*, but these probably formed part of the original Στέφανος of

How long were his poems extant ?

---

[1] Ammian. Marcell. XXV. 4, (Iulianus) recolebat saepe dictum lyrici Bacchylidis, quem legebat iucunde.

Meleager (cf. *Anth. Pal.* IV. i. 34). There are several references to Bacchylides, and quotations of his words, in the scholia on Pindar, Homer, Hesiod, Aristophanes, Apollonius Rhodius, Callimachus, Aristides, and Hermogenes; but we do not know the pedigrees of these anonymous commentaries, nor whence their materials were drawn. Much may have been, and probably was, derived from the commentary of Didymus, as is known to have happened in the case of a reference in Ammonius (Bergk, frag. 10). The claims of the compiler of the *Etymologicum Magnum* and of Tzetzes, our latest authorities for any words of Bacchylides, in the eleventh and twelfth centuries, may safely be dismissed; and an allusion to him by Theophylact (*Ep.* 8, Meursius) probably does not imply an acquaintance with his works. There is no such evidence in the case of Bacchylides, as there is in that of Hyperides, of his having survived in manuscript until the very age of the revival of learning. The continuous tradition breaks off about the year 500, a thousand years after the poet's birth; and since that date we have no certain warrant that any eye has seen a complete poem by Bacchylides for a space of fourteen hundred years.

The veil has at length been lifted by the discovery in Egypt of a papyrus roll which enables us, for the first time in the history of modern scholarship, to judge for ourselves on adequate grounds what manner of poet he was. *Discovery of the manuscript.* The discovery was made by natives, to which fact the unfortunately mutilated condition of the papyrus may be ascribed. When it reached England the manuscript consisted of about 200 torn fragments. The largest of these measured 20 inches in length, and contained four and a half columns of writing; there were fourteen pieces of some considerable size, containing one

b

γ

or more columns; while the rest were small fragments
ranging from pieces measuring a few inches in either
direction to scraps containing barely one or two letters[1].
For the most part the fractures were recent, and were
probably due to the Egyptian discoverers; but in a few
places the completely different colours of adjoining fragments show that the fracture must be of old standing.
If the manuscript was deposited in a tomb (as is *a priori*
probable, though no authentic information on the point is
forthcoming), this might be due to ancient plunderers in
search of treasure; but the matter is not one of great
importance, except as indicating that the modern discoverers are not solely to blame for the present condition
of this precious manuscript.

The identification of the contents of the roll as being
the lost odes of Bacchylides was easily accomplished through the occurrence in it of
several of the known quotations from that poet, and will
be disputed by no one; but the task of establishing the
true order of the *disiecta membra poetae* was one of some
time and difficulty. In the result, however, the manuscript
has been arranged into three sections, each continuous
(though not complete) in itself, but without any immediate connexion with the others. The first measures
9 feet in length, and contains twenty-two columns of
writing; the second measures 2 feet 3 inches, and contains
six columns, with minute traces of another; while the
third measures 3 ft. 6 inches, and contains ten columns.
The total length of the papyrus as at present arranged

Size of the MS.

---

[1] Two fragments were acquired separately in Egypt by Mr. B. P. Grenfell,
who kindly presented them to the British Museum. They contain parts of
III. 8-10 and IX. 82-84; but they do not appear in the photographic
facsimile of the MS., having been received just after the photographs were
taken.

is thus 14 feet 9 inches, with a greatest height of 9¾ inches,
and it contains, in whole or in part, thirty-nine columns.
How much is lost, it is impossible to affirm with certainty.
The fragments for which it has not as yet been possible to
find a place, though amounting to forty in number, are
nearly all very small, and do not indicate a greater loss
than would be sufficient to link together the three main
sections. These considerations would indicate a minimum
length of 17 feet for the complete roll, with a content of
forty-five columns. It cannot well have been less, though
it may have been more.

When complete the papyrus must have been a very hand-
some manuscript. It is written in a fine uncial   Its writing
hand of good size, in columns of varying width, and arrange-
according to the length of the lines in them,   ment.
but ranging between 4 and 5½ inches, including the blank
space between the end of one column and the beginning
of the next, which varies, according to circumstances, from
an inch to nothing. The number of lines in each column
varies between thirty-two and thirty-six, thirty-five being
the commonest total. The lines differ of course in length,
but are throughout decidedly shorter than those which
have been adopted in the current editions of Pindar,—a fact
of some interest to students of metre. Divisions of words
at the ends of lines are not avoided. The subject will have
to be investigated by metrical specialists, but the evidence
of a manuscript so early, and moreover so carefully
written, is a weighty argument in favour of a division into
comparatively short lines, which has, moreover, this decided
advantage, that the rhythm of the lines can be easily
observed in reading them.

The text is written throughout in a single hand, but has
been corrected certainly by one, and probably by two re-

visers, in addition to the original scribe himself. In the
manuscript as originally written no titles were attached to
the poems. In a few cases (Nos. II, XIX, XX) they have
been added in the margin by a contemporary hand, which
may be that of the original scribe, but appears to be different (being finer as well as smaller than the text). The same
hand (denoted in the critical notes to this edition as A^2)
has made some corrections, but not many. Most of the
corrections, as well as the supplements of missing lines in
XVIII and XIX, have been made by a later hand (A^3),
which is not always correct in its alterations, so that its
evidence (though undoubtedly resting upon MS. authority,
as the insertion of missing lines proves) must be received
with caution. The same hand has supplied most of the
titles, though not without omissions, as in the case of
Ode V. In two cases, XI. 23, XVIII. 16, lines or
portions of lines have been supplied by a hand which,
though about contemporary with A^3, does not seem to be
identical.

    The dates of these hands can only be determined on

Its date.
palaeographical evidence, and although the
materials now extant make it possible to date
cursive hands on papyrus within reasonably narrow limits,
the case is not the same with regard to uncial hands, and
a dogmatic decision can seldom be given, except where
there is a really close similarity to a hand of which the
date is known. In the present case the writing is of
a type to which there is no precise parallel; but its
features seem to point to a date about the middle of the
first century B. C. The strongly marked Ptolemaic features
of the manuscripts of the third and second century have
disappeared; but some of their characteristics are preserved. The broad μ, with very shallow depression between

the uprights, is of a distinctly Ptolemaic type, which finds no parallel in later periods until we reach the sloping hands of the third century. The shape of v, too,—a shallow curve on the top of an upright stroke,—resembles that of other MSS. which have been assigned to the first century B. C., and has little in common with the fully-formed Roman character of the succeeding centuries. More decisive than all is the shape of ξ, which is composed of three unconnected strokes, the top and bottom ones being very long, and the middle one little more than a dot. Now, so far as extant evidence goes, the formation of ξ with three unconnected strokes is universal (disregarding the very primitive epigraphic form, where the three parallel strokes are connected by a perpendicular stroke through the middle of them) up to about the middle of the first century B. C., while afterwards it is as regularly formed without lifting the pen. That is, it is a characteristically Ptolemaic form. On these grounds it seems clear that the manuscript falls within the Ptolemaic period, and there is nothing inconsistent with this in the shapes of the other letters. At the same time the other letters have features approximating to the Roman type (e. g. a, ϵ, and σ have much the same characters as in the Harris Homer, Brit. Mus. Pap. CVII), which makes it probable that the manuscript belongs to the transition between the two styles. A date, therefore, somewhere about 50 B. C. seems on the whole the most suitable to the evidence in our present state of knowledge. A much later date could only be maintained on the supposition that the scribe was deliberately imitating an earlier type of hand; and for such an hypothesis there does not seem to be sufficient evidence.

The correctors' hands may be dismissed more briefly.

The earlier (A²) would appear to be contemporary (possibly even identical) with the original scribe. The later (A³) is in the Roman cursive of the end of the first or early part of the second century. It should be added that in the case of small corrections, such as the striking out of a letter, or the insertion of letters which have no very characteristic forms, it is very difficult to distinguish the hands: so that the apportionment of the corrections to the various hands in the critical notes must be regarded as only tentative.

The manuscript is unusually well provided with accents, stops, and other aids to the reader. The **Punctuation, accents, etc.** metrical divisions into strophes are indicated by *paragraphi*, which, however, are sometimes omitted. The accents are in many cases by the first hand, in some, it would appear, by the second, and in many by the third. Not all words, by any means, are accented, but usually the longer words, or those about which there was some possibility of mistake. No manuscript of equal age is so fully supplied with accents, but one which approaches it is the fragment of Alcman at the Louvre; which suggests the possibility that lyric poets were considered to require more aids to the reader than other authors. It is also possible, and indeed probable, that carefully and elaborately written manuscripts, such as this is, were more fully supplied than others with accents and punctuation. Some characteristics of the accentuation deserve mention. Oxytone words, instead of having the acute accent on the final syllable, have grave accents on the preceding syllables; thus κρατός is written ΚΡᾺΤΟC, παγκρατής ΠᾺΓΚΡᾺΤΗC, and so on. Some instances of a similar practice (no doubt arising from the fact that all syllables except the one bearing the acute accent were supposed to have the grave accent) are found in a few other papyri (Brit. Mus. Papp. CVII and CXIV of the Iliad)[1]. In the case of diphthongs, the accent, if circumflex, normally covers parts of *both* letters, while if acute it is placed on the first of the two.

Punctuation, in the form of a single dot just above the level of the tops of the letters, is fairly fully supplied, and generally, it would seem, correctly, so that in cases of doubt considerable weight should be attached to the evidence of the punctuation. Only in one case (XV. 47) is the point placed at the level of the bottom of the writing, and that is probably a slip of the pen.

Breathings (especially the rough breathing) and marks of diaeresis over ι and υ, either at the beginning of a word or when adjoining another vowel with which they do not form a diphthong, are generally, but not universally, added. The breathings are normally square in shape, but are sometimes partially rounded. Long compound words, such as κυανοπλόκαμος, ἀκαμαντορόας, and the like, often have a semicircular stroke placed below the point of junction, so as to show that they form a single word.

The correctness of the manuscript is a matter which can only be determined upon internal evidence, since there is no other copy with which to compare it. It is, of course, not free from *Its correctness.* errors—no manuscript is. Besides simple slips of the pen, such as Ακρσιωι for ᾿Ακρισίωι, or δυοφεον for δυοφερόν, there is a certain number of ordinary errors of transcription, such as αμφεβαλλεν for ἀμφέβαλεν, θελωσιν for λῶσιν, δ᾿εκατι for ἀέκατι, καρτερον for κρατερόν—errors which are easily detected through the metre, and which present no difficulty in restoration. Beyond these, the metre reveals certain

[1] Cf. Thompson, *Greek and Latin Palaeography,* p. 72.

corruptions which are less easy to account for and sometimes less easy to correct; such as missing syllables, as in
V. 8, 169, XVII. 37, 62, 74, 93, imperfect correspondences
between strophes, as in XI. 72 and 114, XVII. 6, 29, 72
and 95, omissions of parts of lines, as in XI. 23, XIII. 52,
XVIII. 48, and even omissions of whole lines, such as
those which the corrector has rectified in XVIII. 55–57
and XIX. 22. There are also a few cases where the MS.
reading is unintelligible, as ασαγενοντα in IX. 13, σοεινειν
in XVII. 90, 91, αιονα in XVII. 112, and τιην in XIX. 15.
Nevertheless the general impression left by a study of the
manuscript is decidedly in favour of its trustworthiness.
The proportion of mistakes is small; and it is not likely
that many have escaped detection, since the metre supplies a test which is difficult to evade. The chances
against an accidental corruption fulfilling the requirements
of metre in a lyric poem are very large indeed; and of
intentional corruption there is no trace. Further, the
manuscript preserves unusual forms which would easily
lend themselves to alteration; e. g. ἀελλοδρόμαν in V. 39,
where the MSS. of the scholia of Pindar which quote the
passage have the commoner, but obviously less authentic,
form ἀελλόδρομον; καλλιρόαν in XI. 26 instead of καλλίροον;
ἐρύκεν in XVII. 41 and φυλάσσεν in XIX. 25, infinitive
forms of a type which has been conjecturally restored in
Pindar, but which has disappeared from the MSS.; and
the dialectic forms are generally observed faithfully. The
carefulness and correctness of the punctuation are also
points in the manuscript's favour. No doubt conjectural
emendation is not only admissible but necessary in
various places; but it will have to be applied with
caution, especially in passages which are partially mutilated.

To pass to the contents of the manuscript. The papyrus, as now restored, contains twenty poems, of which six (including three out of the four longest odes in the collection) are either complete or need only such small restorations as can be made with approximate certainty; of eight more the precise length can be ascertained, but the proportion fully preserved is variable; of one a substantial portion is preserved (sixty-six lines), but an equal amount is probably lost; while five are mere fragments, varying from eight to twenty-three lines in length, of the original size of which nothing is known. In all, the papyrus contains evidence of 1382 lines (including 114 of which no letter remains, though their existence is demonstrated by the metre), without counting the unplaced fragments; and of these about 1070 are either perfect or admit of satisfactory restoration.

Contents of the MS.

In character, fourteen out of the twenty poems are epinikian, and are therefore of a type already familiar from the odes of Pindar; but the remaining six (two of which are perfect and a third nearly so) are examples of a species of Greek literature of which there have hitherto been no complete specimens in existence. The various names of Paean, Dithyramb, and Hymn, which we find in references to the works of the lyric poets, seem to have described compositions of essentially similar character, but differing according to the deity in whose honour they were written. Paeans were, of course, associated with the name of Apollo, Dithyrambs with that of Dionysus, while Hymns might not only be addressed to any deity, but might also, as the exordium to Pindar's earliest hymn shows (frag. 29), be devoted to the celebration of some legendary hero. The

The non-epinikian poems.

six poems which close the manuscript of Bacchylides in its present condition appear to include specimens of all these classes. Two (XVI and XVII) seem to be Paeans; one (XIX) may be a Dithyramb; two (XV and XVIII) contain no addresses to deities, and should therefore probably be classed as Hymns (though as to XVIII there is a further possibility which is mentioned in the introduction to that ode); while one (XX) is too imperfect to allow any certainty with regard to its character. In many respects these six poems form the most interesting feature of the new discovery, and effectively widen our knowledge of Greek literary art.

The beginning and end of the manuscript are both lost, and the sequence of the three sections which **Order of the poems.** survive can only be determined on internal evidence. As arranged in the present edition, the epinikian odes stand first, and begin with two poems (one long and one short) in honour of a fellow-countryman of Bacchylides. Next come three in honour of Hieron, the poet's principal patron; and these are followed by two more in honour of a Cean athlete. Then come poems in honour of athletes of various nationalities, a Phliasian, an Athenian, a Metapontine, and an Aeginetan. The second section contains a long poem for another Aeginetan, and ends with an ode written for a victory won by a Thessalian in some Thessalian games. Thus the present arrangement places at the beginning the poems in honour of the poet's own countrymen and his royal patron, and at the end the only ode not connected with one of the four principal festivals; while in the middle the two Aeginetan odes are brought together. This seems to have the recommendation of probability, and there are no other grounds to go upon. It may be observed that no arrangement will bring together all the poems connected with the same festival, as in the case of Pindar, nor all those relating to the same class of contest.

With regard to the remaining section, that containing the non-epinikian poems, the question is more difficult. It is imperfect at both ends, but the first extant column began with the beginning of a poem, the title of which stands in the upper margin. It is possible that this was actually the beginning of the roll; but there are no means of confirming the suggestion. On the other hand, the relatively well preserved condition of this part of the papyrus suggests that it may have been on the inside of the roll, and therefore near its end; while the mutilated condition of the papyrus containing the first epinikians would be accounted for by its having been on the outside and consequently exposed to damage. The question does not admit of certain solution, and consequently will no doubt be determined differently by different persons. Fortunately it is of no practical importance.

It does not seem probable, even with the fullest allowance for its mutilated condition, that the roll which has now come to light ever contained the complete works of Bacchylides. The Original contents of the MS. fragments collected in Bergk's *Poetae Lyrici Graeci*, which include not only actual quotations, but all references which throw light on the contents of the poems, amount to sixty-nine. Of these only fourteen can be identified with certainty or fair probability in the extant remains of our roll; while of the 107 lines included in Bergk's fragments, only twenty-four can be found here. The manuscript contains examples of Ἐπινίκια (and in this instance the majority of Bergk's fragments can be identified) and apparently of Hymns, Paeans, and Dithyrambs (though only one fragment from these three categories can be identified); but nothing from the Προσῳδίαι, Ὑπορχήματα, Ἐρωτικά, Παροίνια, or Ἐπιγράμματα, and three-fourths of the unclassed fragments are unaccounted for. It is possible, perhaps probable, that the manuscript, when perfect, contained a complete collection of the Ἐπινίκια, and (since the extant fragments to be accounted for are few) it *may* have contained the Hymns, Dithyrambs, and Paeans; but it seems certain that the remaining categories were not represented. However, since these latter poems may fairly be regarded as of minor importance, it is legitimate to conclude that we have, in the manuscript before us, specimens of the best work of Bacchylides, and are justified in forming therefrom a deliberate estimate of his genius.

The titles, dates, state of preservation, and structural

Analysis of the poems.
Ode I.
arrangements of the several poems are discussed in the introductory notes prefixed to them; but the general character of their contents can be more conveniently handled here. The first poem is addressed to Melas of Ceos, in celebration of a victory, probably in the pentathlum, at the Isthmian games. It appears to have been a long poem, of which we now possess the second half, or thereabouts. Of the earlier portion one fragment (frag. 1, at the end of the volume) is preserved, which shows that it contained some part of the story of Minos. Minos, coming to some city (the name is lost) with fifty ships and a host of Cretans, by the favour of Zeus won Dexithea for his bride, and leaving her with half his force he himself sailed away to Cnossus; while she, in the tenth month thereafter, gave birth to Euxantius. Here the fragment breaks off; but the connexion of Euxantius with the subject of the poem may be guessed from Ode II,

in which Ceos is called Εὐξαντὶς νᾶσος, a title hitherto
unknown, but evidently implying a claim to have been
colonized by the son of Minos.   Hence the mention of this
hero leads back to the main subject of the poem, and in
the part which has been more fully preserved the poet is
telling of the victory of Melas.   Melas has followed in the
steps of his father, Panthoides, who was (we gather) an
eminent wrestler, besides being skilled in medicine and
famous for his hospitality.   He, after a happy and enviable
life, has passed away, leaving behind five distinguished sons,
one of whom has now won, among other victories, the
Isthmian crown.   The rest of the poem is occupied with
moral reflections.   Virtue (ἀρετά) hath the greatest glory.
Wealth may be gained by a coward, and tends to conceit ;
but a virtuous life, with health and moderate means, is
a lot that cannot be surpassed.   In any station of life may
happiness be found, if these conditions be granted.   Wealth
is no surety for contentment ; rich and poor alike covet
something more than they have.   But he who is occupied
with trifling cares can have but this present life-time to
enjoy, while virtue, hard though it be to gain, yet when
once gained leaves behind a glorious and undying memorial.

If ἀρετά could be cultivated, as the poet implies, by the
attainment of athletic success, Melas was not
disobedient to his admonitions; for his Isthmian   **Ode II.**
triumph was presently followed up by a similar success at
Nemea.   On this occasion Bacchylides wrote his second
ode ; but it is a very brief composition, probably written
off-hand at the festival itself, for an immediate celebration
of the victory.   The poet bids Fame bear to Ceos the
news of Melas' triumph ; he recalls his Isthmian victory,
and the celebration of it with a choral hymn, adding that
now again the Muse of the victor's native country awakes

the glad music of the flutes to honour the son of Panthoides.

From his countryman, Melas, the poet passes on to his
royal patron Hieron, to whom the next three

Ode III. poems are addressed. They stand in the
manuscript in an inverse chronological order, the latest
first and the earliest last. Ode III celebrates Hieron's
last victory in the games, won by his chariot at Olympia
in 468 B.C., the year before his death. It seems to have
been sung at Delphi, on the occasion of an offering dedicated
there by Hieron in honour of his victory. Clio is summoned
to sing the praise of Demeter, queen of fruitful Sicily, and
her daughter of the violet crown, and the swift horses who
have given Hieron victory at Olympia. Happy is Hieron,
who, seeing that he has received from Zeus a wider sphere
of rule than any other Greek, does not hoard up his wealth,
but spends it in lavish splendour. The temple is now
ablaze with his gifts, the streets filled with his hospitable
distributions. It is right and wise so to win the favour of
the gods, as the story of Croesus shows. He in the days
of his prosperity gave richer gifts to Pythian Apollo than
any living man, and in the day of his misfortune Apollo
saved him from destruction. For when his city was taken
by the Persians, he built a pyre before his palace, and
ascended it with his wife and daughters, and reproaching
the gods with their ingratitude he gave orders that the
pyre should be lighted ; but Zeus sent a great storm,
which extinguished the flames, and Apollo bore him off to
live thereafter in peace among the happy Hyperboreans.
This poem, it may be observed, was written less than
eighty years after the fall of Sardis, and before the publica-
tion of Herodotus' narrative, from which it differs in several
respects, omitting all mention of Solon and making the

immolation of Croesus his own voluntary act, not the sentence of his conqueror. It is the earliest form of the legend of Croesus now extant; but it is noticeable that Pindar, two years previously, in an ode addressed to Hieron (*Pyth.* I. 94), had referred to Croesus as a type of generous profusion. It looks as if Bacchylides had taken up the allusion and expanded it into the central subject of a poem on the next occasion of his writing an ode for the Syracusan monarch.

The legend of Croesus does not, however, occupy the whole poem. It is followed by a passage, mutilated in the MS., in which the poet brings out its applicability to Hieron, and passes on to other mythological allusions which it is not easy to follow in their imperfect condition. In conclusion the poet, like Pindar before him, addresses his patron in tones of consolation and exhortation, which find their explanation in Hieron's ill-health and now approaching death. Mortal man must not look for permanence, but is happy if he can look back upon a well-spent life. Youth, once lost, cannot be regained; but (and here is the point of the admonition) it is otherwise with virtue. The splendour of that grows not dim, but is nourished by the Muse. Hieron's life has been glorious, and should not be lost in silence; so, for its commemoration, may men hereafter be grateful to the 'nightingale of Ceos.' With this little touch of self-laudation, uttered in a far less confident tone than the similar claims of Pindar, Bacchylides closes the series of his odes to Hieron. It is, in fact, the latest utterance of his to which a date can be assigned.

Two years earlier (according to the chronology which seems most probable) he had been called upon to celebrate a chariot-victory won by Hieron at the Pythian games. His rival (if so he is to be called),

Ode IV.

Pindar, was likewise invited to contribute an ode on this occasion; and the result was the splendid first Pythian, with its picture of Zeus' eagle and the description of Aetna in eruption. The task assigned to Bacchylides was more modest, a short ode of twenty lines, perhaps intended for immediate performance at Delphi. Part of the poem is lost, and the rest offers no points of interest (though some of difficulty), being merely an expression of the glory of victory in the great games, and the pleasure which comes to the poet from celebrating them.

The poem which stands next in the manuscript is the earliest in time of the series addressed to Hieron, having been written probably in 476 (see introductory note to

Ode V.

the poem itself) and certainly not later than 472. It is the longest poem in the whole collection, and is preserved intact, with the exception of a few words which can be supplied with practical certainty. Like the preceding ode, it celebrates a victory which was also commemorated by Pindar; but whereas in that case the contribution of Bacchylides was short and insignificant, in this instance both poets alike were commissioned to produce an elaborate ode of victory. The first Olympian of Pindar and the fifth ode of Bacchylides consequently bring the two poets into direct competition (as previously in Pind. *Nem.* V and Bacch. XIII); a competition of which Pindar at any rate was fully conscious when he wrote (*Ol.* I. 111) ἐμοὶ μὲν ὦν Μοῖσα καρτερώτατον βέλος ἀλκᾷ τρέφει and (ll. 115, 116) εἴη σέ τε τοῦτον ὑψοῦ χρόνον πατεῖν, ἐμέ τε τοσσάδε νικαφόροις ὁμιλεῖν, πρόφαντον σοφίᾳ καθ' Ἑλλανας ἐόντα παντᾷ. It was an occasion on which both would be anxious to show their full strength; and it is fortunate that the poem of Bacchylides should have survived in so good a state of preservation. The exordium is less elaborate than Pindar's, consisting of a direct address to the 'fortunate war-lord of the chariot-driving Syracusans,' soliciting his attention to this hymn, sent from the 'divine island' of Ceos by his guest-friend, the renowned servitor of golden-filleted Urania. This confident introduction is followed by a striking passage (forming, in a sense, Bacchylides' answer to Pindar's boasts, quoted above), in which the poet boldly compares himself to an eagle, the messenger of Zeus, who cleaves his way through the upper heights of air, rejoicing in his strength, while lesser fowls crouch in fear below. The heights of earth's mountains set no bounds to his path, nor the rough waves of the sea, but he dwells in the illimitable Chaos of air, far-seen of all. And wide as his range is through the heavens, so wide is the poet's range in praising the sons of Deinomenes for their victories alike in the games and in war. Thence by an easy transition the poet passes to the recent Olympic victory of Pherenicus, the immediate occasion of the ode, describing in animated phrases the speed and the triumphs of this unbeaten race-horse. So far the tone of the poem has been happy and exultant; but the next words suggest an undercurrent that is not so prosperous. 'Blessed is the man to whom the god giveth a portion of good things, and to live a prosperous life through to the end with enviable fortune; for no mortal man may be wholly happy.' And so he passes, without more preface, to the story of the meeting between Heracles and Meleager in the lower world, where Heracles beheld the souls of mortals flitting 'like leaves on Ida' to and fro, and among them one great shade stood forth pre-eminent, so formidable in appearance that the hero seized his bow and prepared to defend himself. But the shade stopped him and, in answer to his inquiries, told his name and sad story; of the hunting of the Calydonian

boar, the strife for its hide, the inadvertent slaying of his
mother's kinsmen, and his mother's vengeance in the
burning of the log on which his life depended. Heracles
weeps to hear his tale, but asks (since lamentations cure
nothing) whether Meleager has a sister living, whom he
might take to wife. Meleager tells him that he left an
unmarried sister at home, Deianira ; and here the poet, with
an abruptness and absence of transition which is characteristic
of him (and is also sometimes found in Pindar at the end of
a story), breaks off his narrative, bidding Calliope stay her
car there and praise Olympian Zeus, and the river Alpheus,
and Pelops, and Pisa, where Pherenicus won glory for Hieron.
Then with a few lines, including a quotation from Hesiod
(perhaps intended as a compliment to the other ' Boeotian
poet,' Pindar), and a prayer for Hieron's peace and prosperity, he winds off his poem to a quiet close. It may not
have the splendour of Pindar, but it has the grace and ease
of an accomplished artist in verse ; and if the story of
Meleager is meant to suggest a consciousness that, in
Hieron's case too, greatness was not unaccompanied by
misfortune, the hint (for which the explanation is easily
found in the known ill-health of the Syracusan ruler) is
lightly and delicately introduced.

The praises of Hieron being concluded the poet returns
to his own countrymen, and the sixth ode

Ode VI.

celebrates the victory of Lachon of Ceos in
the stadium at Olympia. Like Odes II and IV, it is quite
a short poem, apparently written to greet him on his return
to his native island. The rejoicing in Ceos was the greater
because the island had won two victories at the festival,
another of its representatives having been successful in the
boxing. This fact is alluded to in the poem, but otherwise
its contents call for no comment.

Lachon's victory had already been celebrated at Olympia, as a reference in the poem just mentioned proves; and the ode which stands next in the **Ode VII.** manuscript appears to be the poem composed by Bacchylides on that occasion. Unfortunately only the exordium of this ode is preserved, containing an address to the final day of the festival, on which the victors' triumphs were celebrated. It was, however, only a short composition; for one column, now almost entirely lost, contained nearly the whole of this poem and part of another. Of this other, which was also very short, we have only the last six- **Ode VIII.** teen lines, which contain a glorification of its hero's numerous successes at Pytho, Nemea, and the Isthmus, and a prayer that his career may be crowned by a victory at Olympia. The name and nationality of the victor are unknown, as well as the class of contest in which he was victorious.

These three short odes are followed by a poem of over a hundred lines, addressed to Automedes of Phlius in honour of his victory in the pentathlum **Ode IX.** at Nemea. The poet calls upon the Graces to inspire him, that he may sing of Phlius and the plain of Nemea, where Hera nurtured the lion that was to be the first of Heracles' famous labours. There, at a later date, Adrastus and his comrades, before their disastrous expedition against Thebes, founded the Nemean games in honour of the child Archemorus, who was killed by a snake while his nurse, was guiding the army to a fountain. The omen was evil, but Amphiaraus could not turn the heroes back from their doom. From this allusion to the foundation of the Nemean games the poet passes on to the success of Automedes, which is described at some length. His strength is like that of Heracles, who passed through all the earth, over-throwing mighty opponents, reaching in his travels the extremities of Ocean and the Nile, and the passage of the Thermodon, where live the Amazons, the daughters of Ares. This forms a rather artificial transition to the mention of two other daughters of Ares, Thebé and Aegina; but at this point the manuscript is seriously mutilated, so that the connexion of these personages with Phlius and Nemea is left uncertain. Probably it is through the Theban Dionysus, the founder of Phlius, who is mentioned near the end of the poem. The second half of the poem is represented only by tantalizing fragments, of which nothing substantial can be made.

The tenth ode is likewise mutilated, though not to so large an extent. It is addressed to an **Ode X.** Athenian, who had been victorious in the foot-race at the Isthmus. He was a member of the tribe of Oeneis, but his name is lost. The poem contains no myth, being entirely occupied with the praises of the victor. He was a runner of remarkable distinction, and had been twice victorious at the Isthmus and twice at Nemea, besides other successes at Thebes, Argos, Sicyon, Pellene, Euboea, and Aegina. The poet concludes with gnomic reflections on the variety of ways in which a man may strive for distinction, and on the uncertainty that veils the issue of all pursuits. Chance weighs down the scale after all; the admiration of good men is the noblest end to aim at. Wealth too has its advantages;—but here the poet cuts off his admonitions abruptly, and concludes his ode with the reminder that festal celebrations are the accepted sequel to a victory.

The ode which follows next is one of the most interesting among the *epinikia*, both on account of its **Ode XI.** contents and for its allusions to the poet's own lineage. It is addressed to Alexidamus of Metapontum,

victor in the boys' wrestling at Pytho. His success was
a brilliant one, and it served to some extent to compensate
for a disappointment which he had experienced at the
previous Olympian festival, where (as the poet affirms) he
would have been victorious but for an unfair decision on
the part of the judges. The consolation which he had
now received must be ascribed to Artemis, the patroness
of Metapontum ; and the poet passes on to tell of another
act of kindliness on her part, when she healed the daughters
of Proetus. These maidens were smitten with madness by
Hera, because they vaunted that their father was more
wealthy than the consort of Zeus ; and in their madness they
fled from Tiryns (where Proetus ruled, in a fortification built
by the Cyclopes, having quitted Argos on account of a quarrel
with his brother Acrisius, in which much blood was shed).
For thirteen months they wandered over the forests and
rocks of Arcadia, till at last their father prayed to Artemis
to intercede for them with Hera. The intercession was successful, the maidens were restored to sanity, and they built
an altar and a temple to Artemis at Lusus, where the cure
was brought to pass. Thus it was Artemis who wrought
this good ; Artemis, to whom the poet's ancestors, return-
ing from the sack of Troy, established a sacred grove by
the banks of the river Casa, where now Metapontum
stands.

The column which holds the end of the ode to Alexidamus contains also the first eight lines of
a poem addressed to Tisias of Aegina, in **Ode XII.**
honour of a victory in wrestling at Nemea. But after this
column the papyrus breaks off, and it is uncertain how
much is lost. The ode to Tisias may have been a short
one, in which case a single column would have been
sufficient to contain the end of it, with the ten lines which

are missing from the beginning of the following poem; or
it may have occupied several columns of which no trace
now remains. The manuscript has suffered very severely
in this part; for the whole of the second section of it,
which begins here and occupies seven columns, has been
put together out of a number of fragments, of which the
largest only measured a few inches each way. Nearly
the whole of it is occupied by a single poem, addressed
to Pytheas of Aegina, which probably followed immediately
after that to his compatriot Tisias. The special
interest of this poem lies in the fact that it
celebrates the same victory as Pindar's fifth Nemean ode,
a victory won in the boys' pancratium at Nemea. As
in the case of Ode V, we have here Pindar and Bacchylides
competing with elaborate poems of considerable length;
for Bacchylides' poem is only two lines shorter than his
great ode to Hieron. Unfortunately it is not equally
well preserved; and a good deal of restoration has been
necessary in order to bring three-fourths of it into an
intelligible condition. Pindar selected the myth of Peleus
as the central topic for his ode; Bacchylides chose the
more obvious subject (and one frequently used elsewhere
by Pindar in his Aeginetan poems) of Ajax, the great
legendary hero of Aegina. By way of prelude to this, he
seems in the mutilated opening lines of the poem to have
introduced a prophecy of the slaying of the Nemean lion
by Heracles, thus adopting a different legend of the origin
of the Nemean games from that which he employed in
Ode IX. This leads naturally to the usual topic of the
glory to be won by great achievements at the games, and
thence to the victory of Pytheas, who has won great distinction for Aegina. The mutilation of the following lines
leaves it a little uncertain by what exact transition the poet

Ode XIII.

introduces the name of the nymph Endaïs, the wife of
Aeacus and mother of Peleus and Telamon, who became
the fathers of the two great heroes of the Greek host
before Troy, Achilles and Ajax. The body of the poem
is occupied by the story of the defence of the ships by
Ajax, following sufficiently closely the Homeric narrative.
In a swift, picturesque passage is narrated the rout of the
Trojans whenever Achilles appeared on the field, their joy
(like that of storm-tost sailors at the dawn of day) when he
retired in wrath to his tent, their triumphant advance to
the sea-shore and the line of the Greek ships. This part
of the poem is preserved in a fairly complete form, but the
crisis of the narrative, the defeat of the Trojans by Ajax, is
lost. The story must have ended abruptly, as is usual
with Bacchylides, when once the crisis was reached ; and
the concluding portion of the poem reverts to the immortality of glorious achievements, the fame and good govern-
ment of Aegina, the praises of Menander, the trainer of
Pytheas, and (after a lost passage of twelve lines) the hospitality of Lampon, his father. The last is a topic to which
Pindar likewise makes allusion, but otherwise the topics
and structure of the rival odes are quite distinct, and
furnish very fair examples of the different styles of the
two poets.

One more epinikian ode remains, not written for any of
the great games of Hellas, but for a victory
at a festival of local importance in Thessaly, **Ode XIV.**
known as the Petraea. The victor, Cleoptolemus, was
a Thessalian and probably a member of one of the noble
families of Thessaly, since the contest in which he engaged
was the chariot race. Only twenty-three lines of the poem
are preserved, and these are entirely occupied by the exordium. This leisurely rate of progression suggests that

the ode may have been a long one, but the mutilation of
the papyrus leaves this uncertain. The poet begins with
moral reflections, chiefly on his favourite theme, the multi-
farious ways of excellence, among which that of virtue is
alone trustworthy. In this case it is especially justice,
or the observance of the due fitness of things, that is the
object of praise. The music of the lyre and dance is out
of place in a battle, the clang of brass in a festival; taste,
or a right judgement in all things, is the fairest lot. On
this, and presumably as exemplifying this precept, the
poet introduces Cleoptolemus and his victorious horses;
but here the papyrus breaks off, and we have no clue to
the remainder of the poem.

The third section of the papyrus is that which will
The non- probably arouse the keenest interest, on
epinikian account of the novelty of its contents. The
poems. ten columns of which it is composed reveal
to us, for the first time, complete examples of lyrical
poems of a public or festal character, other than epinikian. The precise classification of these six poems
has been discussed elsewhere; but whether they be
Paeans, Dithyrambs, or Hymns, they are all poems
similar in type and general structure. The *occasional*
character, which is essential in epinikian odes, here disappears. If they are addressed to any deity, the reference
to him is of the briefest, occupying but a few lines at the
beginning or end of the poem, and having no bearing on
its topics or character. Putting aside this purely formal and
perfunctory indication of the occasion of the poem, they form
a group of lyrical idylls, each presenting a legendary scene,
without framework, explanation, or moralization. They are
exercises in lyrical scene-painting, brief pictures of dramatic
moments in heroic story. The poet rarely tells his tale to the

end. He paints his picture almost in impressionist style ;
he poses his characters and then drops the curtain. Only
in one case (XVII) is a detailed narrative attempted ; and
there it is a single dramatic scene, with its *dénoûment*,
that is set before us. The pictorial character of the
poem is still preserved, and is emphasized by the fact that
the scenes of this very poem served in several instances
for the subjects of actual paintings. It is this pictorial
character that explains the abruptness, especially in
ending a story, which is characteristic of this group of
poems.

The first among them presents a scene from the story
of Troy, and has a double title: ' The Sons of Antenor,
or the Demand for Helen's Surrender.' The first half of the
poem is almost wholly lost, and therewith the explanation
of the first half of the title. For some reason

Ode XV.

which is not clear, the sons of Antenor apparently serve as the escort of Menelaus when he enters
Troy in order to demand back his stolen wife. His plea
is heard before the assembled people in the agora ; and
this is the scene which the poet wishes to place before us.
The gathering of the Trojans is described in a few lines,
and in a somewhat magniloquent style the Muse is invoked
to declare 'who first began the plea for justice.' Menelaus stands forth to speak, but he has barely opened his
speech with a laudation of justice, which is within the reach
of all, and a condemnation of ὕβρις, which brings the de-
spisers of justice to perdition, when the poem is abruptly
concluded. No word is said of Helen, nor of the result
of the embassy ; that is supposed to be known from
Homer. The poet wishes only to present us his word-
picture of a striking scene, the Greek prince standing up
amid the Trojan crowd to assert his claim for justice.

The title of the second poem in this group is lost, but

Ode XVI.   the central figure in it is Heracles, whose name

may therefore be provisionally attached to it. The second title of the preceding poem (Ἐλένης ἀπαίτησις) is familiar as the name of a play by Sophocles; the second poem presents us a scene which Sophocles has also utilized, the fatal gift of Deianira to Heracles, received by him during his sacrifice on the Cenaean rock. After a proem addressed to Apollo, which seems to indicate that the ode is to be classed as a Paean, the poet plunges at once into his subject. 'We tell how of old Amphitryon's bold-hearted son left Oechalia devoured by fire; and he came to a wave-beaten headland, where he purposed to offer of his spoil to Cenaean Zeus, the cloud-encompassed.' But while he was yet about to sacrifice came the fatal gift of Deianira, sent when she heard that her husband was bringing the white-armed Iolé to his home; little did she know what the future hid, when she received it first by the river Lycormas from the hands of Nessus. There the poem closes, as abruptly as the first.

It is followed by a much longer poem, which is perhaps

Ode XVII.   the most interesting in the whole collection,

and is practically intact. Like the first, it has a double title, Ἠΐθεοι καὶ Θησεύς, 'The Youths and Theseus.' The youths who give the title, and who form, as it were, the chorus of the drama, are the captives brought by Minos from Athens, to be offered to the Minotaur. With them, according to the familiar legend, went Theseus, to save them by slaying the monster in his labyrinth. But the legend given in this poem is far from familiar. It is briefly mentioned by Pausanias and Hyginus, and forms (as we now perceive) the subject of two very important vase-paintings; but otherwise it is wholly unknown. Minos takes a fancy to one of the maidens among the captives, and insults her. She screams to Theseus for protection, and he at once calls on Minos to desist; they may be justly doomed to death, as the penalty of defeat in war, but not to outrage. If Minos is son of Zeus, and thinks he may lord it over them on that ground, Theseus himself is son of Poseidon, and claims to resist him with equal right. Minos takes up the gauntlet thus thrown down, offers to prove his own divine origin by a sign from Zeus, and challenges Theseus to establish his descent from the Sea-god by bringing up from the depths of the sea a ring, which he throws overboard. Zeus responds to his son's prayer by a flash of lightning; whereupon Theseus promptly springs into the sea. Minos rejoices, thinking that he is rid of his rival; but Theseus is carried by dolphins to the halls of Amphitrite, where he receives (presumably in addition to the ring, which, oddly enough, is not mentioned) a robe and a chaplet, with which he returns triumphant from the depths of ocean, reappearing by the side of the ship to the confusion of Minos and the exultation of his companions. Amid their songs of triumph the poem closes, with a perfunctory address to Apollo which serves to label it as a Paean. It is a fine poem throughout; the dramatic colloquy between Minos and Theseus is vigorous, and the several stages of the narrative are vividly and picturesquely delineated without waste of words. The archaeological interest of it is dealt with in the introductory note to the poem itself.

Theseus is likewise the hero of the ode which follows, and gives it its title, though he does not appear on the scene in person. The poem is cast in **Ode XVIII.** dramatic form, being a dialogue between Aegeus, king of Athens, and Medea, his queen. It is possible that the second interlocutor is a chorus of Athenians, but the former view seems to suit the situation and the language better. In performance, each speaker would be represented by a semi-chorus, just as the speeches of Minos and Theseus in the preceding poem were no doubt sung by the chorus, not by single actors. The scene is laid in Athens. Medea asks the meaning of the trumpet which she hears, and of the anxiety which she sees impressed upon her husband's brow. Aegeus answers that a herald has just crossed the Isthmus with news of a wonderful youth, who has done great deeds of strength; he has slain Sinis and the sow of Crommyon and Sciron and Cercyon and Procoptes (more familiar as Procrustes), and Aegeus 'doubts how these things may end.' Medea asks for a fuller description of the youth. Comes he with an army, or alone? Only with the protection of the gods could such deeds be attempted without mishap. Aegeus rejoins that two men only attend him, that he carries sword and javelins, a Laconian helmet on his head, on his body a purple vest and woolly Thessalian cloak. His eyes flash volcanic fire; he is a youth in the first flower of his age, but experienced in the joys of fight; and he is making for glorious Athens. The picture is complete, and with this fourth strophe the poem ends,—a striking and in some respects unique addition to our knowledge of Greek lyrical compositions.

It is the last poem in the manuscript which is complete.

Ode XIX. The ode which follows, entitled 'Io' and stated to have been composed for the Athenians, is complete only in the first half, the second half having lost the terminations of all its lines, though its drift can fairly be made out. It is less striking than the poems which precede it. After an exordium in which the poet exhorts his Muse to strike out some great path of song, suitable to the glory of Athens, he plunges at once into the story of Io, of her flight from the wrath of Hera, of her persecution by Argus and his death at the hands of Hermes, of her coming to Egypt and the birth of Epaphus, who became the ancestor of Cadmus, and thereby of Semelé and Dionysus. It is a slight narrative sketch, with less pictorial effect than its predecessors, and, in spite of its exordium, with no obvious bearing upon Athens or Athenian history.

The twentieth and last ode is a mere fragment. It is entitled 'Idas,' and was composed for the Lacedaemonians. It contained the legend of **Ode XX.** Idas and Marpessa, who eloped, with Poseidon's help, from the palace of Evenus, Marpessa's father, who, failing to overtake them, threw himself into the waters of the Lycormas. But of the manner in which the story was told by Bacchylides we can form no idea; for only the first eleven lines of the poem are preserved, and even they have lost their ends. The papyrus here breaks off abruptly, and so lets the curtain fall once more on the poet whom it, and it alone, has revealed to us.

The foregoing sketch may serve to show the plan and scope of Bacchylides' odes. Of their poetic **Character of** merit no one can as yet claim to give more **Bacchylides'** than a personal opinion; and on that it is not **poetry.** necessary to dwell at length here. One point there is, however, which it may be permitted to emphasize, in order that the poet may receive a just verdict. There is danger that his real merits may be overlooked through pressing the comparison between him and Pindar. Circumstances bring them into inevitable competition, and it is impossible to exclude comparisons from one's mind; but in fact the characteristics of the two poets are wholly dissimilar. In

Pindar (orthodox though his sentiments are in substance) the note of individuality is prominent in all his style. His brilliance, his force, his rapidity, and therewith his difficulty and occàsional obscurity, are marks of a strong and original genius. Like Aeschylus, like Dante, like Shakespeare even at times, like Shelley, like Browning, his fertility of imagination and expression throws stumbling-blocks in the way of the reader's understanding, and he is at once strikingly impressive and markedly difficult. Bacchylides is the negation of all this. He is conventional in the forms of his poems and restrained in the expression of his sentiments. No one will ask what his philosophy of life was, or, asking, will ask in vain. His praises of virtue are conventional, the echo, no doubt, of the gnomic poetry of early Greece; his deities play their conventional parts without question or comment. His merits are merits rather of art than of invention. He has lucidity, grace, picturesqueness, and an easy command of rhythm. He is an artist in verse, rather than a great original genius. If Pindar is associated in our minds with Aeschylus, the affinities of Bacchylides are with Sophocles, in some respects (such as the more conventional treatment of his lyrics) with Euripides. 'It is all triumphant art, but art in obedience to laws.' These are qualities which are liable to be over-looked when placed side by side with poets of greater originative force. Yet the easiness of Bacchylides is not all shallowness. The gift of lucid expression is not one universally possessed. He has a strong sense of natural beauty, which is not too commonly manifested in Greek literature. Witness his fine picture of the eagle (V. 16–30), his vigorous enjoyment of the racehorse's speed (ib. 42–49), the souls of the departed fluttering like leaves' on the gleaming headlands of Ida (ib. 63–67), the triumphant athlete compared to the splendour of the mid-month moon shining among the lesser stars (IX. 27–29), the storm-weary sailors who have 'wished for the day' (XIII. 91–99), the joy of the Trojans at the retirement of Achilles, 'seeing a bright ray of light beneath the storm-cloud's edge' (ib. 105–107), the radiance, as of fire, that shone from the forms of the Nereids (XVII. 103–105), or the picture of Theseus in his youthful beauty (XVIII. 47–59). His vocabulary furnishes further proof of his artistic gifts. Among the hundred and two new words with which Bacchylides enriches our lexicons[1], a large majority consists of compound epithets, which show a real taste for beauty and picturesqueness. Such are the epithets πυριέθειρα, ἀναξιβρόντας, ἱπποδινήτας, ὑψιδαίδαλτος, πολέμαιγις, ἱμεράμπυξ, ἀκαμαντορόας, λιγυκλαγγής, φοινικοκράδεμνος, αἰνόστολος, κυανανθής, ἱμερόγυιος, βροτωφελής, μεγιστοπάτωρ, ξανθοδερκής, πορφυροδίνας, εὐρυνεφής, σεμνοδότειρα, and many more[2]. These are the coinage of a poet with an eye for beauty and colour and effect. If Bacchylides cannot take rank with the greatest of Greek poets, he is yet a true poet and artist, characteristically Greek in his qualities, the recovery of whose works is a real addition to the world's literature.

The metres and dialect of Bacchylides are not to be studied separately from Pindar's, with which they are substantially identical. In metre, as in everything, Bacchylides prefers ease and simplicity.

Metre.

---

[1] See the index, where these words are indicated by an asterisk.

[2] Besides the words which occur only in Bacchylides, there are also several for which there has hitherto been only late authority. Thus πορφυρόζωνος, μενέκτυπος, πολύκρημνος have hitherto been known only in Hesychius, πασιφανής and ὑψίνοος in Nonnus, κυανοπλόκαμος and πανδερκής in Quintus Smyrnaeus, θελξίμβροτος in the Orphic poems, πολύκριθος in Suidas, γυιαλκής in Oppian, χαριτώνυμος in Tzetzes, φερεστέφανος in an inscription, καλυκοστέφανος and ὑψιφανής in late poems in the *Anthology*. ἀτρόμητος (Antipater), βαρυπενθής (Meleager), θυμάρμενος and μενοινά (Callimachus) have attestation in the Alexandrian period.

Only once (in XVII) does he employ a rhythm as complicated as the paeonian. The rest are simple logaoedic metres, with an easy intermixture of dactyls and trochees, or the still simpler dactylo-epitrite. For this reason it has not been thought necessary, in the metrical schemes prefixed to each ode, to employ the complicated notation of Westphal and Schmidt, or to mark off the syllables into feet. The trained student of metres will have no difficulty in perceiving the scientific structure of the verse ; and the ordinary reader will pick up the rhythm more easily than if the schemes included symbols which can only be understood after a study of metrical theory.

In dialect a few varieties only need be noted here. The manuscript appears to be carefully written in this respect,

Dialect. and its evidence emphasizes the composite and conventional character of the Greek lyrical dialect. It is, of course, mixed Doric and Aeolic, but the latter element is less pronounced in Bacchylides than in Pindar. Μοῖσα is found once (V. 4), but Μοῦσα repeatedly ; λαχοῖσαν also occurs once (XIX. 14), and μαρμαίροισιν is given by the editors in a fragment not contained in the present MS. (frag. 56, Bergk 27), but without manuscript evidence. The Boeotian ἐσλός is never found, nor γλέφαρον. On the other hand the Aeolic κλεεννός is used several times, and πεδοιχνέω once. Of Doric forms the use of ᾱ for η is naturally the most marked ; but there are some limitations which are worth noticing. Bacchylides avoids having the ᾱ sound twice in successive syllables, and in such cases retains η in the first. Thus he regularly has φήμα, εἰρήνα, κυβερνήτας, ἀδμήτα (but ἄδματοι in XI. 84, where the final syllable has not an ᾱ). Ἀθάνα and Ἀθᾶναι, however, have the long α in all cases. Compounds of ζῆλος (ἐπίζηλος, πολύζηλος, πολυζήλωτος) regularly keep the η. The Doric third person plural in

-οντι is found occasionally, as πτάσσοντι (V. 22), καρύξοντι (XIII. 198), σεύοντι (XVIII. 10); also the diphthong ευ for εο or ου, as in Δεινομένευς (V. 35), κρατεῦσαν (VI. 7), ὑμνεῦσι (XI. 13). Other Doric forms are ὄρνιχες in V. 22, and λῶσιν (if it be correct) in XVII. 118. ἄ for ε is perhaps found in ἐξαναρίζων (V. 146); in τάμνω (XVII. 4) it is presumably Epic rather than Doric. οὖν occurs twice (XIX. 29, 37), never ὦν. μόνος and μοῦνος, κόρα and κούρα, are used indifferently, as in Pindar; but never Οὔλυμπος. Several Doric infinitives in -εν occur; θύεν (XVI. 18), ἐρύκεν (XVII. 41), ἴσχεν (XVII. 88), φυλάσσεν (XIX. 25).

The grammar and syntax of Bacchylides, like the dialect, are substantially identical with those of Pindar, and the summaries given in Gildersleeve's or Fennell's editions of Pindar will be found to apply in almost all points to Bacchylides. A detailed study of the subject would be out of place here; but it may be hoped that the *index verborum* will facilitate the comparison between the two poets.

The present edition does not attempt to say everything that there is to be said about Bacchylides, which would be absurd, but to provide everything that is necessary to facilitate the first study and appreciation of the newly-recovered poems. The text is printed in two forms; on the left-hand pages is given an exact transcript of the manuscript in **Arrange-ment of this edition.** uncial characters, with the accents, punctuation, *para-graphi*, and corrections of the original, while the right-hand pages contain the text in a readable form, with ordinary characters, division of words, modern accentuation and punctuation, and a moderate amount of restoration. With regard to the latter, a word may be said in explanation. Small restorations, such as single letters and obvious

d

parts of words, are made as a matter of course; but beyond these the amount of restoration admitted into the text is strictly limited. In some cases the evidence of metre and sense combined make restorations, even of words wholly lost, practically certain; but where a passage is much mutilated the chances against the restorer are so great that it seems best, at any rate in an *editio princeps*, not to admit conjectures into the text. The reader will, however, find some proposed reconstructions in the notes, with the additional advantage that they are, in most cases, not by the editor but by Professor Jebb, whose scholarship and skill in composition combine to give him exceptional qualifications for such a task. The only instances in which restorations which are largely conjectural have been admitted into the text are where a moderate amount of reconstruction would complete an otherwise perfect poem or long passage. In such cases, although the restorations must be largely provisional, and no two scholars would independently produce exactly the same results, the advantage of completeness seems to outweigh the disadvantage of slight uncertainty. Instances of this class will be found at the end of Ode V, and in occasional single lines throughout the poems. Those who aspire to larger reconstructions have a wide field left open for the exercise of their genius and poetic divination; subject always to the risk that their efforts may be brought to the test by the recovery of further fragments of the mutilated manuscript. In the words of Bacchylides himself, τὸ μέλλον ἀκρίτους τίκτει τελευτάς.

So far as possible, the text of the original MS. has been adhered to. Obvious errors have, of course, been corrected; and in some places the metre indicates errors which would otherwise have passed unnoticed. In cases of doubt, however, the MS. text has been retained, even when the balance of probability is against it. This is especially the case where the MS. is mutilated. It is often much easier to make a plausible restoration of a mutilated passage if one is allowed to assume that some of the extant readings are wrong; and when a manuscript is so much mutilated as in the present instance, it is probable that in some cases mutilated passages are corrupt. But it is almost certain, judging from experience, that this is the case much less often than restorers are tempted to assume; and in an *editio princeps*, at any rate, the soundest principle seems to be not to alter the extant portions of mutilated passages. Subsequent editors may, no doubt, rightly assume a large liberty in this respect. αἰεὶ τὰ φεύγοντα δίζηνται κιχεῖν.

The critical marks employed in this edition are of the usual kinds. In the ordinary text, square brackets enclose restorations which are due to the mutilations of the MS., angular brackets (⟨ ⟩) words or passages which the MS. never contained, but which the metre shows to be required. Departures from the MS. readings are indicated in the critical notes. Two passages in which relatively large departures from the MS. have been ventured are indicated by asterisks (XVII. 90, 91, XVIII. 35); and four words which appear to be corrupt in the MS., but for which no convincing emendation has been suggested, are marked by daggers (IX. 13, XII. 6, XVII. 112, XIX. 15). In the facsimile text, no restorations have, of course, been made; but dots indicate the *approximate* number of letters missing, except where they are widely spaced, which has been done when the lacuna is too large for a useful estimate to be made. Dots within brackets imply that the papyrus is lost in that place; dots without brackets, that the papyrus is preserved but the reading illegible. It will be seen that in some places the number of dots in the facsimile text does not agree with the number of letters supplied in the restored text. The reason for this is that in the former the number of letters missing in the original is calculated from the indications given in the MS. itself, such as the number of letters contained in an equal space in the lines preceding or following the lacuna. These indications form the basis for conjectural restoration; but it does not appear to be right, when the restoration is made, to modify the basis on which it rests. The indications in the facsimile text can only be approximate, owing to the varying sizes of letters; thus ϵ, θ, ι, o, ρ, σ occupy, in this MS., only about half the space of most other letters, while μ, ξ, π, and occasionally a and ν, are exceptionally broad. Lacunas of equal size in successive lines may in fact have contained four letters in one case and five in the other; but in the facsimile text it is clearly right that they should be indicated as being of equal size. Dots beneath letters (used in the facsimile text only) indicate that the letter in question is very imperfectly preserved in the MS., so that the correctness of the reading must remain doubtful or be determined by other considerations. It is, of course, impossible to indicate the precise degree of uncertainty in each case; for that purpose recourse must be had to the photographic facsimile, published separately. As a rule it may be stated that, the MS. being well and clearly written, there is rarely any doubt as to the MS. reading where the papyrus is not mutilated. The additions made by the correctors are printed above the line in small type; and it may be observed that this occasionally causes unevenness of spacing in the corresponding text on the opposite pages, which must not be laid at the printer's door.

With regard to the commentary, since some readers may think it superfluous, one word may be said. A certain amount of annotation was necessary, in order to explain the readings and restorations adopted in the text; and it appeared possible, without greatly delaying the appearance of the edition, to facilitate the first appreciation of the newly-recovered poems by somewhat extending the scope of the commentary. It does not claim to be exhaustive, but it is hoped it may be found useful, in some cases by solving difficulties, and in others by calling attention to them, and thereby paving the way for future work.

The detached fragments of papyrus, for which it has not been possible to find a place in the restored manuscript (or, in one case, for which the correct place was found too late for it to be transferred thither), are printed at the end of the volume. They are followed (with continuous numeration, but with Bergk's numbers added) by the fragments of Bacchylides given in Bergk's *Poetae Lyrici Graeci*, so far as these do not appear in the newly-discovered manuscript.

References to Bergk (including the numeration of the fragments of Pindar, where quotations are made from these) are to the fourth edition. With regard to Pindar, comparison with whom is everywhere inevitable in a study of his fellow-poet, most use has been made of Rumpel's *Lexicon Pindaricum*, and of Professor Gildersleeve's edition of the Olympian and Pythian odes, which, both now and formerly, has been found most useful as a guide to Pindar's style and characteristics.

The index of words is complete, unless there be accidental omissions. Considerations of space and time operated against making it a systematic Lexicon, on the lines of Rumpel's *Lexicon Pindaricum*, as was at first designed. The inclusion of the fragments from Bergk makes it, however, a complete index to the vocabulary of Bacchylides, so far as his poems are now known to us.

In conclusion, the editor wishes to thank most cordially those scholars whose help has been generously given to him in the preparation of this volume. Professor R. C. Jebb, M.P., Regius Professor of Greek in the University of Cambridge, saw the proofs from the earliest appearance of the text in type, and has most readily and freely contributed suggestions and advice in all subsequent stages. It is satisfactory to know that there is a good prospect of his undertaking an independent edition, in which his admirable scholarship will be free from the trammels of an *editio princeps*, and in which he may do for Bacchylides what he has done for Sophocles. A further debt, of earlier standing, should be acknowledged to Professor Jebb's study of Pindar in the *Journal of Hellenic Studies* (III. 144–183). Professor A. Palmer, Professor of Latin in the University of Dublin, also saw the poems at a very early stage, and helped much in the preliminary processes of reconstruction; but his very serious illness, which will be lamented by all who know him, has deprived this edition of his assistance in the later stages of the work, so that the suggestions to which his name is attached must not in all cases be taken as representing his final and deliberate judgement. Obligations to other scholars, especially Professor F. Blass of Halle (who identified several fragments, especially in Odes VII and IX, which had remained unplaced after the main restoration of the MS.) and Dr. J. E. Sandys of St. John's College, Cambridge, will be found acknowledged in the notes, in which every effort has been made to carry out the principle, *Ius suum cuique*. The elimination of some remaining errors is due to the reader of the Clarendon Press. But while these scholars have contributed much to whatever correctness or usefulness this edition may possess, they must not be held in any way responsible for its defects, whether of plan or of execution.

An *editio princeps*, especially of an imperfect manuscript, is inevitably a chopping-block for the criticisms and reconstructions of other scholars. Its object will be attained if it is found in any way adequate as a basis for subsequent work, and to facilitate the study and enjoyment of the new treasures of Greek literature which fortune has restored to the modern world from their Egyptian grave.

F. G. K.

November 19, 1897.

CRITICAL SYMBOLS.

A = the original text of the manuscript.

A¹ = corrections by the original scribe.

A² = corrections by the second hand.

A³ = corrections by the third hand.

ERRATA.

Ode V, l. 118, *for* ἀδελφίων *read* ἀδελφεῶν.

Ode IX, l. 13, *for* ξανθοδέρκης *read* ξανθοδερκής.

Ode XVI, l. 17, *for* εὑρυνέφει *read* εὑρυνεφεῖ.

ΒΑΚΧΥΛΙΔΗΣ

B

I.

STROPHE.

∪ ∪ — — — ∪ ⏓
— ∪ ∪ — ⏓ — ∪ ⏓
— ∪ — ∪ ∪ —
— — ∪ ∪ — ∪ ∪ — —
5 — ∪ ∪ ∪ — ∪ ∪ —
— — ∪ — ⏓ — ∪ —
— — ∪ — — ∪ —
— ∪ — — — ∪ —

EPODE.

— ∪ ∪ — ∪ ∪ —
— — ∪ ∪ — ∪ ∪ — —
— ∪ — — — ∪ ⏓ — ∪ ∪ — ⏓
— ∪ ∪ — ∪ ∪ — —
5 — ∪ — — — ∪ — —
— ∪ ∪ — ∪ ∪ — —
— ∪ — — — ∪ — — — ∪ — ⏓

1—8 = 9—16 : 17—23
24—31 = 32—39 : 40—46.

I.

[ΜΕΛΑΝΙ(?)ΚΕΙΩΙ]

[πεντάθλῳ(?) Ἴσθμια(?)]

THE beginning of this poem is lost; but a fragment of it (identified after the rest of the poem was in type) will be found below (frag. 1). This fragment, which contains the end of an epode and parts of a strophe and antistrophe, shows that at least two metrical systems are wanting. With the beginning of the poem, the title has, of course, also disappeared. The second ode is, however, entitled τῷ αὐτῷ, and the name of the athlete to whom both poems must consequently be assigned appears to be Melas (II. 4, and note). In II. 14 he is described as Πανθείδα φίλος υἱός, which, if the reading of the MS. is right, gives his father the otherwise unknown name of Pantheides, or son of Pantheus; but since ε and ο are easily confused, and appear to be interchanged elsewhere in this MS. (cf. V. 106, XVII. 66), it is probable that we should read Πανθοίδης. From the second poem it appears further that Melas was a native of Ceos, and consequently a compatriot of Bacchylides. His father, so far as can be gathered from the mutilated beginning of the present poem, had himself been a distinguished wrestler and a physician of high repute; he was now dead, leaving five sons, of whom Melas was one. The victory here commemorated was won at the Isthmian games (I. 17-19); the second ode, besides referring to this Isthmian victory, celebrates a subsequent triumph at Nemea. It is not quite clear in what form of contest these victories were won; but the epithet θρασύχειρος in II. 4 indicates that he was distinguished for his strength, and the references to racing and wrestling in I. 7, 8, seem to point to the pentathlum.

The extant portion of the ode consists of two systems. The first, which is seriously mutilated, deals with the victor and his father, passing in the last three lines of the epode into moral reflections on the superiority of merit to wealth, which, with the praises of contentment with a middle station in life, fill the remainder of the poem. The metre is dactylo-epitrite.

Col. 1]   ΠΟΛ[......]ΝΒΑΘΥ

          ει
       ΔΙΕΛΟ[.....]ΜΕΝΓΕΝΟC

       ΕΠΛΕ[......]ΡΟΧΕΙΡ

       ΑΡΓΕΙΟ[.....]ΛΕΟΝΤΟC

5   ΘΥΜΟ[.....]ΟΠΟΤΕ

       ΑΧΡΕΙ[.....]ΟΛΟῖΜΑΧΑC·

       ΠΟCCΙ[....]ΦΡΟ[...]ΑΤΡΙωΝ

       Τ'ΟΥΚ[..........]ΑΛωΝ

       ΤΟCΑΠΑΝ[   ]

10 ΤΟΞΟCΑΠΟ[........]Ν

       ΑΜΦΙΤ'ΑΤ[   ]

       ΞΕΙΝωΝΤΙ[..]ΛΑΝΟΡΙ[...]ΑΙ·

I. 2. ΔΙ Α, ΔΕΙ or ΔΗ Α³. The letter before ΜΕΝ is perhaps Σ.
6. ΑΧΡΕΙ] the first letter is perhaps cancelled. There are slight traces
of an accent on the Ε, presumably a circumflex.   11. ΑΤ Α, corr. Α¹.

Title. Ἴσθμια : this form, the neuter plural adjective, is regularly employed
in the titles throughout the MS. Cf. the inscription quoted by Pausanias
(VI. 4, 6) μουνοπάλης νικῶ δὶς Ὀλύμπια Πύθιά τ' ἄνδρας.

1–12. The drift of these mutilated lines can hardly be restored with
certainty, but apparently ll. 1–8 refer to Melas himself, and ll. 9–12 (taking
up the allusion in πατρίων) to his father, as ll. 13–16 certainly do.

4. Ἀργεῖο ... λέοντος : these words appear to contain a reference to the
Nemean lion, and consequently suggest the idea that this poem, like No. II,
was written for Melas' Nemean victory, not his Isthmian. On the other
hand, it is dangerous to rely much on a mutilated passage, and the prominent
mention of the Isthmian victory, and that alone, in l. 18 seems quite inconsistent with the view that this is a Nemean ode. The following poem
(II. 6–10), moreover, refers to the choral celebration of Melas' Isthmian
triumph in terms which clearly imply that Bacchylides wrote an ode for
that occasion. Blass and Sandys read Ἀργεῖος here and in II. 5, where see
note.

πολ[.̆ . . . . . .]ν̆ βαθυ-   στρ. α´.

δείελο[.̄ . . . . ̄.] μὲν γένος

ἔπλε[το καρτε]ρόχειρ

'Αργείο[.̆ . . . ̆.] λέοντος

5 θυμο[.̆ . . . ̆.]ο ποτὲ

αχρει[.̄ . . ̆. .]ολοῖ μάχας,

ποσσί[ν τ' ἐλα]φρο[ῖς, π]ατρίων

τ' οὐκ [.̄ . . . . ̄. . π]αλῶν.

τόσα Παν[θοίδᾳ κλυτό]-   ἀντ. α´.

10 τοξος 'Από[λλων ὤπασε]ν

ἀμφί τ' ἰατ[ορίᾳ]

ξείνων τε [φι]λάνορι [τιμ]ᾷ·

6. There are slight traces before -ολοι of a letter which may be β. The other strophes have a long syllable in the place corresponding to ολ here; but a trochee is admissible in place of a spondee.

7. Only a small part of the letter before -τριων remains, but it can be nothing but α, and this makes it almost certain that the word is πατρίων. Otherwise, at first sight it is attractive to read τριῶν, referring to the three bouts by which the wrestling was decided. The combination of wrestling and running seems to imply a reference to the pentathlum. πατρίων παλῶν implies that Melas' father, Panthoides, had been a distinguished wrestler.

8. Professor Jebb suggests ἀπείρατος (Pind. Ol. VIII. 61) or ἀγύμναστος.

9, 10. This restoration substantially agrees with one independently proposed by Dr. Fennell. It is necessary to bring in the name of Panthoides somewhere before l. 13, where he is evidently the subject.

11. ἰατορίᾳ: the remains in the MS., taken in conjunction with the requirements of the metre, leave little room for choice as to the restoration of this word. ἀμφί with the dative is common in Pindar in this sense; e. g. Ol. IX. 14 ἀνδρὸς ἀμφὶ παλαίσμασιν φόρμιγγ' ἐλελίζων.

12. φιλάνορι: in the general sense of 'hospitable,' to which Pind. fr. 236 gives the nearest parallel.

τιμᾷ: other restorations could perhaps be found, but the very slight traces left before -αι seem to suit a μ best.

[.]ΥΔΕΛΑΧωΝ[.]ΑΡΙΤωΝ

ΠΟΛΛΟΙϹΤΕΘ[. .]ΜΑϹΘΕΙϹΒΡΟΤωΝ

15 Α[.]ωΝ’ΕΛΥϹΕΝ[.]ΕΝΤΕΠΑΙ

ΔΑϹΜΕΓΑΙΝΗ[.]ΟΥϹΛΙΠωΝ·

[.]ωΝΕΝΑΟΪΚ[. .]ΝΙΔΑϹ

ΥΨΙΖΥΓΟϹΪϹ[. .]ΙΟΝΙΚΟΝ

ΘΗΚΕΝΑΝΤ[. . .]ΡΓΕϹΙΑΝΛΙΠΑΡωΝΤ’ΑΛ

20 ΛωΝϹΤΕΦΑΝ[. .]ΕΠΙΜΟΙΡῶΝ

ΦΑΜΙΚΑΙΦΑϹῳ[. .]ΓΙϹΤΟΝ

ΚΥΔΟϹΕΧΕΙΝΑΡΕΤΑΝ·ΠΛΟΥ

ΤΟϹΔΕΚΑΙΔΕΙΛΟΙϹΙΝΑΝΘΡωΠωΝΟΜΙΛΕΙ

ΕΘΕΛΕΙΔΑΥΞΕΙΝΦΡΕΝΑϹ

25 ΑΝΔΡΟϹ·ὉΔ’ΕΥΕΡΔωΝΘΕΟΥϹ

ΕΛΠΙΔΙΚΥΔΡΟΤΕΡΑΙ

20. ΕΠΙΜΟΙΡΩΝ Α, corr. Α³. apparently *inter scribendum.* inserted after this line.

23. ΑΝΘΡΩΠΟΙΣ Α, corr. Α¹. 24. A *paragraphus* is erroneously inserted after this line.

13. Χαρίτων : the goddesses who especially presided over success in the games, or rather over the qualities to which such success was due ; since the perfect development of physical strength and skill was a department of art, bringing beauty and grace and a balance of mental and bodily gifts in its train.   Such at least was the theory of athleticism ; though it may be gathered from Euripides that the ideal was very imperfectly realized in his time.   Mr. Bury (*The Nemean Odes of Pindar*, Appendix B) has commented on the mention of the Graces as a special characteristic of Pindar; but Bacchylides is equally full of references to them, and it may be regarded as a commonplace of epinikian poetry.   Mr. Gildersleeve has also noticed this function of the Graces, aptly characterizing them as the goddesses 'who give and grace victories' (*Pindar*, note on *Ol.* II. 55) ; so that their sphere covers alike the victor and the poet.   They are the givers of wisdom and beauty and renown, as Pindar himself says (*Ol.* XIV. 1–7, quoted by Jebb, *Journal of Hellenic Studies*, III. 175 (1882).

14. πολλοῖς: the dative, as though θαυμασθείς were θαυμαστός.

15. αἰῶν’ ἔλυσεν : so Euripides, *Iph. Taur.* 691–2, οὐ κακῶς ἔχει | πράσσονθ’ ἃ πράσσω πρὸς θεῶν λύειν βίον.

[ε]ὖ δὲ λαχὼν [Χ]αρίτων
πολλοῖς τε θ[αυ]μασθεὶς βροτῶν
15 α[ἰ]ῶν' ἔλυσεν, [π]έντε παῖδας μεγαινή[τ]ους λιπών.
[τ]ῶν ἕνα οἱ Κ[ρο]νίδας   ἐπ. α΄.
ὑψίζυγος Ἰσ[θμ]ιόνικον
θῆκεν ἀντ' [εὐε]ργεσιᾶν, λιπαρῶν τ' ἀλ-
20 λων στεφάν[ων] ἐπίμοιρον.
φαμὶ καὶ φάσω [μέ]γιστον
κῦδος ἔχειν ἀρετάν· πλοῦ-
τος δὲ καὶ δειλοῖσιν ἀνθρώπων ὁμιλεῖ,
ἐθέλει δ' αὔξειν φρένας   στρ. β΄.
25 ἀνδρός. ὁ δ' εὖ ἔρδων θεοὺς
ἐλπίδι κυδροτέρᾳ

16. μεγαινήτους : cf. III. 64, and note.

18. Ἰσθμόνικον: the emphatic mention of the Isthmian victory, all other successes being thrown together in λιπαρῶν τ' ἄλλων στεφάνων ἐπίμοιρον, seems decisive as to the ode being Isthmian and not Nemean. In X. 26 the form Ἰσθμιονίκας is used.

20. ἐπίμοιρον: elsewhere only in Stobaeus (103, 27), in a quotation from the philosopher Euryphamus.

21–23. These lines form frag. 30 of Bacchylides in Bergk's *Poetae Lyrici*, being quoted by Plutarch (*de audiend. poet.* 14). The MSS. of Plutarch have φάσωμεν πιστόν, whence Boeckh read πιστὸν φάσομεν, followed by Neue, Schneidewin, and Farnell. Bergk reads φάσομαι πιστόν, and various other corrections have been proposed, all retaining the word πιστόν. There is a lacuna in the papyrus after φασω, but sense and metre are alike against μὲν πιστόν, and the letter before ιστον, of which part is preserved, can only be a γ or a τ. The space does not admit of [κρά]τιστον, and the quotation in Plutarch is strong evidence in favour of a word beginning with με. Hence μέγιστον may be regarded as certain. The corruption of ΜΕΓΙΣΤΟΝ into ΜΕΝΠΙΣΤΟΝ is palaeographically easy.

23. ἀνθρώπων : the MS. has ἀνθρώποις, corrected into ἀνθρώπων. According to Reiske (quoted by Michelangeli, *Frammenti della Melica greca*) some MSS. of Plutarch have ἀνθρώποις, but the genitive is found in most MSS. and all editions. Probabilities are in favour of the genitive, as being somewhat the more unusual phrase, and likely to be altered.

CΑΙΝΕΙΚΕΑΡ·ΕΙΔ·ΥΓ'ΕΙΑC

ΘΝΑΤΟCῈΩΝΕΛΑΧΕΝ

ΖΩΕΙΝΤ'ΑΠΟΙΚΕΙΩΝΕΧΕΙͶ

30 ΠΡΩΤΟ'CΕΡΙΖΕΙΠΑΝΤΙΤΟΙ

ΤΕΡΨΙCΑΝΘΡΩΠΩΝΒΙΩΙ

ΕΠΕΤΑΙΝΟCΦΙΝΓΕΝΟΥ

.. ΝΠΕΝΙΑCΤ'ΑΜΑΧΑΝΟΥ

ΪCΟΝΟΤ'ΑΦΝΕΟCΪ

35 ΜΕΙΡΕΙΜΕΓΑΛΩΝ·ΟΤΕΜΕΙΩ[

Col. 2]   ΠΑΥΡΟΤΕΡΩΝΤΟΔΕΠΑΝ

ΤΩΝΕΥΜΑΡΕ͂Ι ΟΥΔΕΝΓΛΥΚΥ

ΘΝΑΤΟΙCΙΝ·ΑΛΛ'ΑΙΕΙΤΑΦΕΥ

ΓΟΝΤΑΔΙΖΗΝΤΑΙΚΙΧΕΙΝ·

40 ΟΝΤΙΝΑ̣ΚΟΥΦΟΤΑΤΑΙ

ΘΥΜΟΝΔΟΝΕΟΥCΙΜΕΡΙΜΝΑΙ

ΟCCΟΝΑͶΖΩ̇ΗΙΧΡΟΝΟΝΤΟΝΔ'ΕΛΑΧͤΝ·ΤΙ

ΜΑΝ·ΑΡΕΤΑΔ'ΕΠΙΜΟΧΘΟC

---

27. ΥΓΕΙΑΣ Δ, corr. Δ²?   **28.** ΕΛΑΚΕΝ Δ, corr. Δ¹.   **29.** ΕΧΕΙΝ Δ, corr. Δ¹?   **30.** ΠΡΩΤΟΣ Δ, corr. Δ¹?   **37.** ΕΥΜΑΡΕΙ Δ, ΕΥΜΑΡΕΙΝ Δ².

27. σαίνει: in good sense, 'cheers'; cf. Aesch. *Cho.* 194, σαίνομαι δ' ὑπ' ἐλπίδος.

29. ζώειν τ' ἀπ' οἰκείων ἔχει: 'and hath wherewith to live of his own.' This praise of contentment with a moderate lot seems to imply that the family of Melas was of middle station.

33. πενίας τ' ἀμαχάνου: 'irremediable poverty.' A moderate degree of poverty may stimulate to exertion and be consistent with enjoyment; but extreme poverty, against which it is hopeless to struggle, blights and embitters a man's whole life. That and disease are admitted by the poet as fatal to a pleasurable existence.

34. ἴσον: the position is emphatic, lying outside the two branches of the sentence which are marked by τε . . . τε.

37. εὐμαρεῖν: the verb is new.

41. θυμὸν δονέουσι μέριμναι: cf. Pind. *Nem.* VI. 55-57 ᾿τὸ δὲ πὰρ ποδὶ ναὸς

σαίνει κέαρ· εἰ δ' ὑγιείας
θνατὸς ἐὼν ἔλαχεν,
ζώειν τ' ἀπ' οἰκείων ἔχει,
30 πρώτοις ἐρίζει. παντί τοι
τέρψις ἀνθρώπων βίῳ
ἔπεται νόσφιν γε νού-   ἀντ. β'.
[σω]ν πενίας τ' ἀμαχάνου.
ἶσον ὅ τ' ἀφνεὸς ἱ-
35 μείρει μεγάλων, ὅ τε μείω[ν]
παυροτέρων. τὸ δὲ πάν-
των εὐμαρεῖν οὐδὲν γλυκὺ
θνατοῖσιν· ἀλλ' αἰεὶ τὰ φεύγοντα δίζηνται κιχεῖν.
40 ὅντινα κουφόταται   ἐπ. β'.
θυμὸν δονέουσι μέριμναι,
ὅσσον ἄν ζώῃ χρόνον, τόνδ' ἔλαχ[ε]ν. τί
μάν ; ἀρετὰ δ' ἐπίμοχθος

ἐλισσόμενον αἰεὶ | κυμάτων λέγεται παντὶ μάλιστα δονεῖν | θυμόν, and *Pyth.* VI.
36 δονηθεῖσα φρήν.

42. τόνδ': sc. χρόνον. The man whose mind is beset by trifling cares,
hath this life (be it long or short) to enjoy; but he that attains to virtue
leaves behind him an immortal glory. Cf. Browning, *A Grammarian's
Funeral*:

> 'That low man, with a little thing to do,
>   Sees it and does it:
> This high man, with a great thing to pursue,
>   Dies ere he knows it.
> That, hath the world here: should he need the next,
>   Let the world mind him:
> This, throws himself on God, and unperplexed
>   Seeking shall find Him.'

τί μάν : the MS. punctuation after ἔλαχεν seems to show that these are
to be taken as a separate clause, 'Why not ?' Professor Jebb would prefer
to ignore the punctuation, read τιμάν, and translate 'for that space only
hath he the meed of honour.'

[.....]ΕΫΤΑΘΕῖCΑΔ‘ΟΡΘΩC
45 [.....]ΝΕΫΤΕΘΑΝΗΙΛΕΙ
   [.....]ΖΗΛΩΤΟΝΕΥΚΛΕΪΑCΑ[...]ΜΑ

II.

Τωι αυτωι

STROPHE.

EPODE.

Α[.....]ΕΜΝΟΔΟΤΕΙΡΑΦΗΜᾹ[
ΕCΚ[....]ΕΡΑΝΧΑΡΙΤΩ

44. Restored by Blass.   45. ἄφθιτον Jebb. ΛΕΙ om. A., added by A².   II. *Title*. In a hand about contemporary with the MS., apparently A².

46. εὐκλείας ἄγαλμα : cf. Soph. *Ant.* 703, 704 τί γὰρ πατρὸς θάλλοντος εὐκλείας τέκνοις | ἄγαλμα μεῖζον ;

II. 1. σεμνοδότειρα : a ἅπαξ εἰρημένον = ‘giver of glory,’ like ὀλβοδότειρα, which is used by Euripides (*Bacch.* 419). A similar formation from an adjective occurs in αἰνοδότειρα (Orph. *Argon.* 354, ed. Hermann) and βαρυδότειρα (Aesch. *Sept. contr. Theb.* 975, 987).

[μέν, τελ]ευταθεῖσα δ' ὀρθῶς
45 [ἄφθιτο]ν εὖτε θάνῃ λεί-
[πει πολυ]ζήλωτον εὐκλείας ἄ[γαλ]μα.

II.

ΤΩΙ ΑΥΤΩΙ

⟨πεντάθλῳ (?) Νέμεα.⟩

THIS short ode was written probably on the spur of the moment by Bacchylides to celebrate his fellow-countryman's victory at Nemea. Its strophic division consists of very short members, but a parallel will be found in the next ode, in which each system contains precisely the same number of lines as the whole of this poem, namely fourteen.

The strophe proclaims the victory won by Meias in the Nemean games; the antistrophe recalls his former Isthmian success and its celebration in the preceding ode; and the epode reverts to his present triumph, and to its celebration by the 'native-born Muse' of his fellow-countryman. The metre is logaoedic.

ἄ[ϊξον, ὦ σ]εμνοδότειρα Φήμα,   στρ.
ἐς Κ[έον ἱ]εράν, χαριτώ-

Φήμα: it is noticeable that the Doric ā is given in the second syllable alone, and as the MS. appears to have been carefully written in this respect one hesitates to alter it, though the MSS. of Pindar consistently read φάμα. Cf. also V. 194, where φήμα appears again.

For the invocation, compare the similar appeal to Echo in Pindar, *Ol.* XIV. 20–24, and *Nem.* V. 2–5.

2. ἐς Κέον: the remains of the first three letters are slight, but Κέον is confirmed by αὐθιγενής in l. 11.

χαριτώνυμον: the word is otherwise unknown in literature (L. and S. quote it only from an inscription and Tzetzes). The second half of the compound has lost its force.

ΝΥΜ[. .]ΦΕΡΟΥΣ'ΑΓΓΕΛΊΑΝ

ΟΤΙΜ[. .]ΑϹΘΡΑϹΎΧΕΙΡΑΡ

5 ΓΕΊΟ[. .]ΡΑΤΟΝΙΚΆΝ

ΚΑΛΩΝΔ'ΑΝΕΜΝΑϹΕΝΟ̂Ϲ'ΕΝΚΛ[. . .]ΝΩΙ

ΑΥΧΕΝΙΪϹΘΜΟΥΖΑΘΕΑΝ

ΛΙΠΟΝΤΕϹΕΥΞΑΝΤΊΔΑΝΑ

ϹΟΝΕ̣ΠΕΔΕΙΞΑΜΕΝΕΒΔΟΜΗ

10 ΚΟΝΤΑ . . Ν̣ϹΤΕΦΑΝΟΙϹΙΝ·

ΚΑΛΕΙΔΕΜΟ̂Υ̣Ϲ'ΑΥΘΙΓΕΝΗϹ

ΓΛΥΚΕΙΑΝΑΥΛΩΝΚΑΝΑΧΆΝ

ΓΕΡΑΙΡΟΥϹ'ΕΠΙΝΪΚΊΟΙϹ

ΠΑΝΘΕΊΔΑ̣ΫΦΙΛΟΝΥΙΟΝ

4. θρασύχειρος] ΘΡΑΣΥΧΕΙΡ Δ, corr. Jebb.   14. ΠΑΝΘΕΙΔΑΙ Δ,
ΠΑΝΘΕΙΔΑ Δ¹?

4, 5. These lines must contain the name of the athlete to whom these two odes are addressed. There are two alternatives : either the name is to be found in μ . . ας (i. e. either Μέλας or Μέγας), in which case 'Αργεῖον must be read as epithet of νίκαν (since the athlete is plainly a Cean, not an Argive) ; or the name is 'Αργεῖος (found as a proper name in Paus. V. 17. 4, etc.), and μ . . ας can only stand for μέγας. In favour of 'Αργεῖος (proposed by Blass) is its occurrence here and in I. 4 in close connexion with the similar adjectives καρτερόχειρ and θρασύχειρος, while 'Αργεῖον as an adjective of two terminations is unparalleled, though hardly impossible in poetry. In favour of Μέλας, there is a very slight trace of ink before ας, which suits a λ but not a γ : μέγας is not a very pleasing epithet, and unless 'Αργεῖον be read, there is nothing whatever to show to what festival this ode belongs. It cannot be Isthmian, since the poet goes on to say that this new success *recalled* the celebration of the same athlete's triumph at the Isthmus ; and it is incredible that the festival should not be mentioned. These considerations, and especially the last, seem to give the preponderance to Μέλας.

θρασύχειρος : this emendation of the MS. θρασύχειρ seems required by the metre. Cf. ἑκατόγχειρος (Homer) and αὐτόχειρος (Hesychius).

7. 'Ισθμοῦ : this passage supports the claim of an initial digamma in 'Ισθμός, which is maintained by Gildersleeve for the Isthmian odes of Pindar (but not elsewhere), and denied by Bury (*Isthmian Odes*, note on I. 9). But 'Ισθμιόνικος is without it in I. 18 and X. 26, and 'Ισθμός in VIII. 40, and Ίσθμιος in XVIII. 17. The balance of evidence is consequently against

νυμ[ον] φέρουσ᾽ ἀγγελίαν,
ὅτι Μ[έλ]ας θρασύχειρος Ἀρ-
5 γεῖο[ν ἄ]ρατο νίκαν·
καλῶν δ᾽ ἀνέμνασεν ὅσ᾽ ἐν κλ[εεν]νῷ   ἀντ.
αὐχένι Ἰσθμοῦ ζαθέαν
λιπόντες Εὐξαντίδα νᾶ-
σον ἐπεδείξαμεν ἑβδομή-
10 κοντα [σὺ]ν στεφάνοισιν.
καλεῖ δὲ Μοῦσ᾽ αὐθιγενὴς   ἐπ.
γλυκεῖαν αὐλῶν καναχάν,
γεραίρουσ᾽ ἐπινικίοις
Πανθοίδα φίλον υἱόν.

the digamma ; but the instances of hiatus before the word are so strong
as to suggest that some remnant of an original digamma survived in common
pronunciation, sufficient to justify the hiatus to a poet's ear if he required it.
It is well known that Pindar is inconsistent in his observance or neglect of
the digamma (cf. Fennell, *Olympian and Pythian Odes*, p. xxxi).

8. Εὐξαντίδα νᾶσον : there can be no doubt that Ceos is meant, but the
epithet is wholly new. Εὐξαντίς is given in the *Etym. Magn.* as the name of
a family in Miletus, derived from Εὐξάντιος or Εὐξάνθιος, the son of Minos and
Dexithea (Apollod. *Bibl.* III. 1. 2); and that the epithet here is connected
with this personage appears certain from the detached fragment of Ode I
(below, frag. 1, l. 16), where the name Εὐξάντιος is introduced. There must
have been some legendary connexion between Euxantius and Ceos, but
there is no other extant mention of it. See note on frag. 1, l. 16.

9, 10. ἑβδομήκοντα σὺν στεφάνοισιν : this gives the numbers of the chorus
which performed the Isthmian ode.

11. Μοῦσα : the MS. has Μοῦσα habitually, Μοῖσα only once (V. 4).
The latter might be restored throughout, as in Pindar, save that one does
not know how far lyric poets felt bound to be consistent in their conventional dialect. Bacchylides might naturally be less Aeolic than the
Boeotian Pindar.

13. ἐπινικίοις : the earliest example of the word as a substantive = epinikian
odes, Pindar having it only as an adjective.

14. Πανθοίδα : the MS. has Πανθείδα, but there is no evidence for such
forms as Πανθεύς or Πανθείδης, and it seems probable that the ε is simply
a scribe's error for ο, as in V. 106, XVII. 66.

III.

Ιερωνι Συρακοσιωι ιπποις [. . . .]πια

STROPHE.

⏓ – ⏑ ⏕ ⏒ ⏖ ⏑ – ⏑ – ⏓
⏓ – ⏑ ⏑ – ⏑ ⏑ ⏑ – ⏑ – ⏓
⏓ – ⏑ ⏑ – ⏑ ⏑ ⏑ – ⏑ – ⏑
– ⏑ – ⏓ – ⏑ ⏑ ⏑ – ⏑ – ⏓

EPODE.

⏓ – ⏑ ⏑ – ⏑ ⏑ – – –
– ⏑ – ⏓ – ⏑ –
– ⏑ – ⏓ – ⏑ ⏓
– – ⏑ ⏕ – – ⏑ –
5 ⏕ ⏑ – ⏓ – ⏑ – – – ⏑ –
– ⏑ – ⏓ – ⏑ ⏓

1—4 = 5—8 : 9—14
15—18 = 19—22 : 23—28
29—32 = 33—36 : 37—42
43—46 = 47—50 : 51—56
57—60 = 61—64 : 65—70
71—74 = 75—78 : 79—84
85—88 = 89—92 : 93—98

III. *Title.* In a later hand, probably A³.

III.

ΙΕΡΩΝΙ ΣΤΡΑΚΟΣΙΩΙ

ἵπποις [᾿Ολύμ]πια

This ode, the first in the order of the MS. of three addressed to Hieron, is the latest in point of time, being written in honour of Hieron's chariot victory at Olympia, which was won in 468 B.C., the year before his death, thus fulfilling the prayer of Pindar in *Ol.* I. 109-111. The immediate occasion for which it was composed appears to have been the dedication of some golden tripods at Delphi as a thank-offering for the victory (ll. 17-21). The more elaborate thank-offerings for Olympia itself were not completed until after Hieron's death, and were dedicated by his son Deinomenes (Paus. VI. 12. 1; VIII. 42. 8, 9). The poem is, unfortunately, much mutilated, having in fact been put together out of twenty distinct fragments of papyrus. Only nineteen lines are absolutely free from mutilation, but sixty more can be restored either with certainty or with a high degree of probability; and the general drift of the poem is clear, except in one passage.

The poem is written in unusually short metrical divisions, like Pindar's fifth Olympian. Consisting of ninety-eight lines in all, it contains no less than seven systems, the strophes having only four lines each, and the epode six lines. It is noticeable that the second and third lines in each strophe are identical, as also are the second, third and sixth lines in each epode. The first system contains the praises of Hieron, the strophe and antistrophe of the second describe the splendour of the festival at which the ode was sung. The epode of this system introduces the story of Croesus, which is carried through the third and fourth systems, ending in the middle of the fifth antistrophe. A mutilated passage follows, of which it is difficult to discern the drift; but the epode of the sixth system is occupied by gnomic reflections, having especial reference to Hieron, which are continued through the seventh and final system. The metre is logaoedic.

ΑΡ[. .]ΤΟΚΑ̣ΡΠΟΥϹΙΚΕΛΙΑϹΚΡΕΟΥϹΑ̣Ν

Δ[. . . .]ΤΡΑΙΟϹΤΕΦΑΝΟΝΤΕΚΟΥΡΑ̣Ν

Υ[.]ΝΕΙΓΛΥΚΥ̇ΔΩΡΕΚΛΕΙΟΙΘΟᾹϹΤΟ̇

[. . .]ΠΙΟΔΡΟΜΟΥϹΪΕΡΩΝΟϹΙΠΠ[.]ΥϹ·

5 [. . . .]ΤΟΓΑΡϹΥΝΥΠΕΡΟΧΩΙΤΕΝΙΚᾹΙ

[. . . . .]ΛΑΪΑΙΤΕΠΑΡΕΥΡΥΔΙΝΑΝ

[. . . . .]Ε̣ΙΝΟΜΕΝΕΟϹΕΘΗΚΑΝ

[.]Λ̣ΑΒΙΟΝ[. . . . .]ΝΚΥΡΗϹΑΙ·

ΘΡΟΗϹΕΔΕΛ[

10 ᾹΤΡΙϹΕΥΔΑΙΜ[

Col. 3]   Ο̇ϹΠΑΡΑΖΗΝΟϹΛΑΧΩΝ

ΠΛΕΙϹΤΑΡΧΟΝΕΛΛΑΝΩΝΓΕ^{ρα}Ϻ̣ΟϹ

---

6. σὺν Palmer.   **7.** τόθι Palmer.   ΔΕΙΝΟΜΕΝΕΟΣ Α.
12. γέρας] ΓΕΝΟΣ Α, corr. A¹.

1. ἀριστοκάρπου: a word coined by Bacchylides; cf. Pindar (*Nem.* I. 14) ἀριστεύοισαν εὐκάρπου χθονὸς Σικελίαν πίειραν.

κρέουσαν: this feminine of κρέων is not found elsewhere, but the form κρείουσα occurs once in Homer (*Il.* XXII. 48); also in Hesiod (fr. 70, Flach) and Callimachus (*Del.* 219).

2. κούραν: Persephone. Κόρη does not appear as a proper name before Euripides, and it therefore seems best to treat it as an ordinary noun here; 'her daughter of the violet crown.' This address to Demeter and Persephone is especially appropriate here, since Hieron was an hereditary priest of these goddesses (schol. on Pind. *Ol.* VI. 95); and it is noticeable that the scholiast uses the name Κόρη in recording this fact (ἱερωσύνην εἶχεν ὁ Ἱέρων Δήμητρος καὶ Κόρης καὶ Διὸς Αἰτναίου). Pindar (*l.c.*) gives her no name, speaking merely of 'Demeter and her daughter (θυγατρὸς) of the fair steeds.'

3. γλυκύδωρε: the word recurs in XI. 1 as epithet of Victory (Νίκα), and in V. 4 as epithet of Μουσᾶν ἄγαλμα.

Κλειοῖ: notice the scansion Κλειοῖ, ει being short before a vowel, as in Pindar. The Muse's name has the same scansion in Pind. *Nem.* III. 83, but there the MSS. have the form Κλεώ. In V. 13 Bacchylides speaks of himself as the servant of Urania, in XIX. 13 of Calliope.

5. σεύοντο: or ὄρνυντο, but σεύομαι is especially used by Pindar of horses and chariots; cf. *Ol.* I. 20, *Isth.* VII. 61, also frag. 107, where the metaphor is evidently from a chariot.

6. σὺν ἀγλαίᾳ: the termination -λαιαι being clear; and the metre requiring

ἀρ[ισ]τοκάρπου Σικελίας κρέουσαν   στρ. α΄.
Δ[άμα]τρα ἰοστέφανόν τε κούραν
ὔ[μ]νει, γλυκύδωρε Κλειοῖ, θοάς [τ'] Ὀ-
[λυμ]πιοδρόμους Ἱέρωνος ἵππ[ο]υς.
5 [σεύον]το γὰρ σὺν ὑπερόχῳ τε νίκᾳ   ἀντ. α΄.
[σὺν ἀγ]λαΐᾳ τε παρ' εὐρυδίναν
['Αλφεόν, τόθι Δ]εινομένευς ἔθηκαν
[ὅ]λβιον [γόνον στεφάνω]ν κυρῆσαι·
θρόησε δὲ λ[αὸς 'Αχαιῶν].   ἐπ. α΄.
10 ἃ τρισευδαίμ[ων ἀνήρ],
ὃς παρὰ Ζηνὸς λαχὼν
πλείσταρχον Ἑλλάνων γέρας

two syllables with the scansion ⏑ -, ἀγλαΐᾳ is practically certain, and the only doubt is whether it was preceded by a preposition or was compounded in some form not otherwise known, e. g. παναγλαΐᾳ. In the absence of any authority for such a compound, the former alternative seems preferable. For the repetition of the preposition cf. ll. 33, 34.

7, 8. Δεινομένευς ... γόνον: Hieron, who was son of one Deinomenes and father of another. The MS. has Δεινομένεος, and this form of the genitive is also found in IV. 13 and in Pindar (*Pyth.* I. 79); but in V. 35, where, as here, the metre requires a long syllable, the form in -ευς is preserved by the MS., and the same is the case in Simonides (frag. 141, Bergk). εο, even when contracted by synizesis, remains short (e.g. θεός in Pind. *Pyth.* I. 56). The form in -ευς is also said to be particularly characteristic of the Dorian dialects of the islands (Boisacq, *Les Dialectes Doriens*, p. 78), so that it is natural to find it in Simonides and Bacchylides, the poets of Ceos.

ἔθηκαν ... κυρῆσαι: cf. Pindar, *Nem.* X. 48 θῆκε δρόμῳ σὺν ποδῶν χειρῶν τε νικᾶσαι σθένει, though there it is said of the places which granted prizes to be won, here of the horses which won them for the victor.

8-10. The beginnings of these lines are preserved on a detached piece of papyrus, which, on grounds of sense and metre, seems to belong here.

10. ἀνήρ: repeatedly used in a complimentary sense by Pindar; of Hieron himself in *Pyth.* I. 42, 69. ἄναξ is never applied to a contemporary ruler.

12. πλείσταρχον: a new word. Cf. the language of the Greek envoys to Gelon, Hieron's brother and predecessor: μοῖρά τοι τῆς Ἑλλάδος οὐκ ἐλαχίστη μέτα, ἄρχοντί γε Σικελίας (Herod. VII. 157).

C

ΟΙΔΕΠΥΡΓΩΘΕΝΤΑΠΛ[.]ΥΤΟΝΜΗΜΕΛΑΜ

ΦΑΡΕΙΝ̸ΚΡΥΠΤΕΙΝΣΚΟΤΩΙ·

15 ΒΡΥΕΙΜΕΝ ΕΡΑΒΟΥΘΥΤΟΙΣΕΟΡΤΑΙΣ·

ΒΡΥΟΥΣΙΦΙΛΟΞΕΝΙΑΣΑΓΥΙΑΙ·

ΛΑΜΠΕΙΔ·ΥΠΟΜΑΡΜΑΡΥΓΑΙΣΟΧΡΥΣΟΣ

ΥΨΙΔΑΙΔΑΛΤΩΝΤΡΙΠΟΔ̸ΩΝΣΤΑΘΕΝΤΩΝ

ΠΑΡΟΙΘΕΝΑΟΥΤΟΘΙΜΕΓΙ[..]ΟΝΑΛΣΟΣ

20 Φ[..]ΒΟΥΠΑΡΑΚΑΣΤΑΛΙΑ[...]ΕΘΡΟΙΣ

Δ[.]ΛΦΟΙΔΙΕΠΟΥΣΙθΕΟΝΘ[..]ΝΤΙΣ

ΑΓΛΑΪΖΕΘΩΓΑΡΑΡΙΣΤΟ̸[.]ΛΒΩΝ·

ΕΠΕΙΠΟΤΕΚΑΙΔΑΜΑϹΙΠ[.]ΟΥ

13. **ΜΕΛΑΜ—**] ΜΕΛΛΗ Α, apparently, corr. Α¹?   14. **ΦΑΡΕΙΝ Α,** corr. Α¹?   The reading is due to a suggestion by Prof. Palmer. 15. **ΙΕΡΑ**] ΕΡΑ Α, Ι inserted by Α³?   21. θεόν, θεόν Palmer. 22. ἀγλαΐζέτω] so also Jebb. **ΑΓΛΑΙΖΕΘΩ Α. ΑΡΙΣΤΟΝ ΟΛΒΟΝ Α,** **ΑΡΙΣΤΟΣ ΟΛΒΩΝ Α³.**

13. οἶδε κ.τ.λ. : 'hath wisdom not to hide his mounded wealth beneath a black shroud of darkness.' For the sentiment cf. Pindar *Nem.* I. 31 οὐκ ἔραμαι πολὺν ἐν μεγάρῳ πλοῦτον κατακρύψαις ἔχειν, a passage addressed to Hieron's friend, Chromius. μελαμφαρής does not occur elsewhere.

16. φιλοξενίας : there is a shade of difference between the genitive here and the dative in the preceding line, owing to ἑορταί representing certain concrete physical objects, while φιλοξενία is an abstract quality. The same distinction may be felt in English : ' the temples are full with sacrifices, the streets are full of hospitality.'

17. λάμπει κ.τ.λ. : ' the splendour of gold flashes forth from the radiance of the deep-chased tripods, planted before the shrine, where by the streams of Castalia the Delphians minister to Phoebus' holiest grove.' It seems better to make τριπόδων dependent on μαρμαρυγαῖς than on χρυσός, since the former would stand rather awkwardly by itself. ὑπό: ' de re vel conditione comitante atque coniuncta' (Rumpel, *Lex. Pindar.* p. 461); cf. Pind. frag. 48 αἰθομένα δᾳς ὑπὸ ξανθαῖσι πεύκαις.

18. τριπόδων : these must almost certainly be the gift of Hieron, and their dedication the special occasion of the ode. The reference to Delphi, which is repeated in l. 62, would be out of place if the poem were an ordinary song of victory, to be performed at Olympia or Syracuse. Moreover the central portion of the ode deals with the recompense which

οἶδε πυργωθέντα πλ[ο]ῦτον μὴ μελαμ-
φαρεῖ κρύπτειν σκότῳ.

15 βρύει μὲν ἱερὰ βουθύτοις ἑορταῖς,   στρ. β'.
βρύουσι φιλοξενίας ἀγυιαί.
λάμπει δ' ὑπὸ μαρμαρυγαῖς ὁ χρυσὸς
ὑψιδαιδάλτων τριπόδων σταθέντων
πάροιθε ναοῦ, τόθι μέγι[στ]ον ἄλσος   ἀντ. β'.
20 Φ[οί]βου παρὰ Κασταλία[ς ῥε]έθροις
Δελφοὶ διέπουσι. θεόν, θ[εό]ν τις
ἀγλαΐζέτω γάρ, ἄριστον [ὄ]λβον.
ἐπεί ποτε καὶ δαμασίπ[π]ου   ἐπ. β'.

Croesus received for his munificent gifts to the Pythian shrine; and the
point of it lies in the comparison between the munificence of Croesus and
that of Hieron. It is known that a tripod was dedicated at Delphi by
Hieron and his brothers Gelon, Polyzelus, and Thrasybulus, with an inscription by Simonides (Schol. to Pind. *Pyth.* I. 55); but that was in memory
of the battle of Himera, and is quite distinct from the present offering.
Athenaeus (pp. 231 F, 232 A; the reference is due to Dr. Sandys) speaks
of Gelon's dedicating a golden tripod and Victory, and Hieron τὰ ὅμοια. If
Hieron's offering is meant to be distinct from Gelon's, it may be that
mentioned in this poem; but this is questionable. Golden offerings were
unknown at Delphi before the gifts of Gyges; and he was followed by
Croesus, Gelon, and Hieron (Athenaeus, *l. c.*).

21. θεόν, θεόν τις κ.τ.λ.: 'give God the glory—that is the truest prosperity.' The MS. has ἀγλαιζέθω, which, if correct, must be a Doric imperative (cf. ὀπυιέθω in the *Lex Gortyn.* VIII. 32; Boisacq, *Les Dialectes Doriens*,
p. 198), but the middle is unsuitable, and the change to ἀγλαϊζέτω very
slight. γάρ is quite abnormally late, and apparently unnecessarily so, since
τις and γάρ might change places; but cf. Jebb's note on Soph. *Phil.* 1450,
where γάρ stands sixth word in the sentence. ἄριστον ὄλβον, the original
reading of the MS., must be an accusative in apposition to the sentence
in general. ἄριστος ὄλβων, the reading of the reviser, does not seem capable
of a satisfactory sense; but ἄριστος ὄλβῳ is possible and not unattractive,
like ὄλβῳ φέρτατος in Pind. *Nem.* X. 13, 'let a man who is at the height of
prosperity give God the glory.'

23 ff. The story of Croesus, the great benefactor of Delphi (ll. 61-63), is
appropriately introduced into an ode on the occasion of Hieron's gifts to
the same shrine; but in order that the parallel may not be ill-omened, it is

ΛΥΔΙΑСΑΡΧΑΓΕΤΑΝ
25 ΕΥΤΕΤΑΝΠΕΠ[   ]
ΖΗΝΟСΤΕΛΕ[.........]СΙΝ
ÇÁΡΔΙΕСΠΕΡС[..............]ΑΤΩΙ
ΚΡΟΙÇΟΝΟΧΡΥÇ[   ]
ΦΥΛΑΞ·ΑΠΟΛΛΩΝ[.....]ΕΛΠΤΟΝΑ̂ΜΑΡ
30 Μ[.]Δ̲Α̂ΩΝΠΟΛΥΔ[.....]ΟΥΚΕΜΕΛΛΕ
ΜΙΜΝΕΙΝΕΤΙΔ[......].ΑΝ·Π[..]ΑΝΔΕ
ΧΑ...ΤΕΙΧΕΟСΠ[.....]ΘΕΝΑΥ[
Π...·.ΑΤ·ΕΝΘΑСΥ[.....]ΤΕΚΕΔ[
СΥ..ΕΥΠΛΟΚΑΜΟΙ[.]ΕΠΕΒΑΙΝ·ΑΛΑ[
35 [..]..ΤΡΆСΙΔΥΡΟ[.]ΕΝΑΙС·ΧΕΡΑСΔ[
[.]ΠΥ.ΑΙΘΕΡΑС[.]ΕΤΕΡΑСΑΕΙΡΑ[
[...].ΝΕΝ·ΥΠΕΡ[.]ΕΔΑΙΜΟΝ
[...]ΥΘΕΩΝΕСΤΙ[.]ΧΑΡΙС·
[..]ΔΕΛΑΤΟΙ̇Δ[..]ΑΝΑΞ·

40 [.....]ΝΑΛΥΆ[.]ΤΑΔΟΜΟΙ

[. . . . . . .]ΜΥΡΙΩΝ

[. . . . . . .]Ν·

25. πεπρωμέναν Palmer.   27, 28. Restored by Palmer.   29. ὁ δ' ἐς Jebb.   30. μολών Jebb.   31. δουλοσύναν Jebb.   33. The second letter may be an A.   37. ὑπέρβιε Blass, which suits the space better than ὑπέρτατε.

necessary to emphasize the divine favour with which the life of Croesus ended, rather than the overthrow of his earthly prosperity.

26. Ζηνὸς τελειοῦσαι κτίσιν : cf. Pind. *Ol*. XIII. 83 τελεῖ δὲ θεῶν δύναμις καὶ τὰν παρ' ὅρκον καὶ παρὰ ἐλπίδα κούφαν κτίσιν. Here, however, κτίσις (if it be right) would have a meaning still nearer to its common sense. τὰν πεπρωμέναν Ζηνὸς κτίσιν = ' the fated ordinance of Zeus.' τίσιν (Jebb, Sandys) is also possible, but suits the size of the lacuna less well. Moreover, as Croesus is here set forth as a favourite of the gods, it is perhaps more appropriate to represent him as suffering from the *fate* of Zeus than from his *vengeance*.

Λυδίας ἀρχαγέταν,

25 εὖτε τὰν πεπ[ρωμέναν]

Ζηνὸς τελε[ιοῦσαι κτί]σιν

Σάρδιες Περσ[ῶν ἑάλωσαν στρ]ατῷ,

Κροῖσον ὁ χρυσ[άορος]

φύλαξ᾽ Ἀπόλλων· [ὁ δ᾽ ἐς ἄ]ελπτον ἆμαρ   στρ. γ΄.

30 μ[ο]λὼν πολυδ[άκρυον] οὐκ ἔμελλε

μίμνειν ἔτι δ[ουλοσύν]αν· π[υρ]ὰν δὲ

χαλ[κο]τειχέος π[ροπάροι]θεν αὐ[λᾶς]

πο[ιήσ]ατ᾽, ἔνθα σὺ[ν ἀλόχῳ] τε κεδ[νᾷ] ἀντ. γ΄.

σύ[ν τ]᾽ εὐπλοκάμοι[ς] ἐπέβαιν᾽ ἄλα[στον]

35 [θυγα]τράσι δυρο[μ]έναις· χέρας δ[᾽ ἐς]

[αἰ]πὺ[ν] αἰθέρα σ[φ]ετέρας ἀείρα[ς]

[γέγω]νεν· ὑπέρ[βι]ε δαῖμον,   ἐπ. γ΄.

[πο]ῦ θεῶν ἐστὶ[ν] χάρις ;

[ποῦ] δὲ Λατοίδ[ας] ἄναξ ;

40 [. . . . . . .]ν Ἀλυά[τ]τα δόμοι

[‿ ‿ ‿ ‒ ‿ ‒ ‿ ‒ ‒] μυρίων

[‒ ‿ ‒ ‿ ‒ ‿ ‿]ν.

---

28. χρυσάορος : applied to Apollo by Pindar (*Pyth.* V. 104), as well as by Homer.   χρυσάρματος or χρυσόθρονος would equally suit the metre.

30. μολών : the MS. is rubbed here, but this reading (due to a suggestion by Jebb) suits all the requirements except the circumflex which the ω seems to have in the MS. ; and on that Jebb notes that in Soph. *Ant.* 916 λαβών has been corrected from λαβὼν in L.

34. ἄλαστον : with δυρομέναις, cf. Homer, *Od.* xiv. 174, ἄλαστον ὀδύρομαι (Jebb).

36. σφετέρας : in singular sense = 'his,' as occasionally in Pindar (*e. g. Ol.* IX. 84 ; *Pyth.* IV. 83) and elsewhere in poetry.

39. Λατοίδας : to be scanned as a trisyllable (as in Pind. *Pyth.* I. 12 ; IV. 259), in spite of the marks of diaeresis in the MS.

[.   . • • . .]ΝΑΣΤΥ

[.   . • • . .]ΔΙΝΑΣ

Col. 4] 45 ΠΑΚΤωΛΟΣ·Α[.]ΙΚΕΛΙωΣΓΥΝΑΙΚΕΣ

ΕΞΕΥΚΤΙΤ[.]ΝΜΕΓΑΡωΝΑΓΟΝΤΑΙ·

ΤΑΠΡΟΣΘΕΝΔ[. .]ΘΡΑΦΙΛΑΘΑΝΕΙΝΓΛΥΚΙΣΤΟΝ·
^{νυν}

ΤΟΣ·ΕΙΠΕΚΑΙΑΒ[. .]ΒΑΩΤΑΝΚ[. . .]ΥΣΕΝ

ΑΠΤΕΙΝΞΥΛΙΝΟΝΔΟΜΟΝ·ΕΙ[. . .]ΟΝΔΕ

50 ΠΑΡΘΕΝΟΙ·ΦΙΛΑΣΤΑΝΑΜΑΤΡΙΧ[.]ΙΡΑΣ

ΕΒΑΛΛΟΝ·ΟΓΑΡΠΡΟΦΑΝΗΣΘΙΑ

ΤΟΙΣΙΝΕΧΘΙ[. . . .]ΦΟΝωΝ·

ΑΛΛ·ΕΠΕΙΔΕΙΝΟ[. .]ΥΡΟΣ

ΛΑΜΠΡΟΝΔΙΑΪ[. . . . .] . ΟΣ

55 ΖΕΥΣΕΠΙΣΤΑΣΑ[. . . . .]ΘΕΣΝΕΦΟΣ

ΣΒΕΝΝΥΕΝΞΑΝΘΑ[   ]

ΑΠΙΣΤΟΝΟΥΔΕΝΟΤΙΘ[. . . .]ΡΙΜΝΑ

ΤΕΥΧΕΙ·ΤΟΤΕΔΑΛΟΓΕΝΗΙ[. . .]ΛΛωΝ

---

47. ΠΡΟΣΘΕΝ Α, corr. on metrical grounds. ἐχθρά Palmer. ΝΥΝ is added above ΦΙΛΑ by Α³.   48. ΑΒ . . ΒΑΩΤΑΝ Α, corr. Α¹? 51. ΕΒΑΛΛΕΝ Α, corr. Α¹. ΘΝΑ-] ΘΙΑ Α, corr. Α¹.   56. φλόγα Palmer.

44. χρυσοδίνας: the only authority for this word is the late Byzantine rhetorician Nicolaus (Walz, *Rhett.* I. 476) ; but it would be especially appropriate to Pactolus (and is so used by Nicolaus). The fact that the preceding syllable has to be short may seem an argument in favour of the more commonplace εὐρυδίνας, but something like ἐρεύθεται αἵματι χρυσοδίνας would suit both sense and metre.

47. The metre shows that the νῦν which has been written above the line in a later hand is an explanatory gloss, not a word which has been accidentally omitted.

48. ἀβροβάταν: the most obvious explanation is to take this as a synonym for Πέρσην, as it practically is in Aesch. *Pers.* 1072, the only other place where it occurs; but (as Professor Palmer has pointed out) the Persians take no part in the burning of Croesus, according to the version of Bacchy-

[‿ – ‿ ‿ ‿ ‿ ‿ ‿ – ‿   ]ν ἄστυ   στρ. δ΄.

[χρυσο]δίνας

45 Πακτωλός· ἀ[ε]ικελίως γυναῖκες

ἐξ εὐκτίτ[ω]ν μεγάρων ἄγονται.

τὰ πρόσθε δ᾽ [ἐχ]θρὰ φίλα· θανεῖν γλύκιστον.

τόσ᾽ εἶπε καὶ ἀβ[ρο]βάταν κ[έλ]ευσεν   [ἀντ. δ΄.

ἄπτειν ξύλινον δόμον· ἔκ[λαγ]ον δὲ

50 παρθένοι, φίλας τ᾽ ἀνὰ ματρὶ χ[ε]ῖρας

ἔβαλλον· ὁ γὰρ προφανὴς θνα-   ἐπ. δ΄.

τοῖσιν ἔχθι[στος] φόνων.

ἀλλ᾽ ἐπεὶ δεινο[ῦ π]υρὸς

λαμπρὸν διάϊ[σσεν μέν]ος,

55 Ζεὺς ἐπιστάσα[ς μελαγκευ]θὲς νέφος

σβέννυεν ξανθὰ[ν φλόγα].

ἄπιστον οὐδὲν ὅ τ[ι θεῶν μέ]ριμνα   στρ. ε΄.

τεύχει. τότε Δαλογενὴ[ς Ἀπό]λλων

lides. His death is self-sought, and ἀβροβάταν must represent a Lydian attendant, to whom the description is equally applicable. It may be a proper name, like Ἀβροκόμας in Herod. VII. 224 (so Palmer).

51. προφανής: 'the death that is visible before it comes.' This sense is found elsewhere only in Aristotle, *Eth.* III. 8, 15, but is preferable to the common meaning, 'clearly visible.' The word does not occur elsewhere in verse.

54. μένος: so also Jebb; the letter before ος seems to end in a perpendicular stroke, and must therefore be μ, ν, or π.

55. μελαγκευθές: adjectives ending in -θης with this scansion are not common, and μελαγκευθής has the recommendation of being used elsewhere by Bacchylides, viz. in frag. 64 (Bergk 38) μελαγκευθὲς εἴδωλον ἀνδρὸς Ἰθακησίου.

56. ξανθὰν φλόγα: cf. frag. 46 (Bergk 13), l. 4 ξανθᾷ φλογί.

57. ἄπιστον οὐδέν κ.τ.λ.: cf. XVII. 117, and Pind. *Pyth.* X. 48 ἐμοὶ δὲ θαυμάσαι | θεῶν τελεσάντων οὐδέν ποτε φαίνεται | ἔμμεν ἄπιστον.

58. Δαλογενής: the epithet recurs in XI. 15, but elsewhere is found only in a quotation from an unnamed lyric poet (assumed by Bergk to be Simonides) in Aristotle, *Rhet.* III. 8.

ΦΕΡωΝΕΣΥΠΕΡΒΟΡΕΟ[. . .]ΕΡΟΝΤΑ

60 ΣΥΝΤΑΝΙΣΦΎΡΟΙΣΚΑΤ[. . .]ΣΣΕΚΟΥΡΑΙΣ

ΔΙΕΥΣΕΒΕΙΑΝ·ΟΤΙΜΕ[. . . . .]ΝΑΤωΝ

ΕΣΑ[.]ΑΘΕΑΝΕΠΕΜΨΕ[. . .]ω·

ΟΣ[. .]ΜΕΝΕΛΛΑΔ·ΕΧΟΥΣΙΝ[.·]ΥΤΙ[.]

ωΜ[.]ΓΑΙΝΗΤΕΙΕΡωΝΘΕΛΗΣΕΙ

65 [. . . .]Ν . ΕΟΠΛΕΙΟΝΑΧΡΥΣΟΝ

[. . . .]ΑΙΠΕΜΨΑΙΒΡΟΤωΙ

[. . .]ΓΕΙΝΠΑΡΕΣΤΙΝΟ̇Σ

[. . . .]ΗΦΘΟΝωΙ ΪΑΙΝΕΤΑ[.]

[. . . .]ΛΗΦΙΛΙΠΠΟΝΑΝΔΡΑ[.]ΗΙω[

70 [. . . .]ΙΟΥΣΚΑ̑ΠΤΡ[.Ν]ΔΙΟ[

[. . . .]ΚωΝΤΕΜΕΡΟ[

[. . . .]ΜΑΛΕΑΙΠΟΤ[

59, 60. γέροντα was conjectured by Blass and κατένασσε by Palmer; and the former led to the identification of a fragment containing parts of the endings of ll. 59–65.   62. ΕΠΕΜΨΕ A, corr. on metrical grounds.   65. σέο Palmer.   67, 68. ὅστις μή Palmer. ΙΑΙΝΕΤΑΙ A, corr. A³.   72. ΠΟΤ] ΝΟΤ A, apparently, corr. A¹?

59. Ὑπερβορέους: ὧν θαλίαις ἔμπεδον | εὐφαμίαις τε μάλιστ' Ἀπόλλων | χαίρει (Pind. *Pyth.* X. 34). The land of the Hyperboreans, as described in this well-known passage of Pindar, is a land of the blest, and especially beloved of Apollo. There appears to be no other authority for this end to the story of Croesus.

60. τανισφύροις: this form (τανι- for τανυ-) is consistently used in the MS., cf. V. 59 τανισφύρου, XI. 55 τανίφυλλον.

63. ὅσοι μέν: there is no answering δέ, but μέν, as often (*e. g.* after pronouns, ἐγὼ μέν, &c.), has a limiting force much like that of γε. No one

φέρων ἐς Ὑπερβορέο[υς γ]έροντα
60 σὺν τανισφύροις κατ[ένα]σσε κούραις
δι' εὐσέβειαν, ὅτι μέ[γιστα θ]νατῶν   ἀντ. ε'.
ἐς ἀ[γ]αθέαν ἐπέπεμψε [Πυθ]ώ.
ὅσ[οι] μὲν Ἑλλάδ' ἔχουσιν, [ο]ὔτις,
ὦ μ[ε]γαίνητε Ἱέρων, θελήσει

65 [. . . .]ν [σ]έο πλείονα χρυσὸν   ἐπ. ε'.

[. . . .]ᾳ πέμψαι βροτῷ

[. . . .]ειν πάρεστιν ὅσ-

[τις μ]ὴ φθόνῳ πιαίνετα[ι]

[. . . .]λη φίλιππον ἄνδρα [Κ]ηΐω[ν]

70 [. . . .]ιον σκᾶπτρ[ο]ν Διὸ[ς]

[. . . .] Κῶν τε Μερο[π   ]   στρ. ς'.

[. . . .] Μαλέᾳ ποτ[   ]

would send gifts greater than Hieron—of the men at least who inhabit Hellas (Jebb). There is a stop in the MS. at the end of l. 62, which indicates that this is the proper division of the clauses. The paragraphus between ll. 63 and 64 should presumably have come after l. 64, marking the end of the antistrophe.

64. μεγαίνητε: the last syllable is lengthened in arsis, which rather helps than increases the licence of the hiatus. The accent shows that μεγαίνητε is to be regarded as one word (similar in formation to μεγήρατα in Hesiod, *Theog.* 240), not as two, with μέγ' adverbial. Cf. I. 16.

69. Κηίων: or possibly Κήϊον.

71. Κῶν τε Μερο—: Professor Palmer was the first to point out that this mutilated line, with the letters κωντεμερο, probably contains a reference to Cos, which also bore the name of Μεροπίς. Possibly, as Jebb adds, the reference is to the person, Cos the son of Merops. It is not clear, however, in what connexion the name is mentioned here.

72. Μαλέᾳ: perhaps mentioned in connexion with the worship of Apollo there, cf. Thuc. VII. 26, 2; Paus. III. 12, 8 (Jebb).

[. . . .]ΝΟϹΕΦΑΜΕΡΟΝΑ[

[. . . .] . ϹΚΟΠΕΙϹΒΡΑΧ[

7 [. . . .ˈ]ΕϹϹΑΔˈΕΛΠΙϹΥΠ[

[. . .]ΕΡΙѠΝˑΟΔˈΑΝΑΞ[

[. . . .ʹ.]ΟϹΕΙΠΕΦΕΡΗ[

                   v
Col. 5]   ΘΝΑΤΟΝΕΥΤΑ𝍒ΧΡΗΔΙΔΥΜΟΥϹΑΕΞΕΙΝ

          ΓΝѠΜΑϹΟΤΙΤˈΑΥΡΙΟΝΟΨΕΑΙ

80   ΜΟΥΝΟΝΑΛΙˊΟΥΦΑΟϹ

        ΧѠΤΙΠΕΝΤΗΚΟΝΤˈΕΤΕΑ

        ΖѠΑΝΒΑΘΥˊΠΛΟΥΤΟΝΤΕΛΕΙϹˑ

        ΟˊϹΙΑΔΡѠΝΕΥˊΦΡΑΙΝΕΘΥΜΟΝˑΤΟΥΤΟΓΑΡ

        <u>ΚΕΡΔΕˊѠΝΥΠΕΡΤΑΤΟΝˑ</u>

85   ΦΡΟΝΕΟΝΤ[ˑ]ϹΥΝΕΤΑΓΑΡΥˊѠˑΒΑΘΥϹΜΕΝ

78. ΕΥΝΤΑ] ΕΥΤΑΝ Δ, corr. Δ²?

75. Professor Jebb suggests δολόεσσα δ' ἐλπὶς ὑπὸ κέαρ δέδυκεν | ἐπαμερίων. The first and last words were independently proposed by Dr. Sandys.

77. The first word is not Ἀδμητος, the letter before ος being apparently a λ, while there is an accent on the letter immediately preceding it. This suggests the possibility of restoring ὁ δ' ἄναξ Ἀπόλλων | ὁ βουκόλος (or ἑκα-βόλος [Jebb]) εἶπε Φέρητος υἱῷ, with a reference to the time when Apollo served Admetus as his cowherd. In any case it seems better to read υἱῷ than υἱός, making the following passage a declaration to Admetus rather than by him.

78 ff. The following passage is a consolation to Hieron for the approach of old age. The words addressed to Admetus extend as far as l. 84, and in the phrase which follows (φρονέοντι συνετὰ γαρύω) the poet applies them to Hieron. The tone of the whole closely resembles that of the last part of Pindar's third Pythian. There Hieron is ill, and probably it was known that the illness was incurable; so that whether that ode was actually written shortly before his death or a few years earlier, the poet, like Bacchylides here, was certainly contemplating his death and addressing to him words of consolation. In both the consolation takes the same form. Mortal man must not count on length of days nor permanence of prosperity; but virtue

[....]νος ἐφάμερον ἀ[˘ ‾ ‾ ˘   ]

[....] σκοπεῖς βραχ[‾ ˘ ˘ ‾ ˘ ‾ ˘   ]

75 [....]εσσα δ᾽ ἐλπὶς ὑπ[˘ ˘ ˘ ‾ ˘ ‾ ˘   ]   ἀντ. ϛʹ.

[...]εριων· ὁ δ᾽ ἄναξ [˘ ‾ ˘]

[.....]ος εἶπε Φέρη[τος υἱῷ]·

θνατὸν ἐὖντα χρὴ διδύμους ἀέξειν

γνώμας, ὅτι τ᾽ αὔριον ὄψεαι   ἐπ. ϛʹ.

80 μοῦνον ἁλίου φάος,

χὥτι πεντήκοντ᾽ ἔτεα

ζωὰν βαθύπλουτον τελεῖς.

ὅσια δρῶν εὔφραινε θυμόν· τοῦτο γὰρ

κερδέων ὑπέρτατον.

85 φρονέοντ[ι] συνετὰ γαρύω· βαθὺς μὲν   στρ. ζʹ.

preserves its sheen undimmed, and the poet's praise can secure it immortality.

81. πεντήκοντ᾽ ἔτεα : these words form part of the address to Admetus, but it is evident that they are intended to apply, at any rate approximately, to Hieron. The date of Hieron's birth is nowhere stated, but this accords sufficiently well with what can be gathered indirectly as to his age. He had a son sufficiently old in 476 to be made regent of Aetna, and this of itself is sufficient to show that in 468, the date of this ode, he could not have been far short of fifty. On the other hand the tone of Pindar's ode seems to indicate that he was not an old man ; and at the battle of Himera, in 480, he was still in the prime of life. It is therefore safe to accept the words of Bacchylides as giving approximately Hieron's real age in 468, a year before his death.

85. φρονέοντι συνετά : Bacchylides' equivalent for Pindar's φωνάεντα συνετοῖσιν (Ol. II. 93).

85-87. βαθὺς μὲν αἰθὴρ ἀμίαντος, κ.τ.λ. : the form of this passage suggests a comparison with the celebrated exordium of Pindar's first Olympian, which, since it was written either four or eight years previously, Bacchylides must have known. The references to gold and water are common to both, and so is the apophthegmatic form of utterance, though the immediate bearing of the comparisons is different. The point of the comparison in

ΑΙΘΗΡΑΜΙΑΝΤΟΣ·ΫΔΩΡΔΕΠΟΝΤΟΥ

ΟΥΣΑΠΕΤΑ[.]·ΈΥΦΡΟΣΥΝΑΔ'ΟΧΡΥΣΟΣ·

ΑΝΔΡΙΔ'Ο[. .]ΕΜΙΣΠΟΛΙΟΝΠ[. .]ΕΝΤΑ

ΓΗΡΑΣΘΑΛ[. . .]ΝΑΥΤΙΣΑΓΚΟΜΙΣΑΙ

90   ΗΒΑΝ·ΑΡΕΤΑ[. . .]ΕΝΟΥΜΙΝΥΘΕΙ

ΒΡΟΤΩΝΑΜΑΣ[. . .]ΤΙΦΕΓΓΟΣ·ΑΛΛΑ

MΟΥΣΑΝΙΝΤΡ[. . . .]ΪΕΡΩΝΣΥΔ'ΟΛΒΟΥ

ΚΑΛΛΙΣΤ'ΕΠΕΔ[. . .]ΑΟΘΝΑΤΟΙΣ

ΑΝΘΕΑ·ΠΡΑΞΑ[. . .]Δ'ΕΥ

95   ΟΥΦΕΡΕΙΚΟΣΜ[. . . .]Ω

ΠΑ·ΣΥΝΔ'ΑΛΑΘ[. . . .]ΚΑΛΩΝ

ΚΑΙΜΕΛΙΓΛΩΣΣΟΥΤΙΣΥΜΝΗΣΕΙΧΑΡΙΝ

ΚΗΙΑΣΑΗΔΟΝΟΣ

---

89. ΑΓΚΟΜΙΣΑΙ Δ, corr. on metrical grounds.   91. σώματι
J. K. Ingram.   98. ΑΗΔΟΝΟΣ] Ο was at first mis-written for Δ,
but corrected at once.

Bacchylides is not very obvious, but it appears to lie in the contrast between
the permanency of these elemental excellences, and the transiency of
human life ; to which is added the suggestion, not explicitly worked out,
that virtue, cherished by the Muse, may attain to the permanency denied to
man's mortal life. ' The depths of air suffer no stain. The waters of the
sea decay not. Gold is a joy for ever. But man that has reached hoary
age may not win back the bloom of youth. Yet virtue hath a radiance
which faileth not with the mortal frame, but is nourished by the Muse.'

88. παρέντα: the only words which suit the remains visible in the MS.
seem to be προέντα, with the somewhat unusual sense of 'casting away,'
'letting slip,' or παρέντα (proposed by Jebb), 'after·seeing old age go by.'
In support of the latter, Jebb quotes Plato, *Rep.* 460 E, ἀνδρὶ δέ, ἐπειδὰν τὴν

αἰθὴρ ἀμίαντος· ὕδωρ δὲ πόντου
οὐ σάπετα[ι]· εὐφροσύνα δ᾽ ὁ χρυσός·
ἀνδρὶ δ᾽ [οὐ θ]έμις πολιὸν π[αρ]έντα
γῆρας θάλ[εια]ν αὖτις ἀγκομίσσαι   ἀντ. ζ'.
90 ἥβαν. ἀρετᾶ[ς γε μ]ὲν οὐ μινύθει
βροτῶν ἅμα σ[ώμα]τι φέγγος· ἀλλὰ
Μοῦσά νιν τρ[έφει]. Ἱέρων, σὺ δ᾽ ὄλβου
κάλλιστ᾽ ἐπεδ[είξ]αο θνατοῖς   ἐπ. ζ'.
ἄνθεα· πράξα[ντι] δ᾽ εὖ
95 οὐ φέρει κόσμ[ον σι]ω-
πά. σὺν δ᾽ ἀλαθ[είᾳ] καλῶν
καὶ μελιγλώσσου τις ὑμνήσει χάριν
Κηΐας ἀηδόνος.

ὀξυτάτην δρόμου ἀκμὴν παρῇ, and Soph. *O. C.* 1229 εὖτ᾽ ἂν τὸ νέον παρῇ, which strongly confirm it.   The first letter may also be a γ.

90. μινύθει: if the reading is right (and there is nothing suspicious about the word in itself) the υ is here scanned long, of which there is no other example.

95. οὐ φέρει κόσμον σιωπά: contrast Soph. *Aj.* 293 γυναιξὶ κόσμον ἡ σιγὴ φέρει.   Here, however, σιωπά is not the silence of the prosperous man himself, but of his contemporaries.   Bacchylides' sentiment is equivalent to Horace's 'Paullum sepultae distat inertiae Celata virtus.'

96. καλῶν: the participle, agreeing with τις: 'naming him with truth,' i. e. in praising Bacchylides he may truthfully be called the 'honey-tongued nightingale of Ceos.'

97. μελιγλώσσου: apparently a favourite word with Bacchylides, who uses it again, as an epithet of ἀοιδαί, in the well-known fragment on Peace (frag. 46, Bergk 13).

IV.

πύθια.

```
  ⏑ ⏑ ⏑ − ⏑ ⏑ − ⏑ −
  ⏑ ⏑ ⏑ − ⏑ ⏑ − ⏑ − −
  − ⏑ ⏑ − ⏑ ⏑ − ⏑ ⏑ − −
  ⏑ − ⏑ − − ⏑ ⏑ − ⏑ − − ⏑ −
5 − ⏑ ⏑ − ⏑ ⏑ − ⏑ ⏑
  − ⏑ ⏑ − ⏑ ⏑ − ⏑ − −
  ⏑ ⏑ − ⏑ ⏑ − − − −
  ⏑ − − ⏑ − ⏑ ⏑ − ⏑ − −
  ⏑ ⏑ ⏑ − − ⏑ ⏑ −
10 − ⏑ − ⏑ ⏑ − − ⏑ − −
```

I—10 = 11—20

ΕΤΙCΥΡΑΚΟCΊΑΝΦΙΛΕΙ
ΠΟΛΙΝΌΧΡΥCΟΚΟ[.]ΑCΑΠΟΛΛⲰΝ
ΑCΤΎΘΕΜΙΝΘ᾿Ϊ[...]ΝΑΓΕΡΆΙΡΕΙ·
ΤΡΙΤΟΝΓΑΡ[......]ΛΟΝΥΨΙΔΕΊΡΟΥΧΘΟΝΟC
5 ΠΥ[.]ΙΌΝΙΚ[......]ΤΑΙ

IV. *Title*: apparently by A³.   4. ἀμφ᾿ ὀμφαλόν Jebb.

3. ἀστύθεμις: a coinage of Bacchylides, so far as is known, and the only instance (except in proper names) in which θέμις appears as the second part of a compound. It has, of course, a transitive sense = ὁ θεμίζων τὸ ἄστυ.

IV.

ΤΩΙ ΑΥΤΩΙ

⟨ἵπποις⟩ Πυθία.

The following much mutilated little poem is shown by its title to be addressed to Hieron on the occasion of a Pythian victory, and by its contents (l. 6) to be concerned with a victory in the chariot race. The omission of ἵπποις in the title is due to the fact that it had occurred in the title of the preceding poem, so that it is covered, so to speak, by the words τῷ αὐτῷ. Hieron's victory in the chariot race at Delphi was won in Pyth. 29 (Schol. on Pind. *Pyth.* I), which (adopting Clinton's and Bergk's calculation of the Pythiads, which is also that of the Scholiasts, as against that of Pausanias and Boeckh, which places each Pythiad four years earlier) corresponds with the year 470 B.C. The present poem was probably composed on the spot for immediate use, like Pindar's eleventh Olympian. The same victory forms the subject of Pindar's first Pythian, but that was evidently written for a later and more elaborate celebration of the victory, in the presence of Hieron himself. The two poets therefore do not come into direct rivalry here, but the higher task is assigned to Pindar; and if, as seems certain, this is subsequent to the competition between Pindar's first Olympian and the fifth ode of Bacchylides (see below, the introductory note to the latter), the fact is significant.

The poem consists of two strophes in logaoedic metre.

ἔτι Συρακοσίαν φιλεῖ   στρ. α΄.

πόλιν ὁ χρυσοκόμας Ἀπόλλων,

ἀστύθεμίν θ᾽ Ἱ[έρω]να γεραίρει.

τρίτον γὰρ [ἀμφ᾽ ὀμφα]λὸν ὑψιδείρου χθονὸς

5 Π[υθ]ιόνικ[ος ἀείδε]ται,

4. τρίτον: Hieron had previously won two Pythian victories in the single horse race, both with his famous horse Pherenicus (see next ode).

ὑψιδείρου: another ἅπαξ εἰρημένον, compounded from δειράς ('the high-ridged earth'); not, like δολιχόδειρος, ταναύδειρος κ.τ.λ., from δειρή, in the sense of 'neck.' ὑψίδειρος would be very applicable to the region around Delphi.

ω[. .]ΠΟΔ[. . . . .]ϹΥΝΙΠΠΩΝ·

[. . . . .]

[.　.　.　.　.　.]ΑϹΑΛΕΚΤΩΡ

[.　.　.　.　.　.]ΤΙΝΟΩΙ

10 [.　.　.　.　.　.]ΥΜΝΟΥϹ[

[.　.　.　.　.　.　.]

[.　.　.　.　.　.　.]

Col. 6]　　ΔΕΙΝΟΜΕΝΕΟϹΚ'. . ΕΡΑ . . ΜΕΝΥΙΟΝ·

ΠΑΡΕϹΤΊΑΝΑΓΧΙΑ . ΟΙϹ[. . . .]ΑϹΜΥΧΟΙϹ

15 ΜΟΥΝΟΝΕΠΙΧΘΟΝΙΩ[.]ΤΑΔΕ

ΜΗϹΑΜΕΝΟΝϹΤΕΦΑΝΟΙϹΕΡΕΠΤΕΙΝ

ΔΥΟΤ'ΟΛΥΜΠΙΟΝΙΚΑϹ

ΑΕΙΔΕΙΝ·ΤΙΦ[.]ΡΤΕΡΟΝΗ . . . . ΙΝ

18. θεοῖσιν Palmer.

6. ὠκυπόδων . . . . . . σὺν ἵππων : Professor Palmer suggests ἐν ἀγῶσιν ἵππων, which makes excellent sense, but involves an alteration of the reading of the MS. ; and this, in a mutilated passage, must be regarded as inadmissible.　Perhaps καμάτῳ σὺν ἵππων, the preposition having the same almost instrumental significance as in Pindar, *Nem.* X. 48 δρόμῳ σὺν ποδῶν χειρῶν τε νικᾶσαι σθένει : or ἀέθλοις (Jebb), scanned as in Pind. *Nem.* I. 11, &c.

8. ———as ἀλέκτωρ : Professor Palmer suggests ἐνδομάχας ἀλέκτωρ, from Pind. *Ol.* XII. 14, but in the absence of the context it is impossible to say whether the sense would be suitable here.

13. κ' ἐγεραίρομεν : the MS. appears to have a mark of elision after the κ, otherwise κατεραίνομεν would be equally possible, and easier to interpret. As it stands, the interpretation of the passage depends wholly on the missing words.

14. παρ' ἑστίαν : the accusative indicates that some word implying sending or going has been lost before l. 13, on which this clause depends.　In the absence of this word it is impossible to say whether the passage alludes to an actual residence of Bacchylides in Sicily or not.

Αἴτνας : this restoration seems probable, so far as sense is concerned,

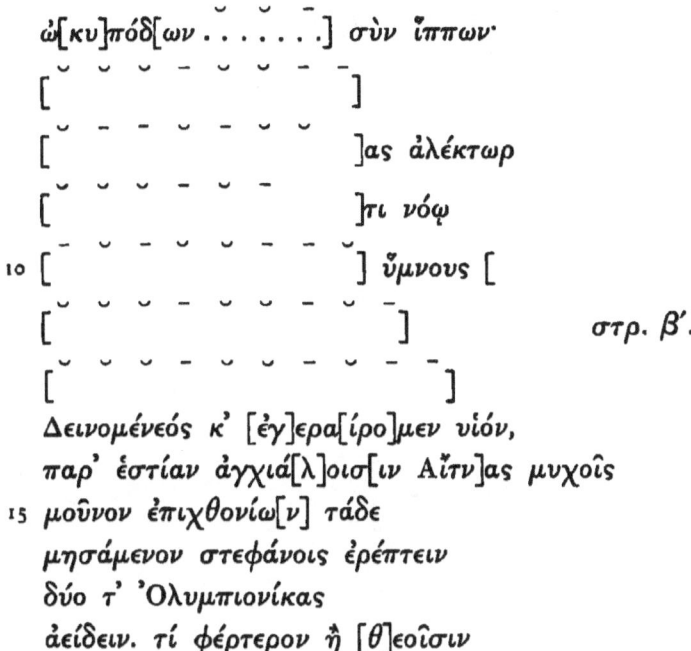

ὠ[κυ]πόδ[ων . . . .] σὺν ἵππων·

[   ]

[   ]ας ἀλέκτωρ

[   ]τι νόῳ

10 [   ] ὕμνους [

[   ]   στρ. β'.

[   ]

Δεινομένεός κ' [ἐγ]ερα[ίρο]μεν υἱόν,
παρ' ἑστίαν ἀγχιά[λ]οισ[ιν Αἴτν]ας μυχοῖς
15 μοῦνον ἐπιχθονίω[ν] τάδε
μησάμενον στεφάνοις ἐρέπτειν
δύο τ' Ὀλυμπιονίκας
ἀείδειν. τί φέρτερον ἢ [θ]εοῖσιν

since Hieron (as appears from Pindar's contemporary poem) at this date liked references to his founding of the city of Aetna (in 476); but it is a little doubtful whether there is room in the lacuna for six letters, even though two of them are iotas. Perhaps the scribe wrote ἀγχιάλοις.

16. μησάμενον: perhaps a corruption of μησάμενοι (Jebb); but the mutilation of the passage leaves its construction obscure.

17. δύο τ' Ὀλυμπιονίκας: in the mutilated condition of the poem it is impossible to say with certainty who are the two Olympic victors here referred to. No other member of Hieron's family is known to have won Olympic victories, except Gelon; and the scholiast on Aristides III, p. 317 (Bergk, Bacch. frag. 5) says that Bacchylides and Pindar celebrated the victories of Gelon and Hieron, which suggests that Bacchylides may have composed an ode in 488, when Gelon and Hieron were both victorious at Olympia. But the words of the scholiast do not necessarily mean that both poets wrote odes for both rulers, and a reference to a victory won eighteen years previously hardly suits the tone of the present passage. A possible explanation is that Hieron's son, Deinomenes, was associated with his father in the Olympic victory of 472; but of this there is no confirmation, and one would have expected to find it mentioned in Pindar's and Bacchylides' poems on the occasion.

D

ΦΙΛΟΝΕΟΝΤΑΠΑΝΤΟ[.] . ΠῶΝ   ·

20 ΛΑΓΧΑΝΕΙΝΑΠΟΜΟΙΡΑ[. . .]ΘΛΩΝ

V.

STROPHE.

19. παντοδαπῶν : not a very satisfactory word in point of sense, but none other seems to answer the requirements of metre and the remains visible in the MS. Hieron won victories at Olympia, Pytho, and Thebes.

20. λαγχάνειν ἀπο μοῖραν : =ἀπολαγχάνειν μοῖραν, cf. Herod. V. 57. For

φίλον ἐόντα παντο[δα]πῶν
20 λαγχάνειν ἄπο μοῖρα[ν ἀέ]θλων ;

V.

⟨ΤΩΙ ΑΥΤΩΙ⟩

⟨κέλητι Ὀλύμπια.⟩

This poem is separated in the MS. from the last merely by a
simple *paragraphus*, such as usually indicates the end of a strophe.
There is no title and no indication that a new poem is being begun.
The fact that it is a new poem is established by the difference in
metre, and also by the character of the contents, which show that it
relates to an Olympian and not a Pythian victory. It is a victory
won by Hieron at Olympia in the single horse race, with his
celebrated horse Pherenicus ; and the scholiast on Pindar, who
quotes lines 37-40, tells us that it is the same victory as that commemorated by Pindar in his great first Olympian ode. The
chronology of this and the other victories won by Hieron is somewhat obscure, but considerable light is thrown upon the subject by
Bacchylides. We know from the scholiast on Pindar (*Pyth.* III)
that Hieron won the single horse race at Delphi in the 26th
and 27th Pythiads, which, according to the reckonings of
Pausanias, followed by Boeckh and most modern editors, correspond with 486 and 482 B.C.; and from *Pyth.* III. 73, 74, we learn
that these victories (there is no record of Hieron having won on
any other occasion in this particular contest) were gained by the
horse Pherenicus. It is also clear from *Ol.* I. 18 that the Olympic
victory there commemorated was won by Pherenicus ; and this
poem is assigned by most editors to 472 B.C. We therefore

the tmesis, with the preposition following the verb, cf. XIX. 7 βάλωσιν ἀμφι
τιμᾶν. It would no doubt be possible to read ἀπόμοιραν, but the word is late
and prosaic.

EPODE.

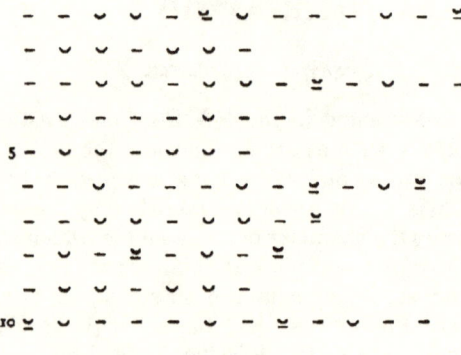

$$1—15 = 16—30 : 31—40$$
$$41—55 = 56—70 : 71—80$$
$$81—95 = 96—110 : 111—120$$
$$121—135 = 136—150 : 151—160$$
$$161—175 = 176—190 : 191—200$$

apparently have the same horse winning races over a period of fourteen years, which is practically impossible; and it has consequently been suggested by Dr. Fennell and others that the Pherenicus of the Pythian victories was the sire or grandsire of the Pherenicus of the Olympian victory. This theory is, however, overthrown by the present poem of Bacchylides, which clearly shows (lines 37-41) that the victor at Olympia had also been victorious at Pytho. The Pythian and Olympian victors must consequently be one and the same, and it becomes necessary to adopt a chronology which will make this possible. The necessary approximation of dates can be made from both sides. On the one hand this evidence is a strong confirmation of the later dating of the Pythiads, followed by the scholiasts on Pindar and by Bergk, and already probable upon other grounds (cf. Wilamowitz-Moellendorff, *Aristoteles und Athen*, II. 324 ff.), according to which the 26th and 27th Pythiads fall in 482 and 478 B.C. On the other hand, the date assigned by Bergk to Pindar's first Olympian is 476 B.C. (the 76th Olympiad instead of the 77th), and there is nothing in the poem itself inconsistent with this date. Indeed, the omission of all reference, either in that poem of Pindar or in this of Bacchylides, to the victory of Kyme (in 474 B.C.), for which Hieron made a special offering at Olympia, is a strong argument in favour of the earlier date. Nor is there any allusion in either to the founding of Aetna, which took place in the course of 476 B.C.; and Didymus (quoted by the Schol. on Pind. *Ol.* I. 23) expressly states that Hieron was Συρακούσιος, not Αἰτναῖος, at the time of this victory.

On this showing, Pherenicus won his victories at Delphi in 482 and 478, at Olympia in 476[1]. A modern racehorse does not continue on the turf for six years, still less win important races over such a period; but the circumstances of Greek racing were different. Horses were not then raced at two years old, nor worked so hard as a modern racehorse at three and four. A fairer analogy may be found among steeplechasers, who do not begin racing so early and are consequently able to continue much longer. These horses frequently race at ten and eleven years old, and one celebrated steeplechaser, The Lamb, won the Grand National (the severest race of the whole year, being $4\frac{1}{2}$ miles in length, and always

---

[1] Any idea that the victory won by Hieron at Olympia with the single horse in 488 might be the one celebrated in this poem is at once put out of court by the fact that Hieron is addressed as ruler of Syracuse, which he was not until 478.

ΕΥΜΟΙΡ[..]ΥΡΑΚ[...]Ν

ΙΠΠΟΔΙΝΗΤ[.]..ϹΤΡΑΤΑ[.]Ε·

ΓΝΩϹΗΙΜΕΝ[.]ΟϹΤΕΦΑΝ[.]Ν

ΜΟΙϹΑΝΓΛΥΚ[.]ΔΩΡΟΝΑΓΑ[.]ΜΑΤΩΝΓΕΝΥΝ

5 ΑΙΤΙϹΕΠΙΧΘΟΝΪΩΝ

ΟΡΘΩϹ·ΦΡΕΝΑΔ'ΕΥΘΥΔΙΚ[.]Ν

ΑΤΡΕΜ'ΑΜΠΑΥϹΑϹΜΕΡΙΜΝᾶΝ

ΔΕΥΡ'ΑΘΡΗϹΟΝΝΟΩ[.]

ΗϹΥΝΧΑΡΙΤΕϹϹΙΒΑΘΥΖΏΝΟΙϹΥΦΑΝΑϹ

10 ΥΜΝΟΝΑΠΟΖΑΘΕΑϹ

ΝΑϹΟΥΞΕΝΟϹΫΜΕΤΕΡΑΝΠϮΕΜ

∇. 8. σὺν νόῳ] ΣΥΝ om. A, inserted on metrical grounds.
9. ῇ] Η A.

2. ἱπποδινήτων: a new word. On the analogy of οἰστροδίνητος, it should
mean 'whirled along by horses,' and there is perhaps a reference to the
coins of Syracuse, with their well-known device of a chariot drawn by four
horses.

4. Μοισᾶν: perhaps Μουσᾶν should be read; cf. note on II. 11.

5. αἰ: the MS. preserves the Doric form, which is not found in Pindar.

6. εὐθύδικον: possibly εὐθυδίκαν, as Bacchylides is fond of feminine forms;
but there is no extant example of the feminine. Pindar (*Pyth.* xi. 9) has
ὀρθοδίκαν as masculine.

8. σὺν νόῳ: 'attentively.' The insertion of σύν is required by the metre;
its omission in the MS. is easily explained by the fact that -σον precedes.

run at a great pace) twice at an interval of three years (1868 and 1871), being nine years old on the last occasion. This will give some indication of what may have been possible for a good horse under the easier circumstances of the Greek hippodrome.

The following poem, the longest of the odes of Bacchylides, consists of five systems. The first system, with the strophe of the second, deals with the praises of Hieron, the poet's comparison of himself to an eagle, and the victories of Pherenicus; the rest of the second system, the third and fourth systems, and the strophe of the fifth, contain the myth of Meleager; while the final antistrophe and epode revert to Hieron and pray for his prosperity. The metre is dactylo-epitritic, of a simple, easy-flowing character.

εὔμοιρ[ε Σ]υρακ[οσίω]ν   στρ. α΄.
ἱπποδινήτ[ων] στρατα[γ]έ,
γνώσῃ μὲν [ἰ]οστεφάν[ω]ν
Μοισᾶν γλυκ[ύ]δωρον ἄγαλμα, τῶν γε νῦν
5 αἴ τις ἐπιχθονίων,
ὀρθῶς· φρένα δ᾽ εὐθύδικ[ο]ν
ἀτρέμ᾽ ἀμπαύσας μεριμνᾶν,
δεῦρ᾽ ἄθρησον ⟨σὺν⟩ νόῳ,
ᾗ σὺν Χαρίτεσσι βαθυζώνοις ὑφάνας
10 ὕμνον ἀπὸ ζαθέας
νάσου ξένος ὑμετέραν πέμ-

9. ᾗ: 'where.' Professor Palmer suggests εἰ, 'whether.' The corruption of εἰ into η would be very easy in the hand of this MS., but the sense seems less satisfactory.

σὺν Χαρίτεσσι βαθυζώνοις : so Pindar, *Pyth.* IX. 1–3 ἐθέλω ... σὺν βαθυζώνοισιν ἀγγέλλων Τελεσικράτη Χαρίτεσσι γεγωνεῖν.

11. This line and the corresponding line in the antistrophe (l. 26) have a syllable more than the corresponding lines in all the remaining strophes, and the same is the case with ll. 14 and 29, the rhythm of which is similar. There is nothing suspicious in the text in either place, and the phenomenon must be left for metrologists to take note of.

νάσου : Ceos.

ξένος : this implies that Bacchylides had himself come to Hieron's court, either now or previously. The word πέμπει in itself might be taken

ΠΕΙΚΛΕΕΝΝΑΝΕCΠΟΛΙΝ

ΧΡΥCΑΜΠΥΚΟCΟΥΡΑΝΙΑC

ΚΛΕΙΝΟCΘΕΡΑΠΩΝ·ΕΘΕΛΕΙΔΕ

15 ΓΑΡΥΝΕΚCΤΗΘΕΩΝΧΕΩΝ

ΑΙΝΕΪΕΡΩΝΑ·ΒΑΘΥΝ

Δ᾽ΑΙΘΕΡΑΞΟΥΘΑΙCΙΤΑΜΝΩΝ

ΥΨΟΥΠΤΕΡΥΓΕCCΙΤΑΧΕΙ

ΑΙCΑΙΕΤΟCΕΥΡΥ͜ΑΝΑΚΤΟCΑΓΓΕΛΟC

20 ΖΗΝΟCΕΡΙCΦΑΡΑΓΟΥ

ΘΑΡCΕΙΚΡΑΤΕΡΑΙΠΙCΥΝΟC

ΙCΧΥΪ·ΠΤΑCCΟΝΤΙΔ᾽ΟΡΝΙ

ΧΕCΛΙΓΥ͜ΦΘΟΓΓΟΙΦΟΙΒΩΙ·

ΟΥΝΙΝΚΟΡΥΦΑΙΜΕΓΑΛΑͣCΙCΧΟΥCΙΓΑΙΑC

25 [.]ΥΔ᾽ΑΛΟCΑΚΑΜΑΤΑC

Col. 7]   ΔΥCΠΑΙΠΑΛΑΚΥΜΑΤΑ·ΝΩΜΑͣ

ΤΑΙΔ᾽ΕΝΑΤΡΥΤΩΙΧΑΕΙ

13, 14. ΟΥΡΑΝΙΑΣ | ΚΛΕΙΝΟΣ Α, altered on account of strophic correspondence. ΚΛΙΝΟΣ Α, corr. Α³.   16. ΑΙΝΕΙ Α, corr. Α²?   22. ΤΑΣΣΟΝΤΙ Α, corr. Α²?   23. φόβῳ] ΦΟΙΒΩΙ Α.   24. ΜΕΓΑ-ΛΑΙΣ Α, corr. Α²?   26. ΝΩΜΑΙ Α, corr. Α²?

to imply that Bacchylides, though he had previously visited Hieron and was consequently entitled to call himself ξένος, was now in Ceos and sent his poem from there.   But it is questionable whether the meaning of πέμπει is to be pressed.   In Pind. *Nem.* IV. 18 Timasarchus is said to 'send' home crowns from the games at Cleonae and Athens, though no doubt he brought them himself.   It is probable that Pindar was at the court of Hieron at this time (cf. *Ol.* I. 10, 16), and it is possible that there was a general assembly of poets in honour of the occasion.

13. χρυσάμπυκος: the same epithet is applied to the Muses generally in Pind. *Pyth.* III. 89.

16-30. Bacchylides, like Pindar in *Ol.* II. 97, claims kinship with the king of birds; and though the comparison, so far as regards the genius of Bacchylides, may be overbold, yet the passage itself, as a description of the

πει κλεεννὰν ἐς πόλιν
χρυσάμπυκος Οὐρανίας κλει-
νὸς θεράπων. ἐθέλει δὲ
15 γᾶρυν ἐκ στηθέων χέων
αἰνεῖν Ἱέρωνα· βαθὺν   ἀντ. α΄.
δ᾽ αἰθέρα ξουθαῖσι τάμνων
ὑψοῦ πτερύγεσσι ταχεί-
αις αἰετός, εὐρυάνακτος ἄγγελος
20 Ζηνὸς ἐρισφαράγου,
θαρσεῖ κρατερᾷ πίσυνος
ἰσχύϊ· πτάσσοντι δ᾽ ὄρνι-
χες λιγύφθογγοι φόβῳ.
οὔ νιν κορυφαὶ μεγάλας ἴσχουσι γαίας,
25 [ο]ὐδ᾽ ἁλὸς ἀκαμάτας
δυσπαίπαλα κύματα· νωμᾶ-
ται δ᾽ ἐν ἀτρύτῳ Χάει,

eagle, may form a companion picture to the celebrated Pindaric eagle of the first Pythian.

19. εὐρυάνακτος: the word does not occur elsewhere, but Callimachus (*Hymn to Demeter*, 121) has εὐρυάνασσα.

20. ἐρισφαράγου: in the Homeric hymn to Hermes (l. 187) of the roaring of the waves of Poseidon; here of the thunders of Zeus.

26. δυσπαίπαλα: in Archilochus (frag. 115, Bergk), the only other pre-Christian instance of the word, it is applied to the glens of mountains; and similarly παιπαλόεις in Homer. There is no other example of this or a kindred word applied to a soft and moving substance like water. This seems to favour the connexion between παιπαλόεις and δυσ-παλής, quoted by L. and S. from Schneidewin, so that the sense would be 'difficult,' rather than 'rocky.'

26, 27. Quoted by the scholiast on Hesiod, *Theog.* 116 Βακχυλίδης δὲ χάος τὸν ἀέρα ὠνόμασε, λέγων περὶ τοῦ ἀετοῦ· Νωμᾶται δ᾽ ἐν ἀτρυγέτῳ χάει (Bergk, Bacch. frag. 47); and what appears to be a misquotation of the same line is given by the scholiast on Aristophanes, *Birds* 192, as from Ibycus (frag. 28 in Bergk). ἀτρυγέτῳ has superseded ἀτρύτῳ in the quotation, as being (in the sense of 'unfruitful' attributed to that word) a more obviously appro-

ΛΕΠΤΟΤΡΙΧΑΣΥΝΖΕΦΥΡΟΥΠΝΟ

ΑΙΣΙΝΕΘΕΙΡΑΝΑΡΙΓΝ

30 ΤΟΣΜΕΤΑΝΘΡΩΠΟΙΣΙΔΕΙΝ·

ΤΩΣΝΥΝΚΑΙΜΟΙΜΥΡΙΑΠΑΝΤΑΙΚΕΛΕΥΘΟΣ

ΥΜΕΤΕΡΑΝΑΡΕΤΑΝ

ΥΜΝΕΙΚΥΑΝΟΠΛΟΚΑΜΟΥΘ·ΕΚΑΤΙΝΙΚΑΣ

ΧΑΛΚΕΟΣΤΕΡΝΟΥΤ·ΑΡΗΟΣ

35 ΔΕΙΝΟΜΕΝΕΥΣΑΓΕΡΩΧΟΙ

ΠΑΙΔΕΣ·ΕΥΕΡΔΩΝΔΕΜΗΚΑΜΟΙΘΕΟΣ·

ΞΑΝΘΟΤΡΙΧΑΜΕΝΦΕΡΕΝΙΚΟΝ

ΑΛΦΕΟΝΠΑΡΕΥΡΥΔΙΝΑΝ

ΠΩΛΟΝΑΕΛΛΟΔΡΟΜΑΝ

40 ΕΙΔΕΝΙΚΑΣΑΝΤΑΧΡΥΣΟΠΑΧΥΣΑΩΣ

ΠΥΘΩΝΙΤ·ΕΝΑΓΑΘΕΑΙ·

ΓΑΙΔ·ΕΠΙΣΚΗΠΤΩΝΠΙΦΑΥΣΚΩ

ΟΥΠΩΝΙΝΥΠΟΠΡΟΤΕ[..]Ν

ΙΠΠΩΝΕΝΑΓΩΝΙΚΑΤΕΧΡΑΝΕΝΚΟΝΙΣ

45 ΠΡΟΣΤΕΛΟΣΟΡΝΥΜΕΝΟΝ·

31. MOI A, corr. Blass, on metrical grounds. 33. ΥΜΝΕΙ A, corr. Palmer. 35, 36. ΑΓΕΡΩΧΟΙ | ΠΑΙΔΕΣ A, altered on account of strophic correspondence.

priate epithet of Chaos; but the metre requires ἀτρύτῳ, which, from meaning 'not worn out,' 'unexhausted,' comes to mean 'inexhaustible,' and so 'illimitable.'

29. ἔθειραν: not elsewhere used of a bird's plumage before Oppian. λεπτότριχα is equally odd as applied to a bird; it must presumably mean 'of fine and delicate plumage.'

31. μυρία παντᾷ κέλευθος: cf. XIX. 1, and Pind. *Isth.* III. 19 (IV. 1) ἔστι μοι θεῶν ἕκατι μυρία παντᾷ κέλευθος; also Bacch. IX. 48 μυρία παντᾷ φάτις.

34. χαλκεοστέρνου τ' Ἄρηος: an allusion to the battle of Himera, in which all the four sons of Deinomenes took part, as appears from the epigram of Simonides on the tripod dedicated by them at Delphi in memory of it (frag. 141, Bergk).

λεπτότριχα σὺν Ζεφύρου πνοαῖσιν ἔθειραν ἀρίγνω-
30 τος μετ' ἀνθρώποις ἰδεῖν.
τὼς νῦν καὶ ἐμοὶ μυρία παντᾷ κέλευθος   ἐπ. α'.
ὑμετέραν ἀρετὰν
ὑμνεῖν, κυανοπλοκάμου θ' ἔκατι Νίκας
χαλκεοστέρνου τ' Ἄρηος,
35 Δεινομένευς ἀγέρω-
χοι παῖδες. εὖ ἔρδων δὲ μὴ κάμοι θεός.
ξανθότριχα μὲν Φερένικον
Ἀλφεὸν παρ' εὐρυδίναν
πῶλον ἀελλοδρόμαν
40 εἶδε νικάσαντα χρυσόπαχυς Ἀώς,
Πυθῶνί τ' ἐν ἀγαθέᾳ.   στρ. β'.
γᾷ δ' ἐπισκήπτων πιφαύσκω,
οὔ πώ νιν ὑπὸ προτέ[ρω]ν
ἵππων ἐν ἀγῶνι κατέχρανεν κόνις
45 πρὸς τέλος ὀρνύμενον.

35. Δεινομένευς: on the form cf. note on III. 7.

37–40. Quoted by the scholiast on Pindar, *Ol.* I. (frag. 6, Bergk). An instance of the difficulty of forming a true judgement from fragments is provided by Bergk's argument that the poem from which these lines were taken is shown to have related to Hieron's victory in Ol. 76 (not to the victory with the chariot in Ol. 78) by the use of the third person εἶδε, to which Hieron is to be supplied as subject ; and that the past tense shows that the poem was written after Hieron's death. The first part of the argument is not very clear, but the whole of it falls to the ground now that it appears that the subject of the verb is not Hieron but χρυσόπαχυς Ἀώς.

39. ἀελλοδρόμαν: the MSS. of the Pindar scholia have ἀελλόδρομον, but Bacchylides is markedly fond of forms in -ης (-ας), so there is no reason to doubt the accuracy of the MS. On the contrary, the fact that it has correctly preserved an otherwise unknown and easily corrupted form is testimony to its trustworthiness.

41. ἀγαθέᾳ: a standing epithet of Pytho, cf. III. 62 and Pind. *Pyth.* IX. 77.

42. γᾷ δ' ἐπισκήπτων: cf. VIII. 3, 4 γᾷ δ' ἐπισκήπτων χέρα κομπάσομαι.

ΡΙΠΑ͞ΙΓΑΡΪϹΟϹΒΟΡЄΑΙ̸
ὉΝΚΥΒЄΡΝΉΤΑΝΦΥΛΑϹϹωΝ
ЇЄΤΑΙΝЄΌΚΡΟΤΟΝ
ΝΙΚΑΝЇЄΡωΝΙΦΙΛΟΞЄ́ΝωΙΤΙΤΎϹΚωΝ·
ΟΛΒΙΟϹὯΙΤΙΝΙΘЄΟϹ
ΜΟΙΡΑΝΤЄΚΑΛωΝЄ́ΠΟΡЄΝ
ϹΥΝΤЄΠΙΖΉΛω͞ΙΤΥΧΑΙ
ΑΦΝ̣ЄΙΟΝΒΙΟΤΑΝΔΙΆΓЄΙΝ·ΟΥ
ΓΑ[. . . .]Є̣ΠΙΧΘΟΝΙωΝ
Π[. . . .]Α̣Γ'ЄΥΔΆΙΜωΝЄΦΥ·
[. . . . . .]Ο̣Τ'ЄΡЄ̸ΙΨΙΠΥΛΑΝ
[. . . . .]Α̣ΤΟΝΛЄΓΟΥϹΙΝ
[. . . . .]ΑΡΓΙΚЄΡΑΥ
Col. 8] ΝΟΥΔωΜΑΤΑΦЄΡϹЄΦΟΝΑϹΤΑΝΙϹΦΥΡΟΥ
ΚΑΡΧΑΡΌΔΟΝΤΑΚΥΝ'Α
ΞΟΝΤ'ЄϹΦΑΟϹЄΞΑΪΔΑ
ΥΙΟΝΑΠΛΆΤΟΙ'ЄΧΙΔΝΑϹ·
ЄΝΘΑΔΥϹΤΆΝωΝΒΡΟΤωΝ
ΨΥΧΑϹЄΔΆΗΠΑΡΑΚωΚΥΤΟΥΡЄЄ́ΘΡΟΙϹ

46. **ΒΟΡΕΑΙ** A, corr. A^1. 49. **ΦΙΛΟΞΕΝΩΙ** A, corr. on metrical grounds. 53. **ΑΦΝΕΙΟΝ** A, Stobaeus, Apostolius; the word must be scanned as a dissyllable, hence **ΑΦΝΕΟΝ** should probably be read. 56. **ΕΡΕΙΨΙΠΥΛΑΝ** A, the second E struck out by A^1? 58. δῦναι Palmer.

48. *νεόκροτον*: the word does not occur elsewhere, and the appropriateness of the compound is not very clear. Its literal sense in this context must apparently be 'new-clamoured,' *i. e.* celebrated with new clamours of applause. *κρότος* is used for applause by Aristophanes and Demosthenes.

49. *τιτύσκων*: the earliest extant example of the active, Homer using only the middle.

50–55. Quoted by Stobaeus (*Flor.* 103, 2), as from Βακχυλίδου 'Επινίκων (frag. 1, Bergk). The first four lines are also quoted by Apostolius (XII. 65 e), and the last two by Stobaeus (*Flor.* 98, 26).

ῥιπᾷ γὰρ ἴσος Βορέα,
ὃν κυβερνήταν φυλάσσων,
ἴεται νεόκροτον
νίκαν Ἱέρωνι φιλοξείνῳ τιτύσκων.
50 ὄλβιος ᾧτινι θεὸς
μοῖράν τε καλῶν ἔπορεν
σύν τ᾿ ἐπιζήλῳ τύχᾳ
ἀφνεὸν βιοτὰν διάγειν· οὐ
γά[ρ τις] ἐπιχθονίων
55 π[άντ]α γ᾿ εὐδαίμων ἔφυ.
[καὶ μάν πο]τ᾿ ἐρειψιπύλαν   ἀντ. β΄.
[παῖδ᾿ ἀνίκ]ατον λέγουσιν
[δῦναι Διὸς] ἀργικεραύ-
νου δώματα Φερσεφόνας τανισφύρου,
60 καρχαρόδοντα κύν᾿ ἄ-
ξοντ᾿ ἐς φάος ἐξ Ἀΐδα,
υἱὸν ἀπλάτοι᾿ Ἐχίδνας.
ἔνθα δυστάνων βροτῶν
ψυχὰς ἐδάη παρὰ Κωκυτοῦ ῥεέθροις,

ᾧτινι : wrongly altered to ᾧτε by Neue (followed by Bergk and some later editors).

51. καλῶν : Neue conjectured κακῶν, and much good ink has been spent by later editors in discussing it.

52. ἐπιζήλῳ : so also the MSS. of Stobaeus and Apostolius. All the editors, from Neue downwards, have altered it to ἐπιζαλῷ, but the compounds of ζῆλος regularly retain η. Cf. πολυζήλωτος (I. 46, X. 48), πολύζηλος (XI. 63).

55. πάντα γ᾿ : so Stobaeus in *Flor.* 98, 26, but in 103, 2 the MSS. have merely πάντ᾿, in consequence of which many emendations have been proposed.

56. ἐρειψιπύλαν : a coinage of Bacchylides, so far as is known, probably referring to Heracles' siege and capture of Troy. Aeschylus has ἐρειψίτοιχος (*Sept. contr. Theb.* 884).

64. ἐδάη : 'he perceived'; rather different from the usual meaning of the verb, 'to learn.'

65 ΟΙΑΤΕΦΥΛΛ'ΑΝΕΜΟC

ΙΔΑCΑΝΑΜΗΛΟΒΟΤΟΥC

ΠΡΩΝΑCΑΡΓΗCΤΑCΔΟΝΕΙ

ΤΑΙCΙΝΔΕΜΕΤΕΠΡΕΠΕΝΕΙΔΩ

ΛΟΝΘΡΑCΥΜΕΜΝΟΝΟCΕΝ

70 ΧΕCΠΑΛΟΥΠΟΡΘΑΝΙΔΑ·

ΤΟΝΔ'ΩCΙΔΕΝΑΛΚΜΗΙΟCΘΑΥΜΑCΤΟCΗΡΩC

[..]ΥΧΕCΙΛΑΜΠΟΜΕΝΟΝ

ΝΕΥΡΑΝΕΠΕΒΑCΕΛΙΓΥΚΛΑΓΓΗΚΟΡΩΝΑC·

ΧΑΛΚΕΟΚΡΑΝΟΝΔΕΠΕΙΤ'ΕΞ

75 ΕΙΛΕΤΟΪΟΝΑΝΑΠΤΥ

ΞΑCΦΑΡΕΤΡΑCΠΩΜΑ·ΤΩΙΔ'ΕΝΑΝΤΙΑ

ΨΥΧΑΠΡ[.]ΦΑΝΗΜΕΛΕΑΓΡΟΥ·

ΚΑΙΝΙΝΕΥΕΙΔΩCΠΡΟCΕΕΙΠΕΝ·

ΥΙΕΔΙΟCΜΕΓΑΛΟΥ

80 ΣΤΑΘΙΤ'ΕΝΧΩΡΑΪΓΕΛΑΝΩCΑCΤΕΘΥΜΟΝ

ΜΗΤΑΥCΙΟΝΠΡΟΪΕΙ

69. ΕΝ— Δ, ΕΓ— Δ³. **70.** ΠΟΡΘΑΝΙΔΑ Δ, corr. Δ²? **71.** ΑΛΚ-ΜΗΙΟΣ Δ. **75, 76.** ΑΝΑΠΤΥ | ΞΑΣ Δ, altered on account of strophic correspondence. **78.** ΠΡΟΣΕΕΙΠΕΝ Δ, corr. on metrical grounds. **80.** ΤΕ] Δ written at first for Τ, but corrected at once.

65-67. οἷά τε φύλλ', κ.τ.λ.: these lines add another to the list of parallel passages which includes Homer, *Il.* II. 468; Apollonius Rhodius, IV. 216, 217; Virgil, *Aen.* VI. 309, 310; and Milton, *Paradise Lost* I. 301-304. Since Homer's comparison does not relate to disembodied spirits, Bacchylides may claim to have furnished the prototype for the later writers. In one respect, the *localization* of the simile (Ἴδας ἀνὰ μηλοβότους πρῶνας), the nearest parallel is Milton's 'leaves *in Vallombrosa*'; and the parallel is the more striking because it is, of course, unconscious.

67. ἀργηστάς: 'the gleaming headlands of Ida.' Professor Jebb, however, proposes ἀργεστάς, as epithet of ἄνεμος.

70. Πορθανίδα: Meleager, son of Oeneus and grandson of Porthaon. Scanned as a quadrisyllable, ᾱο coalescing by synizesis into one long syllable. A trace of this meeting of Heracles and Meleager in the lower

65 οἷά τε φύλλ' ἄνεμος
  Ἴδας ἀνὰ μηλοβότους
  πρῶνας ἀργηστὰς δονεῖ.
  ταῖσιν δὲ μετέπρεπεν εἴδωλον θρασυμέμνονος ἐγ-
70 χεσπάλου Πορθαονίδα.
  τὸν δ' ὡς ἴδεν Ἀλκμήνιος θαυμαστὸς ἥρως   ἐπ. β'.
  [τε]ύχεσι λαμπόμενον,
  νευρὰν ἐπέβασε λιγυκλαγγῆ κορώνας·
  χαλκεόκρανον δ' ἔπειτ' ἐξ-
75 είλετο ἰόν, ἀνα-
  πτύξας φαρέτρας πῶμα. τῷ δ' ἐναντία
  ψυχὰ προφάνη Μελεάγρου,
  καί νιν εὖ εἰδὼς προσεῖπεν·
  υἱὲ Διὸς μεγάλου,
80 στᾶθί τ' ἐν χώρᾳ, γελανώσας τε θυμόν
  μὴ ταύσιον προΐει   στρ. γ'.

world is preserved by Apollodorus (II. 5. 12, 4), who says that when Heracles appeared, all the shades fled, except Meleager and Medusa. Heracles
thereupon drew his sword upon Medusa, but was warned by Hermes that
she was only a shade. Here there is no mention of Medusa, but Heracles
makes the same mistake with regard to Meleager. It would seem that
the subject was also treated by Pindar; since the scholiast on Homer,
Il. XXI. 194, after stating that Heracles met Meleager in Hades and was
requested by him to marry his sister Deianira, which he did after a contest
with her previous suitor Achelous, adds ἡ ἱστορία παρὰ Πινδάρῳ. If the scholiast
is to be followed literally, Pindar's version differed somewhat from that of
Bacchylides, giving the original suggestion of the match to Meleager instead
of to Heracles, and including the subsequent contest with Achelous. It would
be interesting to know which poet was the first to deal with the subject.

80. γελανώσας: an otherwise unknown verb, but evidently connected with
γελάνής, a derivative of γελάω which occurs twice in Pindar (*Ol.* V. 2;
Pyth. IV. 181), in the latter case as an epithet of θυμός.

81. ταύσιον: the Doric form of τηύσιος is also found in Alcman (frag. 92,
Bergk).

ΤΡΑΧΥΝΕΚΧΕΙΡѠΝΟΪϹΤΟΝ

ΨΥΧΑΙϹΙΝΕΠΙΦΘΙΜΈΝѠΝ·

ΟΥΤΟΙΔΕΟϹѠϹΦΑΤΟ·ΘΑΜΒΗϹΕΝΔ'ΑΝΑΞ

85 ΑΜΦΙΤΡΥѠΝΙΆΔΑϹ·

ΕΙΠΕΝΤΕ·ΤΙϹΑΘΑΝΑΤѠΝ

ΗΒΡΟΤѠΝΤΟΙΟΫ́ΤΟΝΕΡΝΟϹ

ΘΡΕΨΕΝΕΝΠΟ͞ΙΑ͞ΙΧΘΟΝΙ·

ΤΙϹΔ'ΕΚΤΑΝΕΝ·ΗΤΑΧΑΚΑΛΛΊΖѠΝΟϹΗΡΑ

90 ΚΕΙΝΟΝΕΦΑΜΕΤΈΡ͞ΑΙ

ΠΕΜΨΕΙΚΕΦΑΛ͞ΑΤ·ΤΑΔΕΠΟΥ

Col. 9] ΠΑΛΛΑΔΙΞΑΝΘ͞ΑΙΜΕΛΕΙ·

ΤΟΝΔΕΠΡΟϹΕΦΑΜΕΛΕΑΓΡΟϹ

ΔΑΚΡΥΌΕΙ̣Ϲ·ΧΑΛΕΠΟΝ

95 ΘΕѠΝΠΑΡΑΤΡΈΨΑΙΝΟΟΝ

ΑΝΔΡΕϹϹΙΝΕΠΙΧΘΟΝΊΟΙϹ·

ΚΑΙΓΑΡΑΝΠΛΆΞΙΠΠΟϹΟΙΝΕΥϹ

ΠΑΥϹΕΝΚΑΛΥ̣ΚΟϹΤΕΦΑΝΟΥ

ϹΕΜΝΑϹΧΟΛΟΝΑΡΤΕΜΙΔΟϹΛΕΥΚѠΛΕΝΟΥ

100 ΛΙϹϹΟΜΕΝΟϹΠΟΛΕѠΝ

Τ'ΑΙΓѠΝΘΥϹΊΑΙϹΙΠΑΤΗΡ

ΚΑΙΒΟѠΝΦΟΙΝΙΚΟ̣Ν͡Ѡ́ΤѠΝ·

ΑΛΛΑΝΙΚΑΤΟΝΘΕΑ

ΕϹΧΕΝΧΟΛΟΝ·ΕΥΡΥΒΙΑΝΔ'ΕϹϹΕΥ[.]ΚΟΥΡΑ

105 ΚΑΠΡΟΝΑΝΑΙΔΟΜΆΧΑΝ·

83. ψυχαῖσιν ἔπι φθιμένων : for ἐπί with the dative in the sense of 'against,' cf. Pind. *Ol.* II. 99 ἐπί τοι 'Ακράγαντι τανύσαις, where the action is again that of aiming an arrow; and l. 90 below ἐφ' ἁμετέρᾳ πέμψει κεφαλᾷ.

90. κεῖνον : sc. the slayer of Meleager. If there is a man alive who could slay such a hero as Meleager, Hera will assuredly make use of so formidable a champion to assail Heracles; a thought dismissed with the reflection that Pallas is committed to his defence.

τραχὺν ἐκ χειρῶν ὀϊστὸν
ψυχαῖσιν ἔπι φθιμένων.
οὔ τοι δέος. ὡς φάτο· θάμβησεν δ᾽ ἄναξ
85 Ἀμφιτρυωνιάδας,
εἶπέν τε· τίς ἀθανάτων
ἢ βροτῶν τοιοῦτον ἔρνος
θρέψεν ἐν ποίᾳ χθονί;
τίς δ᾽ ἔκτανεν; ἦ τάχα καλλίζωνος Ἥρα
90 κεῖνον ἐφ᾽ ἁμετέρᾳ
πέμψει κεφαλᾷ· τὰ δέ που
Παλλάδι ξανθᾷ μέλει.
τὸν δὲ προσέφα Μελέαγρος
δακρυόεις· χαλεπὸν
95 θεῶν παρατρέψαι νόον
ἄνδρεσσιν ἐπιχθονίοις.   ἀντ. γ΄.
καὶ γὰρ ἂν πλάξιππος Οἰνεὺς
παῦσεν καλυκοστεφάνου
σεμνᾶς χόλον Ἀρτέμιδος λευκωλένου
100 λισσόμενος πολέων
τ᾽ αἰγῶν θυσίαισι πατὴρ
καὶ βοῶν φοινικονώτων.
ἀλλ᾽ ἀνίκατον θεὰ
ἔσχεν χόλον, εὐρυβίαν δ᾽ ἔσσευ[ε] κούρα
105 κάπρον ἀναιδομάχαν

97. πλάξιππος: cf. Homer, *Il.* IX. 581 ἱππηλάτα Οἰνεύς.

98, 99. καλυκοστεφάνου σεμνᾶς ... Ἀρτέμιδος λευκωλένου: a rather excessive multiplication of epithets, even for Bacchylides, who is fond of applying two adjectives to a single substantive.

104. χόλον: because Oeneus had omitted to sacrifice to her, though offering hecatombs to all the other gods (Homer, *Il.* IX. 535, 536).

ỎCΚΑΛΛΙΧΟΡΟΝΚΑΛΥΔΩ

Ν᾽ΕΝΘΑΠΛΗΜΥΡΩΝСΘΕΝΕΙ

ỎΡΧΟΥCΕΠΕΚΕΙΡΕΝΟΔΟΝΤΙ

CΦΑΖΕΤΕΜΗΛΑΒΡΟΤΩΝ

110 Θ᾽ΟCΤΙCΕΙCΑΝΤΑΝΜΟΛΟΙ·

ΤΩΙΔΕCΤΥΓΕΡΑΝΔΗΡΙΝΕΛΛΑΝΩΝΑΡΙCΤΟΙ

ÇΤΑCΑΜΕΘ᾽ΕΝΔΥΚΕΩC

ΕΞΑΜΑΤΑCΥΝΕΧΕ͜ΩC·ΕΠΕΙΔΕΔΑΙΜΩΝ

ΚΑΡΤΟCΑΙΤΩΛΟΙCΟΡΕΞΕΝ

115 ΘΑΠΤΟΜΕΝΤΟΥCΚΑΤΕΠΕΦΝΕ

CΥ[.]ΕΡΙΒΡΎΧΑCΕΠΑΪCCΩΝΒΙΑΙ

Α[..]ΑΙΟΝΕΜΩΝΤ᾽ΑΓΓΕΛΟΝ

Φ[...]ΑΤΟΝΚΕΔΝΩΝΑΔΕΛΦΕΩΝ

[.....]ΚΕΝΕΝΜΕΓΑΡΟΙC

120 [......]CΑΛΘΑΙΑΠΕΡΙΚΛΕΙΤΟΙCΙΝΟΙΝΕΟC·

·   [......]ΛΕCΕΧΜΟΙΡ᾽ΟΛΟΑ

[.......]C·ΟΥΓΑΡΠΩΔΑΪΦΡΩΝ

---

106. ἐς] ΟΣ Α, ὸΣ Α³!; corr. Palmer.   113. ΣΥΝΕΧΕΩΣ Α, corr. Α³.   115. ΤΟΥΣ Α; altered on metrical grounds.   115, 116. ΚΑΤΕΠΕΦΝΕΝ | ΣΥΣ Α, altered on grounds of strophic correspondence.   117. Ἀγέλαον] ΑΓΓΕΛΟ Α, against metre.   121. ΛΕΣΕΝ Α, corr. Α³!

106. ἐς: MS. ὸς, but Professor Palmer's emendation is at once simple and effective, and is supported by other cases in which ε and ο seem to be interchanged in this MS.; cf. II. 14, XVII. 66.

Καλυδῶ|ν': a curious division of the word. The rule is that divisions of words at the ends of lines are made after a vowel; and the rule is observed even when the syllable belonging to the next line is elided. Cf. ὑμνοάνασ|σ' in XII. 1.

107. πλημυρῶν: the single μ of the MS. is noticeable, as supporting the derivation from the same root as πίμπλημι, advocated by Buttmann.

113. συνεχέως: the first syllable is long. The same scansion is found in Homer and Hesiod. Liddell and Scott state that the ν was not doubled

ἐς καλλίχορον Καλυδῶ-
ν'· ἔνθα πλημυρῶν σθένει
ὄρχους ἐπέκειρεν ὀδόντι,
σφάζέ τε μῆλα, βροτῶν
110 θ' ὅστις εἴσαντ' ἂν μόλοι.
τῷ δὲ στυγερὰν δῆριν Ἑλλάνων ἄριστοι ἐπ. γ'.
στασάμεθ' ἐνδυκέως

ἐξ ἅματα συνεχέως· ἐπεὶ δὲ δαίμων
κάρτος Αἰτωλοῖς ὄρεξεν,
115 θάπτομεν οὓς κατέπεφ-
νεν σῦς ἐριβρύχας ἐπαΐσσων βίᾳ,
Ἀ[γκα]ῖον ἐμῶν τ' Ἀγέλαον
φ[έρτ]ατον κεδνῶν ἀδελφέων
[οὓς τέ]κεν ἐν μεγάροις
120 [πατρὸ]ς Ἀλθαία περικλειτοῖσιν Οἰνέος.
[τοὺς δ' ὤ]λεσε μοῖρ' ὀλοὰ   στρ. δ'.
[τλάμονα]ς· οὐ γάρ πω δαΐφρων

in writing, and the original reading of this MS. supports this view, while
the corrector is against it.

117. Ἀγκαῖον: cf. Apollodorus (*Bibl.* I. 8. 2, 6). Ἀγέλαον: the MS.
reading, ἄγγελον, is shown by the metre, as well as the sense, to be corrupt,
and the true name is supplied by Antoninus Liberalis (*Metam.* 2). It is
there given as Ἀγέλεως.

122. τλάμονας: this restoration involves the admission of a dactyl in this
foot, corresponding to a trochee (=cyclic dactyl) in the other strophes;
but (1) no other word gives so good a sense; (2) the lacuna requires a word
of seven or eight letters, the s with which it ends coming below (and
slightly after) the first ε in ὤλεσε in the line above.

δαΐφρων: cannot be used in a good sense, = 'prudent,' in this context.
Therefore, if the derivation from the same root as δαῆναι be retained, it
must mean 'wily,' 'designing'; but a better sense, especially in connexion
with the other epithet ἀγροτέρα, is obtainable by connecting it with δάϊς,
'with hostile mind,' 'warlike.' In l. 137 'designing' would be an appropriate
epithet, but a sense corresponding to the Latin *infensus* would be equally
appropriate, and would suit both passages.

[......]ΟΛΟΝΑΓΡΟΤΕΡΑ

Col. 10]   ΛΑΤΟΥϹΘΥΓΑΤΗΡ·ΠΕΡΙΔ·ΑΙΘΩΝΟϹΔΟΡΑϹ

125   ΜΑΡΝΑΜΕΘ·ΕΝΔΥΚΕΩϹ

ΚΟΥΡΗΙϹΙΜΕΝΕΠΤΟΛΕΜΟΙϹ·

ΕΝΘ·ΕΓΩΠΟΛΛΟΙϹϹΥΝΑΛΛΟΙϹ

ΙΦΙΚΛΟΝΚΑΤΕΚΤΑΝΟΝ

ΕϹΘΛΟΝΤ·ΑΦΑΡΗΑΤΑΘΟΟΥϹΜΑΤΡΩΑϹ·ΟΥΓΑΡ

130   ΚΑΡΤΕΡΟΘΥΜΟϹΑΡΗϹ

ΚΡΙΝΕΙΦΙΛΟΝΕΝΠΟΛΕΜΩΙ·

ΤΥΦΛΑΔ·[..]ΧΕΙΡΩΝΒΕΛΗ

ΨΥΧΑΙϹΕΠ[.]ΔΥϹΜΕΝΕΩΝΦΟΙ

ΤΑΙΑΘΑΝΑΤΟΝΤΕΦΕΡΕΙ

135   ΤΟΙϹΙΝΑΝΔΑΙΜΩΝΘΕΛΗΙ·

ΤΑΥΤ·ΟΥΚΕΠΙΛΕΞΑΜΕΝΑ

ΘΕϹΤΙΟΥΚΟΡΑΔΑΙΦΡΩΝ

ΜΑΤΗΡΚΑΚΟΠΟΤΜΟϹΕΜΟΙ

ΒΟΥΛΕΥϹΕΝΟΛΕΘΡΟΝΑΤΑΡΒΑΚΤΟϹΓΥΝΑ·

140   ΚΑΙΕΤΕΔΑΙΔΑΛΕΑϹ

ΕΚΛΑΡΝΑΚΟϹΩΚΥΜΟΡΟΝ

ΦΙΤΡΟΝΕΓΚΛΑΥϹΑϹΑ·ΤΟΝΔΗ

ΜΟΙΡ·ΕΠΕΚΛΩϹΕΝΤΟΤΕ

126. ΚΟΥΡΗΙΣΙ Δ, corr. Δ¹?   129. ΑΦΑΡΗΑΤΑ Δ, corr. Δ¹.
ΟΥ ΓΑΡ om. Δ, inserted by Δ³.   134. ΑΘΑΝΑΤΟΝ Δ, corr. Δ¹.
137. ΚΟΡΑ Δ, altered on metrical grounds.   142. ΕΓΚΛΑΥΣΑΣΑ Δ,
corr. Jebb.

124. περὶ δ' αἴθωνος δορᾶς: it will be observed that, as in Homer, no
mention is made of Atalanta.

128. Ἴφικλον: named as one of the sons of Thestius (and therefore a
brother of Althaea) by Apollonius Rhodius (I. 45 ff.) and Apollodorus
(I. 7. 10. 1, 8. 3. 2). Aphares (or Aphareus, the only extant form of the
nominative) is not elsewhere mentioned among the sons of Thestius, but
cf. Ovid, *Metam.* VIII. 304, where Idas and Lynceus are described as ' duo

[παῦσεν χ]όλον ἀγροτέρα
Λατοῦς θυγάτηρ· περὶ δ' αἴθωνος δορᾶς
125 μαρνάμεθ' ἐνδυκέως
Κουρῆσι μενεπτολέμοις.
ἔνθ' ἐγὼ πολλοῖς σὺν ἄλλοις
Ἴφικλον κατέκτανον
ἐσθλόν τ' Ἀφάρητα θοοὺς μάτρωας· οὐ γὰρ
130 καρτερόθυμος Ἄρης
κρίνει φίλον ἐν πολέμῳ,
τυφλὰ δ' [ἐκ] χειρῶν βέλη
ψυχαῖς ἔπ[ι] δυσμενέων φοιτᾷ θάνατόν τε φέρει
135 τοῖσιν ἂν δαίμων θέλῃ.
ταῦτ' οὐκ ἐπιλεξαμένα   ἀντ. δ'.
Θεστίου κούρα δαΐφρων
μάτηρ κακόποτμος ἐμοὶ
βούλευσεν ὄλεθρον ἀτάρβακτος γυνά.
140 καῖέ τε δαιδαλέας
ἐκ λάρνακος ὠκύμορον
φιτρὸν ἀγκλαύσασα· τὸν δὴ
μοῖρ' ἐπέκλωσεν τότε

Thestiadae, proles Aphareia.' In Homer Meleager is only said to have killed one of his uncles (*Il.* IX. 567).

139. ἀτάρβακτος: this confirms the reading in Pind. *Pyth.* IV. 84, where Hermann (followed by Liddell and Scott) substitutes ἀταρμύκτοιο for ἀταρβάκτοιο.

142. ἀγκλαύσασα: ἐγκλαύσασα, the reading of the MS., does not occur elsewhere, and gives no satisfactory sense. It may seem inconsistent that Althaea should weep for the death which is her own act; but it is an inconsistency true to nature, and a striking touch.

143. τότε: i.e. 'at the time of my birth,' if the reading is right. But perhaps we should read ποτέ.

ΖΩΑϹΟΡΟΝΑΜΕΤΕΡΑϹΕΜΜΕΝ·ΤΥΧΟΝΜΕΝ

145 ΔΑΪΠΎΛΟΥΚΛΎΜΕΝΟΝ

ΠΑΙΔ·ΑΛΚΙΜΟΝΕΞΑΝΑΡΊ

ΖΩΝΑΜΩΜΗΤΟΝΔΕΜΑϹ

ΠΥΡΓΩΝΠΡΟΠΆΡΟΙΘΕΚΙΧΗϹΑϹ·

ΤΟΙΔΕΠΡΟϹΕΥΚΤΙΜΈΝΑΝ

150 ΦΕΥΓΟΝΑΡΧΆΙΑΝΠΟΛΙΝ

ΠΛΕΥΡΩ͂ΝΑ·ΜΙΝΥΝΘΑΔΕΜΟΙΨΥΧΑΓΛΥΚΕΙΑ·

ΓΝΩΝΔ·ΟΛΙΓΟϹΘΕΝΈΩΝ·

ΑΙΑΙ·ΠΥΜΑΤΟΝΔΕΠΝΕΩΝΔΆΚΡΥϹΑΤΛ[

ΑΓΛΑΑΝΗΒΑΝΠΡΟΛΙΠΩΝ·

155 ΦΑϹΙΝΑΔΕΙϹ⌊ΒΌΑΝ

Col. 11]   ΑΜΦΙΤΡΥΩΝΟϹΠΑΙΔΑΜΟΥΝΟΝΔΗΤΟΤΕ

ΤΈΓΞΑΙΒΛΕΦΑΡΟΝΤΑΛΑΠΕΝΘΕΟϹ

ΠΟΤΜΟΝΟΙΚΤΕΊΡΟΝΤΑΦΩΤΟϹ·

ΚΑΙΝΙΝΑΜΕΙΒΟΜΕΝΟϹ

160 Τ̲Ο̲Ι̲Δ·ΕΦΑ·ΘΝΑΤΟΙϹΙΜΗΦΥΝΑΙΦΕΡΙϹΤΟΝ

---

154. ΠΡΟΛΙΠΩΝ Α, altered on metrical grounds.   160. ΤΟΙΔ Α, corr. Α³.

145. Δαϊπύλου Κλύμενον: not otherwise known.

146. ἐξαναρίζων: so MS. It is, of course, easy to alter it to ἐξεναρίζων, but it seems possible that it may be an example of Doric ᾱ=ε, like Ἄρταμις (frequent in Doric inscriptions), φρασί (Pindar), κ. τ. λ.

149. τοὶ δέ: the enemy.

151. μίνυνθα: except in the mutilated line 191, the corresponding lines in the other strophes all have a long syllable in the places corresponding to the last syllable of this word. Hence there is some plausibility in the suggestion, made by Mr. L. C. Purser, that μίνυνθα represents an aorist (ἐ)μινύνθη, from an assumed verb μινύνω, collateral to μινύθω. This would also improve the sense. As the line stands, taking μίνυνθα as an adverb, the meaning must be 'but my pleasant life was but for a short time,' a phrase (as Professor Jebb points out) parallel to, and perhaps reminiscent of, the words of Thetis to Achilles (*Il.* I. 416) ἐπεί νύ τοι αἶσα μίνυνθά περ, οὔ τι μάλα δήν. Mr. Purser's suggestion, besides satisfying the metrical requirements, gives a somewhat

ζωᾶς ὅρον ἀμετέρας ἔμμεν. τύχον μὲν
145 Δαϊπύλου Κλύμενον
παῖδ᾽ ἄλκιμον ἐξαναρί-
ζων, ἀμώμητον δέμας,
πύργων προπάροιθε κιχήσας·
τοὶ δὲ πρὸς εὐκτιμέναν
150 φεῦγον ἀρχαίαν πόλιν
Πλευρῶνα. μίνυνθα δέ μοι ψυχὰ γλυκεῖα· ἐπ. δ´.
γνῶν δ᾽ ὀλιγοσθενέων,
αἰαῖ· πύματον δὲ πνέων δάκρυσα τλ[άμων]
ἀγλαὰν ἥβαν προλείπων.
155 φασὶν ἀδεισιβόαν
Ἀμφιτρύωνος παῖδα μοῦνον δὴ τότε
τέγξαι βλέφαρον, ταλαπενθέος
πότμον οἰκτείροντα φωτός.
καί νιν ἀμειβόμενος
160 τόδ᾽ ἔφα· θνατοῖσι μὴ φῦναι φέριστον,

more natural sense; 'pleasant life ebbed away from me.' It is questionable, however, whether the termination -ᾱ can stand. There is no authority for Doric ᾱ = η in the 1st aorist passive terminations, and probably μινύνθη should be read instead. If this supposed form is inadmissible, then, as Professor Jebb suggests, μίνυνθ᾽ ἦν is possible. The reading in l. 191, however, leaves it doubtful whether the metrical irregularity is not original; and it may be observed that in this form it is identical with the third line of the epode.

153. τλάμων: the λ is partially lost, but is practically certain, the only alternatives being α and δ. There is also a slight trace of what may be the apex of an α following, and of an acute accent upon it.

160–162. θνατοῖσι . . . φέγγος: quoted by Stobaeus (*Flor.* 98, 27) as from Bacchylides, with the addition, however, of another line at the end, ὄλβιος δ᾽ οὐδεὶς βροτῶν πάντα χρόνον (frag. 41, Bergk 2). It is probable that Stobaeus, or the authority from whom he took his quotation, quoted from memory, and appended to the passage from this ode a line in similar metre from another part of Bacchylides' works. A conjecture of Bergk's (as to these words having been spoken by Silenus) disappears through the

ΜΗΤ'ΑΕΛΙΟΥΠΡΟϹΪΔΕΙΝ

ΦΕΓΓΟϹ·ΑΛΛΟΥΓΑΡΤΙϹΕϹΤΙΝ

ΠΡΑΞΙϹΤΑΔΕΜΥΡΟΜΕΝΟΙϹ·

ΚΡΗΚΕΙΝΟΛΕΓΕΙΝΟΤΙΚΑΙΜΕΛΛΕΙΤΕΛΕΙΝ·

165 ΗΡΑΤΙϹΕΝΜΕΓΑΡΟΙϹ

ΟΙΝΗΟϹΑΡΗΪΦΙΛΟΥ

ΕϹΤΙΝΑΔΜΗΤΑΘΥΓΑΤΡΩΝ

ϹΟΙΦΥΑΝΑΛΙΓΚΙΑ·

ΤΑΝΚΕΝΛΙΠΑΡΑΝΘΕΛΩΝΘΕΙΜΑΝΑΚΟΙΤΑΝ

170 ΤΟΝΚΕΜΕΝΕΠΤΟΛΕΜΟΥ

ΨΥΧΑΠΡΟϹΕΦΑΜΕΛΕΑ

ΓΡΟΥΛΙΠΟΝΧΛΩΡΑΥΧΕΝΑ

ΕΝΔΩΜΑϹΙΔΑΪΑΝΕΙΡΑΝ

ΝΗΪΝΕΤΙΧΡΥϹΕΑϹ

175 ΚΥΠΡΙΔΟϹΘΕΛΞΙΜΒΡΟΤΟΥ·

ΛΕΥΚΩΛΕΝΕΚΑΛΛΙΟΠΑ

ϹΤΑϹΟΝΕΥΠΟΙΗΤΟΝΑΡΜΑ

ΑΥΤΟΥ·ΔΙΑΤΕΚΡΟΝΙΔΑΝ

ΥΜΝΗϹΟΝΟΛΥΜΠΙΩΝΑΡΧΑΓΟΝΘΕΩΝ·

180 ΤΟΝΤ'ΑΚΑΜΑΝΤΟΡΟΑΝ

ΑΛΦΕΟΝΠΕΛΟΠΟϹΤΕΒΙΑΝ

---

164. ΚΡΗ Α, corr. Α²?   169. ἐθέλων] ΘΕΛΩΝ Α, altered on metrical grounds.   ΑΚΟΙΤΑΝ Α, corr. Α¹?   170. δέ] ΚΕ Α, corr. Α²? ΧΛΩΡΑΥΧΕΝΑ] the diphthong has a double accent, but the first is perhaps meant to be cancelled.   179. ΟΛΥΜΠΙΟΝ Α, ΟΛΥΜΠΙΩΝ Α³, against metre.

discovery of the true context. The passage adds another to the many forms of a sentiment which was a commonplace in Greek literature, and has found its most famous expression in Sophocles, *Oed. Col.* 1225–1228.

μήτ' ἀελίου προσιδεῖν   στρ. ε΄.
φέγγος. ἀλλ' οὐ γάρ τίς ἐστιν
πρᾶξις τάδε μυρομένοις,
χρὴ κεῖνο λέγειν ὅ τι καὶ μέλλει τελεῖν.
165 ἦ ῥά τις ἐν μεγάροις
Οἰνῆος ἀρηϊφίλου
ἐστὶν ἀδμήτα θυγατρῶν·
σοὶ φυὰν ἀλιγκία;
τάν κεν λιπαρὰν ἐθέλων θείμαν ἄκοιτιν.

170 τὸν δὲ μενεπτολέμου
ψυχὰ προσέφα Μελεά-
γρου· λίπον χλωραύχενα
ἐν δώμασι Δαϊάνειραν,
νῆιν ἔτι χρυσέας
175 Κύπριδος θελξιμβρότου.
λευκώλενε Καλλιόπα,   ἀντ. ε΄.
στᾶσον εὐποίητον ἅρμα
αὐτοῦ, Δία τε Κρονίδαν
ὕμνησον Ὀλύμπιον ἀρχαγὸν θεῶν,
180 τόν τ' ἀκαμαντορόαν
Ἀλφεόν, Πέλοπός τε βίαν,

162. ἀλλ' οὐ γάρ κ.τ.λ.: almost verbally identical with Homer (*Od.* X. 202, 568, ἀλλ' οὐ γάρ τις πρῆξις ἐγίνετο μυρομένοισιν.

172. χλωραύχενα: elsewhere as epithet of a nightingale, in Simonides (frag. 73, Bergk). It is a rather curious epithet to apply to a girl, χλωρός not being generally a complimentary epithet of the complexion. Theocritus has χλοερὰ μέλεα (XXVII. 66), but with reference to youthful freshness rather than complexion.

174. χρυσέας: the first syllable is short, as in Pind. *Pyth.* IV. 4, &c.

176. The transition is very abrupt, and no hint is given as to any special point or applicability in the story or its conclusion.

КΑΙΠΙϹΑΝ·ΕΝΘ'ΟΚΛΕΕΝΝΟϹ

[. .]ϹϹΙΝΙΚΆϹΑϹΔΡΟΜΩΙ

[. . .]ΕΝΦΕΡΕΝΕΙΚΟϹΕΥΠΥΡΓΟΥϹϹΥΡΑΚΟΥϹ

185 ϹΑϹΪΕΡΩΝΙΦΕΡΩΝ

[. . .]ΑΙΜΟΝΊΑϹΠΕΤΑΛΟΝ·

[. . .]Δ'ΑΛΗΘΕΙΑϹΧΑΡΙΝ

Col. 12]   ΑΙΝΕΙΝΦΘΟΝΟΝΑΜΦ[

ΧΕΡϹΙΝΑΠΩϹΆΜΕΝΟΝ

190 ΕΙΤΙϹΕΥΠΡΆϹϹΟΙΒΡΟΤΩ[

ΒΟΙΩΤΟϹΑΝΗΡΤΑΔΕΦΩΝ[

ΗϹΙΟΔΟϹΠΡΟΠΟΛΟϹ

ΜΟΥϹΑΝΌΝΑΘΑΝΑΤΟΙΤΙ[

ΚΑΙΒΡΟΤΩΝΦΗΜΑΝΕΠ[

195 ΠΕΙΘΟΜΑΙΕΥΜΑΡΕΩϹ

ΕΥΚΛΕΑΚΕΛΕΥΘΟΥΓΛΩϹϹΑΝΟ[

ΠΕΜΠΕΙΝΪΕΡΩΝΙ·ΤΟΘΕΝΓΑ[

ΠΥΘΜΕΝΕϹΘΆΛΛΟΥϹΙΝΕϹΘΛ[

182. Πίσαν : the first syllable is short, as in Pindar, whereas Simonides (in an epigram, the authenticity of which is perhaps not beyond question), Euripides, and Theocritus have it long. Of lesser authors there are many on each side ; cf. Pape-Benseler, s. v.

187. ἀληθείας: perhaps ἀλαθείας, as elsewhere in Bacchylides and in Pindar.

192. Ἡσίοδος : no passage answering to the quotation here given occurs in our extant Hesiod, and it must be added to the list of fragments. This pointed reference to Hesiod as a Βοιωτὸς ἀνήρ, and to his reputation, is very noticeable when it is remembered that this ode was to be sung at the same time as one of Pindar's, and probably in his actual presence. It looks like a graceful compliment from the poet to his rival.

193. If the text is sound the foot -σᾶν δν| must be regarded as a cyclic dactyl, answering to a full dactyl in each of the corresponding feet in the other epodes. It is no doubt possible to make the correspondence exact by inserting ποτ' or ἄρ', or some such syllable, but they are not satisfactory in point of sense, and there is no reason why they should have dropped out. A very attractive suggestion is made by Professor Jebb, to read ὃν ἐν ἀθανάτῳ τιμᾷ τ' ἔθεντο, where ἐν might easily have dropped out after ὅν, and

καὶ Πίσαν, ἔνθ' ὁ κλεεννὸς
[πο]σσὶ νικάσας δρόμῳ
[αὖξ]εν Φερένικος ἐϋπύργους Συρακούσ-
185 σας, Ἱέρωνι φέρων
[εὐδ]αιμονίας πέταλον.
[χρὴ] δ' ἀληθείας χάριν
αἰνεῖν, φθόνον ἀμφ[οτέραισιν]
χερσὶν ἀπωσάμενον,
190 εἴ τις εὖ πράσσοι βροτῶ[ν].
Βοιωτὸς ἀνὴρ τάδε φών[ασεν παλαιός],   ἐπ. ε'.
Ἡσίοδος πρόπολος
Μουσᾶν, ὃν ἀθάνατοι τι[μαῖς ὄφελλον]
καὶ βροτῶν φήμαν ἔπ[λησαν].
195 πείθομαι εὐμαρέως
εὐκλέα κελεύθου γλῶσσαν ο[ἰακοστρόφον]
πέμπειν Ἱέρωνι· τόθεν γὰ[ρ]
πυθμένες θάλλουσιν ἐσθλ[οί],

αθανατοι for αθανατωι would be a corruption dating back to the time when o stood for the long vowel as well as the short. The subject of the verb would then be the Muses. As an alternative, retaining ἀθάνατοι, Professor Jebb suggests ὃν ἄρ' (or ποτ') ἀθάνατοι τίον μέγιστα.

194. φήμαν: cf. II. 1.

ἔπλησαν: it is not easy to get a satisfactory word to complete the line. ἐπῆγον, ἐπῆρον, and the like, are excluded by the accent on the first syllable in the MS. ἔπλησαν, in the sense of 'fulfilled,' 'completed,' is perhaps possible. Professor Jebb suggests ὕπασσαν, taking it to be another instance of the confusion of o and ε, as in l. 106.

196. οἰακοστρόφον: supplied from Pind. Isth. III. 89 (IV. 71); 'I trust to send to Hieron an utterance of fair fame to guide his path.' κέλευθος is used of a ship's course in Pind. Pyth. V 88. At the same time it is clear that no high degree of certainty can be claimed for such a conjecture. ο[ἴκοθεν] or ὀ[λβίῳ], with an additional disyllabic word, are also possible. Professor Jebb suggests κέλευθον, 'to send my utterance along an honoured path.'

197. τόθεν: the original sense, as a genitive of ὁ, is preserved here. It is equivalent to τῶν, and is the antecedent to τούς.

ΤΟΥϹΟΜΕΓΙϹΤΟΠΑΤѠΡ
200 ΖΕΥϹΑΚΙΝΗΤΟΥϹΕΝΕΙΡΗΝ[

VI.

Λαχωνι Κειωι σταδιει Ολυμ^π

⏑ – ⏑ – ⏑ – –
⏑ ⏑ – ⏑ – ⏑ – ⏒
– ⏑ ⏑ – – ⏑ ⏑ – ⏑ – –
⏑ – ⏑ ⏑ – ⏑
5 – ⏑ – ⏑ – ⏑ ⏒
⏑ – ⏑ ⏑ ⏑ – ⏑ –
– ⏑ – ⏑ ⏑ – ⏑ – –
⏑ ⏑ – ⏑ – –

1 — 8 = 9 — 16

200. φυλάσσει Palmer.

200. εἰρήνᾳ: the MSS. of Pindar appear generally to retain the η in the stem, though the editors have habitually altered it.

τοὺς ὁ μεγιστοπάτωρ
200 Ζεὺς ἀκινήτους ἐν εἰρήν[ᾳ φυλάσσει].

VI.

ΛΑΧΩΝΙ ΚΕΙΩΙ

σταδιεῖ ᾿Ολύμπ[ια]

After the praises of Hieron, the poet reverts to those of his own countrymen, and the next two odes are, like the first two, addressed to a native of Ceos. In this case the victor to be commemorated is Lachon, son of Aristomenes, who had won the foot-race at Olympia. This is expressly stated in the poem before us, as well as in the title ; yet the name of Lachon of Ceos does not appear in the list of victors in the foot-race which has come down to us through the agency of Eusebius. There is not the least reason to question the authenticity of the poem; and this is consequently a strong proof of the untrustworthiness of the Olympic Register, the compilation of which only goes back to Hippias of Elis, at the end of the fifth century (cf. Mahaffy, *Journal of Hellenic Studies*, II. 164–178). And if the register was wrong with regard to contests which took place only some sixty or seventy years before its compilation, what is its value for the three hundred years which lie yet farther back ?

The first of the two poems to Lachon is a short ode of sixteen lines, arranged in two strophes, sung in Ceos itself, before the doors of his father's house. It refers to another ode which had already been sung at Olympia, at the time of the victory, and it is probable that this is the ode which follows next in the manuscript. It is impossible to be certain, since the papyrus is broken at this point, and only ten lines of the second poem are preserved; but these, so far as they go, are consistent with this theory. The first poem is perfect, except for a few letters at the ends of three lines.

φυλάσσει : supplied by Professor Palmer from XIII. 155-6, ἄστεά τ᾿ εὐσεβέων | ἀνδρῶν ἐν εἰρήνᾳ φυλάσσει.

ΛΑΧΩΝΔΙΟϹΜΕΓΙϹΤΟΥ

ΛΑΧΕΦΕΡΤΑΤΟΝΠΟΔΕϹϹΙ

ΚῩΔΟϹΕΠΑ2ΦΕΙΟΥΠΡΟΧΟΑΙϹ[

ΔΙΟϹϹΑΠΑΡΟΙΘΕΝ

5 ΑΜΠΕΛΟͤΡΌΦΟΝΚΕΟΝ

ἈΕΙϹΆΝΠΟΤ'ΟΛΥΜΠΙᾹΙ

ΠΥΞΤΕΚΑΙϹΤΆΔΙΟΝΚΡΑΤΕΥ[

ϹΤΕΦΑΝΟΙϹΕΘΕΊΡΑϹ

ΝΕΑΝΙΑΙΒΡΥΟΝΤΕϹ·

10 ϹΕΔΕΝΥΝΑΝΑΞΙᵹΌΛΠΟΥ

ΟΥΡΑΝΙΑϹΥΜΝΟϹΈΚΑΤΙΝΙΚ[

ΑΡΙϹΤΟΜΈΝΕΙΟΝ

ΩΠΟΔΆΝΕΜΟΝΤΕΚΟϹ

ΓΕΡΆΙΡΕΙΠΡΟΔΟΜΟΙϹΑΟΙ

15 ΔΑΙϹΌΤΙϹΤΑΔΙΟΝΚΡΑΤΗϹΑϹ

ΚΕΟΝΕΥΚΛΕΪΞΑϹ

*——

VI. *Title* by A³.   3. Ἀλφεοῦ] ΑΛΦΕΙΟΥ A, altered on metrical grounds; the first syllable has been miswritten, and a Λ is added above the line by A³, but the exact form of the blunder is uncertain.

2. λάχε : of course an intentional play upon the victor's name.

3. σεμναῖς : many other words are equally possible, and the adjective may agree with either Ἀλφεοῦ or προχοαῖσι : but the parallels in Pindar are in favour of the latter; *e.g. Nem.* I. 1, ἄμπνευμα σεμνὸν Ἀλφεοῦ, *Ol.* III. 22, ζαθεοῖς ἐπὶ κρημνοῖς Ἀλφεοῦ.

4. δι' ὅσσα : probably not 'has won glory on account of the hymns which they sang,' but 'has won glory, on account of which they sang hymns.' The means by which the glory was won have already been expressed in πύδεσσιν, and the hymns sung at Olympus were a consequence of his victory. Then ll. 4-9 balance ll. 10-15, the general structure of the ode being, 'Lachon has won an Olympic victory, which was celebrated formerly at Olympia, and now is celebrated at his own home in Ceos.'

7. πύξ τε καὶ στάδιον κρατεῦσαν : it was Ceos, not Lachon, that was victorious in these two contests. There is no reason to suppose that Lachon won the boxing; in l. 15 (and in the title) he is simply mentioned as victor in the foot-race, and it is not in the least likely that a competitor in

Λάχων Διὸς μεγίστου   στρ. α'.
λάχε φέρτατον πόδεσσι
κῦδος ἐπ' Ἀλφεοῦ προχοαῖσ[ι σεμναῖς],
δι' ὅσσα πάροιθεν
5 ἀμπελοτρόφον Κέον
ἄεισάν ποτ' Ὀλυμπίᾳ
πύξ τε καὶ στάδιον κρατεῦ[σαν]
στεφάνοις ἐθείρας
νεανίαι βρύοντες.   στρ. β'.
10 σὲ δὲ νῦν ἀναξιμόλπου
Οὐρανίας ὕμνος ἔκατι νίκ[ας],
Ἀριστομένειον
ὦ ποδάνεμον τέκος,
γεραίρει προδόμοις ἀοι-
15 δαῖς, ὅτι στάδιον κρατήσας
Κέον εὐκλέϊξας.

training for a sprint would have entered for a contest of strength. Another
Cean had won the boxing-contest; and Lachon's success in the race caused
Ceos to be celebrated as victorious in both events at the same festival.

10. ἀναξιμόλπου: a word of analogous formation to Pindar's ἀναξιφόρμιγξ
(*Ol.* II. 1). It cannot be said to decide the question as to the derivation of
the first part of the compound from ἀνάσσω or ἀνάγω (cf. Bury, *Isthmian Odes
of Pindar*, p. ix. note), since either 'Urania, queen of song,' or 'Urania that
awakes the song,' makes good sense. Cf. XVII. 66, ἀναξιβρόντας, XX. 8,
ἀναξίαλος.

12. Ἀριστομένειον τέκος: for the adjective formed from a proper name
instead of a genitive, cf. Pindar, *Pyth.* II. 18, Δεινομένειε παῖ, and VIII. 19,
Ξενάρκειον υἱόν.

14. προδόμοις: i. e. songs sung before the door of his home. προδρόμοις,
'songs going before you in procession,' suggests itself as an obvious possibility; but there is no necessity for the change, and προδόμοις, the
commoner word, is far less likely to have been corrupted into προδρόμοις
than vice versa. προδόμοις also provides the contrast to Ὀλυμπίᾳ in the
preceding sentence, which, moreover, stands in the corresponding line
of the strophe.

16. εὐκλέϊξας: so Pindar, *Pyth.* IX. 99, εὐκλεῖξαι, and κλεῖξειν in *Ol.* I. 110.

VII.

Τωι αυτωι

```
 – ∪ – – ∪ ∪ – ∪ – ∪ –
 – – ∪ – – – ∪ [– ×
 – – ∪ ∪ – ∪ ∪ – [∪ –
 [.      .      .  .]
5 [.    .    .        .]
 .]  ∪ – [.    .    .]
 – – ∪ [.  .] – – – ∪ –
 – – ∪ – – ∪ – – – ∪ ×
 – ∪ ∪ – ∪ ∪ – – – ∪ –
10 – – ∪ – – – ∪ – – – ∪ –
 – – ∪ – – – ∪ [.      .]
 [–] ∪ – – [.   .   .   .]
```

ΩΛΙΠΑΡΑΘΥΓΑΤΕΡΧΡΟΝΟΥΤΕϟ[

ΝΥΚΤΟϹϹΕΠΕΝΤΗΚΟΝΤΑΜ[

ΕΚΚΑΙΔΕΚΆΤΑΝΕΝΟΛΥΜΠ[

Col. 13]   [. . . .]ΑΡ[

5 [. .]ΤΟϹΑΙΜ[

ΚΡΙΝΕΙΝΤΑ[. . . . .]ΛΑΙΨΗΡῶΝΠΟΔΩΝ

ΕΛΛΑϹΙΚΑΙΓΥ[. . . .]ΡΙϹΤΑΛΚΕϝΕϹϹΘΕΝΟϹ·

VII. *Title* by A³, **written over an erasure of three lines.**   7.
ΡΙϹΤΑΛΚΕΕϹ Δ, corr. A³?

1. θύγατερ Χρόνου τε καὶ Νυκτός: no daughter of Χρόνος and Νύξ appears to be recognized by the mythologists. Most of the children of Night are of ill omen, such as Θάνατος, the Μοῖραι, and Nemesis (Hesiod. *Theog.* 211–225), and therefore inconsistent with the epithet λιπαρά; but she was also the mother of Αἰθήρ and Ἡμέρα (*ib.* 124), and the latter is probably intended here. See note on l. 3.

2. πεντήκοντα: perhaps the number of the chorus engaged in singing the ode, like ἐβδομήκοντα in II. 9.

3. ἐκκαιδεκάταν: the Olympic festival took place about the middle of the

VII.

ΤΩΙ ΑΥΤΩΙ.

The title in the margin has been written over three washed-out lines, perhaps a repetition of the full title as given at the beginning of the previous poem. The exact length of the poem cannot be ascertained, but it must have been very short, since one column has to contain the whole of it (except the first three lines), together with the beginning of the next poem. It can therefore only have consisted of one metrical system. The extant fragments do not admit of the reconstitution of the metre. It may be observed that lines 9 and 10 may have corresponded with lines 1 and 2 (with only the difference of a spondee for a trochee in the latter half of line 9), but lines 3 and 10 cannot be reconciled, if the text is sound. The metre is dactylo-epitrite.

> ὦ λιπαρὰ θύγατερ Χρόνου τε κ[αὶ]
> Νυκτός, σὲ πεντήκοντα μ[
> ἐκκαιδεκάταν ἐν Ὀλυμπ[ίᾳ
> [. . . .]αρ[
> 5 [. .]τοσαιμ[
> κρίνειν τά[χος τε] λαιψηρῶν ποδῶν
> Ἕλλασι καὶ γυ[ίων ἐ]ριστάλκες σθένος.

month; and Professor Jebb suggests that on this occasion the last day fell on the 16th day of the month (restoring μηνός at the end of l. 2), so that the invocation with which the poem opens is addressed to this last day of the festival, on which the victories won in the games were celebrated.

4–14. The last few letters of ll. 6–14 are on the same piece of papyrus as col. 14, but the rest of these lines has been put together by Professor Blass from several small fragments. The continuity of sense and general resemblance of metre show that they belong to ode VII, and thus a connexion is established between two large portions of the MS. Professor Blass is not responsible for the restorations here printed; but for the most part they are obvious.

F

ωˈΔΕCΥΠΡΕCΒΥ[. . . .]ΝΝΕΙΜΗΙCΓΕ[.]ΑC

ΝΙΚΑCΕΠΑΝΘΡ[. .]ΟΙCΙΝΕΥΔΟΞΟCΚΕΚΛΗ

10 ΤΑΙΚΑΙΠΟΛΥΖΗ[. . . .]C·ΑΡ[. . . . . . .]ΟΝ

[. . .]ˈΕΚΟCΜΗ[. . . .]ΦΑΝ[. . . . . . .]ΝΑ

[.   .   .   .   .   .   .]

[.   .   .   .   .   .   .]

[.   .   .   .   .   .   .]ΟΜΩΙ

[24 lines wanting to complete column.]

VIII.

```
        –  –  ⌣  ⌣  –  ⌣  ⌣  –
        –  –  ⌣  ⌣  –  ⌣  ⌣  –  –
        –  ⌣  –  –  –  ⌣  ⌣
        –  –  ⌣  –  ⌣  ⌣  –
  5  –  –  ⌣  –  –  –  ⌣  ⌣
        –  ⌣  –  –  –  [⌣ –]
        –  ⌣  –  ⌣  –  ⌣  –
        –  ⌣  –  ⌣  –  ≚ [–  ⌣  ⌣]
        ⌣  ⌣  –  ⌣  ⌣  –  –
 10 –  –  ⌣  –  –  –  ⌣  [–]
        –  –  ⌣  –  –  –  ⌣  –  [.  .  .]
        ⌣  ⌣  ⌣  –  –  –  ⌣  ⌣  [.  .  .]
        –  ⌣  –  –  ⌣  ⌣
        –  –  ⌣  –  –
 15 –  ⌣  ⌣  –  ⌣  ⌣  –
        –  –  ⌣  –  –
```

Col. 14]   ΠΥΘΩΝΑΤΕΜΗΛΟΘΥΤΑΝ

        ΥΜΝΕΩΝΝΕΜΕΑΝΤΕΚΑΙΪCΘ[.]ΟΝ·

8. ΝΕΙΜΗΙΣ ΓΕΡΑΣ] the Σ and Γ are written over other letters, apparently Σ Τ, by A³.

8. σύ: the day invoked in ll. 1–3.
VIII. 1. μηλοθύταν : primarily of a person, a priest who sacrifices sheep,

ᾧ δὲ σὺ πρεσβύ[τατο]ν νείμῃς γέ[ρ]ας
νίκας, ἐπ' ἀνθρ[ώπ]οισιν εὔδοξος κέκλη-
10 ται καὶ πολυζή[λωτο]s. ἀρ[. . . . . . .]ον
[. . .] ἐκόσμη[σ . . .]φαν[. . . . . . .]να
[. .   .   .   .]
[. .   .   .   .]
[. .   .   .   .]ομῳ

[The rest is wanting.]

VIII.

This poem, like the last, must have been very short, consisting
of sixteen lines in addition to such part of col. 13 as was left after
the completion of ode VII. The one fact which can apparently
be gathered from its remains is that the athlete commemorated in
it had won victories in the Pythian, Nemean and Isthmian games,
but never at Olympia. Nothing can be determined as to his
name or nationality. The metre is dactylo-epitrite.

Πυθῶνά τε μηλοθύταν
ὑμνέων Νεμέαν τε καὶ Ἰσθ[μ]όν.

as in Eur. *Alc.* 121; but transferred to the altar at which the sheep were
sacrificed, as in Eur. *Iph. Taur.* 1116, βωμοὺς μηλοθύτας, and so to the place
in which such altars stood, as here. This enumeration of places at which
games were held, taken in conjunction with the reference in the following
lines to the number of victories won by the athlete for whom this poem was
written, seems to imply that he had been successful at all these places.

ΓΑ͞ΔΕΠΙCΚΗΠΤѠΝΧΕΡΑ

ΚΟΜΠΑCΟΜΑΙ·CΥΝΑΛΑ

5 ΘΕΙΑ͞ΤΔΕΠΑΝΛΑΜΠΕΙΧΡΕΟ[

ΟΥΤΙCΑΝΘΡѠΠѠΝΚ[

ΝΑCΕΝΆΛΙΚΙΧΡΟΝѠ[

ΠΑΙCΕѠΝΑΝΗΡΤΕΠ[

ΝΑCΕΔΕΞΑΤΟΝΙΚΑC·

10 ѠΖΕΥΚ[.]ΡΑΫΝῈΓΚΕCΚΑ[

       ε
ΟΧΘΑΙCΙΝΑΛΦΙΟΥΤΕΛΕCC[..........]C

ΘΕΟΔΟΤΟ[.]CΕΥΧΑC·ΠΕΡΙΚ[

ΓΛΑΥΚΟΝΑΙΤѠΛΙΔΟ[

       μ᾽
ΑΝΔΉΕΛΑΙΑC

15 ΕΝΠΕΛΟΠΟCΦΡΥΓΙΟΥ

<u>ΚΛΕΙΝΟΙCΑΕΘΛΟΙC·</u>

IX.

Αυτομηδει Φλιασιωι πενταθλωι Νεμεα

STROPHE.

$$
\begin{array}{l}
- \smile - - - \smile \smile - \smile \smile - \\
- \smile - \smile - - \smile - \\
- - \smile \smile \smile - \smile \smile - - - \smile - - \\
- \smile - - - \smile \smile - \smile \smile - - \\
5\ - \smile - - - \smile \smallsmile \\
- - \smile \smile - \smile \smile - - \\
- \smile - - - \smile \smallfrown \\
- - \smile - - - \smile - \\
- \smile - - \smile - - - \smile - \smallsmile
\end{array}
$$

3. ΓΑ **Δ**, corr. **Δ**¹?   6. κλεεννάς Jebb.   9. ΝΟΣ **Δ**, ΝΑΣ **Δ**³?
10. ἀμφ᾽ Jebb.   11. ΑΛΦΙΟΥ **Δ**, corr. **Δ**³.   14. ΑΝΔΗ **Δ**,
ΑΝΔΗΜ᾽ **Δ**³.   IX. *Title* by **Δ**³.

3. γᾷ δ᾽ ἐπισκήπτων χέρα: cf. V. 42.
4, 5. σὺν ἀλαθείᾳ . . . χρέος: parenthetical. χρέος is used in its most general sense; 'every matter is best seen in the light of truth.'

γᾷ δ' ἐπισκήπτων χέρα
κομπάσομαι· σὺν ἀλα-
5 θείᾳ δὲ πᾶν λάμπει χρέο[s]·
οὔτις ἀνθρώπων κ[λεεν]-
νὰς ἐν ἅλικι χρόνῳ
παῖς ἐὼν ἀνήρ τε π[
νας ἐδέξατο νίκας.
10 ὦ Ζεὺ κ[ε]ραυνεγχές, κα[ὶ ἀμφ']
ὄχθαισιν Ἀλφειοῦ τέλεσσ[ον . . . .]s
θεοδότο[υ]s εὐχάς· περὶ κ[ρᾶτά τέ οἱ τίθει]
γλαυκὸν Αἰτωλίδο[s]
ἄνδημ' ἐλαίας
15 ἐν Πέλοπος Φρυγίου
κλεινοῖς ἀέθλοις.

IX.

ΑΥΤΟΜΗΔΕΙ ΦΛΙΑΣΙΩΙ

πεντάθλῳ Νέμεα.

Of this poem, addressed to Automedes of Phlius, about half is
preserved in a form which admits of satisfactory restoration, while
the other half is almost wholly lost, only a few fragments remaining
to indicate its length and character. It commemorates a victory
won in the pentathlum at the Nemean games; but there is no
evidence to show its date. The entire poem consisted of four

8. Perhaps πρὶν πλέο|νας (Jebb) or ποσσὶ πλεῦ|νας (Sandys). The
metre being uncertain, no certain conclusion can be arrived at.

13. Αἰτωλίδος: i. e. Elean, the Eleans and Aetolians being descended,
according to the legend, from two brothers, and Elis having been assigned
to the Aetolian Oxylus after the Dorian conquest of the Peloponnese.
Cf. Pindar, Ol. III. 12, Αἰτωλὸς ἀνήρ.

EPODE.

```
 – – ∪ – – – ∪ – – ∪ ∪ –
 – ∪ – – – ∪ ∪ – ∪ ∪ – – – – ∪ –
 ⏑ – ∪ – – – ∪ – –
 – ∪ – – – ∪ –
5 – ∪ ∪ – ∪ ∪ –
 – – – ∪ – – – ∪ –
 – ∪ – – – ∪ –
 – ∪ – – ∪ – –
```

1—9 = 10—18 : 19—26
27—35 = 36—44 : 45—52
53—61 = 62—70 : 71—78
79—87 = 88—96 : 97—[104]

ΔΟΞΑΝΩΧΡΥCΑΛΑΚΑΤΟΙΧΑΡΙ[.]ΕC

ΠΕΙCΙΝΒΡΟΤΟΝΔΟΙΗΤΕΠΕΙ

ΜΟΥCΑΝΤΕΪΟΒΛΕΦΑΡΩΝΘΕΙΟCΠΡΟΦ[..]ΑC

ΕΥΤΥΚΟCΦΛΕΙΟΥΝΤΑΤΕΚΑΙΝΕΜΕΑΙΟΥ

5 ΖΗΝΟCΕΥΘ[.·.]ΕCΠΕΔΟΝ

ΥΜΝΕΙΝΟΤΙΜΗΛΟΔΑΪΚΤΑΝ

ΘΡΕΨΕΝΑΛΕΥΚΩΛΕ[..]C

ΗΡΑΠΕΡΙ[....]ΤΩΝΑΕΘΛΩΝ

ΠΡΩΤΟΝ[...]ΚΛΕΙΒΑΡΥΦΘΟΓΓ[.]ΝΛΕΟΝΤΑ·

10 ΚΕ[.....]ΝΙΚΑCΠΙΔΕCΗΜΙΘΕΟΙ

ΠΡ[.....]ΝΑΡΓΕΙΩΝΚΡΙΤΟΙ

2. ΠΕΙΣΙΝΒΡΟΤΟΝ Δ, ΠΕΙΣΙΜΒΡΟΤΟΝ Δ³?   6. ὅθι] ΟΤΙ Δ.

3. Μουσᾶν ... θεῖος προφάτας: in Pindar (frag. 90) the poet describes himself as ἀοίδιμος Πιερίδων προφάτας, but here Apollo must be meant, in his character of Μουσηγέτης. 'Grant, O Graces of the golden spindles, a persuasive brilliance to my song,—ye and the divine spokesman of the dark-eyed Muses, that I may sing well-built Phlius and the fertile plain of Nemean Zeus, where white-armed Hera nurtured the ravager of the flocks, the deep-voiced lion, to be the first of the far-famed toils of Heracles.' The expression is, however, strange, since normally a προφήτης is one who

systems. The first system refers to the institution of the Nemean festival by Adrastus, ending with a transition to the victory of Automedes, which occupies the strophe of the second system. The rest of that system contains references to the travels and exploits of Heracles, himself the typical athlete in feats of strength, and thereby to the Amazons whom he conquered ; and these lead up to a mention of Thebes, in the beginning of the third system, the point of which is lost through the disappearance of nearly all the remainder of the poem. The metre is dactylo-epitrite.

δόξαν, ὦ χρυσαλάκατοι Χάρι[τ]ες,   στρ. αʹ.
πεισίμβροτον δοίητ' ἔπει,
Μουσᾶν τε ἰοβλεφάρων θεῖος προφ[άτ]ας,
εὔτυκον Φλιοῦντά τε καὶ Νεμεαίου
5 Ζηνὸς εὐθ[αλ]ὲς πέδον
ὑμνεῖν, ὅθι μηλοδαΐκταν
θρέψεν ἁ λευκώλε[νο]ς
Ἥρα περι[κλει]τῶν ἀέθλων
πρῶτον ['Ηρα]κλεῖ βαρύφθογγ[ο]ν λέοντα.
10 κε[ῖθι γὰρ] νικάσπιδες ἡμίθε[οι]   ἀντ. αʹ.
πρ[ώτιστο]ν Ἀργείων κριτοὶ

speaks for a higher power than himself; but no other interpretation seems possible without considerable alterations to the Greek.

6. μηλοδαΐκταν : a coinage of Bacchylides, so far as is known, to which there is no parallel except the late ψυχοδαΐκτης.

10. νικάσπιδες : a new word. So far as formation goes it might mean either 'with victorious shields,' like χάλκασπις, or 'shield-conquering,' like ῥίψασπις, but the former appears preferable in point of sense.

ἡμίθεοι : Adrastus and his comrades were not demigods, but the word is used inexactly, just as Pindar applies it to the Argonauts (Pyth. IV. 12, 184, 211). So also below, XI. 62.

ΑΘΛΗΣΑΝΠΑΡΜΕΜΟΡΩΙΣΥΝΞΑΝΘΟΔΕΡΚΗC

ΠΕΦΝ'ΑCΑΓΕΥΟΝΤΑΔΡΑΚΩΝΥΠΕΡΟΠΛΟC

CΑΜΑΜΕΛΛΟΝΤΟCΦΟΝΟΥ·

15 ΩΜΟΙΡΑΠΟΛΥΚΡΑΤΕC·ΟΥΝΙΝ

ΠΕΙΘ'ΟΙΚΛΕΙΔΑCΠΑΛΙΝ

CΤΕΙΧΕΙΝΕCΕΥΑΝΔΡΟΥCΑΓ[

ΕΛΠΙCΑΝΘΡΩΠΩΝΥΦΑΙ . [

ακαι
ΔΗΤΟΤ'ΑΔΡΑCΤΟΝΤΑΛ[

Col. 15]   20 ΠΕΜΠΕΝΕCΘΗΒΑCΠΟΛΥΝΕΙΚΕΙΠΛΑ . . [

12. **ΑΘΛΗΣΑΝΠΑΡΜΕΜΟΡΩΙΣΥΝ** Α: the first M is cancelled and X written above by A³, and similarly ΣΥ cancelled and ΤΟ written above. It is impossible to ascertain whether any letter was inserted above the line to precede Π, as the papyrus is mutilated, but the metre requires some such change.   13. **ΑΣΑΓΕΥΟΝΤΑ**]: the Υ is a correction, apparently of an original Ρ, by A³.   16. **ΟΙΛΛΕΙΔΑΣ** Α, corr. A³; both Λ's have been cancelled by the corrector, by mistake. 19. **Α ΚΑΙ**] ΔΗ Α, corr. A³.

12. ἐπ' Ἀρχεμόρῳ: the infant child of Lycurgus, King of Nemea, killed by a snake while his nurse, Hypsipyle, was guiding Adrastus and his comrades to a fountain, of which they and their army stood in need. Amphiaraus declared the accident to be ạn omen of the fate of the expedition against Thebes, and therefore they gave the child, whose proper name was Opheltes, the surname of Ἀρχέμορος, and founded the Nemean games in his memory (Apollod. *Biblioth.* III. 6. 4).

13. ἀσαγεύοντα : for this word as it stands no explanation can be offered ; and, unless it is to be supposed that it is a word which, with all its cognates, has escaped the ancient lexicographers, some emendation is necessary. A simple and possible one is to read ἀσαλεύοντα, connecting it with ἀσαλεῖν, which appears in Hesychius with the explanation ἀφροντιστεῖν· σάλα γὰρ ἡ φροντίς. With regard to the quantity of the first syllable of σάλα there appears to be no direct statement; but it is to be observed that the verb appears as ἀσάλλειν in the MSS. of Hesychius. If the α be long, there can, of course, be no connexion with σάλος and σαλεύω. σάλα is said by Photius to have been used by Aeschylus, and the *Etym. Magn.* quotes ἀσαλής from the same author. In sense such a word would be satisfactory ; the child was seized by the snake while playing carelessly about. If the corruption goes deeper than this, the last part of the word may represent

ἄθλησαν ἐπ' Ἀρχεμόρῳ, τὸν ξανθοδέρκης

πέφν' †ἀσαγεύοντα† δράκων ὑπέροπλος,

σᾶμα μέλλοντος φόνου.

15 ὦ Μοῖρα πολυκρατές· οὔ νιν

πεῖθ' Ὀϊκλείδας πάλιν

στείχειν ἐς εὐάνδρους ἀγ[υιάς].

ἐλπὶς ἀνθρώπων ὑφαιρ[εῖ . . . .]

ἃ καὶ τότ' Ἄδραστον Ταλ[αιονίδαν]　　　　ἐπ. α'.

20 πέμπεν ἐς Θήβας Πολυνείκεϊ πλα[ξίππῳ πέλας]

εὕδοντα, the child having been killed while asleep (so Statius, *Theb.* V. 502–4); but the first part of the word remains unaccounted for. A further suggestion, originally made by Mr. R. A. Neil, is δωτεύοντα. δωτεύειν is given by Hesychius with the paraphrase ἀπανθίζεσθαι, and the suggestion that the child Archemorus was plucking flowers when he met his death derives striking confirmation, as Professor Jebb points out, from a fragment of the 'Hypsipyle' of Euripides (Nauck, *fr. Eur.* 754, ed. 2) which refers to this very incident: ὥσπερ ὁ τῆς Ὑψιπύλης τρόφιμος (says Plutarch, *De Amicorum Multitud.* p. 93 d) εἰς τὸν λειμῶνα καθίσας, ἔδρεπεν

> ἕτερον ἐφ' ἑτέρῳ αἱρόμενος
> ἄγρευμ' ἀνθέων ἡδομένᾳ ψυχᾷ,
> τὸ νήπιον ἄπληστον ἔχων.

(This reference was also independently supplied by Dr. Sandys.) In sense, therefore, δωτεύοντα is quite suitable, and palaeographically the transition from Ω to CA in the hands used on papyrus is not very remote, while that from Τ to Γ is of course quite easy.

16. Ὀϊκλείδας: Amphiaraus.

17. ἀγυιάς: sc. their homes, or the streets of Argos. Cf. Pindar, *Pyth.* VIII. 54 (the words of the same Amphiaraus with reference to the *second* expedition against Thebes) ἀφίξεται λαῷ σὺν ἀβλαβεῖ | Ἄβαντος εὐρυχόρους ἀγυιάς.

18. The last letter before the lacuna is mutilated, but appears to be ρ rather than ν. Some such words as μῆτιν ἐσθλάν would serve to complete the line.

19 Ταλαιονίδαν: cf. Pind. *Ol.* VI. 15, though the scansion is different, the αι being there treated as a disyllable and scanned ∪ —

20. At first sight the papyrus appears to be perfect at the end of this line, though showing only slight traces of one or two letters after πλα. But the metre, as compared with the other epodes, is defective, and a close examination shows that the surface of the papyrus has peeled off, carrying away the ink. The restoration here proposed satisfies the metre and the apparent

ΚΕΙΝΩΝΑΠΕΥΔΟΞΩΝΑΓΩΝΩΝ

ΕΝΝΕΜΕΑΙΚΛΕΙΝΟ[. .]ΟΤΩΝ

ΟΙΤΡΙΕΤΕΙΣΤΕΦΑΝΩΙ

ΞΑΝΘΑΝΕΡΕΨΩΝΤΑΙΚΟΜΑΝ

25 ΑΥΤΟΜΗΔΕΝΥΝΕΝΙΚΑ̈́

CΑΝΤΙΝΙΝΔΑΙΜΩΝΕ[.]ΗΚΕΝ·

ΠΕΝΤΑΕΘΛΟΙCΙΝΓΑΡΕΝ[.']ΠΡΕΠΕΝΩC

ΑCΤΡΩΝΔΙΑΚΡΙΝΕΙΦΑΗ

ΝΥΚΤΟCΔΙΧΟΜΗΝΪΔΟ[. .]ΫΦΕΓΓΗCCΕΛΑΝΑ·

30 ΤΟΙΟ[C]ΕΛΛΑΝΩΝΔΙΑ[. . . .]ΟΝΑΚΥΚΛΟΝ

ΦΑΙΝ[.]ΘΑΥΜ[.]CΤΟΝΔΕ[.]ΑC

ΔΙC[.]ΟΝΤΡΟΧΟΕΙΔΕΑΡΙΠΤῶΝ

ΚΑΙΜΕΛΑΜΦΥΛΛΟΥΚΛΑΔΟΝ

ΑΚΤΕΑCΕCΑΙΠΕΙΝΑΝΠΡΟΠΕΜΠΩΝ

35 ΑΙΘΕΡ'ΕΚΧΕΙΡΟCΒΟΑΝΩΤΡΥΝΕΛΑΩΝ

ΗΤΕ[. .]ΥΤΑΙΑCΑΜΑΡΥΓΜΑΠΑΛΑC

25. ΑΥΤΟΜΗΔΕ Α, corr. Α³: ΓΕ ΝΙΚΑ-] ΕΝΙΚΑΙ Α, corr. Α³.   26.
[Θ]ΗΚΕΝ Α, corr. Α³.   33. ΜΕΛΑΝΦΥΛΛΟΥ Α, corr. in faint ink,
as in l. 2.   36. ΤΑΛΑΣ Α, corr. Α³.

sense, but cannot be called certain. Professor Jebb suggests ἐς Θήβας
πολυνεικέα πλαξίππου πόλιν, taking Θήβας as the genitive singular and comparing Pind. *Ol.* VI. 85 πλάξιππον ἃ Θήβαν ἔτικτεν. This, however, involves
altering the MS. reading πολυνείκει, which seems hardly justifiable in
a mutilated passage.

22. κλεινοὶ βροτῶν κ.τ.λ.: 'famous are they among mortals, who weave
their bright locks with the crown of that biennial festival.' This forms the
transition to the mention of the victor to be commemorated.

23, 24. οἳ . . . ἐρέψωνται: the subjunctive without ἄν, as in Pind. *Ol.* III. 11
and elsewhere (Goodwin, *Moods and Tenses*, 1889, § 540).

26. νιν: sc. στέφανον.

28. διακρίνει: a peculiar use of the word ; lit. 'distinguishes the lights of
the stars,' but with the sense 'distinguishes from herself and sets in a lower
place.'

29. νυκτὸς διχομήνιδος: so Pind. *Isth.* VII. 44 διχομηνίδεσσιν ἑσπέραις, and
in *Ol.* III. 19 of the moon herself.

κείνων ἀπ' εὐδόξων ἀγώνων
ἐν Νεμέᾳ. κλεινο[ὶ βρ]οτῶν,
οἳ τριέτει στεφάνῳ
ξανθὰν ἐρέψωνται κόμαν.

25 Αὐτομήδει νῦν γε νικά-
σαντί νιν δαίμων ἔ[δ]ωκεν.
πενταέθλοισιν γὰρ ἐν[έ]πρεπεν ὡς   στρ. β'.
ἄστρων διακρίνει φάη
νυκτὸς διχομήνιδ[ος ε]ὐφεγγὴς σελάνα.

30 τοῖος Ἑλλάνων δι' ἀ[πείρ]ονα κύκλον
φαῖν[ε] θαυμ[ασ]τὸν δέ[μ]ας,
δίσ[κ]ον τροχοειδέα ῥιπτῶν,
καὶ μελαμφύλλου κλάδον
ἀκτέας ἐς αἰπεινὰν προπέμπων

35 αἰθέρ' ἐκ χειρὸς βοὰν ὤτρυνε λαῶν,
ἢ τε[λε]υταίας ἀμάρυγμα πάλας.   ἀντ. β'.

32–36. Three contests are enumerated, in which Automedes is said to have distinguished himself, viz. the discus, the javelin, and the wrestling. It may therefore be presumed that he was successful in these events, but was beaten in the two remaining contests of the pentathlum, the long jump and the foot-race. This, however, throws no light on the problem as to the principles on which the pentathlum was decided. A competitor who won three events outright must have been the winner, on any reasonable hypothesis. What one wants to know is, how the result was determined when no one won an absolute majority of events, and here Bacchylides does not help us.

32. ῥιπτῶν: the accent in the MS., which is in fainter ink than the writing itself, and therefore probably added by the third hand (A³), shows that the participle is to be taken as from ῥιπτέω, not ῥίπτω.

35. αἰθέρα: feminine, as in *Ol.* I. 6, XIII. 88. Bacchylides, however, like Pindar, fluctuates as to the gender, having it masculine in III. 86.

36. ἢ τελευταίας ἀμάρυγμα πάλας: in a passage so mutilated as that which follows it is impossible to speak with certainty, but apparently τοιῷδ' introduces a fresh subject, a comparison with the hero whose exploits are narrated in the following lines. In that case the present line must go with

ΤΟΙΩ[......]ʹΜΩΙϹ[....]Ι

ΓΥΙΑ[......]ΜΑΤΑ[....]ΓΑΙΑΠΕΛΑϹϹ⊍[

ΙΚΕΤ[.....]ΝΠΑΡΑΠΟΡΦΥΡΟΔΙΝΑ . [

40 ΤΟΥΚ[....]ΑϹΑΝΧΘΟΝΑ

    ͵ͱΛΘΕ[....]ΕΠΕϹΧΑΤΑΝΕΙΛΟΥ·

ΤΑΙΤΕΠ[...]ΑΕΙΠΟΡΩΙ

ΟΙΚΕΫ́ϹΙΘΕΡΜΩΔΟΝ[.....]ΓΧΕΩΝ

ῙϹΤΟΡΕϹΚΟΡΑΙΔΙΩΞΙΠΠ[...]ΡΗΟϹ

45 ϹΩΝΩΠΟΛΥΖΉΛΩΤʹΑΝΑΞΠΟΤΑΜΩΝ

ΕΓΓΟΝΟΙΓΕΫ́ϹΑΝΤΟΚΑΙΥΨΙΠΥΛΟΥΤΡΟΙΑϹῈΔΟϹ·

38. ΠΕΛΑϹϹΩ[.] Α, ΣΩ deleted by Α³, but the correction, written
above, is lost through mutilation of the papyrus: perh. πελάσσας.
41. ΗΛΘΕ] ΜΑΘΕ Α, corr. Α³.   42. εὐναεῖ] so Jebb, and the
conjecture suits the visible remains of the first three letters.   44.
ΚΟΡΑΙ Α, corrected for metrical reasons.

what precedes, ἀμάρυγμα being what is sometimes called an accusative of
respect; 'or in the glancing movements of the final wrestling.' Professor
Jebb suggests punctuating after χειρός, and reading βοὰν δ' ὤτρυνε λαῶν δὴ
τελευταίας κ. τ. λ., which simplifies the construction. The wrestling was the
last contest in the pentathlum, hence τελευταίας. It is to be observed that
the discus is put before the javelin-throwing, as against the suggestion of
Dr. Waldstein (in Fennell's *Nemean and Isthmian Odes*, p. xx) that the
javelin-throwing, which required steadiness of hand, must have preceded
the discus. Dr. Waldstein's *a priori* considerations, which are accepted by
Fennell and Bury, are not decisive. A soldier required steadiness of hand
after the exertion of a charge or march, not merely when fresh; hence the
javelin-throwing may have been placed deliberately after the discus. There
are analogies in modern sports, though of a comic kind, such as threading
a needle after running a hundred yards.

37. τοιῷδ': τοιάδε is used by Pindar (*Isth.* III. 45) in precisely the same
way, comparing a past achievement with a present one.

ὑπερθύμῳ: the second υ is largely conjectural, only the very slightest traces
of the letter being left; but they suit υ better than anything else.

38. γυιαλκέα σώματα κ. τ. λ.: a general reference to such exploits as the
defeats of the Nemean lion, Antaeus, Achelous, &c. For πρὸς γαίᾳ cf. XI. 23
πρὸς γαίᾳ πεσόντα.

39. 'Ωκεανόν: the restoration implies the occurrence of a dactyl in place

τοιῷ[δ᾽ ὑπερθ]ύμῳ σ[θένε]ι
γυια[λκέα σώ]ματα [πρὸς] γαίᾳ πελάσσω[ν]
ἵκετ᾽ ['Ωκεανὸ]ν παρὰ πορφυροδίναν,
40 τοῦ κ[λέος π]ᾶσαν χθόνα

ἦλθε[ν, καὶ] ἐπ᾽ ἔσχατα Νείλου,
ταί τ᾽ ἐπ᾽ [εὐν]αεῖ πόρῳ
οἰκεῦσι Θερμώδον[τος ἐ]γχέων
ἵστορες κοῦραι διωξίππ[οι᾽ ῎Α]ρηος.
45 σῶν, ὦ πολυζήλωτ᾽ ἄναξ, ποταμῶν   ἐπ. β'.
ἔγγονοι γεύσαντο καὶ ὑψιπύλου Τροίας ἕδος.

of a spondee (or the scanning of ἔᾰ as = ἔᾱ), and the same applies to
'Ηριδανόν, which is another possible conjecture. Εὐφράτην is tempting, but
there appears to be no legend of Heracles having reached that river.
Αἴγυπτον (preferred by Professor Palmer) would do, but is unlikely in
immediate proximity to Νείλου. For 'Ωκεανὸν πορφυροδίναν cf. Pind. *Pyth.*
IV. 251 ἔν τ᾽ 'Ωκεανοῦ πελάγεσσι μίγεν πόντῳ τ᾽ ἐρυθρῷ. Heracles reached the
ocean stream when he went to fetch the cattle of Geryones.

40. τοῦ κλέος κ. τ. λ.: the antecedent of the relative, which is also the
subject of the main sentence, is implied, not expressed: 'he, whose fame
has gone out into all the world,' *i. e.* Heracles. It does not seem possible to
devise any reconstruction of the passage which will admit of the name itself
being introduced. Cf. ll. 22, 23, where the antecedent to οἵ is only represented by the predicate of the principal clause, κλεινοί. Professor Jebb
suggests σῶμat᾽ ἀνήρ or σώματα φώς in l. 38.

41. ἐπ᾽ ἔσχατα Νείλου: on the journey to the gardens of the Hesperides.

42. εὐναεῖ: Professor Jebb's conjecture, which suits the visible remains
and gives an excellent sense, implies a form εὐναής side by side with εὐνάεις
and εὐνάων.

44. κοῦραι: the Amazons, who were descended from Ares and Harmonia.

45. σῶν . . . ποταμῶν: the πολυζήλωτος ἄναξ is Ares, and his rivers are,
presumably, rivers of blood, as the κρουνοὶ 'Αφαίστοιο (Pind. *Pyth.* I. 25) are
streams of fire. 'Of thy rivers, much envied king, did thy descendants
drink, they and the site of lofty Troy'; referring to the expedition of the
Amazons to Troy to fight against the Greeks. This is the only sense of
which the passage, as it stands, seems to admit; but it is not satisfactory.
Professor Jebb proposes to read καθ᾽ for καί, which is a very slight change
and greatly improves the sense; and it is possible that the ποταμοί are then
the literal rivers of Troy, Simois and Scamander, though there is no other
evidence to associate them particularly with Ares.

CΤΕΙΧΕΙΔΙΕΥΡΕΙΑCΚΕΛΕ[.]ΘΟΥ

ΜΥΡΙΑΠΑΝΤΑΙΦΑΤΙC

CΑCΓΕΝΕΑCΛΙΠΑΡΟ

50 ΖΩΝΩΝΘΥΓΑΤΡΩΝ·ΑCΘ[..]Ι

CΥΝΤΥΧΑΙCΩΚΙCCΑΝΑΡΧΑΥ

<u>ΓΟΥCΑΠΟΡΘΗΤΩΝΑΓΥΙΑΝ·</u>

ΤΙCΓΑΡΟΥΚΟΙ[...]ΚΥΑΝΟΠΛΟΚΑΜΟΥ

ΘΗΒΑCΕΥΔΜ[.......]Ν

Col. 16]   55 [. . . . .]ΜΧΟΝΑΙΓΙΝΑΝ·ΜΕΓ[

       [. . . . .]ΧΕΙΤΕΚΕΝΗΡΩ

       [. . . . .]ΟΥ·

       [. . . . .]ΑΙΩΝ

       [. . . . .]

     60 [. . . . . . .]

       [. . . . .]ΡΙ.. ΠΛΟΝ[

       Η[. . . .]ΑΝΕΛΙΚΟCΤΕΦΑ[

       Κ[. . . .]CΑΙΤ·ΑΛΛΑΙΘΕΩΝ[

       [. . . .]ΗCΑΝΑΡΙΓΝΩΤ[.]ΙCΕ ... ΛΑΙ[

51. ΑΡΧΑ-] ΑΡΧΑΙ Α, corr. Α².   55. ΜΝΟΝ Α, corr. Α².

48. μυρία παντᾷ φάτις : cf. V. 31, XIX. 1.

50. θυγατρῶν : apparently not now the Amazons exclusively, but the daughters of Ares in general, so as to form a transition to the mention of Thebes.

51. ᾤκισσαν : this form is also found once in Pindar (*Isth.* VII. 20).

54. Θήβας : Thebé and Aegina are not elsewhere described as daughters of Ares, but such a parentage must be implied here, if there is to be any connexion with the preceding passage. Their connexion with a victory of an inhabitant of Phlius at the Nemean games is not clear.

στείχει δι' εὐρείας κελε[ύ]θου
μυρία παντᾷ φάτις
σᾶς γενεᾶς λιπαρο-
50 ζώνων θυγατρῶν, ἃς θ[εο]ὶ
σὺν τύχαις ᾤκισσαν ἀρχα-
γοὺς ἀπορθήτων ἀγυιᾶν.
τίς γὰρ οὐκ οἶ[δεν] κυανοπλοκάμου   στρ. γ'.
Θήβας ἔϋδμ[ατον πόλι]ν

55 [. . . . .]μον Αἴγιναν ; μέγ[ιστον]

[. . . . λέ]χει τέκεν ἥρω

[. . . . .]ον·

[. . . . .]αιων

[. . . . .]

60 [. . . . . . .]

[. . . . . .]ρι[.]πλοϋ[. .]

η[. . . .]αν ἑλικοστέφα[νο .]   ἀντ. γ'.

κ[. . . .]ς αἴ τ' ἄλλαι θεῶν

[. . . .] ἦσαν ἀριγνώτ[ο]ις. ε . . . λαϊ[

55–88. This column has been partly reconstructed from twelve fragments of papyrus, most of which were first combined by Professor Blass. The test of the identification lies, of course, in the metre. Unfortunately the remains are still too fragmentary to establish the drift of the poem.

55. The error in the MS. perhaps points to an epithet ending in -υμον, which a scribe might easily confuse with ὕμνον.

56. Aegina was the mother by Zeus of Aeacus, hence Ζηνί may precede λέχει in this line and Αἴακον begin the following line; but there are not sufficient materials for the restoration of the whole passage.

65 [. . . .] A̦ΙΠΟΤΑΜΟΥΚΕ[.]Á̦ΔΟ̦ΝΤΟC·

    [. . . .]ΑΝΠΟΛΙΝ

    [. . . .]CΙΤΕΝΙΚΑ[

    [. . . .]Λ̦ΩΝΒΟΑΙ[

    [. . . .]Υ̦Ç̣Ι·Μ̦[ᵃ

70 [. . . . . . .]Ṇ·

    [. . . . . . .]ΝΕΟC[

    [. . .]ΘΕΝΤΑΙΟΠΛΟΚΟΝΕΥΕΙΠΕΙΝ[

    [. . .]ΝΑΜ̣[.]ΤΩΝΕΡΩΤΩΝ

    [. . . . . . .]

75 [. . . . . . .]

    [. . . . . . .]

    [. . . .]Y̦ΏΤΑΝ

    [. . . .]ΝΥΜΝΟΝ·

    [. . . .]Ḳ̣ΑΙΑΠΟΦΘΙΜΕΝΩΝ̣̀

80 [. . . .]ΡΥΤΟΝΧΡΟΝΟΝ

    [. . . .]ΙΝΟΜΕΝΟΙCΑΙΕΙΠΙΦΑΥCΚω̣̄ᵒⁱ

    [. . . . . .]Μ̣ΈΑΝΙΚΑΝ·ΤΟ . . ΤΟΙΚΑΛΟΝΕΡΓΟΝ

    . Ṇ̣Ḥ̣Ç̣ΙΩΝΥΜΝΩΝΤΫΧΟΝ .

    ΥΨΟΥΠΑΡΑΔΑΙΜΟCΙΚΕΙΤΑΙ·

85 CΥΝΔ᾽Α[.]ΑΘΕΙΑΙΒΡΟΤΩΝ

69. A added above the line by Δ³.   77. Υ deleted before Ω by Δ³.
79. ΑΠΟΦΘΙΜΕΝΩΝ Δ, corr. Δ³?   81. ΠΙΦΑΥCΚΩ Δ, corr. Δ³?

65 [. ‿ ‾ ‾ .]αι ποταμοῦ κε[λ]άδοντος·

[. ‿ ‾ ‾ .]αν πόλιν

[. ‾ ‾ ‿ ‾ .]σι τε νίκα[

[. ‾ ‾ ‿ .]λων βοαι[

[. ‿ ‾ .]υσαι· μ[. ‾ ‾ .]

70 [. ‾ ‿ ‾ ‾ ‿ ‾ ‿ .]ν

[. ‾ ‿ ‾ ‿ ‿ ‾ .]νέος   ἐπ. γ΄.

[. ‿ ‾]θέντα ἰόπλοκον εὖ εἰπεῖν [. ‿ ‾ .]

[. ‾ ‾ ‿ ἀγ]νάμ[π]των ἐρώτων

[. ‾ ‿ ‿ ‾ .]

75 [. ‾ ‿ ‿ ‾ ‿ .]

[. ‾ ‿ ‾ ‾ ‿ .]

[. ‾ ‾ ‿ .]ώταν

[. ‾ ‿ ‾ ‾ ‿ ο]ν ὕμνον

[. ‿ ‾ ‾ .] καὶ ἀποφθιμένῳ   στρ. δ΄.

80 [. ‾ ‾ ‿ ἄτ]ρυτον χρόνον

[. ‾ ‾ ἐπιγ]ινομένοις αἰεὶ πιφαύσκοι

[. . . . . ‿ .]μέα νίκαν· τό[δε] τοι καλὸν ἔργον,
[γ]νησίων ὕμνων τυχόν,
ὑψοῦ παρὰ δαίμοσι κεῖται.

85 σὺν δ' ἀλαθείᾳ βροτῶν

82. Perhaps Νεμέᾳ, which is scanned as disyllabic in l. 22 and in Pind.
Nem. iv. 75; but if so, the final ι is omitted in the MS.

ΚΑΛΛΙϹΤΟΝΕͿ[

Λ[. .]ͤΠΕΤΑΙΜΟΥϹ[. . . . .]ΡΜΑ·

ΕΝΔ'ΑΝΘΡ[

Col. 17]   [.   .   .   .   .   . .]

90 [.   .   .   .   .   . .]

[.   .   .   .   .   . .]

[.   .   .   .   .   . .]

[.   .   .   .   .   . .]

[.   .   .   .   .   . .]

95 [.   .   .   .   .]ΑΥΡΟΙϹ

[. . .]ΔΡ[.   .   . .]ΤΟΜΕΛΛΟΝ·

[. .]ΜΙϢ[.   .   .]ϢΚΕΧΑΡΙΝ

[.]ΑΙΔΙϢΝ[.   .]ΘΕΟΤΙΜΑΤΟ[.]ΠΟΛΙΝ

[.]ΑΙΕΙΝΑΠΟ[.   .]ΕΥΝΤΈϹ

100 [.]ΡΥϹΕΟϹΚΑΠΤΡ[   ]

[. .]ΤΙΚΑΛΟΝΦΡ[   ]

ΑΙΝΕΟΙΤΙΜΟ[   ]

99. EYNTEΣ A, corr. A³.

87. Μουσᾶν . . . ἄθυρμα : cf. frag. 71 (Bergk 48). The missing word may be an epithet of Μουσᾶν, such as ἀγακλειτᾶν.

95–99. The ends of these lines are on a different piece of papyrus from that which holds the earlier part of the poem, and it was only on metrical grounds that they could be identified as belonging to this poem at all. The material for the identification may seem to be small, but in point of fact these five endings suit the metre of this poem and of no other in the collection. Moreover it was only necessary to suppose that a column of thirty-four lines is

κάλλιστον εἰ[. . . . .]

λ[εί]πεται Μουσ[ᾶν . . . . ἄθυ]ρμα.

ἐν δ' ἀνθρ[ωπ . . . . . .]   ἀντ. δ'.

[. . . . . . .]

90 [. . . . .]

[. . . . . . .]

[. . . . . .]

[. . . . . .]

[. . . . .]

95 [. . . . . π]αύροις

[ἀν]δρ[άσιν . . .] τὸ μέλλον.

[. .]μι[. . . . . δ]ῶκε χάριν   ἐπ. δ'.

[κ]αὶ Διων[ύσου . . .] θεοτίματο[ν] πόλιν

[ν]αίειν ἀπο[. . .]εῦντας

100 [χ]ρυσεοσκάπτρ[. . .]

[. .]τι καλὸν φρ[. . .]

αἰνέοι τιμο[. . . .]

lost after l. 54, to bring these lines into precisely their proper place in the strophic arrangement of the poem; an hypothesis subsequently confirmed by Prof. Blass' identification of additional fragments both of these lines and of the preceding column. The identification of this small fragment is thus of considerable importance, first as indicating the length of the ode to Automedes, and next as determining the true sequence of the fragments of this part of the manuscript, since the beginning of Ode X is on the same piece of papyrus.

98. καὶ Διωνύσου: or τᾷ Διώνυσος.

[...]ỊΔΙϹΥΝΚ.[   ]

[..]ỌΙΤΕΠΕΝΤ[   ]

X.

STROPHE.

EPODE.

1—10 = 11—20 : 21—28
29—38 = 39—48 : 49—56

[..]ΜΑ·ϹΥΓ[.   .   .]ΟΙΧΝΕΙϹ

[..]ΛΑ·ΚẠ[.   .   .]

[.   .   .   .   .]

[.   .   .   .   .]

5 [....]Ν(Ụ)Ṇ̣ṬṆỊ[.   .   .   .]Ι'ωι

Ξ[.·]ỌΝ·ΟΤΙΧΡΥ[   ]

Ọ[....]ΟΦΘΑΛΜΟΙϹΙΝ[   ]

Π̣[....]ẠΝΑΠΡΑΚΤΑΝ·[   ]

[πα]ιδὶ σὺν κ[. . . . .]

[..]οι τε πεντ[. . . . .]

X.

[ΑΝΩΝΤΜΩΙ ΑΘΗΝΑΙΩΙ]

[σταδιεῖ Ἴσθμια]

THE following poem is the only epinikian ode in this collection addressed to an Athenian; and through the mutilation of the beginning the name of the victor himself is lost. It appears from the poem, however, that he was a member of the tribe of Oeneis, and that his victory was won in the foot-race at the Isthmian games. The beginning of the poem is preserved on the same pieces of papyrus as the concluding fragments of the last poem, but the exact point at which it begins has to be determined by metrical considerations. It contains no myth, and its principal topic is the series of successes won by the hero in various games, followed by moral reflections. It consists of two systems, and is written in dactylo-epitrite metre.

[Φή]μα, σὺ γ[ὰρ . . . . .]οιχνεῖς   στρ. α΄.

[..]λα, κα[. . . . .]

[. . . . . . .]

[. . . . . . .]

5 [. . . .]νωνται[. . . .]ῷ

ξ[υν]όν, ὅτι χρυ[σο . .]

ὀ[. . . .] ὀφθαλμοῖσιν[. . .]

π[. . . .]αν ἀπράκταν .[. . .]

Ạ[. . . .]ῙΚΑΙΝΥΝΚΑCΙΓΝΗΤΑCΑΚΟΙΤΑC

10 [.]ΑCΙ .'ΤΙΝΕΚΕΙΝΗCΕΝΛΙΓΎΦΘΟΓΓΟΝΜΕΛΙCCΑΝ

[.]ΧΕΙΡΕCῙΝ˙ΑΘΑΝΑΤΟΝΜΟΥCᾶΝΑΓΑΛΜΑ

[.]ΥΝΟΝΑΝΘΡΩΠΟΙCΙΝΕΙΗΙ

ΧΑΡΜΑΤ[.]ΑΝΑΡΕΤΑΝ

ΜΑΝ͡ΟΝΕΠΙΧΘΟΝῙΟΙCΙΝ

15 ῸCCΑΝΙΚΑCΕΚΑΤΙΑΝΘΕCΙΝΞΑΝ

Θ[. .]ΑΝΑΔΗCΑΜΕΝΟCΚΕΦΑΛΑΝ

ΚΥΔΟ̣CΕΥ̣ΡΕΙΑΙCΑΘΑΝΑΙC

ΘΗΚΑCΟΙΝΕΙΔΑΙCΤΕΔΟΞΑΝ

ΕΝΠΟCΙΔΑΝΟCΠΕΡῚΚΛΕΙΤΟΙCΑΕΘΛΟΙC

Col. 18] 20 [. . . . .]ΑCΕΛΛΑCΙΝΠΟΔΩΝΤΑΧΕΙΑΝΟΡΜ̣ΑΝ·

[. . . . .]ΡΟΙCΙΝΕΠΙCΤΑΔΙΟΥ

11. The letter before ει may be Λ.   12. εἴη] ΕΙΗΙ Δ.   14. ΜΑΝΟΟΝ Δ, corr. Δ³.   15. νῦν om. Δ, inserted on metrical grounds.

9. κασιγνήτας ἀκοίτας : apparently the commission for the production of this ode was given to Bacchylides, not by the victor himself, but by his brother-in-law.

10. There must be some corruption at the beginning of the line, since the syllable which appears as τιν should be long. νασιώταν suggests itself as a possible reading, referring to Bacchylides' Cean nationality. This would account for the corruption, since the feminine form νασιῶτιν, which is found in the tragedians, might have been expected. The only objection is that the slight remains of the first letter suggest π rather than ν.

λιγύφθογγον μέλισσαν : Bacchylides himself. The comparison of a poet to a bee in Pindar's ἄωτος ὕμνων ἐπ᾽ ἄλλοτ᾽ ἄλλον ὦτε μέλισσα θύνει λόγον (Pyth. X. 53), and in Horace's 'apis Matinae more modoque grata carpentis thyma . . . carmina fingo,' is natural enough; but the epithet λιγύφθογγος here seems to make the comparison relate to the voice of the bee, instead of to his collection of honey, in which case it is hardly felicitous.

11. ἵν᾽ ἀθάνατον κ. τ. λ.: lit. 'that the everlasting ornament of the Muses (sc. the poet's song) may be a cause for joy common to mankind at large, arising out of thine excellence'; i. e. that this poem may be a public celebration of the victor's achievement, making known his triumph to the world at large.

ᾱ̆[. .˘. .ˉ.]ι καὶ νῦν κασιγνήτας ἀκοίτας

10 [.]ασι.ˉτιν ἐκείνησεν λιγύφθογγον μέλισσαν

[.]χειρες, ἵν' ἀθάνατον Μουσᾶν ἄγαλμα   ἀντ. α'.
[ξ]υνὸν ἀνθρώποισιν εἴη
χάρμα τ[ε]ᾶν ἀρετᾶν,
μανῦον ἐπιχθονίοισιν

15 ὅσσα ⟨νῦν⟩ Νίκας ἕκατι ἄνθεσιν ξαν-
θ[ὰν] ἀναδησάμενος κεφαλὰν
κῦδος εὐρείαις 'Αθάναις
θῆκας, Οἰνείδαις τε δόξαν,
ἐν Ποσειδᾶνος περικλειτοῖς ἀέθλοις,

20 [ἔνθα προύφην]ας Ἕλλασιν ποδῶν ταχεῖαν ὁρμάν.

[. .˘. .ˉ. . . .ˉ. .]ροισιν ἐπὶ σταδιου   ἐπ. α'.

15. ὅσσα: adverbial, 'how much thou hast brought glory.'

νῦν: the metre is defective, and this supplement provides a palaeographical explanation of the corruption. For Νίκας ἕκατι cf. V. 33. As the lines are divided in the MS. there is a marked hiatus after ἕκατι. Professor Jebb accordingly suggests that the line should be made to end with this word, whereby a regular dactylo-epitritic rhythm is secured both here and in the corresponding lines in the other strophes (ll. 33, 43), where at present there is a diphthong followed by a word beginning with a vowel. Examples of hiatus at the end of a line after a long syllable are frequent (e.g. ll. 51, 53 in this ode); but after a short syllable it is found (ignoring instances at the end of a strophe) only in V. 172, 177, IX. 40, XI. 12, XIII. 82, 120.

ξανθάν: not ξανθοῖς, agreeing with ἄνθεσιν, since the wreath of dry parsley, which was the prize in the Isthmian games, could hardly be so described.

20. Or ἔνθα καὶ δεῖξας (Jebb), ἔνθα προύδειξας (Palmer). For προφαίνειν cf. Pind. Isth. VII. 55.

21. Professor Jebb suggests the following restoration, but ll. 23 and 25 are rendered doubtful by the uncertainty as to the metre of the corresponding ll. 51 and 53 :—

σπεῦδε μὲν κούροισιν ἐπὶ σταδίου
θερμὰν ἐπιπνέων ἄελλαν,

ΘΕΡΜ[. .·. . . .]ΠΝΕωΝΑΕΛΛΑΝ

ΕϹΤΑ[. . . . .] . Δ'ΑΪ͞ΞΕΘΑΤΗΡωΝΕΛΑΙωΙ

ΦΑ͞ΡΕ[. . . . .]ΝΕΜΠΙ͂ΤΝωΝΟΜΙΛΟΝ

25 ΤΕΤΡ[. . . . .]ΝΕΠΕΙ

ΚΑΜ[. . . . .]ΜΟΝΪϹΘΜΙΟΝΙΚΑΝ

ΔΙϹΝ[. . . . .]Α͂ΡΥΞΑΝΞΥΒΟΥ

_.ωΝ[. . . . .]ωΝΠΡΟ͂ΦΑΤΑΙ·

ΔΙϹΔ'Ε[. . . . .]ΑΙΚΡΟΝΙΔΑΖΗΝΟϹΠΑΡΑΓΝΟΝ

30 ΒωΜΟ[. . . . . .]ΝΑΤΕΘΗΒΑ

ΔΕΚΤ[. . . . .]ΥΡΎΧΟΡΟΝ

Τ'ΑΡΓΟ[. . . ;.]ΝΤΕΚΑΤΑΙϹΑΝ·

Ο̇ΙΤΕΠ[. . . . .]Α̣ΝΝΕ̣ΜΟΝΤΑΙ·ΑΜΦΙΤ'ΕΥΒΟΙ

ΑΝΠΟ[. . . . . .].]·Ο̇ΙΘΪ͂ΕΡΑΝ

35 ΝΑϹΟ[. . . . .]ΑΝ·ΜΑΤΕ̣ΥΕΙ

Δ'ΑΛΛ[. . . . .]ΑΝΚΕΛΕΥΘΟΝ

Α̇ΝΤΙ[. . . . .]ωΝΑΡΙΓΝώΤΟΙΟΔΟΞΑϹΤΕΥΞΕΤΑΙ·

ΜΥΡΙΑΙΔ'ΑΝΔΡωΝΕΠΙϹΤΑ͞Ζ̇ΑΙΠΕΛΟΝΤΑΙ·:

23. ΑΪΞΕΘΑΤΗΡΩΝ Α; Α³ has written ΥΤ above ΙΞ, and added Ε between Θ and Α. 27. ἀγκάρυξαν Jebb. ΕΥΒΟΙ Α, corr. Α³. 28. The first letter (now lost) is corrected by Α³? to Λ. 30. ἁ κλεινά Jebb. 37, 38. Lines wrongly divided in Α. 38. ΕΠΙΣΤΑΤΑΙ Α, corr. Α³.

> ἔσταζ' ἱδρῶτι δ' αὖτε θεατήρων ἐλαίῳ
> φάρεα φαίδιμον ἐμπίτνων ὅμιλον,
> τετράκωλον ἐπεὶ
> κάμψεν δρόμον,

comparing for ll. 21, 22 *Il.* xxiii. 380, and for ll 23, 24 *Il.* xviii. 595, and Athen. xiii. p. 582.

28. Χαρίτων: the Graces are the dispensers of success in the games; cf. Pind. *Ol.* IV. 8, Οὐλυμπιονίκαν δέκευ | Χαρίτων ἕκατι τόνδε κῶμον, and see

θερμ[. . . . . .] πνέων ἄελλαν

ἐστα[. . . . . . .] δ' αὖτε θεατήρων ἐλαίῳ

φάρε[. . . . .]ν ἐμπίτνων ὅμιλον

25 τετρ[. . . . .]νεπει

καμ[. . . . . .]μον Ἰσθμιονίκαν

δίς ν[ιν ἀγκ]άρυξαν εὐβού-

λων [Χαρίτων] προφᾶται,

δὶς δ' ἐ[ν Νεμέ]ᾳ Κρονίδα Ζηνὸς παρ' ἁγνὸν

στρ. β'.

30 βωμό[ν· ἁ κλει]νά τε Θήβα

δέκτ[ο νιν, ε]ὐρύχορόν

τ' Ἄργο[ς Σικυώ]ν τε κατ' αἶσαν,

οἵ τε Π[ελλάν]αν νέμονται, ἀμφί τ' Εὔβοι-

αν πο[λυλήϊον], οἵ θ' ἱερὰν

35 νᾶσο[ν Αἴγιν]αν. ματεύει

δ' ἄλλ[ος ἀλλοί]αν κέλευθον,

ἅν τι[ς εὖ τάμν]ων ἀριγνώτοιο δόξας

τεύξεται. μυρίαι δ' ἀνδρῶν ἐπιστᾶμαι πέλονται.

note above on I. 13. Hence the judges in the games may well be called 'the spokesmen of the favouring Graces.'

29. For the following list of athletic successes, cf. Pind. *Ol*. XIII. 32–46, 97–112. The list there given is of the successes, not of a single victor, but of his whole house, and it includes all the places named in the record of the Athenian athlete commemorated by Bacchylides: Isthmus (33, 98), Nemea (34, 98), Thebes (107), Argos (ib.), Sicyon (109), Pellene (ib.), Euboea (112), Aegina (109). The names of the games at these several places are given by Gildersleeve in his note ad loc.

31. εὐρύχορόν τ' Ἄργος: cf. Pind. *Pyth*. VIII. 55, where Argos is called Ἄβαντος εὐρυχόρους ἀγυιάς.

37. τάμνων: cf. Pind. *Isth*. V. 22 μυρίαι δ' ἔργων καλῶν τέτμηνθ' ἑκατόμπεδοι ἐν σχερῷ κέλευθοι. An alternative is χωρῶν (Jebb).

HAP . [. .]ΦΟCΗΧΑΡΙΤωΝΤΙΜᾶΝΛΕΛΟΓΧωC

40 ΕΛΠΙΔΙΧΡΥCΕᾶΙΤΕΘΑΛΕΝ·

ΗΤΙΝΑΘΕΥΠΡΟΠῖΑΝ

ΕΙΔωςΕΤΕΡΟCΔʼΕΠΙΠΑΙCΙ

ΠΟΙΚΙΛΟΝΤΟΞΟΝΤΙΤΑΙΝΕΙ·ΟΙΔʼΕΠΕΡΓΟΙ

CΙΝΤΕΚΑΙΑΜΦΙΒΟωΝΑ . ΕΛΑΙC

45 ΘΥΜΟΝΑΥΞΟΥCΙΝ·ΤΟ . ΕΛΛΟΝ

ΔʼΑΚΡΙΤΟΥCΤΙΚΤΕΙΤΕΛΕΥΤΑC

ΠᾶΙΤΥΧΑΒΡΙCΕΝ ΟΜΕΝΚΑΛΛΙCΤΟΝΕCΕΛωΝ

ΑΝΔΡΑΠΟΛΛωΝΥΠΑΝΘΡωΠωΝΠΟΛΥΖΗΛωΤΟΝ ΕΙΜΕΝ·

ΟΙΔΑΚΑΙΠΛΟΥΤΟΥΜΕΓΑΛΑΝΔΥΝΑΜΙΝ·

50 ᾶΚΑΙΤ[.]ΝΑΧΡΕΙΟΝΤ[. . . .]Ι

ΧΡΗCΤΟΝ·ΤΙΜΑΚΡΑΝ . . ω . ΙΑΝῙΘΥCΑCΕΛΑΥΝω

[. .]ΤΟCΟΔΟΥ·ΠΕΦΑΤΑΙΘ . ΑΤΟΙCΙΝΙΚΑC

39. σοφός Palmer.   47. ΠΑ, apparently, A, corr. A³.   ΒΡΙΣΕΝΟΜΕΝ A, corr. A³.   ἐσθλῶν] ΕΣΕΛΩΝ, apparently, A.   48. ἔμμεν] ΕΙΜΕΝ A. 49. ΔΥΝΑΜΙΝ A, corr. A³.   51. The first letter after MAKPAN seems to be Γ, Π, or Ν.   ΙΘΥΣ] Υ is written over Ι by A² or A³, and Θ is written over some other letter, perhaps Ο. After ΙΘΥΣ, ΑΣ has been struck out.

39. ἢ γὰρ σοφός κ. τ. λ.: six different ways are enumerated in which men may achieve the satisfaction of their aspirations: (1) in intellectual wisdom; (2) in the favour of the Graces (as an athlete); (3) in communion with the gods; (4) in the careers and achievements of their children (a consideration perhaps intended for the parents of the subject of this ode); (5) in the works of their hands; (6) in the multitude of their flocks and herds. σοφός: or στέφος, which perhaps suits the space better.

Χαρίτων τιμάν: the Graces give honour both to poets and to athletes, but the expression ἐλπίδι χρυσέᾳ τέθαλεν seems to fix the application to the latter, whose successes are achieved in youth, and who have life before them.

ἢ γὰρ σ[ο]φὸς ἢ Χαρίτων τιμὰν λελογχὼς

ἀντ. β'.

40 ἐλπίδι χρυσέᾳ τέθαλεν,
ἤ τινα θευπροπίαν
εἰδώς, ἕτερος δ' ἐπὶ παισὶ
ποικίλον τόξον τιταίνει· οἱ δ' ἐπ' ἔργοι-
σίν τε καὶ ἀμφὶ βοῶν ἀ[γ]έλαις
45 θυμὸν αὔξουσιν. τὸ [μ]έλλον
δ' ἀκρίτους τίκτει τε[λευ]τάς.

παῖ, τύχα βρίσει· τὸ μὲν κάλλιστον, ἐσθλῶν
ἄνδρα πολλῶν ὑπ' ἀνθρώπων πολυζήλωτον ἔμμεν.

οἶδα καὶ πλούτου μεγάλαν δύνασιν,   ἐπ. β'.
50 ἃ καὶ τ[ὸ]ν ἀχρεῖον τ[ίθησ]ι
χρηστόν. τί μακρὰν γνῶμ' ἀνευθύνας ἐλαύνω
[ἐκ]τὸς ὁδοῦ; πέφαται θ[ν]ατοῖσι νίκας

41. θευπροπίαν : an oracle or utterance of the gods, teaching the individual to whom it is given how to direct his life.

42. ἐπὶ παισί : ' on the ground of his children,' like ἐπ' ἔργοισιν below.

43. ποικίλον τόξον : the image of the Psalmist, 'Happy is the man that hath his quiver full of them.' ποικίλος, because with many children his aims and hopes are in many different directions. Prof. Jebb, however, suggests a different explanation of the passage ; 'another (i.e. the lyric poet) aims at youths the cunning shaft of song,' comparing frag. 46 (Bergk 13), l. 11, παιδικοί θ' ὕμνοι φλέγονται. Dr. Sandys, coinciding with Jebb's view, adds a reference to Pind. Isth. II. 3 οἱ μὲν πάλαι ... ῥίμφα παιδείους ἐτόξευον μελιγάρυας ὕμνους, which goes far to justify the representation of lyric poetry in general by this special type of it, which might otherwise seem unnatural.

46. ἀκρίτους : apparently ' indiscriminate,' in the sense that the results bear no relation to the zeal with which they have been sought.

51. The readings in this line are doubtful. The restoration here proposed comes close to the remains in the MS., and the corruption may be accounted for by supposing the scribe to have been confused by the likeness of ΓΝωΜΑΝΕΥΘΥΝΑC to the familiar words γνώμαν and εὐθύς. γνῶμα = ' opinion.' The restoration also suits the probable requirements of the metre, giving a dactylo-epitritic line.

[. . . .]ϷΟΝΕΥΦΡΟϹΎΝΑ

Col. 19]   ΑΥΛΩΝ̣[

55 ΜΙΓ[

 ΧΡΗΤΙ . [

XI.

Ἀλεξιδαμωι Μεταποντινωι παιδι παλαιστηι Πυθια

STROPHE.

EPODE.

1—14 = 15—28 : 29—42
43—56 = 57—70 : 71—84
85—98 = 99—112 : 113—126

55. The paragraphus below this line must have been written by mistake.   **XI.** *Title* by A³.

[ὕστε]ρον εὐφροσύνα
αὐλῶν [
55 μιγ[
χρὴ τι[

XI.

ΑΛΕΞΙΔΑΜΩΙ ΜΕΤΑΠΟΝΤΙΝΩΙ

παιδὶ παλαιστῇ Πύθια

THIS poem, complete except for a few words, celebrates a Pythian victory in the boys' wrestling contest, won by Alexidamus of Metapontum, son of Phaïscus. It is the only poem in this collection addressed to a native of Magna Graecia; and no Metapontine victor appears among the odes of Pindar. The Pythian games were not the only occasion on which Alexidamus had made the journey from Italy to Greece in order to take part in an athletic festival; for the poet says that he would have gained a victory at Olympia (no doubt at the festival two years before his Pythian success) if he had had fair treatment from the judges there. There is no indication of the precise date of the poem. It consists of three systems, of which the first (except the last three lines) deals with the victory of Alexidamus at Pytho and his disappointment at Olympia, while the second, with the strophe and antistrophe of the third, narrates the myth of the daughters of Proetus, and, parenthetically, the story of the founding of Tiryns. The final epode reverts to Metapontum, introducing (if a brilliant conjecture by Professor Palmer be accepted) the sole personal allusion by the poet to his own family among the extant odes. The thread of connexion running through the whole poem is the action of Artemis. Artemis gave Alexidamus victory in the Pythian games; Artemis, by her intercession with Hera, restored the daughters of Proetus to sanity; Artemis, to whom the poet's ancestors, after taking part in the destruction of Troy, consecrated a grove by the river Casa, is also the patroness of Metapontum.

The metre is logaoedic, with dactylo-epitritic lines interspersed.

NIKAΓ[

COIΠATΓ[

ΥΨΙΖΥ[

ΕΝΠΟΛ[. . . . .]ΠωΙ

5 ΖΗΝJ[   ]

ΚΡΙΝΕ[. . . . . . .]ΑΘΑΝΑΤΟΙ

CΙΝΤΕ[. . . .]ΝΑΤΟΙCΑΡΕΤΑC·

ΕΛΛΑΘΙ[. . . .]ΠΛΟΚΑΜΟΥ

ΚΟΥΡΑ[. . . . . .]ΘΟΔΙΚΟΥ·CΕΘΕΝΔ'ΕΚΑΤΙ

10 ΚΑΙΝΥ[. . . .]ΑΠΟΝΤΙΟΝΕΥ

ΓΥΙωΝ[. . . . .]ΟΥCΙΝΕωΝ

ΚωΜΟΙΤΕΚΑ[. .]ΥΦΡΟCΥΝΑΙΘΕΟΤΙΜΟΝΑCΤΥ·

10. EY-] EI A, apparently, corr. A¹?

1-3. There seem to be two alternatives for the reconstruction of these lines, so far as the sense is concerned. The poet may have said either 'Victory, giver of sweet gifts to men, thy father is Zeus that sitteth on high, and thou, standing by the side of Zeus in golden Olympus, adjudgest the reward of merit to immortals and mortals alike'; or 'Victory, giver of sweet gifts, to thee hath the father of gods and men, that sitteth on high, granted the highest place, and standing,' &c. It is manifestly impossible to be confident as to the exact form of words where so much is left to conjecture, but in the former sense Professor Jebb has proposed, *exempli gratia*,

Νίκα γλυκύδωρε βροτοῖσιν,
σοὶ πατὴρ ἀρχὸς μέν ἐστιν
ὑψίζυγος οὐρανιδᾶν,

and in the latter sense something like the following might be possible :

Νίκα γλυκύδωρε, κράτιστον
σοὶ πατὴρ ἀνδρῶν θεῶν τε
ὑψίζυγος ὤπασ' ἔδος.

4-7. The restoration of these lines is provided by Ursinus, who quotes Bacchylides through the intermediary of a part of Stobaeus which is now lost: Βακχυλίδης δὲ τὴν Νίκην γλυκύδωρόν φησι καὶ ἐν πολυχρύσῳ Ὀλύμπῳ Ζηνὶ παρισταμένην κρίνειν τέλος ἀθανάτοισί τε καὶ θνητοῖς ἀρετῆς (Bergk, frag. 9). The editors, following Neue, have naturally reconstructed the passage in the third person, Νίκα γλυκύδωρος . . . κρίνει, but it is now clear, from σοί in l. 2, that it must be in the second. The division of lines is also, of course, different, as elsewhere.

Νίκα γ[λυκύδωρε, . . .]   στρ. α΄.

σοὶ πατ[ὴρ . . . . .]

ὑψίζυγ[ος . . . .]

ἐν πολ[υχρύσῳ δ᾽ Ὀλύμ]πῳ

5 Ζηνὶ [παρισταμένα]

κρίνε[ις τέλος] ἀθανάτοι-

σίν τε [καὶ θ]νατοῖς ἀρετᾶς.

ἔλλαθι [βαθυ]πλοκάμου

κούρα [Διὸς ὀρ]θοδίκου· σέθεν δ᾽ ἕκατι

10 καὶ νῦ[ν Μετ]απόντιον εὐ-

γυίων [κελαδ]οῦσι νέων

κῶμοί τε κα[ὶ ε]ὐφροσύναι θεότιμον ἄστυ.

8. ἔλλαθι : Palmer proposed ἵλαθι, which is no doubt the word intended
(the only alternative would be to take Ἕλλα as a proper name, which makes
no sense); but it was independently pointed out by Jebb that ἔλλαθι is
given by the grammarians as the Aeolic form of ἵλαθι (cf. Schneidewin,
Simonidis Carminum Reliquiae, p. 103), so that there is no need to depart
from the testimony of the MS. The only doubt is as to the quantity of
the second syllable. In the fragment of Simonides of which Schneidewin
is speaking (fr. 49 in Bergk), the editors mark the syllable as short; but
it does not appear that there is any convincing reason for this. The whole
fragment consists only of the words καὶ σὺ μέν, εἴκοσι παίδων μᾶτερ, ἵλαθι,
and it is quite possible that a line ended with παίδων, the next beginning
with a dactylo-epitritic foot (– ◡ – –). ἵλαθι properly stands for ἵληθι, and
would have the a long; nor does there seem to be any authority for ἵλᾱθι
earlier than Theocritus. ἔλλᾱθι would then be the Aeolic equivalent of the
Doric ἵλᾱθι and the Epic ἵληθι. Callimachus (frag. 121, quoted by Jebb)
has ἔλλατε, with a short, like ἵλαθι in Theocritus.

βαθυπλοκάμου : the restoration is Professor Jebb's, who, however, proposes to read βαθυπλόκαμ᾽ ὦ, on the ground that the compounds of πλόκαμος
are almost invariably applied to females, and never to Zeus, as is apparently
the case here, since nothing but Διός will suit the lacuna in the next line.

11. κελαδοῦσι : frequently in Pindar in the sense of celebrating a person
or place or achievement; e.g. *Pyth.* XI. 9 ὄφρα Θέμιν ἱερὰν Πυθῶνά τε καὶ
ὀρθοδίκαν γᾶς ὀμφαλὸν κελαδήσετε.

12. εὐφροσύναι : for the plural, meaning concrete festivities, cf. Aesch.
Prom. 540 θυμὸν ἀλδαίνουσαν ἐν εὐφροσύναις.

ΥΜΝΕΥΣΙΔΕΠΥΘΙΟΝΙΚΟΝ

ΠΑΙΔ[.]ΘΑΗΤ[.]ΝΦΑΪΣΚΟΥ·

15 ΙΛΕΩ'[..]ΙΝΟΔ[..]ΟΓΕΝΗΣΥΙ

ΟΣΒΑΘΥΖΩΝ[...]ΛΑΤΟΥΣ

ΔΕΚΤ[..]ΛΕΦ[...]Ν·ΠΟΛΕΕΣ

Δ'ΑΜΦΑΛΕΞ[..]ΑΜΟΝΑΝΘΕΩΝ

ΕΝΠΕΔΙ῟ΩΙΣΤΕΦΑΝΟΙ

20 ΚΙΡΡΑΣΕΠΕΣΟΝΚΡΑΤΕΡΑΣ

ΗΡΑΠΑΝΝΙΚΟΙΠΑΛΧΑΣ·

ΟΥΚ[..]ΔΕΝΙΝΑΕΛΙΟΣ

ΚΕ[..]ΩΙΤ῟ΕΣΥΝΑΜΑΤΙΠΡΟΣΓΑΙΑΤ῏ΠΕΣΟΝΤΑ·

ΦΑΣΩΔΕΚΑΙΕΠ῍ΖΑΘΕΟΙΣ

25 ΑΓΝΟΥΠΕΛΟΠΟΣΔΑΠΕΔΟΙΣ

ΑΛΦΕΟΝΠΑΡΑΚΑΛΛΙΡΟΑΝΔΙΚΑΣΚΕΛΕΥΘΟΝ

ΕΙΜΗΤΙΣΑΠΕΤΡΑΠΕΝΟΡΘΑΣ

ΠΑΓΞΕ'ΝΩΙΧΑΙΤΑΝΕΛΑΙΑΙ

15. ἴλεφ] the word has been corrected (probably by Α¹), but the original reading is uncertain. Λ is apparently written over Σ, and Ι has been added above the line. The alteration in the termination would no doubt correspond to that in l. 17.   17. βλεφάρῳ] the termination has been corrected; the last letter appears originally to have been Ν, perhaps the dual, βλεφάροιν.   21. ΠΑΝΝΙΚΟΙ ΠΑΛΛΑΣ Α; the second Λ is cancelled by Α¹? The accent on ΠΑΝΝΙΚΟΙ points to the true reading, παννίκοιο.   23. ΤΕ Α, corr. Α¹? The rest of this line has been added by a later hand (probably not Α²); cf. XVIII. 16.   24. ΕΠΙ Α, corr. Α².   28. ΠΑΓΞΕΝΩΙ Α, ΠΑΓΞΕΙΝΩΙ Α¹? ΕΛΑΙΑΙ] the last Ι has perhaps been added later.

14. θαητόν: similarly applied by Pindar (*Pyth.* X. 58) to an athlete when celebrated by songs of victory, τὸν Ἱπποκλέαν ἔτι καὶ μᾶλλον σὺν ἀοιδαῖς ἕκατι στεφάνων θαητὸν ἐν ἅλιξι θησέμεν.

16. βαθυζώνοιο Λατοῦς: so Pindar, frag. 58 βαθύζωνον Λατώ.

21. ἦρα: it seems impossible to take this as two words, ἦ ῥα, owing to its very late position in the sentence, and to the absence of any need for such words of special emphasis. Nor can this difficulty be evaded by putting a stop before κρατερᾶς and removing that after πάλας, since the latter is

ὑμνεῦσι δὲ Πυθιόνικον
παῖδα θαητ[ὸ]ν Φαῖσκον.

15 ἵλεῳ [ν]ιν ὁ Δ[αλο]γενὴς υἱ-   ἀντ. α΄.
ὸς βαθυζών[οιο] Λατοῦς
δέκτ[ο β]λεφ[άρῳ]· πολέες
δ' ἀμφ' Ἀλεξ[ίδ]αμον ἀν[θ]έων
ἐν πεδίῳ στέφανοι

20 Κίρρας ἔπεσον κρατερᾶς
ἧρα παννίκοιο πάλας.
οὐκ [εἶ]δε νιν ἀέλιος

κε[ίν]ῳ γε σὺν ἄματι πρὸς γαίᾳ πεσόντα.

φάσω δὲ καὶ ἐν ζαθέοις

25 ἁγνοῦ Πέλοπος δαπέδοις,
Ἀλφεὸν παρὰ καλλιρόαν, δίκας κέλευθον
εἰ μή τις ἀπέτραπεν ὀρθᾶς,
παγξένῳ χαίταν ἐλαίᾳ

supported by the MS. itself, the evidence of which with regard to punctuation seems quite trustworthy. It therefore seems certain that it is one word, ἧρα, used like χάριν governing a genitive, meaning 'on account of.' This use is found in later poets, such as Callimachus (vid. L. and S.), but no such early instance as this has hitherto been known. On the other hand, there is no instance of the use of the word at all between Homer and Callimachus, so that it is impossible to tell when its prepositional use began.

23. σὺν ἄματι : temporal use of σύν, as in Pind. *Pyth.* XI. 10 ἄκρᾳ σὺν ἑσπέρᾳ.

26. δίκας κ. τ. λ. : the words in which this charge of unfairness is expressed may refer to some action by a competitor, but they apply most naturally to the judges, and it is probably a decision of the Hellanodicae that Alexidamus complained of. γνῶμαι in l. 35 also supports this view. To contemporaries, knowing the circumstances, there could be no doubt as to the exact application of the charge, and it is a very outspoken accusation to make in so public a manner. It may safely be presumed that Alexidamus did not intend to compete at Olympia again, or such a declaration would be extremely impolitic.

28. παγξένῳ : i. e. open to all, for which all may compete.

H

ΓΛΑΥΚΑΪΣΤΕΦΑΝΩCΑΜΕ[. .]Ṇ

30 ΠΟΡΤΙΤΡΌΦ[. . . . .] .·ΪΚΕCΘΑΙ·

[. . . . .]

Col. 20]   ΠΑΙΔ'ΕΝΧΘΟΝΙΚΑΛΛΙΧΟΡΩΙ

ΠΟΙΚΙΛΑΙCΤΕΧΝΑΙCΠΈΛΑCCΕΝ·

[. .]Λ'ΗΘΕΟCΑΙΤΙΟCΗ

35 [.]ΝΩΜΑΙΠΟΛΎ∏ΛΑΓΚΟΙΒΡΟΤΩΝ

[.]ΜΕΡCΑΝΥΠΈΡΤΑΤΟΝΕΚΧΕΙΡῶΝΓΕΡΑC·

[. .]ΥΝΔ'ΑΡΤΕΜΙCΑΓΡΟΤΕΡΑ

[. .]ΥCΑΛΆΚΑΤΟCΛΙ[.]ΑΡΑΝ

[. . .]'ΡΑΤΟΞΌΚΛΥΤΟCΝΙΚΑΝΕΔΩΚΕ·

40 [. .]ΙΠΟΤ'ΑΒΑΝΤΙΆΔΑC

[.]ΩΜΟΝΚΑΤΈΝΑCCΕΠΟΛΎΛ

[. .]CΤΟΝΕΎΠΕΠΛΌΙΤΕΚΟΥΡΑΙ·

Τ̣ẠCΕΞΕΡΑΤΩΝΕΦΟΒΗCΕ

ΠᾺΓΚΡᾺΤΗCΉΡΑΜΕΛΆΘΡΩΝ

45 ΠΡΟΙ̣ΤΟΥΠΑΡΆΠΛΗΓΙΦΡΕΝΑC

<hr>

30. ἐς χθόνα κ' Jebb.   35. πολύπλαγκτοι] ΠΟΛΥΠΛΑΓΚΟΙ Α.
36. ἄμερσαν] the reading is due to a conjecture by Palmer.   39.
ἀμέρα Purser.

30. πορτιτρόφον : Metapontum was famous for agriculture, as is shown by
the ear of corn on its coins. The exact restoration of the rest of the line is
doubtful, because the two corresponding lines (72, 114) in the other epodes
differ in scansion, and it is uncertain which is correct. Cf. note on l. 72.
If, as seems probable, l. 72 is correct, then, having regard to the fact that
a mark of elision is visible in the MS. before ἱκέσθαι, the line may have run
as it has been here printed. If l. 114 is correct, then πορτιτρόφον κέν νιν ἐς
πατρίδ' ἱκέσθαι is possible here, but the traces of letters before ἱκέσθαι suit νθ'
better.

31. Palmer suggests ἀλλὰ τύχα φθονερά, as answering the requirements of
metre and sense.

33. πέλασσεν : 'made him acquainted with,' cf. Homer, *Il.* V. 766, ἥ ἑ
μάλιστ' εἴωθε κακῇς ὀδύνῃσι πελάζειν.

34. ἢ θεὸς αἴτιος : sc. by favouring the other candidate, which the Greek

γλαυκᾷ στεφανωσάμε[νο]ν, ἐπ. αʹ.

30 πορτιτρόφ[ον ἐς χθόνα κʼ εὐτυχέονθ]ʼ ἱκέσθαι.

[˙ · · · · · ·]

παῖδʼ ἐν χθονὶ καλλιχόρῳ

ποικίλαις τέχναις πέλασσεν.

[ἀλ]λʼ ἢ θεὸς αἴτιος, ἢ

35 [γ]νῶμαι πολύπλαγκτοι βροτῶν

[ἄ]μερσαν ὑπέρτατον ἐκ χειρῶν γέρας.

νῦν δʼ Ἄρτεμις ἀγροτέρα

[χρ]υσαλάκατος λι[π]αρὰν

[ἀμέ]ρα τοξόκλυτος νίκαν ἔδωκε.

40 [τᾷ] ποτʼ Ἀβαντιάδας

[β]ωμὸν κατένασσε πολύλ-

[λι]στον εὔπεπλοί τε κοῦραι.

τὰς ἐξ ἐρατῶν ἐφόβησε στρ. βʹ.

παγκρατὴς Ἥρα μελάθρων

45 Προίτου, παραπλῆγι φρένας

gods were apt to do in ways which are hardly consistent with our ideas of fairness; e. g. Athena and Apollo in the chariot race in *Il.* XXIII. 383–393, and Athena again in the foot race, ib. 774. This reference to the gods is, however, only a formal alternative, not a real one.

39. ἀμέρα: this restoration is due to Mr. L. C. Purser, who observes that it was a title given to Artemis in special reference to her having calmed the madness of the daughters of Proetus, and therefore especially appropriate here; cf. Callimachus, *Hymn.ad Dian.* 233–6 :—

> ἢ μέν τοι Προῖτός γε δύω ἐκαθίζετο νηούς,
> ἄλλον μὲν Κορίης, ὅτι οἱ συνελέξατο κούρας
> οὔρεα πλαζομένας ἀφείνια· τὸν δʼ ἐνὶ Λούσοις
> Ἡμέρῃ, οὕνεκα θυμὸν ἀπʼ ἄγριον εἵλετο παίδων.

Cf. also Pausanias, VIII. 18. 3. It may be observed that no less than four epithets are here applied to one substantive.

40. Ἀβαντιάδας: Proetus, son of Abas and brother of Acrisius.

41. κατένασσε: not elsewhere applied to inanimate objects.

45. παραπλῆγι: apparently in active sense 'a compulsion which brings madness,' lit. 'driving (the mind) aside.'

ΚΑΡΤΕΡΑΙΖΕΥΞΑC·ΑΝΑΓΚΑΙ·

ΠΑΡΘΕΝΙΑΙΓΑΡΕΤΙ

ΨΥΧΑΙΚΙΟΝΕCΤΕΜΕΝΟC

ΠΟΡΦΥΡΟΖΩΝΟΙΟΘΕΑC·

50 ΦΑCΚΟΝΔΕΠΟΛΥCΦΕΤΕΡΟΝ

ΠΛΟΥΤΩΙΠΡΟΦΕΡΕΙΝΠΑΤΕΡΑΞΑΝΘΑCΠΑΡΕΔΡΟΥ

CΕΜΝΟΥΔΙΟCΕΥΡΥΒΙΑΙ·

ΤΑΙCΙΝΔΕΧΟΛΩCΑΜΕΝΑ

CΤΗΘΕCΙΝΠΑΛΙΝΤΡΟΠΟΝΕΜΒΑΛΕΝΟΜΜΑ·

55 ΦΕΥΓΟΝΔ·ΟΡΟCΕCΤΑΝΙΦΥΛΛΟΝ

CΜΕΡΔΑΛΕΑΝΦΩΝΑΝΙΕΙCΑΙ

ΤΙΡΥΝΘΙΟΝΑCΤΥΛΙΠΟΥCΑΙ

ΚΑΙΘΕΟΔΜΑΤΟΥCΑΓΥΙΑC·

ΗΔΗΓΑΡΕΤΟCΔΕΚΑΤΟΝ

60 ΘΕΟΦΙΛΕCΛΙΠΟΝΤΕCΑΡΓΟC

ΝΑΙΟΝΑΔΕΙCΙΒΟΑΙ

ΧΑΛΚΑCΠΙΔΕCΗΜΙΘΕΟΙ

CΥΝΠΟΛΥΖΗΛΩΙΒΑCΙΛΕΙ·

ΝΕΙΚΟCΓΑΡΑΜΑΙΜΑΚΕΤΟΝ

65 ΒΛΗΧΡΑCΑΝΕΠΑΛΤΟΚΑCΙΓΝΗΤΟΙCΑΠΑΡΧΑC

Col. 21]   ΠΡΟΙΤΩΙΤΕΚΑΙΑΚΡCΙΩΙ·

ΛΑΟΥCΤΕΔΙΧΟCΤΑCΙΑΙC

ΗΡΙΠΟΝΑΜΕΤΡΟΔΙΚΟΙCΜΑΧΑΙCΤΕΛΥΓΡΑΙC·

54. **ΣΤΗΘΕΣΙΝ** A, corr. on metrical grounds.   νόημα] **ΟΜΜΑ** A, against sense and metre.   66. Ἀκρισίῳ] **ΑΚΡΣΙΩΙ** A.   68. **ΗΡΙΠΟΝ** A, corr. on metrical grounds.

49. πορφυροζώνοιο: elsewhere only in Hesychius, who gives it as the explanation of λύζωνος.

51. πάρεδρος: 'consort'; not elsewhere used of a wife. Pindar calls Themis Διὸς πάρεδρος (*Ol.* VIII. 22), also Rhadamanthus (*ib.* II. 84).

54. ἔμβαλεν νόημα: the MS. reading, εμβαλεν ομμα, is wrong in metre as well as difficult in sense, and the correction here given is palaeographically

καρτερᾷ ζεύξασ' ἀνάγκᾳ.
παρθενίᾳ γὰρ ἔτι
ψυχᾷ κίον ἐς τέμενος
πορφυροζώνοιο θεᾶς·
50 φάσκον δὲ πολὺ σφέτερον
πλούτῳ προφέρειν πατέρα ξανθᾶς παρέδρου
σεμνοῦ Διὸς εὐρυβία.
ταῖσιν δὲ χολωσαμένα
στήθεσσι παλίντροπον ἔμβαλεν νόημα.
55 φεῦγον δ' ὄρος ἐς τανίφυλλον
σμερδαλέαν φωνὰν ἱεῖσαι,
Τιρύνθιον ἄστυ λιποῦσαι   ἀντ. β'.
καὶ θεοδμάτους ἀγυιάς.
ἤδη γὰρ ἔτος δέκατον
60 θεοφιλὲς λιπόντες Ἄργος
ναῖον ἀδεισιβόαι
χαλκάσπιδες ἡμίθεοι
σὺν πολυζήλῳ βασιλεῖ.
νεῖκος γὰρ ἀμαιμάκετον
65 βληχρᾶς ἀνέπαλτο κασιγνήτοις ἀπ' ἀρχᾶς
Προίτῳ τε καὶ Ἀκρισίῳ·
λαούς τε διχοστασίαις
ἤρειπον ἀμετροδίκοις μάχαις τε λυγραῖς.

simple. The archetype having ΕΜΒΑΛΕΝΝΟΗΜΑ, one of the two Ν's dropped out, and εμβαλεν οημα very easily became εμβαλεν ομμα.

58. θεοδμάτους : as having been built by the Cyclopes at the order of Zeus.

59. γάρ : explaining the mention of Tiryns in l. 57, rather than Argos, which was the native home of Proetus.

65. βληχρᾶς ... ἀπ' ἀρχᾶς: cf. Apollod. *Bibl.* II. 1. 1 οὗτοι (Ἀκρίσιος καὶ Προῖτος) καὶ κατὰ γαστρὸς μὲν ἔτι ὄντες ἐστασίαζον πρὸς ἀλλήλους, ὡς δὲ ἀνετράφησαν περὶ τῆς βασιλείας ἐπολέμουν.

68. ἤρειπον : sense, as well as metre, requires this emendation of the MS.

ΛΙϹϹΟΝΤΟΔΕΠΑΙΔΑϹΑΒΑΝΤΟϹ

70 ΓΑΝΠΟΛΎΚΡΙΘΟΝΛΑΧΟΝΤΑϹ

     ΤΙΡΥΝΘΑΤΟΝΟΠΛΌΤΕΡΟΝ

     ΚΤΊΖΕΙΝΠΡΙΝΕϹΑΡΓΑΛΈΑΝΠΕϹΕΙΝΑΝΑΓΚΑΝ·

     ΖΕΥϹΤ῾ΕΘΕΛΕΝΚΡΟΝΙΔΑϹ

     ΤΙΜΩΝΔΑΝΑΟΥΓΕΝΕΑΝ

75 ΚΑΙΔΙΩΞ[.]῾ΠΠΟΙΟΛΥΓΚΕΟϹ

     ΠΑΥϹΑΙϹΤΥΓΕΡΩΝΑΧΈΩΝ·

     ΤΕΙΧΟϹΔΕΚΥΚΛΩΠΕϹΚΑΜΟΝ

     ΕΛΘΟΝΤΕϹΥΠΕΡΦΊΑΛΟΙΚΛΕΙΝΑῙΠ[. . .]ΕΙ

     ΚΑΛΛΙϹΤΟΝΙΝ῾ΑΝΤΙΘΕΟΙ

80 ΝΑΙΟΝΚΛΎΤΟΝΙΠΠΌΒΟΤΟΝ

     ΑΡΓΟϹΗΡΩΕϹΠΕΡΊΚΛΕῙΤΟΙΛΙΠΟΝΤ[. .]

     ΕΝΘΕΝΑΠΕϹϹΎΜΕΝΑΙ

     ΠΡΟΙΤΟΥΚΥΑΝΟΠΛΌΚΑΜΟΙ

     <u>ΦΕΥΓΟΝΆΔΜΑΤΟΙΘΥΓΑΤΡΕϹ·</u>

85 ΤΟΝΔ῾ΕΙΛΕΝΑΧΟϹΚΡΑΔΙΑΝ·ΞΕΙ

     ΝΑΤΕΝΙΝΠΛΑΞΕΝΜΕΡΙΜΝΑΧ·

---

69. **ΠΑΙΔΕΣ** Δ, corr. Δ³.   83. **ΚΥΑΝΟΠΛΟΚΑΜΟΣ** Δ, corr. Δ¹.
86. **ΜΕΡΙΜΝΑΙ** Δ, corr. Δ¹.

ἤριπον, the aorist being intransitive. For the metaphorical sense, cf. Soph. *Ant.* 596 οὐδ' ἀπαλλάσσει γενεὰν γένος, ἀλλ' ἐρείπει θεῶν τις.

μάχαις τε λυγραῖς: Pausanias (II. 25. 7) mentions a monument of a battle between Proetus and Acrisius, on the road between Argos and Epidaurus.

70. πολύκριθον: elsewhere only in Suidas (s. v. κρίμνον), who may have known it from this passage.

72. There is some doubt as to the readings of this line. Of the two corresponding lines in the other epodes, one (l. 30) is mutilated, and the other (l. 114) scans – – ◡ – ◡̆ ◡ – ◡ ◡ ◡ – –. It would be possible to make the present line correspond with that scansion by introducing two emendations, both of them palaeographically easy, viz. εἰς for ἐς and πεσέν (Doric infin.) for πεσεῖν: ἀργαλέαν being scanned as a trisyllable. But, as Professor Jebb has pointed out, the metre of the line as it stands is much more natural and probable than that of l. 114; and he has consequently proposed to emend the latter line, by reading ἄνδρεσσιν ἐς ἱπποτρόφον πόλισμ' 'Αχαιοῖς. These

λίσσοντο δὲ παῖδας Ἄβαντος
70 γᾶν πολύκριθον λαχόντας
     Τίρυνθα τὸν ὁπλότερον   ἐπ. β΄.
     κτίζειν, πρὶν ἐς ἀργαλέαν πεσεῖν ἀνάγκαν.
     Ζεύς τ᾽ ἔθελεν Κρονίδας,
     τιμῶν Δαναοῦ γενεὰν
75 καὶ διωξ[ί]πποιο Λυγκέος,
     παῦσαι στυγερῶν ἀχέων.
     τεῖχος δὲ Κύκλωπες κάμον
     ἐλθόντες ὑπερφίαλοι κλεινᾷ π[όλ]ει,
     κάλλιστον ἵν᾽ ἀντίθεοι
80 ναῖον κλυτὸν ἱππόβοτον
     Ἄργος ἥρωες περικλειτοὶ λιπόντ[ες].
     ἔνθεν ἀπεσσύμεναι
     Προίτου κυανοπλόκαμοι
     φεῦγον ἄδματοι θύγατρες.
85 τὸν δ᾽ εἷλεν ἄχος κραδίαν, ξεί-   στρ. γ΄.
     να τέ νιν πλᾶξεν μέριμνα·

changes are less explicable on palaeographical grounds, but the rhythmical gain is clear. On the whole, since the third line which would have decided the point is unhappily mutilated, it has seemed best to leave the MS. reading in each case, though warning the reader that one or other requires alteration.

κτίζειν : not a first foundation, since it was already a κλεινὰ πόλις (l. 78), but a new settlement ; cf. note on l. 77.

75. Λυγκέος: Lynceus was the father of Abas.

77. τεῖχος δὲ Κύκλωπες κάμον : the 'Cyclopean' origin of the massive walls of Tiryns is often mentioned; e. g. Paus. II. 16. 5, 25. 8. In the former passage Pausanias speaks of the Cyclopes as building 'the wall in Tiryns' for Proetus, but in the latter he refers the name of Tiryns, and presumably therefore the foundation also, to Tiryns, the son of Argus ; so that τὸ τεῖχος τὸ ἐν Τίρυνθι must be interpreted literally, as 'the wall in (the already existing) Tiryns.' This agrees with the version of Bacchylides. Tiryns already existed and was a πόλις, but presumably was not hitherto fortified.

85. ξεῖνα : 'strange,' like our 'outlandish' : cf. Aesch. *Prom.* 707 οὔποτ᾽, οὔποτ᾽ ηὔχουν ξένους μολεῖσθαι λόγοις ἐς ἀκοὰν ἐμάν.

ΔΟΙΑΞΕΔΕΦΑΣΓΑΝΟΝΑΜ

ΦΑΚΕΣΕΝΣΤΕΡΝΟΙΣΙΠΑΞΑΙ·

ΑΛΛΑΝΙΝΑΙΧΜΟΦΟΡΟΙ

90 ΜΥΘΟΙΣΙΤΕΜΕΙΛΙΧΙΟΙΣ

ΚΑΙΒΙΑΙΧΕΙΡΩΝΚΑΤΕΧΟΝ·

ΤΡΙΣΚΑΙΔ[...]ΜΕΝΤΕΛΕΟΥΣ

ΜΗΝΑΣ[..]ΤΑΔΑΣΚΙΟΝΗΛΥΚΤΑΞΟΝΥΛΑΝ

ΦΕΥΓΟΝΤΕΚΑΤΑΚΑΡΔΙΑΝ

95 ΜΗΛΟΤΡΟΦΟΝ·ΑΛΛ'ΟΤΕΔΗ

ΛΟΥΣΟΝΠΟΤΙΚΑΛΛΙΡΟΑΝΠΑΤΗΡΙΚΑΝΕΝ

ΕΝΘΕΝΧΡΟΑΝΙΨΑΜΕΝΟΣΦΟΙ

ΝΙΚΟΚ[.......]ΟΛΑΤΟΥΣ

ΚΙΚΛ[..........]ΒΟΩΠΙΝ

*του δ' εκλυ' αριστοπατρα

Col. 22] 100 ΧΕΙΡΑΣΑΝΤΕΙΝΩΝΠΡΟΣΑΥΓΑΣ

ΙΠΠΩΚΕΟΣΑΕΛΙΟΥ

ΤΕΚΝΑΔΥΣΤΑΝΟΙΟΛΥΣΣΑΣ

ΠΑΡΦΡΟΝΟΣΕΞΑΓΑΓΕΙΝ·

ΘΥΣΩΔΕΤΟΙΕΙΚΟΣΙΒΟΥΣ

105 ΑΖΥΓΑΣΦΟΙΝΙΚΟΤΡΙΧΑΣ·

*

93. ἠλύκταζον] ΗΛΥΚΤΑΞΟΝ Α.   94. ΚΑΤΑΚΑΡΔΙΑΝ Α, corr.
Palmer.   106. Om. Α, added in upper margin by Α³.

93. ἠλύκταζυν: MS. ἠλύκταξον, by false analogy from such forms as δοίαξε above. It is possible that ἠλύκταξαν is intended, but the imperfect is more suitable in sense.

96. Λοῦσον: the accent is in the MS. Pausanias (VIII. 18. 7) calls the place Λουσοί, and says that it was there that Melampus cured the daughters of Proetus, in a temple of Artemis. Bacchylides says nothing of the intervention of Melampus. Pausanias, in fact, seems to be confusing two forms of the legend, the healing by Melampus having consisted of driving the frenzied women across the borders of Argos into Sicyon (and Pausanias himself mentions a temple in the territory of Sicyon built on the spot where

δοίαξε δὲ φάσγανον ἄμ-
φακες ἐν στέρνοισι πᾶξαι.
ἀλλά νιν αἰχμοφόροι
90 μύθοισί τε μειλιχίοις
καὶ βίᾳ χειρῶν κατέχον.
τρισκαίδ[εκα] μὲν τελέους
μῆνας [κα]τὰ δάσκιον ἠλύκταζον ὕλαν,
φεῦγόν τε κατ᾿ Ἀρκαδίαν
95 μηλοτρόφον· ἀλλ᾿ ὅτε δὴ
Λοῦσον ποτὶ καλλιρόαν πατὴρ ἵκανεν,
ἔνθεν χρόα νιψάμενος φοι-
νικοκ[ραδέμνοι]ο Λατοῦς
κίκλ[ησκε θύγατρα] βοῶπιν,   ἀντ. γ.

100 χεῖρας ἀντείνων πρὸς αὐγὰς
ἱππώκεος ἀελίου,
τέκνα δυστάνοιο λύσσας
πάρφρονος ἐξαγαγεῖν·
θύσω δέ τοι εἴκοσι βοῦς
105 ἄζυγας φοινικότριχας.
τοῦ δ᾿ ἔκλυ᾿ ἀριστόπατρα

the cure was effected, II. 7. 8), while in the other version the women
wander about in Arcadia and are cured at Lusus or Lusi, which is in
the hills between Cleitor and Cynaetha (Curtius, *Peloponnesos* I. 397, quoting
Polyb. IV. 18 ; the reference is due to Dr. Sandys).

97. φοινικοκραδέμνοιο : a Bacchylidean word, cf. XIII. 189.

104. 105. This short break into the first person is curious.

106. ἀριστόπατρα : 'child of the best father.'   L. and S. give ἀριστότοκος
as possessing the same sense in [Eur.] *Rhes.* 909 ; but this interpretation of
the passage is questionable.   When a mother is lamenting her dead son, as
is there the case, she is more likely to dwell on his excellence than her
own ; hence γέννας ἀριστοτόκοιο would seem to mean 'an offspring that was
the best of children,' just as ἀριστόμαντις means 'the best of prophets,' and
μεγιστοάνασσα 'greatest of queens.'

ΘΗΡΟϹΚΌΠΟϹЄΥΧΟΜЄΝΟΥ·ΠΙΘΟΥϹΑΔ'ΗΡΑΝ
ΠΑΥϹЄΝΚΑΛΥΚΟϹΤЄΦΆΝΟΥϹ
ΚΟΥΡΑϹΜΑΝΙΑ͂ΝΑΘЄΩΝ·
ΓΑΙΔ'ΑΥΤΙΚΑὈΙΤЄΜЄΝΟϹΒΩΜΟΝΤЄΤЄ́ΤЄΥΧΟΝ
ΧΡΑΙΝΟΝΤЄΜΙΝΑΙΜΑΤΙΜΗΛΩΝ
ΚΑΙΧΟΡΟΥϹἹϹΤΑΝΓΥΝΑΙΚΩΝ·
ЄΝΘЄΝΚΑΙΑΡΗΪΦΙΛΟΙϹ
ΑΝΔΡЄϹϹΙΝΙΠΠΟΤΡΌΦΟΝΠΟΛΙΝΑΧΑΙΟΙϹ
Є́ϹΠЄΟ·ϹΥΝΔЄΤΥΧΑ͞Ι
ΝΆΙЄΙϹΜЄΤΑΠΌΝΤΙΟΝΩ
ΧΡΥϹЄ́ΑΔЄϹΠΟΙΝΑΛΑΩ͂Ν·
ΑΛϹΟϹΤЄΤΟΙῙΜЄΡΌЄΝ
ΚΆϹΑΝΠΑΡЄΎΥΔΡΟΝΠΡΟΓΟ
ΝΟΙЄϹϹΆΜЄΝΟΙΠΡΙΑΜΟΙ'ЄΠΙΧΡΟΝΩΙ
ΒΟΥΛΑΙϹΙΘЄΩΝΜΑΚΑΡΩΝ

110. ΤΕΤΕΤΕΥΧΟΝ A, corr. A^1? 120. ἔσσαν ἐμοί] ΕΣΣΑΜΕΝΟΙ A, corr. Palmer. ΕΠΙ A, corr. A^3.

107. *θηροσκόπος*: also applied to Artemis in the two other instances of its use, *Hymn. Hom.* XXVII. 11, and *Anth. Pal.* VI. 240.

πιθοῦσα: the second aorist is rare, but is found in Pindar and elsewhere. It would be easy to read *πείθουσα*, and this would be in accordance with the metre in ll. 23, 51, 65, and 93; but l. 9 supports the short syllable, so that the change is not necessary.

110. *γᾷ*: perhaps *τᾷ*, 'there.'

τέμενος: Pausanias mentions a temple in Sicyonian territory erected by Proetus (see note on l. 96), but not at Lusus, where, he says, no remains at all were visible in his time. Polybius, however (see note on l. 96), mentions a temple of Artemis in the neighbourhood.

114. For the metre see note on l. 72. *ἱπποτρόφον*: Metapontum is called *πορτιτρόφος* in l. 30.

115. *ἔσπεο*: so far as the form goes, this may be either indicative or imperative; but in the latter case it would be necessary to read *ναίοις* for *ναίεις* in the next line. Moreover *ἔνθεν* would be awkward with the imperative.

116. *ναίεις Μεταπόντιον*: no special connexion of Artemis with Metapontum is elsewhere recorded; but it is possible that the large temple, the ruins of which are almost the only visible remains of Metapontum, was a temple

θηροσκόπος εὐχομένου· πιθοῦσα δ' Ἥραν
παῦσεν καλυκοστεφάνους
κούρας μανιᾶν ἀθέων.
110 γᾷ δ' αὐτίκα οἱ τέμενος βωμόν τε τεῦχον,
χραῖνόν τέ μιν αἵματι μήλων
καὶ χοροὺς ἵσταν γυναικῶν.
ἔνθεν καὶ ἀρηϊφίλοις   ἐπ. γ'.
ἄνδρεσσιν ἱπποτρόφον πόλιν Ἀχαιοῖς
115 ἔσπεο· σὺν δὲ τύχᾳ
ναίεις Μεταπόντιον, ὦ
χρυσέα δέσποινα λαῶν.
ἄλσος τέ τοι ἱμερόεν
Κάσαν παρ' εὔυδρον πρόγο-
120 νοι ἔσσαν ἐμοί, Πριάμοι' ἐπεὶ χρόνῳ
βουλαῖσι θεῶν μακάρων

of Artemis. It is also noticeable that the Metapontines dedicated at Olympia a statue of Endymion, the beloved of Artemis (Paus. VI. 19. 11).

119. Κάσαν : the name is otherwise unknown, but Suidas mentions a river Κῆσος, without any indication of locality. Presumably it is one of the two rivers (now the Bradano and the Basiento) which run through Metapontine territory. Dr. Sandys adds (from Pliny, *N. H.* III. 11, 16) that the Latin name of the Basiento was Casuentus, which completes the identification.

120. ἔσσαν ἐμοί : the MS. ἐσσάμενοι is impossible, unless the passage be altered elsewhere, so as to introduce the finite verb which is needed. Professor Palmer's emendation, ἔσσαν ἐμοί, is palaeographically excellent, giving a complete sense with the slightest possible change of reading. It is true that Bacchylides does not elsewhere refer to his own family, but there is no reason why he should not do so, as Pindar does in *Pyth.* V. 76. Moreover πρόγονοι by itself would be obscure, and needs some word to show whose ancestors are meant. With regard to the ancestors of Bacchylides, nothing is recorded elsewhere; but the legends of Metapontum spoke of the settlement there of a portion of Nestor's Pylian followers, who were carried thither on their return from Troy (Strabo, VI. p. 264). It must apparently be to this descent that Bacchylides alludes. For the form ἔσσαν, cf. Pind. *Pyth.* IV. 273 ἔσσαι, and V. 42 κάθεσσαν (according to Hermann's reading).

ΠΕΡCΑΝΠΟΛΙΝΕΥΚΤΙΜΈΝΑΝ
ΧΑΛΚΟΘΩΡΆΚΩΝΜΕΤΑΤΡΕΙΔᾺΝ·ΔΙΚΑΙΑC
ΟCΤΙCΕΧΕΙΦΡΕΝΑCΕΥ
125 ΡΉCΕΙCΥΝΑΠΑΝΤΙΧΡΟΝΩΙ
ΜΥΡΊΑCΑΛΚΑCΑΧΑΙΩΝ·

XII.

Τισίαι Αἰγινήτηι παλαιστῆι Νεμεα

STROPHE.

```
 _  _  ᴗ  _  _  _  ᴗ  ᴗ  _  ᴗ  ᴗ  _
 _  _  ᴗ  _  _
 _  ᴗ  ᴗ  _  ᴗ  ᴗ  _
 _  _  ᴗ  ᴗ  _  ᴗ  ᴗ  _  ᴗ  _  ᴗ  _
5 _  _  ᴗ  ᴗ  _  ᴗ  ᴗ  _  _
 ᴗ  ᴗ  _  _  _  ᴗ  _  _
 _  _  ᴗ  _  _  _  ᴗ  _  ᴗ  _
 _  _  ᴗ  ᴗ  _  _  ᴗ  ᴗ  _  ᴗ  ᴗ  _
```

ΩCΕΙΚΥΒΕΡΝΉΤΑCCΟΦΟCΥΜΝΟΆΝΑC
C·ΈΥΘΥΝΕΚΛΕΙΟΙ
ΝΥΝΦΡΕΝΑCΆΜΕΤΈΡΑC
ΕΙΔΗΠΟΤΕΚΑΙΠΑΡΟC·ΕCΓΑΡΟΛΒΙΑΝ
5 ΞΕΙΝΟΙCΙΜΕΠΌΤΝΙΑΝΙΚΑ
ΝᾶCΟΝΑΙΓΕΙΝΑCΑΠΆΡΧΕΙ

1. ὑμνοάνασσα: the word is apparently coined by Bacchylides. Cf. μεγιστοάνασσα (XIX. 21), and the proper name Πλειστοάναξ. For the division of the word at the end of the line, cf. V. 106.

2. Κλειοῖ: cf. note on III. 3. Here the absence of any antistrophe leaves the quantity of the first syllable doubtful.

5. ξείνοισι: in Pindar (according to Rumpel) ξεῖνος, when applied to the person *to* whom another comes, always implies the pre-existence of ties of hospitality. If the same rule applies to Bacchylides, he here represents himself as coming to host-friends and not to strangers, which suggests that

πέρσαν πόλιν εὐκτιμέναν
χαλκοθωράκων μετ᾽ Ἀτρειδᾶν. δικαίας
ὅστις ἔχει φρένας εὐ-
125 ρήσει σὺν ἅπαντι χρόνῳ
μυρίας ἀλκὰς Ἀχαιῶν.

XII.

ΤΙΣΙΑΙ ΑΙΓΙΝΗΤΗΙ

παλαιστῇ Νέμεα.

OF this poem only eight lines are left at the foot of the column, after which the papyrus breaks off. It is interesting as showing, in conjunction with the poem which follows, that Pindar, in spite of the number of his Aeginetan odes and the evident closeness of his connexion with the island, did not have a monopoly of the celebration of the athletic victories won by members of Aeginetan families. Of the victor here commemorated, Tisias, who had won the wrestling contest at the Nemean games, nothing more is known; nor is there anything to show the original length of the poem.

ὡσεὶ κυβερνήτας σοφὸς ὑμνοάνασ-
σ᾽ εὔθυνε Κλειοῖ
νῦν φρένας ἀμετέρας,
εἰ δή ποτε καὶ πάρος· ἐς γὰρ ὀλβίαν
5 ξείνοισί με πότνια Νίκα
νᾶσον Αἰγίνας †ἀπάρχει†

this was not his first visit to Aegina nor his first celebration of an Aeginetan victory. This ode may consequently be later than that to Pytheas.

6. ἀπάρχει: the reading must be corrupt. A sense such as 'leads me' (cf. Pind. Nem. IV. 46, according to Mommsen's interpretation) or 'commands me' is possible, but the accusative με is inconsistent with either of these. Jebb suggests ἀπαιτεῖ, 'bids me,' 'requires me,' which supplies a satisfactory sense with a small change, though there is no obvious palaeographical explanation of the corruption; or ἐπαίρει, which is slighty further from the MS.

ΕΛΘΟΝΤΑΚΟCΜΗCΑΙΘΕΟΔΜΑΤΟΝΠΟΛΙΝ·
ΤΑΝΤ'ΕΝΝΕΜΕΛΙΓΥΑΛΚΕΑΜΟΥΝΟΠΑΛΑ[

*   *   *   *   *

Col. 23]   . . . . . .]ΛΕΙω

[3 lines wanting]

. . . . .]ΔΑΝ

[rest of column wanting]

XIII.

STROPHE.

```
   — — ◡ ◡ — ◡ ◡ —
   ⌣ — ◡ — ◡
   — ⌣ — ◡ ◡ — ⌣
   — ◡ — ⌣ — ◡ — ⌣
 5 ⌣ — ◡ ◡ — ◡ ◡ — ⌣
   — ◡ — — — ◡ ⌣
   — — ◡ ◡ — ◡ ◡ —
   ⌣ — ◡ — ⌣
   — ◡ ◡ — ◡ ◡ — ⌣
10 — ◡ ◡ — ◡ ◡ — ⌣
   — ◡ ◡ — ◡ ◡ —
   — — ◡ — ⌣ — ◡ — ⌣
```

---

8. μουνοπάλαν : as distinguished from the wrestling which formed part of the pentathlum and pancratium. The word is not known elsewhere. but μουνοπάλης occurs in an inscription recorded by Pausanias (VI. 4. 6), and quoted in the note on the title of Ode I, above.

ἐλθόντα κοσμῆσαι θεόδματον πόλιν,
τάν τ᾽ ἐν Νεμέᾳ γυιαλκέα μουνοπάλα[ν]

[The rest is wanting.]

XIII.

[ΠΤΘΕΑΙ ΑΙΓΙΝΗΤΗΙ]

[παιδὶ παγκρατιαστῇ Νέμεα]

THE following ode has been put together out of some twenty-two fragments, none of them being of any great size; and the fact that absolute continuity of the papyrus between the larger pieces cannot be re-established leaves the metrical evidence the sole decisive proof of their identity as portions of the poem, and of their position in it. This evidence, however, has been sufficient to establish the entire framework, and a large part of the contents, of a poem originally containing 198 lines, being thus second in length to the long ode to Hieron alone, and sharing with that the interest of commemorating a victory which also forms the subject of an ode by Pindar. The title is lost, with the first ten lines of the poem; but the internal evidence leaves no doubt that the ode is addressed to Pytheas, son of Lampon of Aegina, and celebrates his victory in the boys' pancratium at Nemea, with which we are already familiar from Pindar's fifth Nemean. The date of the victory is unknown, but it was before 480 B.C. In that year, and again in 478 B.C., Phylacidas, the younger brother of Pytheas, won victories in the same class of competition at the Isthmus; but apparently Pindar's poem on the earlier occasion had been preferred to that of Bacchylides, and it was to the elder poet that the family then had recourse to celebrate these new triumphs, the result being seen in the fourth and fifth Isthmian odes of Pindar.

EPODE.

$$
\begin{array}{l}
- \; - \; \smile \; \smile \; - \; \smile \; \smile \; - \; \underline{\smile} \; - \; \smile \; - \\
- \; - \; \smile \; \smile \; - \; \smile \; \smile \; - \\
\smile \; - \; \smile \; - \; - \\
- \; \smile \; - \; - \; - \; \smile \; \smile \; - \; \smile \; \smile \; - \\
5 \;\; - \; - \; \smile \; - \; - \; - \; \smile \; \underline{\smile} \\
- \; - \; \smile \; \smile \; - \; \smile \; \smile \; - \; \underline{\smile} \\
- \; \smile \; - \; \underline{\smile} \; - \; \smile \; - \; - \; - \; \smile \; \underline{\smile} \\
- \; \smile \; \smile \; - \; \smile \; \smile \; - \; \underline{\smile} \\
- \; \smile \; - \; \underline{\smile} \; - \; \smile \; - \; \underline{\smile}
\end{array}
$$

$$
\begin{array}{l}
1—12 = 13—24 : 25—33 \\
34—45 = 46—57 : 58—66 \\
67—78 = 79—90 : 91—99 \\
100—111 = 112—123 : 124—132 \\
133—144 = 145—156 : 157—165 \\
166—177 = 178—189 : 190—198
\end{array}
$$

The family was a noble one, that of the Psalychidae, and had won other athletic distinctions, to which Pindar alludes. Bacchylides likewise speaks of the glory to be won in the games, but if he made any more express reference, it is lost in the mutilation of the papyrus.

The mutilation is indeed very considerable, for of the 198 lines of the poem only 66, or exactly one-third, can be reckoned as complete, though many more can be plausibly, or even certainly, restored. Metrical considerations show that ten lines are lost from the beginning, and there are slight traces of the column which contained them, in the shape of the letters -λειω and -δαν, forming the ends of two lines; but these belong to the upper part of the column, being respectively the second and fifth lines in it. It is useless to speculate whether the poem to which they belong is that ode to Pytheas' fellow-countryman, Tisias, of which the first few lines have been given above.

The poem consists of six systems, in logaoedic metre. The first system seems to have been devoted to the foundation of the Nemean games by Heracles, while the second addresses Pytheas in person, proclaims the honour which he has conferred upon Aegina, and thence glides off to the ancient history of that island. This forms the transition to the exploits of Ajax, which, as Pindar's Aeginetan odes show, was the almost inevitable topic of odes in honour of his countrymen. It so happens (and it may be more than a coincidence) that Pindar's ode to Pytheas is an exception to this rule. To Pindar, Ajax is the favourite representative of disappointed or ill-treated merit, on account of the decision which deprived him of the arms of Achilles; but here it is of Ajax triumphant, not of Ajax defeated, that the poet speaks, the scene being the defence of the Greek ships from the attack of Hector. This is the central topic of the poem, occupying the third and fourth systems, and perhaps the beginning of the fifth. The strophe of the fifth system is, however, almost wholly lost; and when the text reappears, the poet has passed on to moralizations on the eternal glory to be won by valour, which brings him back, in the epode, to Pytheas, and to his trainer, the Athenian Menander. The final system is much mutilated, the antistrophe in particular having almost entirely disappeared; but it seems to have contained moral reflections and a final reference to Lampon and his family, and to the poet's friendship with them.

I

Col. 24]   ΥΒΡΙΟCΥΨΙΝΟΟΥ

         ΠΑΥCΕΙΔΙΚΑCΘΝΑΤΟΙCΙΚΡΑΙΝШΝ·

         ΟΙΑΝΤΙΝΑΔΥCΛΟΦΟΝШ

         ΜΗCΤΑͨΛΕΟΝΤΙ

    15 ΠΕΡCΕΙΔΑCΕΦΙΗCΙ

         ΧΕΙΡΑΠΑΝΤΟΙΑΙCΙΤΕΧΝΑΙC·

       [. . . .]ΔΑΜΑϹΙΜΒΡΟΤΟCΑΙΘШΝ

       [. . . .]ΟCΑΠΛΑΤΟΥΘΕΛΕΙ

       [. . . .]ΙΝΔΙΑCШΜΑΤΟC·Ε

    20 [. . . . .]ΦΘΗΔ΄ΟΠΙCϘШ

       [. . . . .]ΝΟΝ·ΗΠΟΤΕΦΑΜΙ

       [. . . . .]ΠΕΡΙCΤΕΦΑΝΟΙCΙ

       [. . . . .]ΑΤΟΥΠΟΝΟΝΕΛ

       [. . . . . .]ΝΙΔΡШΕΝΤ΄ΕCΕCΘΑΙ·

    25 [. . . . . . .]ΑΒШΜΟΝΑΡΙCΤΑΡΧΟΥΔΙΟC

       [. . . . .]ΥΔΕΟCΑΝ

       [. . . . .]CΙΝΑ[.]ΘΕΑ

19. πείρειν Jebb. E added at end of line by A³.   20. ἐστρέφθη Jebb. ΟΠΙΣΣΩ A, wrongly altered by A³?   22. κεῖθι Jebb.

11. ὑψινόου: another instance of the occurrence in Bacchylides of a word which hitherto has only been known in late authors (in this case Nonnus).

12. παύσει: Professor Jebb suggests that this part of the poem, as far as ἔσεσθαι in l. 24, is a prophecy (doubtless by Teiresias) of the career of Heracles, especially of his victory over the Nemean lion and the consequent institution of the Nemean games; cf. Pind. *Nem.* I. 61 ff.

15. Περσείδας: Heracles, so called from Amphitryon and Alcmena being grandchildren of Perseus. Heracles, finding his sword would not pierce the hide of the Nemean lion, strangled him with his hands.

17. δαμασίμβροτος: cf. Pind. *Ol.* IX. 85 δαμασιμβρότου αἰχμᾶς.

[10 lines wanting.]
ὕβριος ὑψινόου
παύσει, δίκας θνατοῖσι κραίνων.
οἵαν τινα δύσλοφον ὠ-   ἀντ. α΄.
μηστᾷ λέοντι
15 Περσείδας ἐφίησι
χεῖρα παντοίαισι τέχναις·
[οὐ γὰρ] δαμασίμβροτος αἴθων
[χαλκ]ὸς ἀπλάτου θέλει
[πείρε]ιν διὰ σώματος· ἐ-
20 [στρέ]φθη δ᾽ ὀπίσσω
[φάσγα]νον. ἦ ποτε φαμὶ
[κεῖθι] περὶ στεφάνοισι
[παγκρ]ατίου πόνον Ἑλ-
[λασίν τι]ν᾽ ἱδρώεντ᾽ ἔσεσθαι.
25 [οὕτω παρ]ὰ βωμὸν ἀριστάρχου Διὸς   ἐπ. α΄.
[. . . . . ˘ ˘]υδεος ἀν
[. ˘ ─ ─]σιν ἄ[ν]θεα

18. There is a slight trace of a letter before ος which seems to be κ or χ.

25. ἀριστάρχου Διός : apparently this is the passage referred to by Apollonius (De Constr. 186), where, in speaking of certain kinds of compounds, he quotes this as an example, καθὼς ἔχει τὸ ἀρίσταρχος Ζεὺς παρὰ τοῖς περὶ Βακχυλίδην (Bergk, frag. 52). Athenaeus also quotes Simonides as using the word (III. 99 B), οἶδα δ᾽ ὅτι καὶ Σιμωνίδης που ὁ ποιητὴς ἀρίσταρχον εἶπε τὸν Δία (Bergk, frag. 231).

25-30. The following restoration is proposed by Professor Jebb :—

[τοῖς δὴ παρ]ὰ βωμὸν ἀριστάρχου Διὸς
[νίκας ἐρικ]υδέος ἀν-
[άγου]σιν ἄνθεα
[ἀγλα]ὰν δόξαν πολύφαντον ἐν αἰ-
[ῶνι] τρέφει παύροισι βροτῶν [Ζεύς] κ.τ.λ.

I 2

[.....]ΑΝΔΟΞΑΝΠΟΛΎΦΑΝΤΟΝΕΝΑΙ[

[....]ΤΡΕΦΕΙΠΑΥΡΟΙCΙΒΡΟΤѠΝ

30 [.]ΕΙΚΑΙΟΤΑΘΑΝΑΤΟΙΟ

ΚΥΑΝΕΟΝΝΕΦΟCΚΑΛΎΨΗ ΛΕΙΠΕΤΑΙ

ΑΘΑΝΑΤΟΝΚΛΕΟCΕΥΕΡ

ΧΘΕΝΤ[.]CΑCΦΑΛΕῖCΥΝΑΙCΑῑ·

ΤѠΝΚ[...]ΥΤΥΧѠΝΝΕΜΕᾱΤ

35 ΛΑΜΠѠΝΟ̣CΥΙΕ

ΠΑ̣ΝΘΑΛΕѠΝCΤΕΦΑΝΟΙCΙΝ

[.......]ΑΙΤΑΝ[..]Ε̣ΦΘΕΙC

[......]ΠΟΛΙΝΥ[.]ΙΆΓΥΙΑΝ

[......]ΡΨΙΝ̣[..]ΌΤѠΝ

40 [......]Α[.....]ΟѠΝ

ΚѠ[.....]Α̣ΤΡ[....]Ν

ΝΑCΟ[.]ΥΠΕΡΒΙ[..]ῙCΧΥΝ

ΠΑΜΜᾼΧῙΑΝΑΝΑΦΑΙΝѠΝ·

ѠΠΟΤΑΜΟΥΘΥΓΑΤΕΡ

45 ΔΙΝΑΝΈΟCΑΙΓΙΝ῾ΗΠΙΌΦΡΟΝ

Col. 25]   ΗΤΟΙΜΕΓΑΛΑ[

29, 30. ΒΡΟΤΩΝ | . ΕΙ Δ, altered on grounds of strophic corre-
spondence.   30. ΟΤΑΘΑΝΑΤΟΙΟ Δ, corr. Δ³.   31. ΚΑΛΥΨΗ Δ,
corr. Δ¹.   40. ἀδυπνόων Jebb.   45. ΔΙΝΑΝΕΟΣ Δ, corr. Δ¹.

30. καὶ ὅταν θανάτοιο κ.τ.λ. : cf. Wordsworth, *The Happy Warrior,*
            ' And while the mortal mist is gathering, draws
            His breath in confidence of Heaven's applause.'
35. Λάμπωνος υἱέ: cf. Pindar, *Nem.* V. 4, Λάμπωνος υἱὸς Πυθέας εὐρυσθενής.
39–41. Perhaps [σὺν χορῶν τε]ρψι[μβρ]όταν
            [ὕμνοισι καὶ] ἀ[δυπν]όων
            κώ[μων]. (Jebb).

40. ἀδυπνόων : used by Pindar (*Isth.* II. 25) with the same scansion ; in
Ol. XIII. 22 with ῡ.

[. . . . .]αν δόξαν πολύφαντον ἐν αι-

[. . . .] τρέφει παύροισι βρο-

30 τῶν [. . .] καὶ ὅταν θανάτοιο

κυάνεον νέφος καλύψῃ, λείπεται

ἀθάνατον κλέος εὖ ἐρ-

χθέντ[ο]ς ἀσφαλεῖ σὺν αἴσᾳ.

τῶν καὶ σὺ τυχὼν Νεμέᾳ,   στρ. β΄.

35 Λάμπωνος υἱέ,

πανθαλέων στεφάνοισιν

[ἀνθέων χ]αίταν [ἐρ]εφθεὶς

[αὔξεις] πόλιν ὑ[ψ]ιάγυιαν

[. . . . . τε]ρψι[μβρ]ότων

40 [. . . . . . .] ἁ[δυπν]όων

κώ[μων π]ατρ[ῴα]ν

νᾶσο[ν], ὑπέρβι[ον] ἰσχὺν

παμμαχιᾶν ἀναφαίνων.

ὦ ποταμοῦ θύγατερ

45 δινᾶντος Αἴγιν᾽ ἠπιόφρον,

ἦ τοι μεγάλα[ν ὅδε παῖς]   ἀντ. β΄.

43. παμμαχιᾶν : gen. plur. The MS. has the word accented paroxytone, but there can be no adjective παμμάχιος. It is possible to retain the MS. reading with a simple alteration of the accent, though the plural is not used elsewhere. It may be observed that there is some confusion as regards the accent in the MS., since it is combined with what appears to be a mark of a long syllable over the ι, which is impossible. If an alteration is required, παμμαχίας or παμμαχίαις would admit of easy palaeographical explanation. παμμαχία = παγκράτιον, cf. L. and S., s. v. παμμάχιον and παμμάχος. Professor Jebb suggests the possibility of taking ὑπέρβιον as epithet of παμμαχίαν, and ἰσχύν as an accusative of respect.

44. ποταμοῦ : Asopus.

46. ὅδε παῖς : cf. Pind. *Nem.* II. 3, *Isth.* III. 88, ὅδ᾽ ἀνήρ.

ΕΔΩΚΕΤΙΜΑΝ[
ΕΝΠΑΝΤΕΣΣΙΝ[
ΠΥΡΣΟΝΩϹΕΛ͞[
50 ΦΑΙΝΩΝ·ΤΟΓΕϹΟ[.......]ΝΕΙ
    ΚΑˈΤΙϹΥΦΑΥΧΑϹΚΟ[......]Ρ͞ΑΝ

    ΠΟΔΕΣΣΙΤΑΡΦΕΩ[   ]
    ΗΫΤΕΝΕΒΡΟϹΑΠΕΝ[   ]
55 ΑΝΘΕΜΟΕΝΤΑϹΕΠ[   ]
    ΚΟΥΦΑϹΥΝΑΓΧΙΔΟ[   ]
    ΘΡΩϹΚΟΥϹˈΑΓΑΚΛΕΙΤΑ[......]ΙϹ·

    ΤΑΙΔΕϹΤΕΦΑΝΩϹΑΜΕ[.........]ΕΩΝ
    ΑΝΘΕΩΝΔΟΝΑΚΟϹΤˈΕ[   ]
60 ΡΙΑΝΑΘΥΡϹΙΝ

    ΠΑΡΘΕΝΟΙΜΕΛΠΟΥϹΙΤ[.........]ω

    Δ[.]ΠΟΙΝΑΠΑΙΞΕ[
    [...]ΑΙΔΑΤΕΡΟΔΟ[

    ΑΤ[......]ΝΕΤΙ[

65 ΚΑ[.]ΕΛΑ[...]Α[

51. ΚΑΤΙϹΥΦΑΥΧΑϹ Α, Ι after ΚΑ added by Α²? Η written above last Α by Α³; ὑψαυχὰς Jebb, who would correct it to ὑψαύχην.   54. νεβρὸς] ΝΕΚΡΟϹ Α, corr. Α².   56. ἀγχιδόμοις Jebb.   58. Jebb suggests χρυσαυγέων.   59. ἐπιχωρίαν Jebb.   61. τεὸν (or τὸ σὸν) κλέος ὦ Jebb.   63–66. Reconstructed from suggestions by Palmer and Jebb.   64. ἃ τὸν αἰχματὰν Jebb.

51, 52. The text is seriously corrupt here. Besides the corruptions of καί and ὑψαυχάς (see crit. note) several words have been omitted in the MS. After ὑψαυχάς a single word of two syllables is needed to complete the line (probably κόρα, with which θρώσκουσα in line 57 agrees), and the next line

ἔδωκε τιμὰν
ἐν πάντεσσιν [ἀέθλοις,]
πυρσὸν ὡς Ἑλλ[ασιν ἀλκὰν]
50 φαίνων· τό γε σὸ[ν κλέος αἰ]νεῖ.

καί τις ὑψαυχὰς κο[   ]ραν
< - - ◡ ◡ - ◡ ◡ - >
πόδεσσι ταρφέω[ν]
ἠύτε νεβρὸς ἀπεν[θὴς]
55 ἀνθεμόεντας ἐπ' [ὄχθους]
κοῦφα σὺν ἀγχιδό[μοις]
θρώσκουσ' ἀγακλειτα[ῖς ἑταίρα]ις.

ταὶ δὲ στεφανωσάμε[ναι . . . . . .]εων   ἐπ. β.
ἀνθέων δόνακός τ' ἐ[πιχω]-
60 ρίαν ἄθυρσιν

παρθένοι μέλπουσι τ[. . . . .]ω

δ[έσ]ποινα παῖ ξε[. . .]
['Ενδ]αΐδα τε ῥοδό[παχυν]

ἀπ[. . . . .]ν ἔτι[κτεν Πηλέα]
65 κα[ὶ Τ]ελα[μῶν]α [. . .]

should consist of eight syllables, scanning - - ◡ ◡ - ◡ ◡ - . The lacuna in the MS. between κο and ραν is insufficient to account for more than a small portion of this, being slightly smaller than that in the preceding line, which contains about seven letters ; cf. also l. 57, where the number of missing letters is probably the same. Jebb suggests καί τις ὑψαύχην κόρα | βαίνει προφέρουσ' ἑτεράν (or κοράν).

54. ἀπενθής: a Bacchylidean word, cf. frag. 48 (Bergk 19). There is some doubt as to the accentuation intended in the MS., but apparently it has ἀπέν—, altered to ἀπὲν—, the latter implying an oxytone word.

60. ἄθυρσιν : 'game,' 'sport.' The word is not otherwise known.

65. The last word may be κραταιόν, the epithet applied to Telamon in Pind. Nem. IV. 25 ; but many other epithets are equally possible.

ΑΙΑΚѠΙΜΙΧΘΕΙС'ΕΝΑ[

ΤѠΝΥΙΕΑСΑΕΡСΙΜΑΧ[

ΤΑΧΥΝΤ'ΑΧΙΛΛΕΑ

ΕΥΕΙΔΕΟСΤ'ΕΡΙΒΟΙΑС

70 ΠΑΙΔ'ΥΠΕΡΘΥΜΟΝΒΟΑ[

ΑΙΑΝΤΑСΑΚΕСΦΟΡΟΝΗ[

ΟСΤ'ΕΠΙΠΡΥΜΝΑΙСΤΑΘ[

ΕСΧΕΝΘΡΑСΥΚΑΡΔΙΟΝ[

ΜΑΙΝΟΝΤΑΝ[

75 ΘΕСΠΕСΪѠΙΠ[

ΕΚΤΟΡΑΧΑΛ[

ΟΠΟΤΕΠ[

[. .]Α[. .]ΤΑ . [

ѠΡΕΙΝΑΤ[

80 Τ'ΕΛΥСΕΝΑ[

ΟΙΠΡΙΝΜΕΝ[

Col. 26]   [. .]ΙΟΥΘΑΗΤΟΝΑСΤΥ

[.]ΛΕΙΠΟΝ·ΑΤΥΖΟΜΕΝΟΙ[

.. ΑССΟΝΟΞΕΙΑΝΜΑΧΑ[

66. ἄντροις Jebb.   67. θ' om. Α, inserted by Jebb.   77. ὁππότε]
ΟΠΟΤΕ Α, corr. on metrical grounds.   79. Δαρδανιδᾶν Jebb.
80. ἀλκάν Jebb.

67. τῶν θ' υἱέας : the insertion of θ', which is not in the MS., is necessitated
by there being no verb following which can govern υἱέας. The pedigree is
as follows :

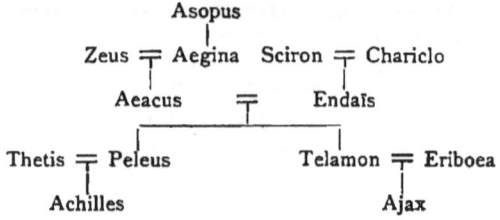

Αἰακῷ μιχθεῖσ' ἐν ἄ[ντροις],
τῶν ⟨θ'⟩ υἱέας ἀερσιμάχ[ους]   στρ. γ'.
ταχύν τ' Ἀχιλλέα
εὐειδέος τ' Ἐριβοίας
70 παῖδ' ὑπέρθυμον βοαθόον
Αἴαντα σακεσφόρον ἥ[ρω]·
ὅστ' ἐπὶ πρύμνᾳ σταθ[εὶς]
ἔσχεν θρασυκάρδιον [ὁρ]-
μαίνοντα ν[ᾶας]
75 θεσπεσίῳ π[υρὶ καίειν]
Εκτορα χαλ[κεομίτραν],
ὁππότε Π[ηλεΐδας]

[. .]α[. .]τα . [. . . . . .]
ὠρείνατ[ο Δαρδανιδᾶν]   ἀντ. γ'.
80 τ' ἔλυσεν ἀ[λκάν].

οἳ πρὶν μὲν [. . . .]
['Ιλ]ίου θαητὸν ἄστυ
[ἔ]λειπον· ἀτυζόμενοι [δὲ]
[θρ]άσσον ὀξεῖαν μάχα[ν],

71. σακεσφόρον : so Soph. *Aj.* 19, Αἴαντι τῷ σακεσφόρῳ. The word being rare, it is possible that Sophocles was consciously following Bacchylides, as in XVI. 16 ff. Its special point as descriptive of Ajax appears from Homer, *Il.* XI. 526,

Αἴας δὲ κλονέει Τελαμώνιος· εὖ δέ μιν ἔγνων·
εὐρὺ γὰρ ἀμφ' ὤμοισιν ἔχει σάκος.

76. χαλκεομίτραν : cf. Pind. *Nem.* X. 90. χαλκεοχάρμαν is also possible, being applied to the Trojans in Pind. *Pyth.* V. 82.

78. Professor Jebb suggests [ἐπ]α[ύε]τ' α[ἰχμάζων, ὁ δ' οἷος].

79. ὠρείνατο : the middle is not found elsewhere.

81. μεγαλαυχεῖς or μεμαῶτες (both suggested by Jebb) will serve to complete the line.

85 ΕΥΤ·ΕΝΠΕΔΙΟ͠ΝΚΛΟΝΕΩ[

ΜΑΙΝΟΙΤ·ΑΧΙΛΛΕΥC

ΛΑϘΦΟΝΟΝΔΟΡΥCΕΙωΝ

ΑΛΛ[.]ΤΕΔΗΠΟΛΕΜΟΙ[

ΛΗΞΕΝΙΟCΤΕΦΑΝϘ[

90 ΝΗΡΗΙ͠ΔΟCΑΤΡΟΜΗΤϘ[

ωCΤ·ΕΝΚΥΑΝΑΝΘΕΪΘ[

ΠΟΝΤ[....]ΕΑCΥΠΟΚΥ

ΜΑCΙ[.]ΔΑΙ͠ΖΕΙ

ΝΥΚΤϘCΑΝΤΑC ΑΝΧ̸Μ̸[

95 ΛΗΞΕΝ̸ΤΕCΥΝΦΑΕCΙΝ[

ΑϘΙ·CΤΟΡΕCΕΝΔΕΤΕΠϘ[

ΟΥΡ͜ΑΝΙΑ·ΝΟΤΟΥΔΕΚΟΝ[

ΙCΤΙΟΝ͜ΑΡΠΑΛΕωΤΑ

ϘΛΠΤΟΝΕΞ[.'..]ΝΤΟΧ[

100 ωCΤΡωΕCΕΠ[.]ΚΛΥΟΝ[

ΧΜΑΤΑΝ͜ΑΧΙΛΛΕͺ

85. ΠΕΔΙΟΝ Δ, corr. Δ³.   94. ΑΝΤΑCΑΝΥΜ Δ, corr. Δ³.
95. ΤΕ Δ, corr. Δ³?   97. ΟΥΡΑΝΙΑ Δ, corr. Δ¹?   98. ΑΡΠΑ-
ΛΕωΤΑ Δ, corr. Δ³?

85. ἐν πεδίῳ κλονέων : cf. Homer, *Il.* XI. 496, ὡς ἔφεπε κλονέων πεδίον τότε
φαίδιμος Αἴας. The MS. had originally πεδίον, which the corrector has altered
to πεδίῳ : but it is a question whether the original reading should not be
retained, taking ἐν as the Aeolic form of ἐς, as in Pind. *Pyth.* V. 38 and
elsewhere. It would make the picture more vivid,—the Trojan array
breaking up as soon as Achilles rushed into the field.

91. A long parenthesis begins here, extending to l. 99, and containing the
most elaborate simile in the whole of Bacchylides. Professor Jebb's restoration of the end of the line, Θρᾴκιος νέα, completes the sense admirably,
supplying an object to δαίζει and a local detail like Ἴδας in V. 66.

94. The MS. is corrupt here, and (the end being lost) it is difficult to

85 εὖτ' ἐν πεδίῳ κλονέω[ν]
    μαίνοιτ' Ἀχιλλεὺς
    λαοφόνον δόρυ σείων.
    ἀλλ' [ὅ]τε δὴ πολέμοι[ο]
    λῆξεν ἰοστεφάν[ου]
90 Νηρῆδος ἀτρόμητο[ς υἱός],

    ὥς τ' ἐν κυανανθέϊ θ[. ‾ ˘ ˘ ‾ .]   ἐπ. γ'.
    πόντ[ῳ Βορ]έας ὑπὸ κύ-
    μασι[ν] δαΐζει
    νυκ[τὸ]ς ἀντάσας ἀναπ[. ‾ ˘ ˘ ‾ .]

95 λῆξεν δὲ σὺν φαεσιμ[βρότῳ]
    Ἀοῖ, στόρεσεν δέ τε πό[ντον]

    οὐρία, νότου δ' ἑκόν[τος ‾ ˘ ‾ .]
    ἱστίον ἁρπαλέως ἄ-
    ελπτον ἐξ[ίκο]ντο χ[έρσον]·
100 ὡς Τρῶες ἐπ[έ]κλυον [αἰ]-   στρ. δ'.
    χματὰ[ν Ἀχ]ιλλέα

gather the intention either of the original reading or of the corrections (see critical note). Jebb suggests ἀναπαυομένων.

95. φαεσιμβρότῳ: cf. Homer, *Il.* XXIV. 785, ϥαεσίμβροτος ἠώς.

97. It is not clear on what lines this passage is to be restored. The accent on ἑκόν— in the MS. seems to show that the original reading was some part of ἑκών, and since we require, in this lacuna, a word to govern or accompany νότου and also a word to govern ἱστίον, it is almost inevitable to read ἑκόντος, with the unparalleled sense 'by the good will of the south wind,' i.e. with a favourable south wind. Then the line can be completed by Professor Jebb's conjecture, ἡρμένοι (= ἡρμένον ἔχοντες, as in Soph. *El.* 54). If an emendation of the extant part of a mutilated passage be admissible, then Jebb's ἔχοντες ἔμπλεον provides a perfectly satisfactory sense with the least possible change.

100. ἐπέκλυον: constructed with an accusative participle, like κλύω in Aesch. *Sept. c. Theb.* 837 νεκροὺς κλύουσα δυσμόρως θανόντας.

[.]ΙΜΝΟ[. .]ΕΝΚΛΙΣΙΗΙΣΙΝ

ΕΙ[.]ΕΚ[.]ΝΞΑΝΘΑΣΓΥΝΑΙΚΟΣ

[. . .]ΗΙΔΟΣΙΜΕΡΟΓΥΙΟΥ

105 Θ[.]ΟΙΣΙΔΑΝΤΕΙΝΑΝΧΕΡΑΣ

. ΟΙΒΑΝΕ[.]ΙΔΟΝΤΕΣΥΠΑΙ

ΧΕΙΜΩΝΟΣΑΙΓΛΑΝ·

ΠΑΣΣΥΔΙΑΣ͞Μ͞ΕΛΠΟΝΤΕΣ

ΤΕΙΧΕΑΛΑΟΜΕΔΟΝΤΟΣ

110 [.]ΣΠΕΔΙΟΝΚΡΑΤΕΡΑΝ

ΑΙΞΑΝΥ[.]ΜΙΝΑΝΦΕΡΟΝΤΕΣ·

ΩΡΣΑΝΤ[.]ΦΟΒΟΝΔΑΝΑΟΙΣ·

ΩΤΡΥΝΕΔ᾽ΑΡΗΣ

[.]ΥΕΓΧΗΣ[.]ΥΚΙΩΝΤΕ

115 [.]ΟΞΙΑΣΑΝΑΞΑΠΟΛΛΩΝ·

ΙΞΟΝΤ᾽Ε[.]ΙΘΕΙΝΑΘΑΛΑΣΣΑΣ·

Col. 27]   [.]ΑΥΣΙΔ᾽ΕΥΠΡΥΜΝΟΙΣΠΑΡ[

ΜΑΡΝΑΝΤ᾽·ΕΝΑΡΙΖ[. . . . .]ΩΝ

[. . .]ΕΥΘΕ͞Τ͞Ο ΦΩΤΩΝ

120 [. . . .]ΤΙΓΑΙΑΜΕΛΑ[   ]

[. . . . .]ΕΑΣΥΠΟΧΕΙ[   ]

---

105. ΘΕΟΙΣΙ] ΟΙΣ is written above an erasure.   108. δὲ λιπόντες]
ΜΕΛΠΟΝΤΕΣ Α, corr. Α¹?   119. ἔρευθε] . . . ΕΥΘΕ Α, ΤΟ added above
line by Α³. ἔρευθε Palmer.

106. φοίβαν : the accentuation in the MS. is noticeable, the word being
treated as oxytone, like other adjectives in -βος. The phrase is picturesque,
'seeing a bright gleam of light beneath the storm-cloud.'

113-115. In Homer the encouragement of the Trojans in their assault of
the Greek camp is exclusively the work of Zeus, Ares and Apollo being held
back from the war and confined to the position of spectators.

114. Λυκίων . . ἄναξ 'Απόλλων : cf. Pind. Pyth. I. 39 Λύκιε καὶ Δάλου
ἀνάσσων Φοῖβε, but the phrase of Bacchylides is more explicit.

119. ἔρευθε : the intransitive use is not otherwise known, but intransitive

[μ]ίμνο[ντ'] ἐν κλισίῃσιν
εἴ[ν]εκ[ε]ν ξανθᾶς γυναικὸς
[Βρισ]ηΐδος ἱμερογυίου,
105 θ[ε]οῖσι δ' ἄντειναν χέρας
φοίβαν ἐ[σ]ιδόντες ὑπαὶ
χειμῶνος αἴγλαν.

πασσυδίᾳ δὲ λιπόντες
τείχεα Λαομέδοντος
110 [ἐ]ς πεδίον κρατερὰν
ἄϊξαν ὑ[σ]μίναν φέροντες,
ὦρσάν τ[ε] φόβον Δαναοῖς.   ἀντ. δ'.
ὤτρυνε δ' Ἄρης
[ἐ]ὐεγχὴς [Λ]υκίων τε
115 [Λ]οξίας ἄναξ Ἀπόλλων·
ἷξόν τ' ἐ[π]ὶ θῖνα θαλάσσας.
[ν]αυσὶ δ' εὐπρύμνοις πάρ[α]
μάρναντ'· ἐναριζ[ομέν]ων

[δ' ἔρ]ευθε φωτῶν
120 [αἵμα]τι γαῖα μέλα[ινα]
['Εκτορ]έας ὑπὸ χει[ρός],

uses of transitive verbs are sufficiently common for this to cause no difficulty. An instance may in fact be found in the only other word which suits the MS., viz. κεύθω, which is normally transitive but occasionally intransitive. It is, however, less appropriate than ἐρεύθω, since the earth could hardly be said to be hidden by the blood of slain men, while the colour contrast, the black earth reddened with blood, is both appropriate and effective. ἐρεύθω is also supported by Homer, *Il.* XI. 394 (from the part of the Iliad which Bacchylides must have had in his mind when composing this ode), αἵματι γαῖαν ἐρεύθων. That the intransitive use might cause some misunderstanding is shown by the corrector's addition of -το above the line, turning the verb into the passive ; though the metre shows that the alteration is wrong.

120. αἵματι : only a small part of the penultimate letter is preserved, but it is certainly τ and not σ, so that σώμασι is impossible.

[.....]ΕΓ·ΗΜΙΘΕΟΙC[   ]

[.....]ΪCΟΘΕШΝΔ·|=ΟΡΜΑΝ·

[.....]ΟΝΕC·ΗΜΕΓΑΛΑΙCΙΝΕΛΠΙCΙΝ

125 [...]ΟΝΤΕCΥΠΕΡΦ[..]ΛΟΝ

[.   .   .   .   .   .]CΙΠΠΕΥΤΑΙΚΥΑΝШΠΙΔΑCΕΚ

[.   .   .   .   .]ΝΕΑC

[.   .   .   .   .]ΠΙΝΑCΤ·ΕΝ

130 [...]Ρ[.]ΙCΕΞΕΙΝΘ[...]ΜΑΤΟΝΠΟΛΙΝ·

[.]ΕΛΛΟΝ·ΑΡΑΠΡΟΤ[...]ΝΔΙ

[.]ΑΝΤΑΦΟΙΝΙΞ[.....]ΑΜΑΝΔΡ[

[.]ΝΑCΚΟΝΤΕCΥΠ[...]ΚΙΔΑΙC

ΕΡΕΙΨ[

135 ΤШΝΕΙΚΑΙ[

ΗΒΑΘΥΞΥΛ[

[.   .   .   .   .   .   .]

123. ΙΣΟΘΕΩΝ] the Ο is written above an erasure. After Δ΄Ι two
nearly horizontal lines are drawn, apparently to fill space accidentally
left vacant.   130–133. Fragment identified and text restored by Blass.

122, 123. Professor Jebb proposes to restore as follows :

πῆμα μέγ' ἡμιθέοις
φέροντος ἰσοθέων δι' ὁρμάν.

123. δι' ὁρμάν : the decipherment of the MS. is not quite clear, ὁρμάν being
preceded by two nearly horizontal strokes which resemble no letter.
Probably the phenomenon is the same as in XIX. 48, where the name
Σεμέλην is written ΓΕ—ΜΕΛΗΝ, through a scribe's blunder. In the present
case the confusion is increased by some one (not the original scribe) having
inserted an inverted comma after the δ, making the ι (if it is one) appear
part of one character with the two nearly horizontal strokes. Removing

[. . . . μ]έγ' ἡμιθέοις

[. . . . .] ἰσοθέων δι' ὁρμάν.

[ἆ τλάμ]ονες· ἢ μεγάλαισιν ἐλπίσιν   ἐπ. δ'

125 [. . .]οντες ὑπερφ[ία]λον

[.   .   .   .   .   .]

[.   .   ]ς ἱππευταὶ κυανώπιδας ἐκ

[.   .   .   .   .] νέας

[.   .   .   .   ]πινας τ' ἐν

130 [ἀμέ]ρ[α]ις ἕξειν θ[εόδ]ματον πόλιν.

[μ]έλλον ἄρα πρότ[ερο]ν δι-

[ν]ᾶντα φοινίξ[ειν Σκ]άμανδρ[ον]

[θ]νάσκοντες ὑπ' [Αἰα]κίδαις   στρ. ε'.

ἐρειψ[ιτοίχοις·]

135 τῶν εἰ καὶ[. . .]

ἢ βαθυξύλ[. . .]

•   •   •   •   •   •

this comma, or placing it after the ι, and regarding the horizontal strokes as meaningless, the reading is simple, and a correct metre is arrived at.

125. Perhaps χαίροντες or κλάζοντες.

126, 127. These two lines are written as one in the MS., the result being an abnormally long line, which breaks into the following column, displacing the beginning of a line there. Cf. ll. 51, 52.

127. ἱππευταί : cf Pind. *Pyth.* IX. 133. This must be the subject (or in apposition with the subject) of the sentence which begins with ἆ τλάμονες, and stands for the Trojans, corresponding to the Homeric ἱππόδαμοι. Hence [Τρῶε]ς ἱππευταί is a probable restoration. Lines 124-130 describe their hopes, while the mutilated passage, ll. 131-142, must have described their repulse by Ajax. According to Bacchylides' manner, the conclusion of the narrative must have been briefly told, and then cut off abruptly, being followed by the gnomic reflections with which the text recommences after the lacuna.

129. εἰλαπίνας will suit the metre, but the meaning is not clear.

[.　　·　·　　　.]

[.　·　　　·　·　.]

140 [.　·　·　　·　　.]

[.　·　·　　　.]

ΟΥΓΑΡΑΛΑΕΠΙΝΥ[

ΠΑCΙΦΑΝΗCΑΡΕΤ[

ΚΡΥΦΘΕΙC'ΑΜΑΥΡΟ[

145 ΑΛΛΕΜΠΕΔΟΝΑΚ[

ΒΡΥΟΥCΑΔΟΞΑΙ

CΤΡΩΦΑΤΑΙΚΑΤΑΓΑΝ[

ΚΑΙΠΟΛΥΠΛΑΓΚΤΑΝΘ[

ΚΑΙΜΑΝΦΕΡΕΚΥΔΕΑΝ[

150 ΑΙΑΚΟΥΤΙΜΑΙ·CΥΝΕΥ

ΚΛΕΙΑΙΔΕΦΙΛΟCΤΕΦ[

Col. 28]　ΠΟΛΙΝΚΥΒΕΡΝΑΙ

ΕΥΝΟΜΙΑΤΕCΑΟΦΡΩΝ

[.˙.]ΑΛΙΑCΤΕΛΕΛΟΓΧ[.]Ν

155 ΑCΤΕΑΤ'ΕΥCΕΒΕΩΝ

ΑΝΔΡΩΝΕΝΕΙ[.]ΗΝΑΙΦΥΛΑCC[.]Ι·

ΝΙΚΑΝΤ'ΕΡΙΚ[....]ΜΕΛΠΕΤ'ΩΝΕΟΙ

[..]ΘΕΑΜΕΛΕΤ[....]ΒΡΟΤΩ

---

142. ἀλαμπέσι] ΑΛΑΕΠΙ Α; Π has been cancelled and some letters written above, both before and after it, of which only the slightest vestiges remain.　　　148. ΠΟΛΥΠΛΑΓΚΤΑΝ Α, —ΤΟΝ Α³. 153. ΕΥΝΟΜΙΑ Α, corr. Jebb.

142. ἀλαμπέσι : see crit. note, and cf. Plutarch, *Phoc.* 1 (quoted by L. and S.) ἀρετὴν . . . ἀμαυρὰν καὶ · ἀλαμπῆ, which almost looks like a reminiscence of this passage.

143. πασιφανής : hitherto known only in Nonnus.

148. πολυπλάγκταν : the corrector has altered the termination to -ον,

οὐ γὰρ ἀλα[μπέσ]ι νυ[κτὸς]
πασιφανὴς ἀρετ[ὰ]
κρυφθεῖσ᾽ ἀμαυρο[ῦται σκότοισιν],
145 ἀλλ᾽ ἔμπεδον ἀκ[άματος]   ἀντ. ε᾽.
βρύουσα δόξᾳ
στρωφᾶται κατὰ γᾶν [τε]
καὶ πολυπλάγκταν θ[άλασσαν].
καὶ μὰν φερεκυδέα ν[ᾶσον]
150 Αἰακοῦ τιμᾷ, σὺν εὐ-
κλείᾳ δὲ φιλοστεφ[άνῳ]
πόλιν κυβερνᾷ
εὐνομίᾳ τε σαόφρων·
[ἁ] θαλίας τε λέλογχεν
155 ἄστεά τ᾽ εὐσεβέων
ἀνδρῶν ἐν εἰρήνᾳ φυλάσσ[ε]ι.
νίκαν τ᾽ ἐρικ[υδέα] μέλπετ᾽, ὦ νέοι,   ἐπ. ε᾽.
[Πυ]θέα μελέτ[αν τε] βροτω-

perhaps rightly, the feminine not being known elsewhere; but Bacchylides
has such a marked fondness for first declension forms that it seems better to
follow the original scribe.

149. φερεκυδέα : hitherto known only as a proper name. The 'honour-
bearing island of Aeacus' is, of course, Aegina. ἀρετά continues to be the
subject.

153. εὐνομίᾳ : the MS. εὐνομία can only be retained by supposing it to be
brought in, almost like an afterthought, to be coupled with ἀρετά as subject
of the sentence. It stands much more naturally as a dative coupled with
εὐκλείᾳ, and the scribe's error is easily accounted for by the neighbourhood
of σαόφρων.

[. .]ΛΈΑΜΕΝΑΝΔΡ[.]Υ·

160 ΤΑΝΕΠΑΛΦΕΙΟΥΤΕΡΟ[. .]Ϛ[.]ΜΑΔΗ

ΤΙΜΑϹΕΝᾶΧΡΥϹᾺΡΜΑΤΟϹ

ϹΕΜΝΑΜΕΓΆΘΥΜΟϹΑΘΑΝΑ·

ΜΥΡΙѠΝΤʼΗΔΗΜΙΤΡΑΙϹΙΝΑΝ . ΡѠΝ

[.]ϹΤΕΦΆΝѠϹΕΝΕΘΕΊΡΑϹ

165 ΕΝΠΑΝΕΛΛΑΝѠΝΑΕΘΛΟΙϹ·

[.·]ΙΜΗΤΙΝ·ΑΘΕΡϹ[.˙.ʼ]ΠΗϹ

[.]ΘΟΝΟϹΒΙᾶΤΑΙ

ΑΙΝΕΙΤѠϹΟΦΟΝΑΝΔΡΑ

[.]ΥΝΔΙΚΑῖ·ΒΡΎΟΤѠΝΔΕΜѠΜΟϹ

170 ΠΑΝΤΕϹϹΙΜΕΝΕϹΤΙΝΕΠΕΡΓΟΙ[

[.]Δʼ ΑΛΑΘΕΙΑΦΙΛΕΙ

ΝΙΚᾶΝΟΤΕΠΑΝΔ[.]ΜΆΤ[

ΧΡΟΝΟϹΤΟΚΑΛѠϹ

[.]ΡΓΜΕΝΟΝΑῖΕΝΑ[

175 [. . . . .]ΝΕ[.]ΝΔΕΜ[

---

169. βροτῶν] ΒΡΥΩ—Δ, corr. Δ¹.

---

159. Μενάνδρου : the Athenian trainer of Pytheas. He is similarly mentioned in Pindar's ode (*Nem.* V. 48), ἴσθι γλυκεῖάν τοι Μενάνδρου σὺν τύχᾳ μόχθων ἀμοιβὰν | ἐπαύρεο. χρὴ δ᾽ ἀπ᾽ Ἀθανᾶν τέκτον᾽ ἀεθληταῖσιν ἔμμεν. It may be that a reference to his services was included in the instructions given to the two poets; but as there are other personal references in Pindar's ode which do not find their counterparts in Bacchylides, it is not safe to insist on this. Βροτωφελής is a new word.

160-165. A reference to the successes won by Menander's pupils in the various festivals. It is his βροτωφελὴς μελέτα that Athena has honoured, not his own athletic prowess.

162. Ἀθάνα : Menander being an Athenian, it is Athena who has given him success.

163. μυρίων : so, but with more literal accuracy, Pindar speaks of the

[φε]λέα Μενάνδρ[ο]υ·
160 τὰν ἐπ' Ἀλφειοῦ τε ῥο[αῖ]ς [ἄ]μα δὴ
τίμασεν ἁ χρυσάρματος
σεμνὰ μεγάθυμος Ἀθάνα,
μυρίων τ' ἤδη μίτραισιν ἀν[έ]ρων
[ἐ]στεφάνωσεν ἐθείρας
165 [ἐ]ν Πανελλάνων ἀέθλοις.

. [ε]ἰ μή τινα θερσ[οε]πὴς   στρ. ϛ'.
[φ]θόνος βιᾶται,
αἰνείτω σοφὸν ἄνδρα
[σ]ὺν δίκᾳ· βροτῶν δὲ μῶμος
170 πάντεσσι μὲν ἐστὶν ἐπ' ἔργοι[ς],
[ἁ] δ' ἀλαθεία φιλεῖ
νικᾶν, ὅ τε πανδ[α]μάτ[ωρ]
χρόνος τὸ καλῶς
[ἐ]ργμένον αἰὲν ἀ[έξει].

175 [. . . . .]ν δὲ μ[. . .]

victory of Alcimedon at Olympia as the thirtieth won by pupils of the other
famous trainer, Melesias, who was an Athenian like Menander (*Ol.* VIII. 66).

166–170. This passage reads just like Pindar's prelude to the praise of
Melesias mentioned in the preceding note (*Ol.* VIII. 53), and may be, as
that has been held to be, a sort of apology for praising an Athenian in
Aegina.

θερσοεπής : a new word, 'bold-speaking,' θέρσος being Aeolic for θάρσος :
cf. Θερσίτης. The MS. has a dot between the N and A of TINA, which at
first sight seems intended to indicate the true division of words as τιν'
ἀθερσοεπής, in which case the first part of the word might conceivably be
connected with ἀθερές (Hesych., = ἀνόητον, ἀνόσιον). But the dot to indicate
divisions of words is not used in this MS., and the scribe could have attained
his object more naturally by a mark of elision after τιν'.

172. πανδαμάτωρ χρόνος : so Simonides (Bergk, frag.4), οὔθ' ὁ πανδαμάτωρ
ἀμαυρώσει χρόνος.

173. καλῶς ; the a is long, a scansion never found in Pindar.

174. ἀέξει : cf. Homer, *Od.* XV. 372, ἔργον ἀέξουσιν μάκαρες θεοί.

K 2

[........]CΜΙΝ[

[.   .   .   .   .   .   .]

[.   .   .   .   .   .   .]

[.   .   .   .   .   .   .]

180 [.   .   .   .   .   .   .]

[.   .   .   .   .   .   .]

[.   .   .   .   .   .   .]

[.   .   .   .   .   .   .]

[.   .   .   .   .   .   .]

185 [.   .   .   .   .   .   .]

[.   .   .   .   .   .   .]

Col. 29]   ΕΛΠΙΔΙΘΥΜΟΝΙΑΙΝ[

ΤΑΙΚΑΙΕΓΩΠΙCΥΝΟ[

ΦΟΙΝΙΚΟΚΡΑΔΕΜΝΟΙ[

190 ΥΜΝΩΝΤΙΝΑΤΑΝΔΕ[

ΦΑΙΝΩΝΞΕΝΙΑΝΤΕ[

ΓΛΑΟΝΓΕΡΑΙΡΩ·

ΤΑΝΕΜΟΙΛΑΜΠΩΝ[

ΒΛΗΧΡΑΝΕΠΑΘΡΗCΑΙCΤ[

195 ΤΑΝΕΙΚ'ΕΤΥΜΩCΑΡΑΚΛΕΙ[

ΠΑΝΘΑΛΗCΕΜΑΙCΕΝΕCΤΑ[

ΤΕΡΨΙΕΠΕΙCΝΙΝ . . ΔΑΙ

ΠΑΝΤΙΚΑΡΥΞΟΝΤΙΛΑ[

191. ΦΑΙΝΩΝ A, corr. A¹?   195. ἄρα Κλειὼ] the reading is
originally due to a suggestion by Jebb.   196. ἐνέσταξεν φρεσίν
Jebb, Blass (to whom is due the identification of a fragment containing a few letters from the ends of ll. 194–7).

191. ξενίαν : apparently a reference to the hospitality shown by Lampon

180 . . . . .

· · · · · ·

· · · · · ·

· · · · · ·

· · · · · ·

185 . . . . .

· · · · · ·

ἐλπίδι θυμὸν ἰαίν[ει].

τᾷ καὶ ἐγὼ πίσυνο[ς]

φοινικοκραδέμνοι[. . .]

190 ὑμνῶν τινα τὰν δε[. . . . . .]

φαίνω, ξενίαν τε [φιλά]-

γλαον γεραίρω·

τὰν ἐμοὶ Λάμπων[. . . . . .]

βληχρὰν ἐπαθρῆσαι στ[. .]

195 τὰν εἴ κ' ἐτύμως ἄρα Κλει[ὼ]

πανθαλὴς ἐμαῖς ἐνέστα[ξεν φρεσίν],

τερψιεπεῖς νιν [ἀοι]δαὶ

παντὶ καρύξοντι λα[ῷ].

towards the poet. Cf. Pind. *Isth.* V. 70, where Pindar says of Lampon, ξένων εὐεργεσίαις ἀγαπᾶται.

189. Probably φοινικοκραδέμνοις Χάρισσιν (Jebb).

193, 194. Jebb restores as follows :—

τὰν ἐμοὶ Λάμπων παρέχων κε χάριν (or δόσιν)
βληχρὰν ἐπαθρῆσαι στίχων.

XIV.

Κλεοπτολεμ[. .] Θεσσαλωι ιπποις Πετραι[.]

STROPHE.

‿ ⏑ ‿ ‿ ‿ ‿ ⏑ ‿ ‿ ⏑ ⏑ ‿
‿ ‿ ‿ ⏑ ‿ ‿
‿ ⏑ ‿ ‿ ⏑ ‿ ‿
[‿] ⏑ ‿ ‿ ‿ ⏑ ‿ ⏑
5 [‿] ‿ ⏑ ⏑ ⏑ ‿ ⏑ ‿ ⏑ ‿ ‿
[‿] ⏑ ‿ ‿ ‿ ⏑ ‿ ‿
[‿] ⏑ ‿ ‿ ‿ ⏑ ‿

EPODE.

‿ ‿ ⏑ ⏑ ‿ ⏑ ⏑ ‿
⏑ ‿ ⏑ ⏑ ‿ ⏑ ⏑ ‿ ‿
[. .] ‿ ‿ ‿ ⏑ ⏑ ‿
‿ ⏑ ‿ ‿ ‿ ⏑ ⏑ ‿ ⏑ ⏑ ‿ [.]
5 ⏑ ‿ ⏑ ⏑ ‿ ⏑ ⏑ ‿
‿ ‿ ⏑ ‿ ‿ ‿ ⏑ ‿ ‿
‿ ⏑ ⏑ ‿ ⏑ ⏑ ‿
‿ ⏑ ‿ ‿ ‿ ⏑ ‿ ‿

1—7 = 8—14 : 15—22

ΕΫΜΕΝΕΙΜΑΡΘΑΙΠΑΡΑΔΑΙ[
ΘΡΏΠΟΙϹΑΡΙϹΤΟΝ·

XIV. *Title* by A³.

XIV.

ΚΛΕΟΠΤΟΛΕΜΩΙ ΘΕΣΣΑΛΩΙ

ἵπποις Πετραῖα

THE ode which stands last among the *epinikia* as they have been here arranged is the only one which does not relate to one of the four great festivals. It is natural that such an ode should have held the last place in the collection, and affords a fair ground for the presumption that no large portion of the MS. has been lost at this point. It celebrates a victory won by a Thessalian, Cleoptolemus, in the chariot race at the Petraea. These games have not previously been known, but there can be no doubt as to their nature and locality. Πετραῖος was the surname of Poseidon in Thessaly, in commemoration of his having cloven the rocks which enclosed the plain and so given an outlet to the imprisoned waters through the gorge of Tempé. The shrine of Ποσειδῶν Πετραῖος is specifically mentioned (l. 20), and the victor, as would be likely in games of merely local importance, is a Thessalian. There is nothing to show in what part of Thessaly the games were held, but the neighbourhood of Tempé is not improbable.

Only the beginning of the poem has been preserved, and that very imperfectly. The last line of the column begins a second metrical system, so that the poem must have extended into at least one other column. One of the unplaced fragments (no. 11), which makes mention of Thessaly, no doubt belongs to this lost column. The extant portion of the poem consists merely of general reflections on good fortune and victory, breaking off just as the specific success of Cleoptolemus is reached.

The metre is dactylo-epitrite.

εὖ μὲν εἱμάρθαι παρὰ δαι[μοσιν ἀν]- στρ. α΄.
θρώποις ἄριστον·

[.]ΥΜΦΟΡΑΔ'ΕCΘΛΟΝΑΜΑΛΔΥ[

[. . . .]ΑΡΥΤΛ[. .]ΟCΜΟΛΟΥCΑ·

       κα_ι [. . .]

5 [. . . .]ΟΝΗΔΗΥΨΙΦΑΝΗΤΕ[

[. . .]ΑΤΟΡΘΩΘΕΙCΑ·ΤΙΜΑΝ

[. . .]ΛΟCΑΛΛΟΙΑΝΕΧΕΙ·

[. . . .]ΑΙΔ'ΑΝΔΡΩΝΑΡΕ[. . .]ΜΙΑΔ'Ε[

[. . . .]ΝΠΡΟΚΕΙΤΑΙ

10 [. . . .]ΠΑΡΧΕΙΡΟCΚΥΒΕΡΝΑΙ

[. . . . .]ΚΑΙΑΙCΙΦΡΕΝΕCCΙΝ·

[. . . . .]ΙΒΑΡΥΠΕΝΘΕCΙΝΑΡΜΟ

[. . . .]ΑΧΑΙCΦΟΡΜΙΓΓΟCΟΜΦΑ

[. . . .]ΓΥΚΛΑΓΓΕΙCΧΟΡΟΙ

15 [. . . .]ΝΘΑΛΙΑΙCΚΑΝΑΧΑ

[. . . .]ΟΚΤΥΠΟC·ΑΛΛΕΦΕΚΑCΤΩΙ

[. . . . .]ΑΝΔΡΩΝΕΡΓΜΑΤΙΚΑΛ

ΛΙCΤΟC[.]ΥΕΡΔΟΝΤΑΔΕΚΑΙΘΕΟCΟ[

ΚΛΕΟΠΤΟΛΕΜΩΙΔΕΧΑΡΙΝ

20 ΝΥΝΧΡΗΠΟCΙΔΑΝΟCΤΕΠΕΤΡ[

3. ἐσθλοὺς] ΕΣΘΛΟΝ Α, corrected by Jebb on metrical grounds. 5. ΗΔΗ Α, ΚΑΙ . . . Α³: the metre shows that some word followed ΚΑΙ, but it is now lost in a lacuna. 8. εὐδαίμων Jebb. 10. ΚΥΒΕΡΝΑΙ Α, corr. Α¹. 13. μάχαις and ὀμφά Jebb, which led to the identification of a fragment containing the ends of ll. 8-15. 17. καιρὸς Jebb. 18. ΕΡΔΟΝΤΙ Α, corr. Α³?

3-6. Professor Jebb proposes the following restoration :—

συμφορὰ δ' ἐσθλόν τ' ἀμαλδύ-   λαμπρόν τε καὶ ὑψιφανῆ τε-
νει βαρύτλατος μολοῦσα·   λεῖ κατορθωθεῖσα·

3. ἐσθλούς: MS. εσθλον, but the metre (which should plainly be two dactylo-epitritic feet, $- \cup - - \mid - \cup - -$) suggests that the termination is corrupt, and this suspicion is confirmed by the remains of l. 10, which holds the corresponding place in the antistrophe. Jebb's restoration, ἐσθλόν τ', implies the loss of τε before καί in l. 5, whereas the MS. testimony rather points to

[σ]υμφορὰ δ' ἐσθλοὺς ἀμαλδύ-
[νει β]αρύτλ[ατ]ος μολοῦσα.

5 [. . . .]ον καὶ [. . .] ὑψιφανῆ τε
[. . . κ]ατορθωθεῖσα· τιμὰν
[δ' ἄλ]λος ἀλλοίαν ἔχει.
[μυρί]αι δ' ἀνδρῶν ἀρε[ταί]· μία δ' ε[ὐ]-		ἀντ. α'.
[δαίμω]ν πρόκειται,

10 [ὅς γε] πὰρ χειρὸς κυβερνᾶ-
[ται δι]καίαισι φρένεσσιν.
[οὐκ ἐ]ν βαρυπενθέσιν ἁρμό-
[ζει μ]άχαις φόρμιγγος ὀμφὰ
[καὶ λι]γυκλαγγεῖς χοροί,

15 [οὐδ' ἐ]ν θαλίαις καναχὰ		ἐπ. α'.
[χαλκ]όκτυπος· ἀλλ' ἐφ' ἑκάστῳ
[καιρὸς] ἀνδρῶν ἔργματι κάλ-
λιστος· [ε]ὖ ἔρδοντα δὲ καὶ θεὸς ὀ[ρθοῖ].
Κλεοπτολέμῳ δὲ χάριν

20 νῦν χρὴ Ποσιδᾶνος τε Πετρ[αί]-

the loss of a word after καί. It is noticeable that Bacchylides does not use the form ἐσλός, which is found in Pindar ; this supports Bergk's view that the form in question is peculiarly Boeotian, and not a part of the common lyric dialect.

10. ὅς γε: explanatory of μία, 'manifold are the forms of merit, but one is blessed above all, the merit of him whose life is guided in uprightness of mind.' ἅ γε would also be possible, but goes less well with κυβερνᾶται, and ὅς is perfectly intelligible and idiomatic. πὰρ χειρός is odd, standing by itself, but no other interpretation seems possible.

18. ὀρθοῖ: this, which was also conjectured by Professor Jebb, seems the only word which ends both the sense and the rhythm satisfactorily.

20. Πετραίου: see introductory note. The name also occurs in Pind. Pyth. IV. 138, παῖ Ποσειδᾶνος Πετραίου, where the scholiast, as Dr. Sandys points out, says φασὶ δὲ καὶ ἀγῶνα διατίθεσθαι τῷ Πετραίῳ Ποσειδῶνι, ὅπου ἀπὸ τῆς πέτρας ἐξεπήδησεν ὁ πρῶτος ἵππος, while another note connects the name with the cleaving of the gorge of Tempé.

ΟΥΤΕΜΕΝΟϹΚΕΛΑΔΗϹΑΙ

ΠΥΡΡΙΧΟΥΤΈΥΔΟΞΟΝΙΠΠΟΝ[

ΟϹΦΙΛΟΞΕΙΝΟΥΤΕΚΑΙΟΡΘΟΔ[

*   *   *   *   *

XV.

]τηνοριδαι
]ς απαιτησις

STROPHE.

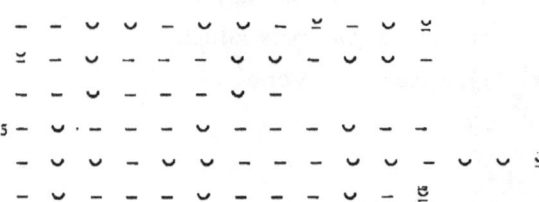

XV. *Title* by A³, in margin above column.

22. Πυρρίχου : perhaps the father of Cleoptolemus, unless it is a mistake for Πυρρίχου, in which case it would be the name of a horse, with an allusion to its colour (πυρρός, bay).

XV. *Title.* At the top of the column, in a small cursive hand, is the mutilated inscription :

]τηνοριδαι
]ς απαιτησις

Elsewhere in the MS. titles are written in the margins at the sides of the columns, never above the first line of the poem, while lines which have been accidently omitted are occasionally inserted at the top or bottom of the papyrus. This cannot be the case here, however, since ἀπαίτησις, besides being a prosaic word, will not fit into the metrical structure of the poem. It is therefore nearly certain that the inscription is a mutilated title, which admits of an easy restoration as ['Αν]τηνορίδαι : ['Ελένη]ς ἀπαίτησις. A similar double title occurs in Ode XVII. The title 'Αντηνορίδαι belongs to the first part of the poem, being confirmed by the mention in l. 7 of Theano, the wife of Antenor. The patronymic is applied by Pindar (*Pyth.* V. 83) to Glaucus, Acamas, and Hippolochus, the heroes worshipped at Cyrene ; while Homer names no less than ten sons of Antenor. It is impossible to say who are the individuals referred to here, nor what is their connexion with the

ου τέμενος κελαδῆσαι,
Πυρρίχου τ' εὔδοξον ἵππον [
ὃς φιλοξείνου τε καὶ ὀρθοδ[ίκου]   στρ. β'.
[The rest is wanting.]

XV.

ΑΝΤΗΝΟΡΙΔΑΙ : ΕΛΕΝΗΣ ΑΠΑΙΤΗΣΙΣ

THE transition from the 'Επινίκια to the miscellaneous poems is lost through the mutilation of the papyrus, and we cannot tell whether the distinction between them was in any way marked in the MS. Nor have we any direct evidence as to the size of the lacuna which now exists between the extant portion of the ode to Cleoptolemus and the first of the miscellaneous poems. It may be observed, however, that if the ode to Cleoptolemus consisted of two metrical systems, it would have occupied only two-thirds of a second column, the rest of which must have been left blank ; while if it consisted of four systems, it would have extended nearly, but not quite, to the bottom of a third column. It is not at all likely to have been longer than this, and therefore it seems probable that the conclusion of the 'Επινίκια was marked by a blank space at the end, in which a title *may* have been written.

It is practically certain that, in the words which begin the fourth main section of the papyrus, we have portions of the first lines of the ode with which the new section commences. Metrical considerations prove that they belong to the same poem as that which occupies the greater part of col. 31, and that a metrical system begins with the first line of col. 30. Considering the lengths of most of these poems, it is improbable that another system preceded this, and it is natural that a new section should begin on a new column. In addition, at the top of the column there is what appears (see note below) to be the title of the poem.

second part of the poem, which is described as 'Ελένης ἀπαίτησις, a title quite suitable to the portion of the poem preserved in the papyrus. It is interesting to note that this is also the title of one of the lost plays of Sophocles, who was certainly acquainted with this part of the poetry of Bacchylides.

```
 _  _  ⏑  _  _  _  ⏑  ⏑  _  ⏑  ⏑  _
 _  _  ⏑  _  _  _  ⏑  _  _
 _  ⏑  _  _  _  ⏑  ⏑  _  _  ⏑  ⏑  _
 _  _  ⏑  ⏑  _  ⏑  ⏑  _  _
5_  ⏑  _  _  _  ⏑  _
 _  _  ⏑  ⏑  _  ⏑  ⏑  _
 _  _  ⏑  _  _  _  ⏑  _  _
```

1—7 = 8—14 : [15—21
22—28=29—35 :] 36—42
43—49 = 50—56 : 57—63

Col. 30]   [. . . . .]ΑΝΤΙΘΕΟΥ

          [. . . . .]ϹΑΘΑΝΑϹΠΡΟϹΠΟΛΟϹ

          [. . . . .]ΑΛΛΑΔΟϹΟΡϹΙΜΑΧΟΥ

          [. . . . .]ΡΥϹΕΑϹ

    5 [. . . . . .]ΑΡΓΕΙѠΝΟΔΥϹϹΕΙ

          [. . . . .]ѠΙ ΑΤΡΕΙΔΑΙΒΑϹΙΛΕΙ

          [. . . . .]ΖѠΝΟϹΘΕΑΝѠ

6. Τ' added above line by A³.

1. 'Αντήνορος: this conjecture seems extremely probable, both as fitting the metre and from the mention in the next line of the 'Αθάνας πρόσπολος, who can only be Theano, the wife of Antenor. There are no materials, however, for the reconstruction of the rest of the passage.

Assuming this to be so, the poem is one of three systems, or sixty-three lines, of which the latter half, or rather less, is practically complete, while of the first half only the scantiest remains have been preserved.

The title of the poem is discussed in the note below, and its contents have been described in the Introduction. The continuous portion of it in its present state begins in the epode of the second system, and this, with the strophe of the third, describes the gathering of the Trojan assembly, and the rising of Menelaus to address it. His speech, or rather sermon, since it consists solely of moral precepts, occupies the antistrophe and epode, after which the poem breaks off with extreme abruptness. With regard to the classification of the poem, the entire absence of any specific reference to any deity, either at the end or (according to appearances) at the beginning, forbids its being regarded as a Paean or a Dithyramb, and makes it probable that it should be reckoned as a Hymn. These, as the fragments of Pindar show, might be devoted to the celebration of the actions of some hero, without (so far as appears) any express association with a deity.

The metre is dactylo-epitrite.

[Ἀντήνορος] ἀντιθέου   στρ. α΄.

[   ]ς Ἀθάνας πρόσπολος

[Π]αλλάδος ὀρσιμάχου

[χ]ρυσέας

5 [   ] Ἀργείων Ὀδυσσεῖ

[   ]ῳ τ᾽ Ἀτρείδᾳ βασιλεῖ

[   ]ζωνος Θεανὼ

2. Ἀθάνας πρόσπολος: cf. Homer, Il. VI. 297–300,
αἱ δ᾽ ὅτε νηὸν ἵκανον Ἀθήνης ἐν πόλει ἄκρῃ,
τῇσι θύρας ὤιξε Θεανὼ καλλιπάρῃος,
Κισσηίς, ἄλοχος Ἀντήνορος ἱπποδάμοιο·
τὴν γὰρ Τρῶες ἔθηκαν Ἀθηναίης ἱέρειαν.

7. Either εὔζωνος or βαθύζωνος would suit the metre.

Θεανώ: it is, no doubt, to this poem that the scholiast on Homer,

[. . . . .]ON

[. . . . .]ΝΠΡΟΣΗΝΕΠΕΝ·

10 [. . . .]ΫΚΤΙΜΕΝΑΝ

[. . . . .]

[. . . . .]ΩΝΤΥΧΟΝΤΆC

[. . . . . . .]ΥΝΘΕΟΙC

[. . . . . . .]ΟΥC

[22 lines wanting]

Col. 31]   Α̂ΓΟΝ·ΠΑΤΗΡΔ΄ΕΥΒΟΥΛΟCΗΡΩC

ΠΑΝΤ[.]C̣ΆΜΑΙΝΕΝΠΡΙΑΜΩΙΒΑCΙΛΕΙ

ΠΑΙΔΕCC̣[.]ΤΕΜΥΘΟΝΑΧΑΙΩΝ·

40   ΕΝΘΑΚΑΡΥΚΕCΔΙΕΥ

ΡΕ̂ΙΑΝΠΟΛΙΝΟΡΝΥΜΕΝΟΙ

ΤΡΩΩΝΑΟΛΛΙΖΟΝΦΑΛΑΓΓΑC

ΔΕΞΊCΤΡΑΤΟΝΕΙCΑΓΟΡᾹΝ·

ΠΆΝΤᾹΙΔΕΔΙΕΔΡΑΜΕΝΑΥΔᾹΕΙCΛΟΓΟC

45   ΘΕΟΙCΔ΄ΑΝΙCΧΟΝΤΕCΧΕΡΑCΑΘΑΝΑΤΟΙC

ΕΥΧΟΝΤΟΠΑΥCΑCΘΑΙΔΥΑ̂Ν·

ΜΟΥCΑ·ΤΙCΠΡΩΤΟCΑ̂ΡΧΕΝΛΟΓΩΝΔΙΚΑΙΩΝ .

ΠΛΕΙCΘΕΝΊΔΑCΜΕΝΕΛΑΟCΓΑ̂ΡΥΪ̈ΘΕΛΞΙΕΠ[.^.]

12. ΤΥΧΟΝΤΑΣ Α, corr. Α³.   47. ΑΡΧΕΝ ΛΟΓΩΝ Α, transposed
on metrical grounds.

Il. XXIV. 496 refers, when he says that Βακχυλίδης πεντήκοντα τῆς Θεανοῦς
ὑπογράφει παῖδας (Bergk, frag. 59).

9. προσήνεπεν: the same form appears in the MSS. of Pindar in *Pyth.*
IV. 97, IX. 31, but has generally been altered by editors to προσέννεπεν.

37. ἥρως: probably Antenor, father of the Antenoridae to whom the first
part of the poem relates. This would give a sort of link between the two parts.

[   ]ον   ἀντ. α΄.

[   ]ν προσήνεπεν·

10 [ἐ]ϋκτιμέναν

[   ]

[   ]ων τυχόντες

[σ]ὺν θεοῖς

[   ]ους

[22 lines wanting.]

ἆγον· πατὴρ δ᾽ εὔβουλος ἥρως
πάντ[α] σάμαινεν Πριάμῳ βασιλεῖ
παίδεσσί τε μῦθον Ἀχαιῶν.
40 ἔνθα κάρυκες δι᾽ εὐ-
ρεῖαν πόλιν ὀρνύμενοι
Τρώων ἀόλλιζον φάλαγγας
δεξίστρατον εἰς ἀγοράν.   στρ. γ΄.
παντᾷ δὲ διέδραμεν αὐδάεις λόγος,
45 θεοῖς δ᾽ ἀνίσχοντες χέρας ἀθανάτοις
εὔχοντο παύσασθαι δυᾶν.
Μοῦσα, τίς πρῶτος λόγων ἆρχεν δικαίων ;
Πλεισθενίδας Μενέλαος γάρυϊ θελξιεπ[εῖ]

39. μῦθον Ἀχαιῶν: evidently a proposal for a conference, in which
Menelaus should formulate his demand for the surrender of Helen.

43. δεξίστρατον: a new compound. Cf. δεξίμηλος, δεξίπυρος, but compounds
of δέχομαι in this form are not common.

47. λόγων ἆρχεν: in spite of the slight uncertainty of the text in the
corresponding line of the antistrophe (l. 54), there can be no doubt that
this transposition of the MS. reading (first suggested by Mr. Purser) is
right, as it brings the metre into the familiar form of three dactylo-epitritic
feet. It is also confirmed by the extant portion of l. 5.

ΦΘΕΓΞΑΤ·ΕΥΠΕΠΛΟΙCΙΚΟΙΝΏCΑCΧΆΡΙCϚΙΝ

50 ΩΤΡΩΕϚΑΡΗΪΦΙΛΟΙ

ΖΕΥCΥ[.........]Π̣ΑΝ[..]ΔΕΡΚΕΤΑΙ

ΟΥΚΆΙ[.....]ΑΤΟΙCΜΕΓΑΛΩΝΑΧ[.]ΩΝ

ΑΛΛ·ΕΝ[.....]ΚΕΙΤΑΙΚΙΧΕΙΝ

ΠᾹCΙΝΑΝΘΡΩΠΟΙCΔΙΚΑ̸Χ̸Η̸ΘΕΪΑΝΑΓΝΑC
$\overset{v\ \ddot{\iota}}{}$

$\overset{ακολουθον}{}$
55 ΕΥΝΟΜῙΑCΚΑ̣Ι̣Π̣Ι̣Ν̣ῩΤᾹCΘΕΜΙΤΟC

ΟΛΒΙΩΝΠ̣[....]ΝΙΝΑΙΡΕ̄ΥΝΤΑΙCῩΝΔ̊ΙΚΟΝ

Α̲Δ·ΑΙΟΛΟΙ[.] . ΥΔΕCCΙΚΑΙΑΦΡΟCΥΝΑΙC

ΕΞΑΙCΙΟΙϚΘ̣Α̣Λ̣Λ̣ΟΥC·ΑΘΑΜΒΗC

ΥΒΡΙCᾹΠ̣Λ..[...]ΔΥΝΑΜΙΝΤΕΘΟΩC

60 ΑΛΛΌΤΡΙΟΝΩΠ̣ΑϚΕΝΑΥΤΙC

[.]᾿ ΕCΒΑΘΥΝΠΕΜΠΕΙΦΘΟΡΟΝ·

[..]ΝᾹΚΑΙΫΠΕΡΦΙΑΛΟΥC

[...]ΠΑΙ[.]ΑϚΩΛΕCΕΝΓΙΓΑΝΤΑC

51-56. Restored from Clem. Alex., Strom. v. 731.   54. ΔΙΚΑΛΗ-
ΘΗΑΝ Α, corr. A³.   δίκαν ὁσίαν ἀγνάν Clem., ἀγνᾶς Bergk, ὁσίας ἀγνᾶς
Blass.   55. ΑΚΟΛΟΥΘΟΝ om. Α, added above line by A³.   θέμιτος]
θέμιδος Clem., θέμιτος conj. Bergk.   56. παῖδές νιν] παῖδες ὦ
νιν Clem., παῖδες οἵ νιν Brunck, παῖδές νιν Neue.   σύνδικον Α, corr.
A¹.   57. αἰόλοις ψεύδεσσι Palmer.   59. πλοῦτον Palmer.
63. ΩΛΕΣΕΝ Α, corr. on metrical grounds.

49. κοινώσας Χάρισσιν: 'having taken the Graces into his counsel.' Cf.
Pind. Pyth. IV. 115 νυκτὶ κοινάσαντες ὁδόν, well translated by Gildersleeve,
'having made night privy to the journey.'

50-56. These lines are quoted by Clement of Alexandria (Strom. V. 731).
He does not name Bacchylides as the author, calling him simply ὁ λυρικός,
and their inclusion among the fragments of Bacchylides is a curious example
of a right conclusion drawn from wrong premises. Sylburg (followed
by Boeckh, Bergk, and practically all subsequent writers) assigns them to
Bacchylides on the ground that Porphyry, in commenting on the prophecy
of the fall of Troy which Horace (Odes, I. 15) puts into the mouth of

φθέγξατ' εὐπέπλοισι κοινώσας Χάρισσιν·
50 ὦ Τρῶες ἀρηΐφιλοι,   ἀντ. γ΄.
   Ζεὺς ὑ[ψιμέδων, ὃς ἅ]παν[τ]α δέρκεται,
   οὐκ αἴ[τιος θν]ατοῖς μεγάλων ἀχ[έ]ων·
   ἀλλ' ἐν [μέσῳ] κεῖται κιχεῖν
   πᾶσιν ἀνθρώποις Δίκαν ἰθεῖαν, ἁγνᾶς
55 Εὐνομίας ἀκόλουθον καὶ πινυτᾶς Θέμιτος.
   ὀλβίων π[αῖδές] νιν αἱρεῦνται σύνοικον.
   ἁ δ' αἰόλοι[ς ψε]ύδεσσι καὶ ἀφροσύναις   ἐπ. γ΄.
   ἐξαισίοις θάλλουσ' ἀθαμβὴς
   ὕβρις, ἁ πλ[οῦτον] δύναμίν τε θοῶς
60 ἀλλότριον ὤπασεν, αὖτις
   [δ]' ἐς βαθὺν πέμπει φθόρον.
   [κεί]να καὶ ὑπερφιάλους
   [γᾶς] παῖ[δ]ας ὤλεσσεν γίγαντας.

Nereus, says that Horace is there imitating Bacchylides, who put a similar prophecy into the mouth of Proteus; from which prophecy these lines are accordingly supposed to be drawn. The argument, as now appears, is false, but the conclusion is correct. This is the longest of the previously extant fragments of Bacchylides which finds a place in the present manuscript (frag. 29 Bergk). The division of lines is, as usual, different from any of those adopted by previous editors. For the variations of reading found in Clement's quotation, see critical notes.

55. Θέμιτος: the same form occurs in Pindar (*Ol.* XIII. 8). Θέμις, according to Hesiod (*Theog.* 901, 902) and an unidentified lyric poet (Bergk, *fragm. adesp.* 140), is the mother of Δίκη, Εὐνομίη, and Εἰρήνη, hence a similar personification is probably intended here.

57. αἰόλοις ψεύδεσσι: cf. Pind. *Nem.* VIII. 25, αἰόλῳ ψεύδει.

59. ἁ: demonstrative, resuming ἁ δ' . . . ὕβρις. This gives a better balance to the sentence than to take ἅ as relative, which involves treating δέ in the next line as marking an apodosis (this, however, is preferred by Jebb), or to regard the apodosis as beginning with κεῖνα in l. 62, which is also barred by the punctuation of the MS.

STROPHE.

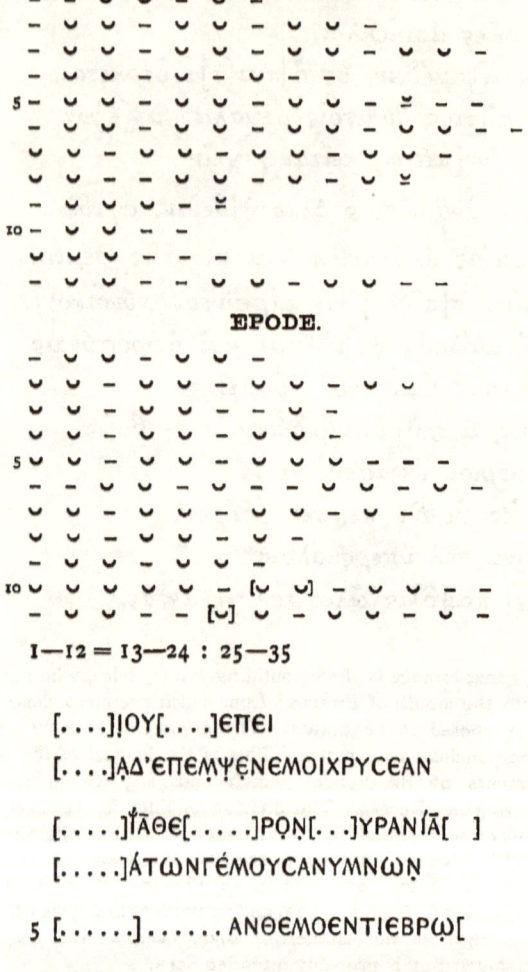

EPODE.

1—12 = 13—24 : 25—35

[. . . .]ỊΟΥ[. . . .]ΕΠΕΙ

[. . . .]ΑΔ᾽ΕΠΕΜΨΕΝΕΜΟΙΧΡΥϹΕΑΝ

[. . . . .]ΪΑΘΕ[. . . . .]ΡΟΝ[. . .]ΥΡΑΝΙΑ[ ]

[. . . . .]ΑΤⲰΝΓΕΜΟΥϹΑΝΥΜΝⲰΝ

5 [. . . . .]. . . . . . ΑΝΘΕΜΟΕΝΤΙΕΒΡⲰ[

2. ὀλκάδ᾽ Sandys.   3. ἀγγελία Jebb, Sandys.

3. θε . . . . . . ρον . . : θεμερόφρονος, a word hitherto known only from
Hesychius, but having the appearance of a lyric compound, would suit the
remains here, and there is a slight trace of ink after θε which suits μ.

XVI.

[ΗΡΑΚΛΗΣ]

The left-hand margin of the papyrus at this point is lost, and with it all indication of the beginning of a new poem and of its title. The former is, however, established by metrical considerations, while the latter must be supplied by conjecture. The main subject of the poem is the last sacrifice and death of Heracles, which occupies the antistrophe and epode, while the strophe, which is mutilated, contains introductory matter, including an invocation of Pythian Apollo. This feature would seem to show that the poem is to be classed as a Paean; it may also indicate that it was intended to be sung at the Pythian festival. A special feature of interest connected with it is the obvious reminiscence of a passage in it by Sophocles (see notes on l. 13 ff.). Like the preceding poem, it ends very abruptly.

The poem consists of a single system in logaoedic metre.

[. . . .]ου[. . . .]επει   στρ.

[ὁλκ]άδ᾽ ἔπεμψεν ἐμοὶ χρυσέαν

['Αγγελ]ία θε[. . . . .]ρον[. . Ο]ὐρανία[s]

[ἀθαν]άτων γέμουσαν ὕμνων

5 [. . . . . .]. . . . . ἀνθεμόεντι Ἕβρῳ

4. ἀθανάτων or ἀβροτάτων (Jebb); πολυφάτων would be attractive, cf. Pind. *Ol.* I. 8 ὁ πολύφατος ὕμνος, *Nem.* VII. 81 πολύφατον θρόον ὕμνων, but it has not the required scansion.

L 2

[.....]ΓΑΛΛΕΤΑΙΗ͂ΔΟΛΙΧΑΥΧΕΝΙΚΥ[

[....]ΔΕΪΑΦ[.]ΕΝΑΤΕΡΠΟΜΕΝΟC

[....]Ν̣Κ ... Τ̣Α̣ΙΗΟΝωΝ

Col. 32] ΑΝΘΕΑΠΕΔΟΙΧΝΕΙ͂Ν

10 ΠΥΘΙˈΑΠΟΛΛΟΝ

ΤΟCCΑΧΟΡΟΙΔΕΛΦωΝ

CΟΝΚΕΛΑΔΗCΑΝΠΑΡΑ̅Κ̅ΛΕΑΝᾺΟΝ
        ^{γα}

ΠΡΙΝΓΕΚΛΕΟΜΕΝΛΙΠΕΙΝ

ΟΙΧΑΛΙΑΝΠΥΡΙΔΑΠΤΟΜΕΝΑ̅Ν

15 ΑΜΦΙΤΡΥωΝΙΑΔΑ̅ΝΘΡΑCΥΜ[.]ΔΕΑΦω

ΘˈΪΚΕΤΟΔˈΑΜΦΙΚΥ͂ΜΟΝˈΑΚΤ[.]Ν·

ΕΝΘˈΑΠΟΛΑΪ͂ΔΟCΕΥΡΥΝΕΦΕΙ͂Κ̣ΗΝΑΙωΙ

ΖΗΝΙΘΥΕΝΒΑΡΥΑ̅ΧΕΑCΕΝΝΕΑ̣ΤΑΥΡΟΥC

ΔΥΟΤˈΟΡCΙΑΛωΙΔΑΜΑCΙΧΘΟΝΙΜ̣Ε̣[

20 ΛΕΚΟΡΑ̅Ι͂ΔΟΒΡΙΜΟ̣Δ̣Ε̣ΡΚΕΙΑΖΥΓΑ[
        ^{τ'}

---

6. ὀπὶ ἡδεΐᾳ Palmer.   11. ΤΟΣΣΑ Α, altered on metrical grounds.
12. ΑΚΛΕΑ Α, corr. Α³.   19, 20. μέλλε Palmer.   20. Δ Α, Τ' Α²?

6. ἀγάλλεται: the subject (which τερπόμενος shows to be masculine) is probably Apollo, to whom the swan was sacred.

8. The visible remains of this line do not seem long enough to fulfil the requirements of the metre.

13. The transition is abrupt, and apparently without any connecting link. The scene which follows is that described in the speech of Hyllus in Sophocles' *Trachiniae* (750 ff.) and it is evident that the younger poet has had Bacchylides in his mind. The passage may be quoted for the sake of convenient comparison—

> ὅθ' εἷρπε κλεινὴν Εὐρύτου πέρσας πόλιν,
> νίκης ἄγων τροπαῖα κἀκροθίνια,
> ἀκτή τις ἀμφίκλυστος Εὐβοίας ἄκρον
> Κήναιόν ἐστιν, ἔνθα πατρῴῳ Διὶ
> βωμοὺς ὁρίζει τεμενίαν τε φυλλάδα·
> οὗ νιν τὰ πρῶτ' ἐσεῖδον ἄσμενος πόθῳ.
> μέλλοντι δ' αὐτῷ πολυθύτους τεύχειν σφαγὰς
> κῆρυξ ἀπ' οἴκων ἵκετ' οἰκεῖος Λίχας, κ.τ.λ.

[. . . . ἀ]γάλλεται ᾷ δολιχαύχενι κύ[κνῳ]

[ὀπὶ ἡ]δείᾳ φ[ρ]ένα τερπόμενος

[. . . .]νκ . . . ται ἠόνων

ἄνθεα πεδοιχνεῖν.

10 Πύθι᾽ Ἄπολλον,

τόσα χοροὶ Δελφῶν

σὸν κελάδησαν παρ᾽ ἀγακλέα ναόν.

πρίν γε κλέομεν λιπ[εῖν]   ἀντ.

Οἰχαλίαν πυρὶ δαπτομέναν

15 Ἀμφιτρυωνιάδαν θρασυμ[ή]δεα φῶ-

θ᾽. ἵκετο δ᾽ ἀμφικύμον᾽ ἀκτ[ά]ν,

ἔνθ᾽ ἀπὸ λαΐδος εὐρυνέφει Κηναίῳ

Ζηνὶ θύεν βαρυαχέας ἐννέα ταύρους

δύο τ᾽ ὀρσιάλῳ δαμασίχθονι μ[έλ]-

20 λε, κόρᾳ τ᾽ ὀβριμοδερκεῖ ἄζυγα

The ἀμφικύμων ἀκτά, the Κήναιος Ζεύς, and the μέλλε of Bacchylides have obvious counterparts here.

15. φῶθ': for the division of the word, cf. V. 106 and note.

18. θύεν: not the imperfect, but the Doric infinitive, =θύειν, dependent on μέλλε, which otherwise would be intolerably prosaic. The poet does not intend to say that Heracles was actually sacrificing nine bulls to Zeus and was going to sacrifice two to Poseidon and one to Athena, but (just as in Sophocles, μέλλοντι . . . τεύχειν σφαγάς) that he was about to begin the whole sacrifice, when the fatal gift from Deianira was brought to him.

ἐννέα: Sophocles gives the number as twelve (ταυροκτονεῖ μὲν δώδεκ᾽ ἐντελεῖς ἔχων | λείας ἀπαρχὴν βοῦς), but the same total is arrived at here by including the two animals offered to Poseidon and the one to Athena, which are not separately specified by Sophocles. The words λείας ἀπαρχήν, just quoted, correspond to ἀπὸ λαΐδος here, just as ταύρους is reproduced in ταυροκτονεῖ.

19. ὀρσιάλῳ δαμασίχθονι: neither epithet occurs elsewhere, but they are obviously titles of Poseidon, the latter being merely a variant of the Homeric ἐνοσίχθων and the Pindaric σεισίχθων, which is also used by Bacchylides himself (XVII. 58).

20. ὀβριμοδερκεῖ: another new epithet.

ΠΑΡΘΕΝΩΙΑΘΑΝΑῙ

ΥΨΙΚΕΡΑΝΒΟΥΝ·

ΤΟΤ'ΑΜΑΧΟΣΔΑΙΜΩΝ

ΔΑῙΑΝΕΙΡΑ͞ΠΟΛ[. .]ΑΚΡΥΝΥΦΑ̣[

25 ΜΗΤΙΝΕΠΙΦΡΟΝ'ΕΠΕΙ

ΠΥΘΕΤ'ΑΓΓΕΛΙΑΝΤΑΛΑΠΕΝΘΕΑ[

ῙΟΛΑ͞ΝΟΤΙΛΕΥΚΩΛΕΝΟΝ

ΔΙΟΣΥΙΟΣΑΤΑΡΒΟ[.]ΑΧΑΣ

ΑΛΟΧΟΝΛΙΠΑΡΟ[. . .]|ΟΤΙΔΟΜΟΝΠΕ̣Ι[. .]Ο̣Ι·

30 Α̂ΔΥΣΜΟΡΟΣΑ̂ΤΑΛ̣[. .]Ν̣'ΟῙΟΝΕΜΗΣΑΤ[ ]

ΦΘΟΝΟΣΕΥΡΥΒΙΑ[. .]ΙΝΑΠΩΛΕΣΕΝ

ΔΝΟΦΕΟΝΤΕΚΑΛΥΜΜΑΤΩΝ

ΫΣΤΕΡΟΝΕΡΧΟΜΕΝΩΝ·

ΟΤ'ΕΠΙΠΟΤΑΜΩΡΟΔΟΕΝΤΙΛΥΚΟΡΜΑ͞Ι[

35 ΔΕΞΑΤΟΝΕΣΣΟΥΠΆΡ(a)ΔΑΙΜΟΝΙΟΝΤΕΡ[

---

24. ΔΑΙΑΝΕΙΡΑ A, corr. A¹. 32. δνοφερόν] ΔΝΟΦΕΟΝ A.
35. ΠΑΡ A, a added above line by A².

22. ὑψικέραν: the a, which is marked long in the MS., is for ω, like Ποσειδᾶν for Ποσειδῶν. Cf. καλλικέραν, XIX. 24. Both words are accented paroxytone in the MS.

23. ἄμαχος δαίμων: probably 'irresistible fate,' rather than any specific deity, such as Ἔρως.

25. ἐπίφρονα: a Homeric epithet of μῆτις (in Odyssey), also used by Hesiod of βουλή (Theog. 122, 661, 896); but always in good sense, whereas here it must mean 'crafty,' 'designing.'

31. εὐρυβίας: in Pindar always applied to a person, not to a personification.

32. δνοφερόν τε κάλυμμα κ.τ.λ.: 'and the dark veil which hid the things to come,' τῶν ὕστερον ἐρχομένων being an objective genitive.

παρθένῳ Ἀθάνᾳ
ὑψικέραν βοῦν.
τότ' ἄμαχος δαίμων
Δαϊανείρᾳ πολ[ύδ]ακρυν ὕφα[νεν]
25 μῆτιν ἐπίφρον', ἐπεὶ   ἐπῳδ.
πύθετ' ἀγγελίαν ταλαπενθέα
Ἰόλαν ὅτι λευκώλενον
Διὸς υἱὸς ἀταρβο[μ]άχας
ἄλοχον λιπαρὸ[ν π]οτὶ δόμον πέμ[π]οι.
30 ἆ δύσμορος, ἆ τάλ[αι]ν', οἷον ἐμήσατ[ο]·
φθόνος εὐρυβία[ς ν]ιν ἀπώλεσεν,
δνοφερόν τε κάλυμμα τῶν
ὕστερον ἐρχομένων·
ὅτ' ἐπὶ ποταμῷ ῥοδόεντι Λυκόρμᾳ
35 δέξατο Νέσσου πάρα δαιμόνιον τέρ[ας].

34. ῥοδόεντι : the fragment of papyrus containing the first syllable of this word was identified by Blass. The application of the epithet to a river is novel.

Λυκόρμᾳ : the original name of the river Evenus in Aetolia, before Evenus, in his pursuit of Idas and Marpessa, drowned himself in it (Apollod. *Bibl.* I. 7. 8). Sophocles, in narrating the same incident, uses the later name (*Trach.* 559).

35. τέρας : there seems to be no other possible word beginning with τε-, and the remains of the third letter resemble a ρ; but the sense is unusual, denoting as it must the blood or shirt of Nessus. Dr. Sandys, however, compares Pind. *Ol.* XIII. 73, where it is used of the bit given by Athena to Bellerophon. Professor Jebb suggests that possibly γέρας should be read, Nessus having made the gift to Deianira as a mark of honour, because she was the last passenger whom he carried across the stream (Soph. *Trach.* 570, 571).

XVII.

]ϊθεοι
]θησευς

STROPHE.

XVII. *Title* by A³.

Title. The marks of diaeresis over the first ι leave no doubt that the first word must be restored as ἤϊθεοι, otherwise ἡμίθεοι is attractive, on the ground that the point of the poem lies in the controversy between Minos and Theseus as to their divine parentages. Ἤϊθεοι must refer to the Athenian youths and maidens whom Theseus was conducting to Crete,

XVII.

ΗΪΘΕΟΙ [ΚΑΙ] ΘΗΣΕΥΣ.

THE two poems which follow are perhaps the most interesting, as they are the most perfect in preservation, of the whole collection. Both are concerned with the legend of Theseus; a subject so intimately associated with Athens that they must almost certainly have been composed for some occasion closely connected with that city.

The first is especially interesting for its contents, the second for its form. The story contained in the first has hitherto been known only from a short passage in Pausanias (I. 17. 2, 3) and another in Hyginus (*Poet. Astron.* II. 5). From the former we learn that it was the subject of one of the paintings of Micon upon the walls of the Theseum; and since the painting did not fully tell its own story (and, as is implied, the legend itself was not commonly known, at least in Pausanias' time), he gives a short summary of it. The passage is as follows: τοῦ δὲ τρίτου τῶν τοίχων ἡ γραφὴ μὴ πυθομένοις ἃ λέγουσιν οὐ σαφής ἐστιν, τὰ μέν που διὰ τὸν χρόνον, τὰ δὲ Μίκων οὐ τὸν πάντα ἔγραψε λόγον. Μίνως ἡνίκα Θησέα καὶ τὸν ἄλλον στόλον τῶν παίδων ἦγεν ἐς Κρήτην, ἐρασθεὶς Περιβοίας, ὥς οἱ Θησεὺς μάλιστα ἠναντιοῦτο, καὶ ἄλλα ὑπὸ ὀργῆς ἀπέρριψεν ἐς αὐτὸν καὶ παῖδα οὐκ ἔφη Ποσειδῶνος εἶναι, ἐπεὶ οὐ δύνασθαι τὴν σφραγῖδα, ἣν αὐτὸς φέρων ἔτυχεν, ἀφέντι ἐς θάλασσαν ἀνασῶσαί οἱ. Μίνως μὲν λέγεται ταῦτα εἰπὼν ἀφεῖναι τὴν σφραγῖδα· Θησέα δὲ σφραγῖδά τε ἐκείνην ἔχοντα καὶ στέφανον χρυσοῦν, Ἀμφιτρίτης δῶρον, ἀνελθεῖν λέγουσιν ἐκ τῆς θαλάσσης. Pausanias does not say from what source he derived his story (possibly only from local guides), and there are no verbal parallels to indicate that he had Bacchylides in his mind; some details also are omitted (such as the sign shown to Minos by Zeus), but in substance the stories are identical. The date of the building of the Theseum (circ. 468–460 B.C., the internal decoration of the walls of course being one of the latest stages) falls well within the probable limits of Bacchylides' life, but there is no evidence to show whether the poet was inspired by the painter, or the painter by the poet.

The passage in Hyginus is fuller than that in Pausanias, and corresponds even more closely with Bacchylides. 'Dicitur enim cum Theseus Cretam ad Minoa cum septem virginibus et sex

$$\cup\ -\ \cup\ \cup\ \cup\ -\ \cup\ -\ -\ -$$
$$\cup\ -\ \cup\ -\qquad -$$
$$-\ \cup\ \cup\ \cup\ -\ \cup\ -$$
$$-\ \cup\ \underset{\smile}{\cup}\ \cup\ -\ \cup\ -\ -\ \cup\ -\ \cup\ -\ \cup$$
5 $$\cup\ -\ \cup\ \cup\ \cup\ -\ \cup\ -$$
$$-\ \cup\ -\ -\ \cup\ \cup\ \cup\ -\ \cup\ -$$
$$-\ \cup\ \cup\ \cup\ -\ \cup\ -\ -\ \cup\ -\ -$$
$$-\ -\ \cup\ -\ -\ \cup\ -\ -\ \cup\ \cup$$
$$-\ \cup\ -\ \cup\ -\ \cup\ -\ \cup\ -$$
10 $$\cup\ \cup\ \cup\ -\ \cup\ -\ \cup\ -$$
$$-\ \cup\ -\ -\ \cup\ -$$
$$\cup\ -\ \cup\ -\ -\ \cup\ -\ -\ -\ \cup\ \cup$$
$$\cup\ -\ \cup\ -\ -\ \cup\ -$$
$$-\ \cup\ -\ \cup\ -\ \cup\ -$$
15 $$-\ \cup\ -\ \cup\ -$$
$$\cup\ -\ \cup\ -\ \cup\ -\ \cup\ \underset{\smile}{\cup}\ -\ \cup\ -$$
$$\cup\ -\ \cup\ -\ -\ \cup\ \underset{\smile}{\cup}\ -\ \cup\ \cup$$
$$-\ \cup\ \underset{\smile}{\cup}\ -\ \cup\ -\ \cup\ -$$
$$\cup\ \cup\ \cup\ -\ -$$
20 $$\cup\ -\ \cup\ -\ -\ \cup\ -\ -\ \cup\ -$$

$$1\text{—}23 = 24\text{—}46 : 47\text{—}66$$
$$67\text{—}89 = 90\text{—}112 : 113\text{—}132$$

on whose behalf he intervened against Minos, and whom ultimately he saved from the Minotaur. They form, as it were, the chorus to the piece, and, as so often in the tragedies, give it their name. They are called ἤιθεοι in ll. 93, 128. It is uncertain whether the Θησεύς which appears in the second line of the title is a separate secondary title (as seems to be the case in Ode XV) or is part of a single title, a καί being lost in the lacuna. As Θησεύς by itself is the title of the following poem, the latter alternative is perhaps the more probable.

(probably only a corruption of vi for vii, which is read by one MS.)
pueris venisset, Minoa de virginibus Eriboeam quandam nomine,
candore corporis inductum, comprimere voluisse; quod Theseus
se passurum negavit, ut qui Neptuni filius esset et valeret contra
tyrannum pro virginis incolumitate disceptare. Itaque cum iam
non de puella, sed de genere Thesei controversia facta esset,
utrum is Neptuni filius esset necne, dicitur Minos anulum aureum
de digito sibi detraxisse et in mare proiecisse, quem referre iubet
Thesea, si vellet se credi Neptuni filium esse; se enim ex Iove
procreatum facile posse declarare. Itaque comprecatus patrem
petiit aliquid signi, ut satisfaceret se ex eo natum; statimque
tonitrum et fulgorem caeli indicium significationis fecisse. Simili
de causa Theseus, sine ulla precatione aut religione parentis, in
mare se proiecit, quem confestim delphinum magna multitudo
mari provoluta lenissimis fluctibus ad Nereidas perduxit; a quibus
anulum Minois, et a Thetide coronam, quam nuptiis a Venere
muneri acceperat, retulit, compluribus lucentem gemmis. Alii
autem a Neptuni uxore accepisse dicunt coronam.' Hyginus'
mention of 'alii' shows that he derived the story from various
authorities, but among them, directly or indirectly, must have
been Bacchylides.

The story has also received artistic illustration in two well-
known and very remarkable vases, the one being the famous cylix
of Euphronius in the Louvre, the other the great amphora of
Clitias and Ergotimus at Florence, which goes by the name of the
François vase. The former[1] represents the scene of Theseus'
interview with Amphitrite. In the centre, and slightly in the
background, stands Athena, armed and wearing the aegis, and
holding her owl in her right hand. On her right front stands
Theseus, a beardless youth, his feet supported by a Triton, whose
fish's tail lies along the bottom of the picture. On the left sits
Amphitrite, whose right hand is stretched out to meet the right
hand of Theseus, either in greeting, or to give him the ring of
Minos. The margin, where there is room, is occupied by dolphins,

[1] *Monuments grecs* 1872, pl. 1; *Wiener Vorlegeblätter* V. 1; Klein, *Eu-
phronios*, p. 182. Mr. A. van Branteghem has kindly lent me a large
drawing of the inside of the cylix, containing the scene in question.
A small reproduction, with a description, will be found in *Mythology and
Monuments of Ancient Athens*, by Miss Jane Harrison and Mrs. Verrall,
pp. 147-9. For the original reference to the vase I am indebted to
Mr. A. H. Smith.

which, besides indicating that the scene is beneath the sea, suggest a reference to the dolphins mentioned in the poem (l. 97), though their special function as carriers is transferred to the Triton. Names are attached to each figure, so there is no room for doubt about the identifications, and the artist's signature is in the margin.

Three other vases (to which references will be found in Hitzig and Blumner's Pausanias, vol. I, p. 207) likewise depict the submarine excursion of Theseus. One (a crater at Bologna) is clearly connected with the story now in question, representing as it does the gift of a wreath by Amphitrite to Theseus, who is borne by a Triton; in the remaining two, Poseidon is the principal figure.

The François vase [1] depicts two scenes from a later stage in the poem, the reappearance of Theseus from his submarine excursion, and the landing in Crete. The first scene shows a ship with sailors, whose attitudes express amazement and excitement; by the side of the ship a man is swimming. This figure has never been understood, and has been explained as a sea-god, or a mere accessory; but it is plainly Theseus, returned from the bottom of the sea, and the sailors' emotion is that which is described in l. 123 ff. of the poem. The second scene represents Theseus (his name is here attached to the figure) landing at the head of the youths and maidens whom he has brought with him. They are fourteen in number, as in the poem, seven youths and seven maidens, ranged alternately. All have names attached to them, and the first, whom Theseus holds by the hand, bears a mutilated name which has been variously read as 'Επίβοια or 'Ερίβοια (see note on l. 14). The joyful attitudes of the whole group correspond with the words which close the description in the poem.

The relations of these vases to the poem of Bacchylides and the painting of Micon belong rather to the sphere of archaeology than to that of literature; but in the case of the François vase at least, it is difficult not to trace a direct indebtedness of the poet to the artist. It certainly adds an interest to the discovery of this poem, to find it illustrating and illustrated by two of the masterpieces of Greek vase-painting.

Apparently the poem should be classed as a Paean, on account of the invocation of Apollo with which it concludes, and which otherwise is pointless. Servius seems to refer to it as a Dithyramb

---

[1] *Wiener Vorlegeblätter* 1888, Taf. III; cf. an article by Reichel in *Archäologisch-epigraphische Mittheilungen*, XIII. 58. I owe the reference to this vase to Mr. A. van Branteghem.

ΚΥΑΝΟΠΡШΡΑΜ[.]ΝΝΛΥϹΜΕΝΕΚΤΥ[

ΘΗϹΕΑΔΙϹΕΠΤ[.]Τ’ΑΓΛΑΟΥϹΑΓΟΥϹΑ

ΚΟΥΡΟΥϹΙΑΌΝШ[.]

ΚΡΗΤΙΚΟΝΤΑΜΝΕΝΠΕΛΑΓΟϹ·

5 ΤΗΛΑΥΓΕΪΓΑΡ[. .]ΦΑΡΕΪ

ΒΟΡΗΪΑΪΠΙΤΝΟ[.]ΑΥΡΑΙ

ΚΛΥΤΑϹΕΚΑΤΙΠ[.]ΛΕΜΑΙΓΙΔΟϹΑΘΑΝ[

Col. 33]   ΚΝΙϹΕΝΤ . ΜΙΝШΚΕΑΡ

ΙΜΕΡΑΜ . . ΚΟϹΘΕΑ

10 ΚΥΠΡΙΔΟ . . . . ΑΔШ[.]Α·

4. TAMNEN Δ, corr. on metrical grounds.

1. κυανόπρῳρα: the accent in the MS., as well as the scansion, shows that the form is not quite identical with κυανοπρῷρα, which the *Etym. Mag.* attributes to Simonides, with the remark that Herodian wrote it κυανοπρώειρα.

2. δὶς ἑπτά: this may be the passage referred to by Servius (on Virg. *Aen.* VI. 21; quoted by Bergk as frag. 17): quidam septem pueros et septem puellas accipi volunt, quod et Plato dicit in Phaedone, et Sappho in Lyricis, et Bacchylides in Dithyrambis, et Euripides in Hercule, quos liberavit secum Theseus. Bacchylides does not here expressly say that there were seven youths and seven maidens, but the gender of κούρους implies the presence of youths and the mention of Eriboia that of maidens. The only interest of the quotation lies in its use of the title Dithyrambi, and that is apparently an error.

6. Βορήϊαι: the mark of short quantity placed over the final syllable in the MS. refers to its value for accentual purposes, not for scansion.

7. ἕκατι: 'by favour of' Athena, the original Homeric sense of the word.

(see note on l. 2), but this can only be correct if the original meaning of the title had been quite lost, so that it could be used in a general sense which would cover the Paeans and probably the Hymns as well. It was performed by a Cean chorus (l. 130), perhaps on the occasion of a deputation being sent from Ceos to attend an Athenian festival.

The poem consists of only two systems, of unusual length, each consisting of sixty-six lines. It is practically perfect, the few mutilations admitting of almost certain restoration in every case. The metre is paeonian.

κυανόπρωρα μ[ὲ]ν ναῦς, μενέκτυ[πον]   στρ. α´.
Θησέα δὶς ἐπτ[ά] τ᾽ ἀγλαοὺς ἄγουσα
κούρους Ἰαόνω[ν],
Κρητικὸν τάμνε πέλαγος·
5 τηλαυγεῖ γὰρ [ἐν] φάρεϊ
Βορήϊαι πίτνο[ν] αὖραι
κλυτᾶς ἕκατι π[ο]λεμαίγιδος Ἀθάν[ας].
κνίσεν τε Μίνωϊ κέαρ
ἱμ[ερ]άμ[πυ]κος θεᾶς
10 Κύπριδο[ς αἰν]ὰ δῶρα·

πολεμαίγιδος : the word is new and rather curious. χρύσαιγις occurs in frag. 52 (Bergk 23). The accent in the MS. has been retained.

8. It is to be observed that the following scene takes place on board the ship which was conveying Theseus to Crete. This is recognized by Pausanias (Μίνως ἡνίκα Θησέα . . . ἦγεν ἐς Κρήτην), and illustrated by the François vase; whereas Hyginus lays the scene in Crete, after the arrival of the ship (cum Theseus Cretam . . . venisset), and the ordinary version of the Minotaur story says nothing of Minos himself being on board the ship which brought the victims. Hellanicus, however (in Plut. *Thes.* 17, quoted by Jebb), represents Minos as fetching the captives from Athens in person.

Μίνωϊ: the metre shows that this must be regarded as a trisyllable, like μάτρωϊ in Pind. *Isth.* VI. 24 (Jebb). Μίνωϊ occurs in Nonnus VII. 361 and other late writers (cf. Pape-Benseler, s. v.). See also l. 68.

9. ἱμεράμπυκος : this restoration involves the hypothesis of an otherwise unknown adjective, like πολέμαιγις, but the MS. seems to require it. Cf. Pindar's Μναμοσύνας λιπαράμπυκος (*Nem.* VII. 15), which is equally a ἅπαξ λεγόμενον, except for a parody by Aristophanes.

10. αἰνά : the restoration is uncertain, but suits the slight traces of letters in the MS.

ΧΕΙΡΑΔ'ΟΥ[. . . .]ΠΑΡΘΕΝΙΚÂC

ΑΤΕΡΘΕΡÃ . . ΕΝ·ΘΙΓΕΝ

ΔΕΛΕ[.]ΚÂΝΠΑΡΗΪ̂ΔѠΝ·

ΒΟΑ[. . . .]ΊΒΟΙΑΧΑΛΚΟ̦

15 ΘΟ̂̕ΡÃ[. . . . .]ΔΙΟΝΟC

ΕΚΓ[.] . ΟΝΪ̈ΔΕΝΔΕΘΗCΕΥC·

ΜΕΛ[.]ΝΔ'ΥΠΟΦΡΎѠΝ

ΔΙ . ΑΓ[.]ΕΝΟΜΜΑΚΑΡΔΊΑΝΤΕΘ̂Ι

CΧΕ[. .]ΙΟΝΆΜΥΞΕΝΑ̦ΓΟC·

20 ΕΙ̂ΡΕ̦Ν[.]ΕΔΙΟCΥ̓ΙΕΦΕΡΤ̦ΑΤΟΥ̓

ΟCΙΟΝ̦ΟΥΚΕΤΙΤΕΑΝ

ΕCѠ̦ΚΥΒΕΡΝÂ'CΦΡΕΝѠΝ

Θ[. . . .] · Ϊ̈CΧΕΜΕΓΑΛΟΥΧΟΝΉΡѠCΒΙΑΝ

ΟΤΙ̦[. .]ΝΕΚΘΕѠΝΜΟ̂ΙΡΑΠΑΓΚΡΑΤΗC

25 ἈΜΜΙ̦ΚΑΤΕΝΕΥCΕΚΑΙΔΙΚΑCΡΈΠΕΙΤΆ

16. ἔκγονον **Palmer, van Branteghem.**   22. **ΚΥΒΕΡΝΑΣ Δ,**
corr. A²?

11. *παρθενικᾶς*: substantive, as in Alcman, frag. 26, *παρθενικαὶ μελιγάρυες ἱμερόφωνοι.*

14. *'Ερίβοια*; there is some doubt as to the name of this maiden. Pausanias gives it as *Περίβοια*, Hyginus as *'Ερίβοια*, while the name on the François vase has been variously read as *'Ερίβοια* and *'Επίβοια* (the reproduction given in the *Wiener Vorlegeblätter* seems to support the latter reading, which is that of Klein, *Meistersignaturen*, p. 33; Reichel gives *'Ερίβοια* without comment). Since a *δέ* is required in the lacuna by the sense, *Περίβοια* is excluded; and of the other alternatives *'Ερίβοια* seems preferable, on the grounds (1) that it is supported by Hyginus, whose version of the story is so close to that of Bacchylides, (2) that the reading of the François vase is doubtful, (3) that the name *'Επίβοια* does not occur elsewhere. The maiden in question is probably to be regarded as the same as the daughter of Alcathous and wife of Telamon, whose name is also given variously as *Περίβοια* and *'Ερίβοια*. (Cf. Plut. *Thes.* 29, where Theseus is said to have married the mother of Ajax, γῆμαι δὲ (λέγεται) καὶ Περίβοιαν τὴν Αἴαντος μητέρα καὶ Φερέβοιαν αὖθις, a sort of confused echo of this story.) Her home was in Megara, but Megara in early times was held to be part of Attica, so that she may have been among the maidens sent to Minos. Pindar uses the

χεῖρα δ' οὐ[κέτι] παρθενικᾶς
ἄτερθ' ἐρά[τυ]εν· θίγεν
δὲ λε[υ]κᾶν παρηΐδων.
βόα[σε δ' Ἐρ]ίβοια χαλκο-
15 θώρα[κα Παν]δίονος
ἔκγ[ον]ον. ἴδεν δὲ Θησεύς,
μέλ[α]ν δ' ὑπ' ὀφρύων
δί[ν]α[σ]εν ὄμμα, καρδίαν τέ οἱ
σχέ[τλ]ιον ἄμυξεν ἄλγος,
20 εἰρέν τε· Διὸς υἱὲ φερτάτου,
ὅσιον οὐκέτι τεᾶν
ἔσω κυβερνᾷς φρενῶν
θ[υμόν]· ἴσχε μεγαλοῦχον ἥρως βίαν.
ὅ τι [μὲ]ν ἐκ θεῶν μοῖρα παγκρατὴς   ἀντ. α'.
25 ἄμμι κατένευσε καὶ δίκας ῥέπει τά-

---

form Ἐρίβοια (*Isth.* V. 45) which may be taken as another argument in favour of the same form here.

15. Πανδίονος ἔκγονον : Theseus, cf. Eur. *Heracl.* 35 Θησέως παῖδας . . . ἐκ γένους Πανδίονος.

20. εἰρεν : this imperfect of the Homeric present εἴρω (itself somewhat rare) has not hitherto been met with; but it occurs twice in this poem (here and in l. 74), and there is no sufficient reason for rejecting it. The MS. reading is clear in both cases; there is no sort of reason why εἶπεν (the inevitable alternative) should have been corrupted into the unfamiliar εἶρεν, while the converse change may easily have taken place elsewhere; and εἶρεν may well have been preferred in order to avoid the monotonous repetition of εἶπεν, which occurs in ll. 47, 52, 81.

22. κυβερνᾷς : for the metaphor, cf. Aesch. *Pers.* 767 φρένες γὰρ αὐτοῦ θυμὸν ᾠακοστρόφουν.

23. μεγαλοῦχον : the word does not occur elsewhere, and μεγάλαυχον is an easy emendation; but 'grasping' is a more appropriate epithet in this context than 'boastful.'

24. ὅ τι μὲν ἐκ θεῶν κ.τ.λ. : referring to the doom of slaughter by the Minotaur which lay before them. To that it was the will of the gods that they should be exposed, and just in so far that it was in payment of the accepted penalty of defeat. But personal insult and outrage were not in the bond.

M

ΤΑΛΑΝΤΟΝΠΕΠΡΩΜΕΝ[.]Ν

ΑΙCΑΝ[.]ΚΠΛΗCΟΜΕΝΟΤ[.]Ν

ΕΛΘΗ·[. .]ΔΕΒΑΡΕΙΑΝΚΑΤΕ

ΧΕΜ[.]ΤΙΝΕΙΚΑΙCΕΚΕΔΝΑ

30 ΤΕΚΕΝΛΕΧΕΙΔΙΟCΥΠΟΚΡΟΤΑΦΟΝΙΔΑC

ΜΙΓΕΙCΑΦΟΙΝΙΚΟCΕΡΑ

ΤΩΝΥΜΟCΚΟΡΑΒΡΟΤΩΝ

ΦΕΡΤ[. .]ΟΝ·ΑΛΛΑΚΑΜΕ

ΠΙΤΘ[.]ΟCΘΥΓΑΤΗΡΑΦΝΕΟΥ

35 ΠΛΑΘΕΙCΑΠΟΝΤΙΩΙΤΕΚΕΝ

ΠΟCΙΔΑΝΙ·ΧΡΥCΕΟΝ

ΤΕΘΙΔΟCΑΝΙΟΠΛΟΚΟΙ

ΚΑΛΥΜΜΑΝΗΡΗΙΔΕC·

ΤΩCΕΠΟΛΕΜΑΡΧΕΚΝΩCCΙΩΝ

40 ΚΕΛΟΜΑΙΠΟΛΥCΤΟΝΟΝ

ΕΡΥΚΕΝΥΒΡΙΝ·ΟΥΓΑΡΑΝΘΕΛΟΙ

Col. 34]   Μ·ΑΜΒΡΟΤΟΙ·ΕΡΑΝΝΟΝΑΟ[

ΙΔΕΙΝΦΑΟCΕΠΕΙΤΙΝ·ΗΙΘΕ[

CΥΔΑΜΑCΕΙΑCΑΕΚΟΝ

45 ΤΑΠΡΟCΘΕΧΕΙΡΩΝΒΙΑΝ

ΔΕ[.]ΞΟΜΕΝ·ΤΑΔ·ΕΠΙΟΝΤΑΔΑ[. . .]ΝΚΡΙΝΕΙ·

[. . . . .]ΠΕΝΑΡΕΤΑΙΧΜΟCΗΡΩ[.]

26. **ΤΑΛΑΝΤΟΝ Δ** (ΤΑ repeated by mistake), corr. Δ¹?   43. ἠθέων]
ΗΙΘΕΩΝ Δ, corr. on metrical grounds ; cf. l. 128.

32. κόρα : Europa, here, as in *Il.* XIV. 321, called daughter of Phoenix, not of Agenor.

34. Πιτθέος θυγάτηρ : Aethra.

ἀφνεοῦ : scanned as an anapaest, as in Pind. frag. 218.

35. πλαθεῖσα : cf. Pind. *Nem.* X. 81 ματρὶ τεᾷ πελάσαις.

37. The metre of this line is deficient, an additional syllable being wanted at the end. The simplest correction palaeographically (and the sense requires no addition) would be to read ἰόπλοκοί τοι, to which the chief

λαντον, πεπρωμέν[α]ν
αἶσαν [ἐ]κπλήσομεν, ὅταν
ἔλθῃ. [σὺ] δὲ βαρεῖαν κάτεχε μ[ῆ]τιν. εἰ καί σε κεδνὰ
30 τέκεν λέχει Διὸς ὑπὸ κρόταφον Ἴδας
μιγεῖσα Φοίνικος ἐρα-
τώνυμος κόρα βροτῶν
φέρτ[ατ]ον, ἀλλὰ κἀμὲ
Πιτθ[έ]ος θυγάτηρ ἀφνεοῦ
35 πλαθεῖσα ποντίῳ τέκεν
Ποσειδᾶνι, χρύσεόν
τέ οἱ δόσαν ἰόπλοκοι
κάλυμμα Νηρηΐδες.
τῷ σέ, πολέμαρχε Κνωσσίων,
40 κέλομαι πολύστονον
ἐρύκεν ὕβριν· οὐ γὰρ ἂν θέλοι-
μ' ἀμβρότοι' ἐραννὸν ἀο[ῦς]
ἰδεῖν φάος, ἐπεί τιν' ἠθέ[ων]
σὺ δαμάσειας ἀέκον-
45 τα. πρόσθε χειρῶν βίαν
δε[ί]ξομεν· τὰ δ' ἐπιόντα δα[ίμων] κρινεῖ.
[τόσ' εἶ]πεν ἀρέταιχμος ἥρω[ς],   ἐπ. α'.

objection is that in the other strophes this line ends with a short syllable.
ἰόπλοκος = ἰοπλόκαμος has hitherto been extant only in two emendations
introduced by Bergk into Pind. *Ol.* VI. 30, *Isth.* VI. 23, in both of which
places he substitutes it for an unmetrical ἰοπλόκαμος.

39. Κνωσσίων : scanned as a dissyllable.

41. ἐρύκεν : the Doric infinitive, like γαρύεν, τράφεν in Pindar (*Ol.* I. 3,
Pyth. IV. 115, V. 72). In Pindar, as Gildersleeve remarks, these forms
have 'the authority of MSS., not the cogency of metre'; but in the present
passage the latter testimony is added. Cf. l. 88 and XIX. 25, where the
metre requires ἴσχεν and φυλάσσεν respectively.

47. ἀρέταιχμος : a somewhat strange compound. Presumably the first

[. .]ΦΟΝΔΕΝΑΥΒΑΤΑΙ

[. .]Ρ[. .]ΥΠΕΡΑ̊ΦΝΟΝ

50 . Α[.]ϹΟϹ·ΑΛΙΟΥΤΕΓΑΜΒΡΩΙΧΟΛΩ[

ΥΦΑΙΝΕΤΕΠ[.]ΤΑΙΝΙΑΝ

ΜΗΤΙΝ·ΕΙΠΕΝΤΕΜΕΓΑΛΟϹΘ[

ΖΕΥΠΑΤΕΡΑΚΟΥϹΟΝ·ΕΙΠΕΡ[

ΦΟΙΝΙϹϹΑΛΕΥΚΩΛΕΝΟϹϹΟΙΤΕΚ[

55 ΝΥΝΠΡΟΠΕΜΠ·ΑΠΟΥΡΑΝΟΥΘ[

ΠΥΡΙ̣ΕΘΕΙΡΑΝΑϹΤΡΑΠΑΝ

ΓΑ̂Μ·ΑΡΙΓΝΩΤΟΝ·ΕΙ

ϙ̣ΙΔΕΚΑΙϹΕΤΡΟΙΖΗΝΙΑϹΕΙϹ[. . .]ΟΝΙ

ΦΥΤΕΥϹΕΝΑΙΘΡᾹΠΟϹΕΙ

60 ΔΑ̂ΝΙΤΟΝΔΕΧΡΥϹΕΟΝ

ΧΕΙΡΟϹΑΓΛΑΟΝ

ΔΙ̂ΚΩΝΘΡΑϹΕΙϹΩΜΑΠΑΤΡΟϹ[.]ϹΔΟΜΟΥϹ

ΕΝΕΓΚΕΚΟϹΜΟΝΒΑΘΕῙΑϹΑΛΟϹ·

ΕΙϹΕΑΙΔ·ΑΙΚ·ΕΜΑϹΚΛΎΗΙ

65 ΚΡΟΝΙΟϹΕΥΧΑ̂Ϲ

ΑΝΑΞΙΒΡΕΝΤΑϹΟ̂ΠΑΝΤΩ[. . . . ´.]Ν·

---

49. ΥΠΕΡΑΦΝΟΝ Α, corr. Α³.   53–55. Restored by Palmer.
58. ΕΙ wrongly repeated at beginning of line by Α, corr. Α¹?   62.
ΘΡΑΣΕΙ] the Θ is written over another letter (perhaps Ι) by Α³?
τό] om. Α, inserted on metrical grounds.   66. ἀναξιβρόντας]
ΑΝΑΞΙΒΡΕΝΤΑΣ Α.

part of the word is the verb ἀρετάω, not the noun ἀρετή, and the meaning is
'valorous with the spear.'

49. ὑπεράφανον : in good sense, the earliest instance of its occurrence. It
would of course be possible to translate 'but the sailors were afraid of the
overweening boldness' of Minos, taking the clause as describing the silence
of the crew on hearing Theseus' speech, and giving the reason of it. But it is
not likely that ἀνδρός and ἀλίου γαμβρῷ refer to the same person, and the
clause may more naturally be taken to mean that the sailors were astounded

[τά]φον δὲ ναυβάται

[ἀνδρὸς] ὑπεράφανον

50 [θ]ά[ρ]σος· 'Αλίου τε γαμβρῷ χολώ[σατ' ἦτορ],

ὕφαινέ τε π[ο]ραινίαν

μῆτιν, εἶπέν τε· μεγαλοσθ[ενὲς]

Ζεῦ πάτερ, ἄκουσον· εἴπερ [μ' ἀλαθέως]

Φοίνισσα λευκώλενός σοι τέκ[ε],

55 νῦν πρόπεμπ' ἀπ' οὐρανοῦ θ[οὰν]

πυριέθειραν ἀστραπάν,

σᾶμ' ἀρίγνωτον· εἰ

δὲ καί σε Τροιζηνία σεισ[ίχθ]ονι

φύτευσεν Αἴθρα Ποσει-

60 δᾶνι, τόνδε χρύσεον

χειρὸς ἀγλαόν,

δικὼν θράσει ⟨τὸ⟩ σῶμα πατρὸς [ἐς] δόμους,

ἔνεγκε κόσμον βαθείας ἁλός.

εἴσεαι δ' αἴ κ' ἐμᾶς κλύῃ

65 Κρόνιος εὐχᾶς

ἀναξιβρόντας ὁ πάντω[ν μεδέω]ν.

at the courage of Theseus. θάρσος also suits Theseus better; it did not require much courage to insult a captive.

50. 'Αλίου γαμβρῷ : Pasiphaë, wife of Minos, was the daughter of Helios.

χολώσατ' ἦτορ: the passive is more common, but the metre will not admit of it. For the middle cf. Hesiod, *Op. et D.* 47, χολωσάμενος φρεσὶν ᾗσιν, *ib.* 53 χολωσάμενος προσέφη, Homer, *Il.* XXI. 136 and *Od.* IX. 480 χολώσατο κηρόθι μᾶλλον. For ἦτορ in this connexion cf. Hesiod. *Theog.* 568 ἐχόλωσε δέ μιν φίλον ἦτορ.

61. χειρὸς ἀγλαὸν . . . κόσμον : a ring, as the stories in Pausanias and Hyginus show.

62. δικών, κ.τ.λ. : 'casting thy body boldly into thy father's halls.' There is a touch of sarcasm in the last words, πατρὸς ἐς δόμους. θράσει is adverbial.

66. ἀναξιβρόντας : cf. ἀναξιμόλπου, VI. 10, and note there as to the derivation. The present example seems to be in favour of the derivation from ἀνάσσω, since it may be doubted whether ἀνάγειν βροντήν is a natural

ΚΛΥΕΔ·ΑΜΕΙΤΡΟΝΕΥΧΑΝΜΕΓΑΣΘΕΝΗ[　]

ΖΕΥΣΫΠΕΡΟΧΟΝΤΕΜΙΝΩΙΦΥΤΕΥΣΕ

ΤΙΜΑΝΦΙΛΩΙΘΕΛΩΝ

70　ΠΑΙΔΙΠΑΝΔΕΡΚΕΑΘΕΜΕΝ·

ΑΣΤΡΑΨΕΘ'·ΟΔΕΘΫΜΑΡΜΕΝΟΝ

ΙΔΩΝΤΕΡΑΣΧΕΙΡΑΣΠΕΤΑΣΣΕ

ΚΛΥΤΑΝΕΣΑΙΘΕΡΑΜΕΝΕΠΤΟΛΕΜΟΣΗΡΩΣ

ΕΙΡΕΝΤΕ·ΘΗΣΕΥΤΑΔΕ·

75　ΜΕΝΒΛΕΠΕΙΣΣΑΦΗΔΙΟΣ

ΔΩΡΑ·ΣΥΔ·ΟΡΝΥ'ΕΣΒΑ

ΡΥΒΡΟΜΟΝΠ[.]ΛΑΓΟΣ·ΚΡΟΝΙ[

Col. 35]　ΔΕΤΟΙΠΑΤΗΡΑΝΑΞΤΕΛΕΙ

ΠΟΣΕΙΔΑΝΫΠΕΡΤΑΤΟΝ

80　ΚΛΕΟΣΧΘΟΝΑΚΑΤΕΥΔΕΝΔΡΟΝ·

ΩΣΕΙΠΕ·ΤΩΙΔ'ΟΥΠΑΛΙΝ

ΘΥΜΟΣΑΝΕΚΑΜΠΤΕΤ'ΑΛΛΕΥ

ΠΑΚΤΩΝΕΠΙΚΡΙΩΝ

ΣΤΑΘΕΙΣΟΡΟΥΣΕ·ΠΟΝΤΙΟΝΤΕΝΙΝ

85　ΔΕΞΑΤΟΘΕΛΗΜΟΝΑΛΣΟΣ·

67. ἄμετρον] **ΑΜΕΙΤΡΟΝ Δ.**　　　72. **ΧΕΙΡΑΣ ΠΕΤΑΣΣΕ Δ**, corr. on metrical grounds.　　　74. σύ] om. **Δ**, inserted by Jebb on metrical grounds.　　　80. ἠΰδενδρον] **ΕΥΔΕΝΔΡΟΝ Δ**, corr. on metrical grounds.

phrase, while 'lord of the thunder' is both a natural and picturesque epithet of Zeus. The MS. αναξιβρεντας is an example of the confusion of ε and ο in this MS.

67. ἄμετρον : 'immoderate,' 'excessive.'

μεγασθενής : cf. the parallel form μεγαλοσθενής, fifteen lines above (l. 52'.

68. Μίνωΐ : see note on l. 8. Here, however, the ι is lengthened in arsis, which is a somewhat strange licence, but not impossible. Jebb compares Homer, *Il.* I. 283 λίσσομ' 'Αχιλλῆϊ μεθέμεν χόλον.

70. πανδερκέα : intransitive, 'visible to all.' Hitherto only known in late writers (as is also the case with θυμάρμενος in the next line), and in active sense, 'all-seeing.'

κλύε δ' ἄμετρον εὐχὰν μεγασθενὴ[ς]   στρ. β'.
Ζεύς, ὑπέροχόν τε Μίνωϊ φύτευσε
τιμάν, φίλῳ θέλων
70 παιδὶ πανδερκέα θέμεν·
ἄστραψέ θ'. ὁ δὲ θυμάρμενον
ἰδὼν τέρας χεῖρε πέτασε
κλυτὰν ἐς αἰθέρα μενεπτόλεμος ἥρως,
εἶρέν τε· Θησεῦ, ⟨σὺ⟩ τάδε
75 μὲν βλέπεις σαφῆ Διὸς
δῶρα· σὺ δ' ὄρνυ' ἐς βα-
ρύβρομον π[έ]λαγος, Κρονί[δας]
δέ τοι πατὴρ ἄναξ τελεῖ
Ποσειδᾶν ὑπέρτατον
80 κλέος χθόνα κατ' ἠΰδενδρον.
ὣς εἶπε· τῷ δ' οὐ πάλιν
θ[υ]μὸς ἀνεκάμπτετ', ἀλλ' εὐπάκτων ἐπ' ἰκρίων
σταθεὶς ὄρουσε, πόντιόν τέ νιν
85 δέξατο θελημὸν ἄλσος.

72. χεῖρε πέτασε : the MS. reading, χεῖρας πέτασσε, is unmetrical, and the emendation here printed seems the simplest which will restore the metrical correspondence. The question is complicated by the fact that the corresponding line in the antistrophe (l. 95) differs from those in the first system (ll. 6, 29). In those the line ends with a spondee, in l. 95 with a dactyl, while l. 72, as here printed, ends with an anapaest.

74. εἶρεν : see note on l. 20.

82. ἀνεκάμπτετο : not elsewhere used in poetry, except late comedy.

84. πόντιον . . . ἄλσος : cf. Aesch. *Pers.* 111 ἐσορᾶν πόντιον ἄλσος.

85. θελημόν : the accentuation in the MS. is oxytone, hence the word is not to be regarded as the neuter of θελήμων, but as that of θελημός, a parallel form to θελεμός and ἐθελημός. Cf. L. and S., s. v. θελεμός, quoting the *Etym. Mag.* and Arcadius on the connexion between these forms. It is to be observed that θελεμός, in the sole case of its occurrence, is applied to water, like θελημός here ; vid. Aesch. *Suppl.* 1026 ποταμοὺς δ' οἳ διὰ χώρας θελεμὸν

ΤΑ . ΕΝΔΕΔΙΟϹΥΙΟϹΕΝΔΟΘΕΝ

ΚΕΑΡ·ΚΕΛΕΥϹΕΤΕΚΑΤΟΫ

[.]ΟΝΙΟΧΕΙΝΕΥΔΑΙΔΑΛΟΝ

<u>ΝΑΑ·ΜΟΙΡΑΔ</u>'ΕΤΕΡΑΝ£ΠΟΡϹΥΝ'ΟΔΟΝ

90 ΙΕΤΟΔ'ωΚΥΠΟ^{μπ}ΔΟΝΔΟΡΥ·ϚΟΕΙ

ΝΕΙΝΒΟΡΕ^ᾰΟΥϹΕΞΟΠΙΘΕΝΠΝΕΟΥϹ'ΑΗΤΑ·

ΤΡΕϹϹΑΝΔ'ΑΘΑΝΑΙωΝ

ΗΙΘΕωΝΓΕΝΟϹΕΠΕΙ

ΗΡωϹΘΟΡΕΝΠΟΝΤΟΝΔΕ·ΚΑ

95 ΤΑΛΕΙΡΙωΝΤ'ΟΜΜΑΤωΝΔΑΚΡΥ

86. ταξεν] ΤΑ . ΕΝ Α, γᾶθεν Jebb.   88. ΙϹΧΕΙΝ Α, corr. on
metrical grounds.   89. ΕΠΟΡϹΥΝ'] so Α; the Ε has been wrongly
cancelled by Α²?   90. ΩΚΥΠΟΔΟΝ Α, corr. Α³.   90, 91.
ϹΟΕΙ | ΝΕΙΝ Α, σθένει δ' ἦν Jebb.   91. ἐξόπιν] ΕΞΟΠΙΘΕΝ Α, corr.
on metrical grounds.   ΒΟΡΕΟΥϹ Α, corr. Α³.   93. πᾶν] om.
Α, inserted on metrical grounds.

πῶμα χέουσιν. Hesychius' gloss on θελεμός is οἰκτρόν, ἥσυχον. The former is
unintelligible, but the latter gives a good sense. Here it may perhaps be
translated ' yielding.'

86. ταξεν : the third letter is wholly lost in the MS., but the beginning τα—
is certain. If it is correct, ταξεν would seem to be the only word, and the
meaning is that Minos was taken aback and scared at Theseus' ready
acceptance of his challenge (cf. Hom. Od. XIX. 264 μηδέ τι θυμὸν τῆκε).
A better sense is, however, given by Professor Jebb's emendation γᾶθεν
(from γήθω = γηθέω) : Minos rejoiced at Theseus having fallen into his trap,
and ordered the ship to proceed without waiting; but fate ordained a different
ending. γᾶθεν, being unfamiliar, may easily have been altered by a scribe
(without much consideration of the sense) into ταθεν, and it is possible that
this is what the MS. actually had. γᾶθεν has only not been inserted in the
text on the ground of a general objection to emending the extant portions of
mutilated words.

88. ἴσχεν : the metre requires this alteration of the MS. ἴσχειν into the
Doric infinitive.

90. ἵετο : intransitive, ' the ship sped swiftly on its way.' For δόρυ = ' ship '
cf. Pind. Pyth. IV. 27, 38, where, however, the substantive is qualified, and
the metaphor explained, by the epithet εἰνάλιον. Aeschylus' use of the term
in the Persae (l. 411) is earlier than either, but there the context makes the

τᾶ[ξ]εν δὲ Διὸς υἱὸς ἔνδοθεν
κέαρ, κέλευσέ τε κατ' οὖ-
[ρ]ον ἴσχεν εὐδαίδαλον
νᾶα· μοῖρα δ' ἑτέραν ἐπόρσυν' ὁδόν.

90 ἵετο δ' ὠκύπομπον δόρυ· * σθένει   ἀντ. β'.
δ' ἦν * Βορεὰς ἐξόπιν πνέουσ' ἀήτα.
τρέσσαν δ' Ἀθαναίων
ἠθέων ⟨πᾶν⟩ γένος, ἐπεὶ
ἥρως θόρεν πόντονδε, κα-
95 τὰ λειρίων τ' ὀμμάτων δάκρυ

metaphor easier; ἐπ' ἄλλην δ' ἄλλος ἴθυνεν δόρυ. Bacchylides is the first to use it as a mere synonym for ναῦς.

σθένει δ' ἦν: the MS. reading (ϹΟΕΙ | ΝΕΙΝ) is plainly corrupt, and it is not easy to find a satisfactory correction. What is wanted is a reading which will (1) make sense, (2) account for the quantity of the last syllable of δορύ, which must be long. These requirements are brilliantly satisfied by Professor Jebb's conjecture, which also has a considerable amount of palaeographical probability. The root of the corruption would be the substitution of Ο for Θ as the second letter, which would lead to the disorganization of the passage. It may be observed that the punctuation of the MS. shows that a new sentence begins after δόρυ, so that a conjunction such as δ' is almost necessary. The periphrasis ἦν πνέουσα is sufficiently common in the tragedies to need no defence.

91. Βορεάς: adjective, as the accent shows. The feminine ἀήτα occurs elsewhere only in Hesiod.

93. The metre is defective, an additional long syllable being required between ἠθέων and γένος. ΠΑΝ may have been accidentally omitted through its resemblance to ΓΕΝ.

94. θόρεν: an exact correspondence with the other strophes could be restored by reading ἔθορε, as proposed by Mr. Purser; but a long syllable may be accepted for the two short.

95. λειρίων: an odd use of the epithet, unless ὀμμάτων is to be taken as meaning 'faces' or 'cheeks.' λείριος is elsewhere applied only to the complexion or voice, but perhaps it is no greater a stretch to apply it to the eye. The metre is irregular, the line ending with a dactyl instead of a spondee or anapaest (cf. note on l. 72). Jebb suggests that the final syllable should be carried on to the next line, χέον being scanned as a mono-syllable. If it may be supposed that the line-division is wrong, and that ll. 95 and 96 may be regarded as a single line, no alteration will be needed,

XÉONBAPEÎANEΠIΔEΓMENOIANAΓKAN·

ΦEPΟNΔEΔEΛΦINECÉNÃΛÌ

ΝAΙÉTÃIMEΓANΘOωC

ΘH[.]EAΠATPOCIΠΠI

100 OYΔΟMON·EMOΛENTEΘEωN

ME . . PON·TOΘIKΛYTAÇÏΔωN

ÉΔEΙCE,NHPEOCOΛ

BÍOYKOPAC·AΠOΓAPAΓΛA

ωNΛAMΠEΓYIωNCEΛAC

105 ωÇTEΠYPOC·AMΦIXAITAIC

ΔEXPYCEOΠΛOKOI

Δ∉ΙNE῏NTOTAINÍÃI·XOPωIΔETEP

ΠONKEAPÝΓPOICINEΠΠOCIN·

ÍΔ`.`NTEΠATPOCAΛOXONΦIΛAN

110 CEMNANBOωΠΪEPATOI

CINAMΦITPITANΔOMOIC·

ÃNINAMΦEBAΛΛENÃΪONAΠOPΦYPEAN·

---

97. After **ΔEΛΦINEΣ Δ** adds **ΕΝ**, against the metre.   102. **ΕΔΕΙΣΕ ΝΗΡΕΟΣ Δ**, the division of words being marked by a comma after **ΕΔΕΙΣΕ**: corr. on metrical grounds.   107. **ΔΕΙΝΕΥΝΤΟ Δ**, corr. Δ²?
108. **ΥΓΡΟΙΣΙΝ ΕΝ ΠΟΣΙΝ Δ**, corr. on metrical grounds.   109. εἶδεν] **ΙΔ . Ν Δ** (qu. **ΙΔΟΝ**?), corr. Δ³.   110. **ΒΟΩΠΙ Δ**, corr. Δ³?
112. **ΑΜΦΕΒΑΛΛΕΝ Δ**, corr. on metrical grounds.

as it will simply be a case of a dactyl in place of a spondee in the middle of a line, or rather (since the metre is paeonian) of a fourth paeon (◡ ◡ ◡ –) in place of a cretic.

97. ἀλιναιέται : a new word, the first reading of which is partly due to Professor Palmer. The scribe of the MS. (or of one of its ancestors) misunderstood it, reading it as two words and inserting ἐν, against the metre ; but the accents on ἀλὶ are a survival from the original correct reading, showing that the acute accent was on one of the following syllables.

99. ἱππίου : rather an inappropriate epithet in this context.

102 The MS. reading is unmetrical. The corresponding lines in the other strophes (ll. 13, 36, 79) all scan ◡ – – ◡ – ◡ –. The restoration printed

χέον βαρεῖαν ἐπιδέγμενοι ἀνάγκαν.
φέρον δὲ δελφῖνες ἁλι-
ναιέται μέγαν θοῶς
Θη[σ]έα πατρὸς ἱππί-
100 ου δόμον. ἔμολέν τε θεῶν
μέγαρον· τόθι κλυτὰς ἰδὼν
ἔδεισεν Νηρῆος ὀλ-
βίου κόρας. ἀπὸ γὰρ ἀγλα-
ῶν λάμπε γυίων σέλας
105 ὥστε πυρός, ἀμφὶ χαίταις
δὲ χρυσεόπλοκοι
δινεῦντο ταινίαι· χορῷ δὲ τέρπον κέαρ ὑγροῖσι ποσσίν.

εἶδέν τε πατρὸς ἄλοχον φίλαν
110 σεμνὰν βοῶπιν ἐρατοῖ-
σιν Ἀμφιτρίταν δόμοις·
ἅ νιν ἀμφέβαλεν †ἀϊόνα† πορφυρέαν,

in the text agrees with this, except that it has a long syllable in the fourth place. This variation is admissible, but one would like to find a form Νερῆος = Νηρέος. Of this, however, there is no evidence.

106. χρυσεόπλοκοι: an addition to the scanty list of compounds of πλέκω in which the verbal part is passive; 'fillets of plaited gold.'

108. ὑγροῖσι: 'supple.' No doubt their feet were also ὑγροί in the literal sense, but that cannot be what is meant here.

110. The metre is irregular, σεμνάν standing where there should be one long syllable or two short ones. Jebb conjectures σεμνοπρόσωπον (the corruption beginning with the loss of the second σ), or possibly σεμνοβοῶπιν, the first three syllables being scanned as a cyclic dactyl.

112. ἀϊόνα: the MS. is quite clear, but the reading is corrupt, suiting neither sense nor metre. The verb ἀμφιβάλλω and the epithet πορφυρέαν point to a word denoting a garment of some kind; on the other hand the passages in Pausanias and Hyginus mention only the ring of Minos (to which no allusion is made here) and a wreath, the ἀμεμφὴς πλόκος of l. 114. One would therefore have expected to find the ring mentioned in this line, but πορφυρέαν seems inconsistent with this, and the recovery of the

ΚΟΜΑ[. .]ΙΤ'ΕΠΕΘΗΚΕΝΟΥΛΑΙC

Col. 36]　ΑΜΕΜΦΕΑΠΛΟΚΟΝ·

115　ΤΟΝΠΟΤΕΘΙΕΝΓΑΜΩΙ

ΔΩΚΕΔΟΛΙ̊CΑΦΡΟΔΙΤΑΡΟΔΟΙCΕΡΕΜΝΟΝ·

ΑΠΙCΤΟΝΟΤΙΔΑΙΜΟΝΕC

ΘΕΛΩCΙΝΟΥΔΕΝΦΡΕΝΟΑ̊ΡΑ̈ΙCΒΡΟΤΟΙC·

ᾸΑΑΠΑΡΑΛΕΠΤΟ̂ΠΡΥΜΝΟΝΦΑΝΗ·ΦΕΥ

120　Ο̈ΙΑΙCΙΝΕΝΦ̊ΟΝΤΙ∅CΙΚΝΩ̈CΙΟΝ

ΕCΧΑCΕΝCΤΡΑΤᾹΓΕΤΑΝΕΠΕΙ

ΜΟΛ·ΑΔΙΑΝΤΟCΕΞΑ̈ΛΟC

ΘΑΥΜΑΠΑΝΤΕCCΙ·ΛΑΜ

ΠΕΔ·ΑΜΦΙΓΥΟΙCΘΕΩΝΔΩ̂Ρ·ΑΓΛΟ

125　ΘΡΟΝΟΙΤΕΚΟΥΡΑΙCΥΝΕΥ

ΘΥΜΙΑ̈ΙΝΕΟΚΤΙΤΩΙ

ΩΛΟΛΥΞΑΝ·Ε

ΚΛΑΓΕΝΔΕΠΟΝΤΟC·ΗϊΘΕΟΙΔ'ΕΓΓΥΘΕΝ

ΝΕΟΙΠΑΙΑ̈ΝΙΞΑΝΕΡΑΤΑ̂ΙΟΠΙ

130　ΔΑΛΙΕΧΟΡΟΙCΙΚΗϊΩΝ

---

116. **ΔΟΛΙΣ Δ**, corr. **Δ²**?　　118. λῶσιν] **ΘΕΛΩΣΙΝ Δ**, against metre;
λῶσιν Palmer.　　119. νᾶα] **ΑΑΑ Δ**, corr. **Δ²**?　　120. φροντίσι]
ΦΟΝΤΙΣΣΙ Δ, corr. **Δ¹**?　　124. γυίοις] **ΓΥΟΙΣ Δ**.　ἀγλαό-] ΑΓΛΟ Δ.

ring must be taken for granted. No satisfactory solution of the difficulty
has yet presented itself. Professor Jebb suggests εἱανόν, which is tolerably
near the MS., but involves the alteration of πορφυρέαν to πορφύρεον : or
possibly ἀμβολάν, which a moderate amount of mutilation in a papyrus MS.
might convert into αιονα.

115. *οἱ* : to Amphitrite, cf. the passage in Hyginus.

117. ἄπιστον, κ.τ.λ.: 'to sensible men nothing that the gods will is
incredible'; the same sentiment as in III. 57, and Pind. *Pyth.* X. 48.

118. λῶσιν : the MS. θέλωσιν is unmetrical and the subjunctive irregular.
Professor Palmer's restoration of the Doric form gives sense and metre
and a simple palaeographical explanation of the corruption.

κόμα[ισ]ί τ᾽ ἐπέθηκεν οὔλαις   ἐπ. β΄.
ἀμεμφέα πλόκον,
115 τόν ποτέ οἱ ἐν γάμῳ
δῶκε δόλιος ᾿Αφροδίτα ῥόδοις ἐρεμνόν.
ἄπιστον ὅ τι δαίμονες
λῶσιν οὐδὲν φρενοάραις βροτοῖς.

νᾶα παρὰ λεπτόπρυμνον φάνη.   φεῦ,
120 οἴαισιν ἐν φροντίσι Κνώσιον
ἔσχασεν στραταγέταν, ἐπεὶ
μόλ᾽ ἀδίαντος ἐξ ἁλός,
θαῦμα πάντεσσι· λάμ-
πε δ᾽ ἀμφὶ γυίοις θεῶν δῶρ᾽, ἀγλαό-
125 θρονοί τε κοῦραι σὺν εὐθυμίᾳ νεοκτίτῳ
ὠλόλυξαν· ἔ-
κλαγεν δὲ πόντος· ἤθεοι δ᾽ ἐγγύθεν
νέοι παιάνιξαν ἐρατᾷ ὀπί.
130 Δάλιε, χοροῖσι Κηΐων

φρενοάραις :=φρενήρεσι, but the form is strange. The mark of a short
syllable over the first α is evidently added in order to warn the reader
against a natural mistake, while the first declension form (of which there
is no other extant example) is in accordance with the predilection shown by
Bacchylides in several other instances, e. g. ἀελλοδρόμας. Jebb observes
that the hiatus in the compound follows the analogy of words in which the
second element is a word which once had the digamma (e. g. μεγιστοάνασσα,
ὀρθοεπής).

119. νᾶα παρὰ λεπτόπρυμνον φάνη : this is the moment illustrated by the
first scene on the François vase : see introductory note above (p. 157).

121. ἔσχασεν : the reappearance of Theseus pricked the bubble of Minos'
self-gratulation. (This further tends to confirm γᾶθεν in l. 86.)

129. παιάνιξαν : the diphthong in the first syllable, coming before a vowel,
is allowably scanned short.

130-132. These lines, having nothing to do with the myth that occupies
all the rest of the poem, are evidently introduced pro forma, to satisfy

ΦΡΕΝΑΪΑΝΘΕΙϹ
ΌΠΑΖΕΘΕΌΠΟΜΠΟΝΕϹΘΛΩΝΤΥΧΑΝ

XVIII.

Θησευς

$$1-15 = 16-30 = 31-45 = 46-60$$

XVIII. *Title* by A³.

the requirements of the occasion for which the poem was composed. The references to Apollo and to the χοροὶ Κηΐων show that it is a hymn to Apollo, sung by a Cean chorus; and a hymn to Apollo would probably be classed as a Paean. The verb παιάνιξαν, with which the myth concludes, helps the transition.

φρένα ἰανθείς,
ὅπαζε θεόπομπον ἐσθλῶν τυχάν.

XVIII.

ΘΗΣΕΥΣ.

THE second Theseus-poem is peculiar, not only among the writings of Bacchylides, but in all extant Greek literature, in respect of its form. It is a dramatic lyric in the strictest sense of the term, being lyric in structure and dramatic in expression. It is a dialogue between two speakers, the divisions of the speeches corresponding with those of the strophes, so that each interlocutor speaks a strophe in turn. The substance of the dialogue has been described in the Introduction. With regard to the class of poem to which it should be assigned, it is impossible to be certain. There is no reference to Apollo or Dionysus, to justify its denomination as a Paean or Dithyramb. It may be a Hymn, which is a sufficiently general term to cover such a lyric exaltation of a hero as this is. It has also been suggested by Mr. A. van Branteghem that it may be an example of the compositions which are classed in the extant list of Pindar's works as τραγικὰ δράματα. It is not to be supposed that Pindar wrote tragedies in the ordinary sense of the term, and the name, which has never been satisfactorily explained, may refer to such dramatic lyrics as the present. It is impossible to verify this conjecture, but it is worth considering. Whatever it is, it is clear that the poem was written for performance at Athens, or on some occasion (such as the Isthmian games) when Athenians were predominant. In preservation it is the most perfect in the collection, only two letters having to be supplied, and those admitting of certain restoration. The metre is logaoedic.

131. φρένα ἰανθείς: the hiatus is strong, ἰαίνω not having a digamma, unless it is to be supposed that Bacchylides followed the analogy of ἰόπλοκος, Ἰόλαος, κ.τ.λ. Jebb proposes to read φρένας.

132. ὅπαζε, κ.τ.λ.: 'grant a god-sent fortune of good things.' θεόπομπον is appropriate in connexion with the literal meaning of ὅπαζε, 'send us a companion.'

ΒΑCΙΛΕΥΤΑΝΙΕΡΑΝΑΘΑΝΑΝ

ΤΩΝΑΒΡΟΒΙΚΩΝΑΝΑΞΙΕΡΩΝΩΝ·

ΤΙΝΕΟΝΕΚΛΑΓΕΧΑΛΚΟΔΩΔΩΝ

ΣΑΛΠΙΓΞΠΟΛΕΜΗΙΑΝΑΟΙΔΑΝ·

5 ΗΤΙΣΑΜΕΤΕΡΑΣΧΘΟΝΟΣ

ΔΥΣΜΕΝΗΣΟΡΡΙ·ΑΜΦΙΒΑΛΛΕΙ

ΣΤΡΑΤΑΓΕΤΑΣΑΝΗΡ·

ΗΛΗΣΤΑΙΚΑΚΟΜΑΧΑΝΟΙ

ΠΟΙΜΕΝΩΝΔ·ΕΚΑΤΙΜΗΛΩΝ

10 ΣΕΥΟΝΤ·ΑΓΕΛΑΣΒΙΑΙ

ΗΤΙΤΟΙΚΡΑΔΙΑΝΑΜΥΣΣΕΙ·

ΦΘΕΓΓΟΥΔΟΚΕΩΓΑΡΕΙΤΙΝΙΒΡΟΤΩΝ

ΑΛΚΙΜΟΥΕΠΙΚΟΥΡΙΑΝ

ΚΑΙΤΙΝΕΜΜΕΝΑΙΝΕΩΝ

15 ΩΠΑΝΔΙΟΝΟΣΥΙΕΚΑΙΚΡΕΟΥΣΑΣ

. . ΟΝΗΛΘΕΔΟΛΙΧΑΝΑΜΕΙΨΑΣ

2. ΑΒΡΟΒΙΚΩΝ . . . ΙΕΡΩΝΩΝ Α, corr. Α³?   3. ΤΙ Α, ΤΙΣ Α³. ΧΑΛΚΟΔΩΔΩΝ Α, corr. Α³?   6. ΟΡΡΙ' Α, corr.Α¹?   9. ἀέκατι] Δ' ΕΚΑΤΙ Α, corr. Palmer, van Branteghem.   10. ΣΕΥΟΝΤΙ Α, corr. Α¹.   13. ΑΛΚΙΜΟΥ Α, corr. Α³.   16. The line is added in a different hand, the same as has added the termination of XI. 23. νέον Palmer.

1–15. Of the two interlocutors, one is Aegeus, king of Athens, as the first line of the poem shows. The other is nowhere named or described. It is clear, however, that the tone of ll. 1–15, 31–45, is not that of an attendant or courtier, but of some one who questions Aegeus as an equal, and to whose queries he replies in detail. It therefore seems probable that this first speaker is Medea, at that time Aegeus' queen, who had consequently good reason to be apprehensive as to the arrival of formidable strangers, and who, according to the legends, did actually try to destroy Theseus on his arrival. This also gives an additional point to ἀμετέρας in l. 5.

2. τῶν ἀβροβίων ἄναξ Ἰώνων: quoted by various commentators on Her-

βασιλεῦ τᾶν ἱερᾶν Ἀθανᾶν,   στρ. α΄.

τῶν ἀβροβίων ἄναξ Ἰώνων,

τί νέον ἔκλαγε χαλκοκώδων

σάλπιγξ πολεμηΐαν ἀοιδάν;

5 ἦ τις ἁμετέρας χθονὸς

δυσμενὴς ὄρι᾽ ἀμφιβάλλει

στραταγέτας ἀνήρ;

ἦ λησταὶ κακομάχανοι

ποιμένων ἀέκατι μήλων

10 σεύοντ᾽ ἀγέλας βίᾳ;

ἦ τί τοι κραδίαν ἀμύσσει;

φθέγγου· δοκέω γὰρ εἴ τινι βροτῶν

ἀλκίμων ἐπικουρίαν

καὶ τὶν ἔμμεναι νέων,

15 ὦ Πανδίονος υἱὲ καὶ Κρεούσας.

[νέ]ον ἦλθεν δολιχὰν ἀμείψας   στρ. β΄.

mogenes περὶ Ἰδεῶν, Book I. (Walz, *Rhett. Graec.* V. 493, VI. 241, VII. 982). The text here confirms the judgement of Wilamowitz-Moellendorff (*Isyllos*, p. 143, *Phil. Unters.* part 9), in preferring the reading given by an anonymous scholiast and by Planudes (τῶν ἀβροβίων Ἰώνων ἄναξ, which he rightly emends by transposing the last two words) to that of Johannes Siceliota (ἀβρότητι ξυνέασιν Ἴωνες βασιλῆες), which Bergk (frag. 42) retains with only the change of Ἴωνες into Ἰώνων.

3. τί: the metre confirms the original reading of the MS., as against the corrector's τίς.

6. ἀμφιβάλλει: 'besets' or 'encompasses.'

9. ἀέκατι: metre and sense alike require the correction of the MS. δ᾽ ἕκατι.

10. σεύοντ᾽: for the Aeolic third person plural, cf. V. 22 πτάσσοντι, XIII. 198 καρύσσοντι.

15. Πανδίονος υἱὲ καὶ Κρεούσας: Aegeus was son of Pandion in the literal sense, but only a descendant of Creusa, the daughter of Erechtheus, wife of Xuthus, and mother of Ion. His actual mother was Pelia (Apollod. *Bibl.* III. 15. 5).

16-30. The answer of Aegeus to Medea's inquiries.

N

178   *ΒΑΚΧΥΛΙΔΗΣ*   [XVIII. 17–

Col. 37]   ΚᾹΡΥΞΠΟCΙΝΪCΘΜΙΑΝΚΕΛΕΥΘΟΝ·

           ΑΦΑΤΑΔ'ΕΡΓΑΛΕΓΕΙ͵ΚΡΑΤΑΙΟΥ

           ΦΩΤΟC·ΤΟΝΥΠΕΡΒΙΟΝΤ'ΕΠΕΦΝΕΝ

20   CΙΝΙΝΟ̈CΪCΧΥΪΦΕΡΤΑΤΟC

           ΘΝΑΤΩΝΗΝΚΡΟΝΙΔΑΛΥΤΑΙΟΥ

           CΕΙϹΊΧΘΟΝΟCΤΕΚΟC·

           CῩΝΤ'ΑΝΔΡΟΚΤΟΝΟΝΕΝΝΑΠΑΙϹ

           ΚΡΕΜΥΩ͂ΝΟCΑΤΆCΘΑΛΟΝΤΕ

25   CΚΙΡΩΝΑΚΑΤΕΚΤΑΝΕΝ·

           ΤΑΝΤΕΚΕΡΚΥ°ΝΟCΠΑΛΑΙCΤΡΑΝ

           ΕCΧΕΝ·ΠΟΛΥΠΉΜΟΝΟCΤΕΚΑΡΤΕΡΑΝ

           CΦΥΡΑΝΕΞΈΒΑΛΛΕΝΠΡΟΚΟ

           ΠΤΑCΑΡΕΙΟΝΟCΤΥΧΩΝ

30 <u>ΦΩΤΟC·ΤΑΥΤΑΔΕΔΟΙΧ'ΟΠΑΙΤΕΛΕΙΤΑΙ·</u>

---

18. ΛΕΓΕΙΝ Δ, corr. Δ¹.   24. ΚΡΕΜΥΩΝΟΣ Δ, corr. on metrical grounds.   26. ΚΕΡΚΥΝΟΣ Δ, corr. Δ³.   28. ΕΞΕΒΑΛΛΕΝ Δ, corr. on metrical grounds.

21. Κρονίδα : Poseidon, not Zeus, as the epithet σεισίχθονος shows. Sinis is called the son of Polypemon in Apollodorus (*Bibl.* III. 16. 2), but the son of Poseidon in Hyginus (*Fab.* 38).

Λυταίου : epithet of Poseidon, διὰ τὸ λῦσαι τὰ Τέμπη Ποσειδῶνα καὶ σκεδάσαι τὸ ἀπὸ τοῦ κατακλυσμοῦ ὕδωρ. This is the explanation given by Steph. Byz. of Λυταί as the name of a place in Thessaly, but it applies equally well to the epithet, which does not occur elsewhere. Hesychius gives Λυταίη as a synonym for Thessaly.

24. Κρεμμυῶνος : an alternative form of Κρομμυών (cf. Pape-Benseler s.v.). The latter is more likely to be the original form, being derived from κρόμυον, but the variant is so well established that it is not permissible to alter the text.

26. παλαίστραν ἔσχεν : 'he put an end to the wrestling-school of Cercyon,' who compelled all comers to wrestle with him. The spot where Cercyon is said to have wrestled with his victims was called παλαίστρα Κερκυόνος in the time of Pausanias (Paus. I. 39. 3). It was near Eleusis, on the road between Eleusis and Megara.

27–30. The explanation of this passage, setting aside any alteration of

κᾶρυξ ποσὶν Ἰσθμίαν κελευθον·
ἄφατα δ' ἔργα λέγει κραταιοῦ
φωτός. τὸν ὑπέρβιόν τ' ἔπεφνεν
20 Σίνιν, ὃς ἰσχύι φέρτατος
θνατῶν ἦν, Κρονίδα Λυταίου
σεισίχθονος τέκος.
σὺν τ' ἀνδροκτόνον ἐν νάπαις
Κρεμμυῶνος, ἀτάσθαλόν τε
25 Σκίρωνα κατέκτανεν.

τάν τε Κερκυόνος παλαίστραν
ἔσχεν· Πολυπήμονός τε καρτερὰν
σφῦραν ἐξέβαλεν Προκό-
πτας, ἀρείονος τυχὼν
30 φωτός. ταῦτα δέδοιχ' ὅπᾳ τελεῖται.

the text, is far from clear. In the ordinary form of the legend, only one
person is mentioned, namely Polypemon, surnamed Procrustes (Paus. I.
38. 5); neither in literature nor in any of the various representations of
the Theseus-legend in art (cf., for example, *Mus. Ital. d' Antich. class.* III. 1)
is more than one actor introduced into the scene. Here, however, there
seem to be two, Procoptes (a name formed in exactly the same way as
Προκρούστης) and Polypemon, the former being apparently the servant of
the latter. The passage would then be translated, 'and Procoptes dropped
the mighty mallet of Polypemon, meeting a man stronger than himself.'
The above explanation is that proposed by Professor Palmer. The difficulty
of two persons being mentioned instead of one is, however, a real one,
especially as no mention is made of the fate of the one who was, *ex hypothesi,*
the principal.   Two other alternatives are possible: (1) that Procoptes
is represented as the son of Polypemon, as Sinis is in some accounts (see
note on l. 21), or as his successor in these malpractices; (2) Professor
Jebb's interpretation, taking πολυπήμονος as an adjective agreeing with φωτός,
and supposing that a play upon words is intended, 'Procoptes dropped his
mallet, having met his own πολυπήμων, or woe-bringer.'   Such a play upon
words would be quite in accordance with Greek usage, but the order of the
words seems against it.

28. σφῦραν: the mallet or hammer with which Procrustes beat out his
victims, if they were too short to fit his bed. Cf. Hyginus, *Fab.* 38 (the
reference is due to Mr. L. C. Purser), 'incudibus suppositis extendebat.'

ΤΙΝΑΔ˙ΕΜΜΕΝΠΟΘΕΝΑΝΔΡΑΤΟΥΤΟΝ

ΛΕΓΕΙ˙ΤΙΝΑΤΕΣΤΟΛΑΝΕΧΟΝΤΑ˙

ΠΟΤΕΡΑΣΥΝΠΟΛΕΜΗΊΟΙΣΟ

ΠΛΟΙΣΙΣΤΡΑΤ˙ΑΝΑΓΟΝΤΑΠΟΛΛΑΝ˙

35 ΗΜΟΥΝΟΝΣΥΝΟΠΛΟΙΣΙΝ

ΣΤΙΧΕΙΝΕΜΠΟΡΟΝΌΙ˙ΑΛΑΤΑΝ

ΕΠΑΛΛΟΔΑΜΊΑΝ

ΪΣΧΥΡΟΝΤΕΚΑΙΑΛΚΙΜΟΝ

ὨΔΕΚΑΙΘΡΑΣΥΝ˙ΟΣΤΟΥΤῺΝ

40 ΑΝΔΡῺΝΚΑΡΤΕΡΟΝΣΘΕΝΟΣ

ΕΧΕΝΗΘΕΟΣΑΥΤΟΝΟΡΜᾹῙ

ΔΙΚΑΣΑΔΊΚΟΙΣΙΝΌΦΡΑΜΉΣΕΤΑΙ

ΟΥΓΑΡΡΑΙΔΙΟΝΑῚΕΝΕΡ

ΔΟΝΤΑΜΗΝΤΥΧΕῖΝΚΑΚῺΙ˙

45 ΠΑΝΤ˙ΕΝΤῺΙΔΟΛΙΧῺΙΧΡΟΝῺΙΤΕΛΕΙΤΑΙ˙

ΔΥΟΟΙΦῺΤΕΜΟΝΟΥΣΑΜΑΡΤΕῖΝ

34. ΣΤΡΑΤΑΝ Α, corr. Α¹.   **35.** Η ΜΟΥΝΟΝ ΣΥΝ ΟΠΛΟΙΣΙΝ Α, corr. on grounds of metre and sense.   **36.** στείχειν] ΣΤΙΧΕΙΝ Α. **39.** ὅστε] ΟΣ Α, corr. Palmer.   **40.** ΚΑΡΤΕΡΟΝ Α, corr. on metrical grounds.   **41.** ΕΧΕΝ Α, corr. Α³?   **46.** ὁμαρτεῖν] ΑΜΑΡΤΕΙΝ Α.

31–45. Medea renews her inquiries, in a way which implies anxiety and apprehension.

35. The MS. reading of this line, ἢ μοῦνον σὺν ὅπλοισιν, is unmetrical, beginning with a spondee instead of a trochee, and being a syllable short at the end. These defects might be altered simply by reading ἢ μόνον σὺν ὅπλοισί νιν, but there is a further difficulty as to the sense, σὺν ὅπλοισι being exceedingly weak after σὺν πολεμηΐοις ὅπλοισι just above, and also inconsistent with the character of an ἔμπορος ἀλάτας. The restoration given in the text satisfies the demands of sense, with only a slight amount of departure from the MS. ; but it is not quite convincing. It should be added that Professor Palmer prefers to retain the MS. reading (with the slight correction required by the metre), explaining that even a travelling merchant would carry arms in a country infested by robbers ; but even on this view the repetition of σὺν ὅπλοισιν is very weak.

τίνα δ' ἔμμεν πόθεν ἄνδρα τοῦτον   στρ. γ΄.
λέγει; τίνα τε στολὰν ἔχοντα;
πότερα σὺν πολεμηΐοις ὅ-
πλοισι στρατιὰν ἄγοντα πολλάν,
35 ἢ μόνον *τ' ἄνοπλόν τέ νιν*
στείχειν, ἔμπορον οἶ' ἀλάταν,
ἐπ' ἀλλοδαμίαν,
ἰσχυρόν τε καὶ ἄλκιμον
ὧδε καὶ θρασύν, ὅστε τούτων
40 ἀνδρῶν κρατερὸν σθένος

ἔσχεν· ἢ θεὸς αὐτὸν ὁρμᾷ,
δίκας ἀδίκοισιν ὄφρα μήσεται.
οὐ γὰρ ῥᾴδιον αἰὲν ἔρ-
δοντα μὴ 'ντυχεῖν κακῷ.
45 πάντ' ἐν τῷ δολιχῷ χρόνῳ τελεῖται.
δύο οἱ φῶτε μόνους ὁμαρτεῖν   στρ. δ΄.

---

39. ὅστε τούτων: so Palmer, for the unmetrical ὃς τούτων of the MS. ὃς τοιούτων, the first syllable being scanned short, is also possible. Either corruption would be easily explicable on palaeographical grounds; but perhaps ὅστε would be the most likely to be corrupted, the τε being liable to be misunderstood.

43, 44. The reason why Theseus' continued successes seem to imply divine protection.

45. τελεῖται: the echo of the τελεῖται with which Aegeus' speech ended (l. 30) is very noticeable. Aegeus says apprehensively, 'I fear how this may end'; Medea answers in effect, 'Time will show,' perhaps with something of a sinister meaning.

46. ὁμαρτεῖν: as Professor Palmer has pointed out, it is possible that the MS. ἁμαρτεῖν is right, ἅμα and ὁμοῦ being from the same root. It is moreover supported by the existence of the adverb ἁμαρτῇ. No doubt the reason why ὁμαρτεῖν was the form in normal use is the fear of confusion with the aorist of ἁμαρτάνω, but it does not follow that this objection weighed with Bacchylides. On the other hand ὁμαρτεῖν was not unlikely to be corrupted in transcription into the more familiar word ἁμαρτεῖν, without reference to the sense; and this seems the more probable explanation.

ΛΕΓΕΙΠΕΡΙΦΑΙΔΙΜΟΙΣΙΔ'ΩΜΟΙΣ

ΞΙΦΟΣΕΧΕΙΝ·

ΞΕΣΤΟΥΣΔΕΔΥ'ΕΝΧΕΡΕΣΣ'ΑΚΟΝΤΑΣ

55 *στιλβειναπολαμνιαν
φοινισσανφλογαπαιδαδ'εμεν
πρωθηβον· αρηϊωνδ'αθυρματων

Col. 38] 50 ΚΗΥΤΥΚΤΟΝΚΥΝΕΑΝΛΑΚΑΙ

ΝΑΝΚΡΑΤΟΣΥΠΕΡΠΥΡΣΟΧΑΙΤΟΥ·

ΧΙΤΩΝΑΠΟΡΦΥΡΕΟΝ

ΣΤΕΡΝΟΙΣΙΤ'ΑΜΦΙΚΑΙΟΥΛΙΟΝ

ΘΕΣΣΑΛΑΝΧΛΑΜΥΔ'·ΟΜΜΑΤΩΝΔΕ

*

ΜΕΜΝΑΣΘΑΙΠΟΛΕΜΟΥΤΕΚΑΙ

ΧΑΛΚΕΝΚΤΥΠΟΥΜΑΧΑΣ

60 ΔΙΖΗΣΘΑΙΔΕΦΙΛΑΓΛΑΟΥΣΑΘΑΝΑΣ

50. ΚΗΥΤΥΚΤΟΝ A, corr. on metrical grounds.   53. ΣΤΕΡΝΟΙΣ A (rightly), ΣΤΕΡΝΟΙΣΙ A¹.   55-57. Om. A, added in upper margin by A³.   56. ΕΜΕΝ A³, corr. on metrical grounds. 59. ΧΑΛΚΕΝΚΤΥΠΟΥ A, corr. A³.

47. λέγει: an echo of the λέγει in l. 32, in the corresponding place in the third strophe.

48. The papyrus is perfect here, and the loss of the latter part of this line must go back to an earlier stage in the transmission of the text. The missing words must either have contained a description of the sword, or named some other weapon which Theseus bore on his shoulders; e. g., since the club was Theseus' characteristic weapon, κορύναν τε πυκνάν.

51. The metre of this line is noticeable, having (after the initial spondee) an anapaest instead of a dactyl; but it does not seem possible to emend the reading. περί for ὑπέρ would restore the metre, but that involves the use of περί with the genitive in the local sense proper to the dative.

λέγει, περὶ φαιδίμοισι δ' ὤμοις
ξίφος ἔχειν < ◡ ◡ – ◡ – – >,
ξεστοὺς δὲ δύ' ἐν χέρεσσ' ἄκοντας

50 κηΰτυκον κυνέαν Λάκαι-
ναν κρατὸς ὕπερ πυρσοχαίτου,
χιτῶνα πορφύρεον
στέρνοις τ' ἄμφι καὶ οὔλιον
Θεσσαλὰν χλαμύδ'· ὀμμάτων δὲ
55 στίλβειν ἄπο Λαμνίαν
φοίνισσαν φλόγα· παῖδα δ' ἔμμεν
πρώθηβον, Ἀρηΐων δ' ἀθυρμάτων
μεμνᾶσθαι πολέμου τε καὶ

χαλκεοκτύπου μάχας,
60 δίζησθαι δὲ φιλαγλάους Ἀθάνας.

53. The position of τε is exceptionally late, as it belongs to the whole clause, not to στέρνοις.

οὔλιον : = οὖλον, 'woolly.' The metre shows that the form is right, and there can be no question as to the sense.

55. Λαμνίαν : 'volcanic.' Λήμνιον βλέπειν is given as a proverbial phrase in Hesychius and elsewhere.

56. φοίνισσαν : the corresponding lines in the other strophes begin with a trochee, and it would no doubt be possible to read φοινίαν, but a spondee is admissible, and φοίνισσαν is much superior in sense. Cf. Pind. *Pyth.* I. 24· φοίνισσα κυλινδομένα φλόξ, describing a literal, as this does a metaphorical, volcanic flame.

57. Ἀρηΐων ἀθυρμάτων : of the joys of war, but the literal sense of the adjective, 'the delight of Ares,' is retained, as in Ἀπολλώνιον ἄθυρμα (Pind. *Pyth.* V. 23), Ἀφροδίσιον ἄθυρμα (Pseud-Anacreon, 53), ἀθύρμασι Μουσᾶν (Bacchyl. frag. 71, Bergk 48).

XIX.

Ἰω Ἀθηναίοισι

STROPHE.

```
   ‿ – ‿ – ‿ – ‿ – ‿
   – ‿ ‿ – ‿ ‿ –
   ‿ – ‿ ‿ – ‿ ‿ – ⹀
   – ‿ – ‿ – ⸱
 5 ‿ – ‿ ‿ – ‿ –
   ‿ – ‿ ‿ – ‿ ‿
   ‿ – ‿ – ‿ – –
   – ‿ ‿ – ‿ ‿ –
   – ‿ ‿ – ‿ – ‿ – ‿
10 – ‿ – ‿ – –
   – – ‿ ‿ – ‿ – ‿ – –
   ‿ – ‿ – ‿ – ‿ ⹂
   ‿ – ‿ ‿ – ‿ ‿ – ‿
   – ‿ – ‿ – ‿ –
15 – ‿ – ‿ ‿ – ‿ – ‿ – ‿
   – ‿ – ‿ – –
   – – ‿ ‿ – ‿ – ‿ – ‿ ‿ ‿
   – ‿ – ‿ ‿ – ‿ – ‿ –
```

EPODE.

```
‿ – ‿ –
```

The rest is mutilated.

1—18 = 19—36 : 37—51

ΠΑΡΕΣΤΙΜΥΡΙΑΚΕΛΕΥΘΟϹ

ΑΜΒΡΟϹΙΩΝΜΕΛΕΩΝ

ὈϹΑΝΠΑΡΑΠΕΙΕΡΙΔΩΝΛΑ

ΧΗΙϹΙΔΩΡΑΜΟΥϹᾶΝ

XIX. *Title* by A².   3. Πιερίδων] ΠΕΙΕΡΙΔΩΝ Α.

1. μυρία κέλευθος : cf. V. 31, and note.
3. ὃς ἄν, κ.τ.λ. : the antecedent is not expressed ; ' manifold is the

XIX.

ΙΩ

Ἀθηναίοισι.

THE following poem is expressly stated in the title to have been written for the Athenians, and it begins with a laudation of Athens and the poet's exhortation of his own genius to rise to the occasion, and justify the gifts bestowed by the Muses. The occasion on which it was to be performed is neither stated nor implied; nor does the subject of the poem throw any light upon it. As is generally the case with Bacchylides, the myth is introduced abruptly, without any attempt to connect it with the occasion of the poem or the persons to whom it is addressed. Io had no special connexion with Athens, nor does Bacchylides try to establish one. By what appears to be an equally abrupt transition at the end, the poet introduces a reference to Thebes, concluding with a mention of the birth of Dionysus from Semele. This last feature suggests that the poem should be classed as a Dithyramb, there being no apparent reason for the introduction of Dionysus, unless it were to satisfy the traditional requirements of this class of composition.

The poem is written in very short lines, and consists of only a single metrical system. Half of it is preserved intact in the MS., but the concluding half comes within the final column of the MS. in its present condition, which has lost the ends of all its lines. The metre is logaoedic.

πάρεστι μυρία κέλευθος   στρ.

ἀμβροσίων μελέων,

ὃς ἂν παρὰ Πιερίδων λά-

χῃσι δῶρα Μουσᾶν,

lyric songs *for him* who has received the Muses' gifts, and *for whom* the Graces shower honour on his hymns.' The subject changes in l. 5, but the subjunctive βάλωσιν shows that the construction is carried on, ᾧ ἄν being understood from ὃς ἄν above. τε, of course, in l. 5 couples the clause to its predecessor, not ἰοβλέφαροι to φερεστέφανοι.

5 ΪΟΒΛΕΦΑΡΌΙΤΕΚΑΙ

ΦΕΡΕΣΤΕΦΑΝΟΙΧΑΡΙΤΕC

ΒΆΛΩCΙΝΑΜΦΙΤΙΜΑΝ

ΥΜΝΟΙCΙΝ·ΥΦΑΙΝΕΝΥΝΕΝ

ΤΑΙCΠΟΛΥΗΡΆΤΟΙCΤΙΚΑΊΝΟΝ
^ε

10 ΟΛΒΪΑΙCΑΘΑΝΑΙC

ΕΥΆΙΝΕΤΕΚΗΪΑΜΈΡΙΜΝΑ·

ΠΡΕΠΕΙCΕΦΕΡΤΑΤΑΝΊΜΕΝ

ΟΔΟΝΠΑΡΑΚΑΛΛΙΟΠΑCΛΑ

ΧΟΊCΑΝΕΞΟΧΟΝΓΕΡΑC·

15 ΤΙΗΝΑΡΓΟCΟΘ'ΙΠΠΈΙΟΝΛΙΠΟΥCΑ

ΦΕΥΓΕΧΡΥCΈΑΒΟΥC

ΕΥΡΥCΘΕΝΕΟCΦΡΑΔΑΪCΙΦΕΡΤΆΤΟΥΔΙΟC

ΪΝΑΧΟΥΡΟΔΟΔΆΚΤΥΛΟCΚΟΡΑ·

ΌΤ'ΑΡΓΟΝΟΜΜΑCΙΒΛΕΠΟΝΤΑ

20 ΠΆΝΤΟΘΕΝΑΚΑΜΆΤΟΙC

ΜΕΓΙCΤΟΆΝΑCCΑΚΕΛΕΥCΕΝ

9. κλεινόν] **KAINON** Α, corr. Α³.   15. δθ'] **OT** Α, corr. Α³.
ΪΠΠΕΙΟΝ Α, corr. Α³?

7. βάλωσιν ἀμφι : tmesis, for ἀμφιβάλωσιν.   It might be possible to take ἀμφί with ὕμνοισιν, but the interposition of a word which is neither an epithet nor in an epithetal relation (such as a genitive or an adverb) would be unprecedented, and βάλλειν τιμάν is a less natural expression than ἀμφιβάλλειν τιμάν.   Pindar has many examples of tmesis, but in all the preposition precedes the verb.

9. κλεινόν : the original reading of the MS. is καινόν, and it is not clear that it is wrong.   After saying that the ways of song are manifold, the poet might proceed to call on his Muse to sing a new song, as well as a brilliant one.   κλεινόν, on the other hand, is in accordance with φερτάταν and ἔξοχον in ll. 12 and 14.

11. εὐαίνετε : a ἅπαξ λεγόμενον, =εὐαίνητε, which is similarly a ἅπαξ λεγόμενον in Pindar (Pyth. IV. 177).

μέριμνα : so Pindar calls his song a πόνος, Nem. III. 12.   Pindar also uses μέριμνα of the care taken by athletes in the preparation for their contests ; here it is of the poet's care in the preparation of his poems.

5 ἰοβλέφαροί τε καὶ
  φερεστέφανοι Χάριτες
  βάλωσιν ἄμφι τιμὰν
  ὕμνοισιν. ὕφαινέ νυν ἐν
  ταῖς πολυηράτοις τι κλεινὸν
10 ὀλβίαις Ἀθάναις,
  εὐαίνετε Κηΐα μέριμνα.
  πρέπει σε φερτάταν ἴμεν
  ὁδὸν παρὰ Καλλιόπας λα-
  χοῖσαν ἔξοχον γέρας.
15 †τι ην† Ἄργος ὅθ᾿ ἵππιον λιποῦσα
  φεῦγε χρυσέα βοῦς,
  εὐρυσθενέος φραδαῖσι φερτάτου Διός,
  Ἰνάχου ῥοδοδάκτυλος κόρα·
  ὅτ᾿ Ἄργον ὄμμασι βλέποντα   ἀντ.
20 πάντοθεν ἀκαμάτοις
  μεγιστοάνασσα κέλευσεν

15. τι ην : the reading of the MS. is plain, but corrupt, and it is not easy to see how it is to be corrected. The stop in the MS. after γέρας indicates that the previous sentence is closed, and that a new departure must be made here ; and the metre requires a trochee. ἦν is apparently required as a principal verb, since there is none other within reasonable distance, a series of relative clauses being carried on by ὅθ᾿ (l. 15), ὅτ᾿ (l. 19), and οὐδέ (l. 25), as far as l. 28. If ἦν, therefore, is correct, it must stand at the beginning of the line, for metrical reasons, τι must be abolished as a copyist's error (ΤΙ is very like Η in the MS), and a word must be supplied after ἦν to complete the verse. These considerations seem to point to some-thing like ἦν ποτ᾿, 'there was a time when . . . ,' an abrupt beginning of which Bacchylides is quite capable. Jebb suggests, however, πῖον, as epithet of Ἄργος, with a comma after γέρας in the line before. If the stop after γέρας be retained (as the MS. rather indicates), τότ᾿ may be read for ὅτ᾿ in l. 19.

16. χρυσέα : with golden horns, like Taygeta in Pind. Ol. III. 29.

21. μεγιστοάνασσα : cf. ὑμνοάνασσα, XII. 1.

*

ΑΚΟΙΤΟΝΑΫΠΝΟΝΕΟΝ

ΤΑΚΑΛΛΙΚΕΡΑΝΔΑΜΑΛΙΝ

25 ΦΥΛΑΣΣΕΝ·ΟΥΔΕΜΑΙΑΣ

ΥΙΟΣΔΫΝΑΤ'ΟΥΤΕΚΑΤΕΥ

ΦΕΓΓΕΑΣΑΜΕΡΑΣΛΑΘΕΙΝΝΙΝ

*χρυσοπεπλος Ηρα

Col. 39]   ΟΫΔΕΝΥΚΤΑΣΑΓ[

ΕΙΤΟΥΝΓΕΝΕΤ'Α[

30 ΠΟΔΑΡΚΕ'ΑΓΓΕΛΟ[

ΚΤΑΝΕῖΝΤΟΤ[

ΟΒΡΙΜΟΣΠΟΡΟΥ[

ΑΡΓΟΝ·ῆΡΑΚΑΙ[

ΑΣΠΕΤΟΙΜΕΡΙΜ[

35 ΗΠΕΙΕΡΙΔΕΣΦΥΤΕΥ[

ΚΑΔΕΩΝΑΝΑΠΑΥΣ[

ΕΜΟΙΜΕΝΟΥΝ

ΑΣΦΑΛΕΣΤΑΤΟΝΑΠΕ[

22. Om. A, added in lower margin by A³.   28. ΟΥΔΕ A, corr. A³?   32.
ΟΒΡΙΜΟΣΠΟΡΟΥ A, ΟΜΒΡΙΜΟΣΠΟΡΟΥ A³.   35. Πιερίδες] ΠΕΙΕΡΙΔΕΣ A.

24. καλλικέραν : cf. ὑψικέραν, XVI. 22.

25. φυλάσσεν : Doric infinitive, cf. ἔρυκεν, XVII. 41, and note.

28. The last column of the MS. in its present condition begins here, but
the papyrus is torn away through its whole height in the middle of the lines,
so that it is hopeless to restore the poem to a continuous shape. After l. 37,
moreover, where the epode begins, the assistance of the metre is lost, and
there is nothing to show the length of the lines.

αγ—: the last letter is either γ or π. In the first case ἀγνάς (Jebb,
Sandys), ἀγνώς or ἀγρεῖν would satisfy the requirements of the MS. and the
metre; in the latter case, ἀπλῶς would seem to be the only word.

32. ὀβριμοσπόρου : probably epithet of Γαῖα, mother of the Titans aud
other formidable offspring. According to some authors (Aeschylus, *Prom.*

χρυσόπεπλος Ἥρα,
ἄκοιτον ἄϋπνον ἐόν-
τα, καλλικέραν δάμαλιν
25 φυλάσσεν· οὐδὲ Μαίας
υἱὸς δύνατ' οὔτε κατ' εὐ-
φεγγέας ἀμέρας λαθεῖν νιν

οὔτε νύκτας ᾱγ[. .]
εἶτ' οὖν γένετ' ᾱ[. . . . .]
30 ποδάρκε' ἄγγελο[ν Διὸς]
κτανεῖν τοῇ[. . . . .]
ὀβριμοσπόρου [. .]
Ἄργον· ἦ ῥα καὶ [. . . . .]
ἄσπετοι μέριμ[ναι]
35 ἢ Πιερίδες φύτευ[σαν . . . .]
καδέων ἀνάπαυσ[ιν . . .]
ἐμοὶ μὲν οὖν   ἐπῳδ.
ἀσφαλέστατον ἀπε[

677, Acusilaus *ap.* Apollod. *Bibl.* II. 1. 3), Argus was γηγενής.   The passage
may have run γαίας | ὀβριμοσπόρου γόνον.

33. ἦ ῥα: apparently two alternatives are given to explain the final success
of Hermes.   Either his own unceasing efforts ultimately outwitted Argus,
or else the Muses helped him.   The latter alternative refers to the form of
the story which represents Hermes as having lulled Argus to sleep by the
music of his flute and then killed him (Ovid, *Metam.* I. 677 ff.).   Jebb, taking
the ἄσπετοι μέριμναι to be the vigils of Argus, would restore the passage
(*exempli gratia*) thus :

εἶτ' οὖν γένετ' αἶσα μοιρόκραντος	ἄσπετοι μέριμναι,
ποδάρκε' ἄγγελον Διὸς	ἢ Πιερίδες φύτευσαν ἀδύμῳ μέλει
κτανεῖν τότε Γᾶς ὑπέροπλον	καδέων ἀνάπαυσιν ὄμμασιν.
ὀβριμοσπόρου τέκος	ἐμοὶ μὲν οὖν
Ἄργον· ἦ ῥα καὶ ἐς τέλος σφ' ἔτειρον	ἀσφαλέστατον ἅπερ εἰλικρινῆ λέγειν.

ΕΠΕΙΠΑΡΑΝΘΕΜΩ[

40 ΝΕΙΛΟΝΑΦΙΚΕΤ'[

ΪΩΦΕΡΟΥΣΑΠΑΙΔ[

ΕΠΑΦΟΝ·ΕΝΘΑΝΙ[

ΑΙΝΟͺΣΤΟΛΩΝΠΡΥ[

ΥΠΕΡΟΧΩΙΒΡΥΟΝΤ[

45 ΜΕΓΙΣΤΑΝΤΕΘΝ[

ΟΘΕΝΚΑΙΑΓΑΝΟΡΙ[

ΕΝΕΠΤΑΠΥΛΟΙ[

ΚΑΔ͡ΟϹϹΕ—ΜΕΛ[

ἈΤΟΝΟΡϹΙΒΆΚΧΑͺ[

50 ΤΙΚΤΕΔΙΟΝΥϹΟΝ[

ΚΑΙΧΟΡΩΝϹΤΕΦΑ[

XX.

Ιδας Λακεδαιμονιοις

42. ΕΝΘΕΝΙ Α, corr. Α³ʔ   48. Κάδμος] ΚΑΔΟΣ Α, corr. Α³. Between the letters ΣΕ and ΜΕΛΗΝ there is a space of half an inch, across which a horizontal line has been drawn.

39, 40. ἀνθεμώδεα Νεῖλον: cf. frag. 65 (Bergk 39) δονακώδεα Νεῖλον.
41–48. The following is Jebb's restoration, though in the absence of

ἐπεὶ παρ' ἀνθεμώ[δεα
40 Νεῖλον ἀφίκετ' [
’Ιὼ φέρουσα παῖδ[α
῎Επαφον· ἔνθα νί[ν
αἰνοστόλων πρύ[
ὑπερόχῳ βρύοντ[
45 μεγίσταν τε θνί[ατ
ὅθεν καὶ ἀγανορε[
ἐν ἑπταπύλοι[ς
Κάδμος Σεμέ[λαν
ἃ τὸν ὀρσιβάκχα[ν
50 τίκτε Διόνυσον [
καὶ χορῶν στεφα[ν

XX.

ΙΔΑΣ

Λακεδαιμονίοις.

As the preceding poem was composed for the Athenians, so
this, the last in the manuscript as we now have it, was written for
the Lacedaemonians. Unfortunately eleven mutilated lines are
all that is left of it, and these are only sufficient to show the
beginning of the myth of Idas and Marpessa. Probably the poem
is to be classed as a Dithyramb, like its predecessor; and the
evidence as to the metre any reconstruction must be more than usually
precarious. It serves, however, to indicate the sense.

'Ιὼ φέρουσα παῖδ' ὑπὸ κόλποις
῎Επαφον· ἔνθα νιν Ζεὺς ἐκ πλανᾶν ἔθηκεν
αἰνοστόλων πρύτανιν γένεος
ὑπερόχῳ βρύοντος ὄλβῳ,
μεγίσταν τε θνατῶν κτίσε σποράν,
ὅθεν καὶ ἀγανόρειος
ἐν ἑπταπύλοισι Θήβαις
Κάδμος Σεμέλαν φύτευσεν.

ϹΠΑΡΤΑΙΠΟΤ˙ΕΝ[

ΞΑΝΘΑΙΛΑΚΕΔΑ[

ΤΟΙΟΝΔΕΜΕΛΟϹΚ[

ΟΤ˙ΑΓΕΤΟΚΑΛΛΙΠΑ[

5 ΚΟΡΑΝΘΡΑϹΥΚΑΡ[

ΜΑΡΠΗϹϹΑΝΪΟΥ[

ΦΥΓΩΝΘΑΝΑΤΟΥ[

ΑΝΑΞΊΑΛΟϹΠΑ̊ϹΙ[

ΙΠΠΟΥϹΤΕ̊ΙΙϹΑΝ[

10 ΠΛΕΥΡΩΝ˙ΕϹΕΫΚΤ[

ΧΡΥϹΑϹΠΙΔΟϹΥΙΟ[

XX. *Title* by Α². 　　　 8. ΠΑΣΙ Α, ΠΟΣΙ Α² ?

4. The story told in the following lines is evidently that of which Apollodorus gives a summary (*Bibl.* I. 7. 8, 9): Εὖηνος μὲν οὖν ἐγέννησε Μάρπησσαν,
ἣν Ἀπόλλωνος μνηστευομένου Ἴδας ὁ Ἀφαρέως ἥρπασε, λαβὼν παρὰ Ποσειδῶνος
ἅρμα ὑπόπτερον. διώκων δὲ Εὖηνος ἐφ᾽ ἅρματος ἐπὶ τὸν Λυκόρμαν ἦλθε ποταμόν,
καταλαβεῖν δὲ οὐ δυνάμενος τοὺς μὲν ἵππους ἀπέσφαξεν, ἑαυτὸν δὲ εἰς τὸν ποταμὸν
ἔβαλε. καὶ καλεῖται Εὖηνος ὁ ποταμὸς παρ᾽ ἐκείνου. Ἴδας δὲ εἰς Μεσσήνην
παραγίνεται, καὶ αὐτῷ ὁ Ἀπόλλων περιτυχὼν ἀφαιρεῖται τὴν κόρην. μαχομένων
δὲ αὐτῶν περὶ τῶν τῆς παιδὸς γάμων Ζεὺς διαλύσας ἐπέτρεψεν αὐτῇ τῇ παρθένῳ
ἑλέσθαι ὁποτέρῳ βούλεται συνοικεῖν· ἡ δέ, δείσασα ὡς ἂν μὴ γηρῶσαν αὐτὴν
Ἀπόλλων καταλίπῃ, τὸν Ἴδαν εἵλετο ἄνδρα. Probably this story would have
sufficed for a single poem, so there is no reason to suppose that Bacchylides

metre, like that of most of the miscellaneous poems, appears to be logaoedic. It is presumably to this poem that the scholiast on Pindar, *Isth*. III. 72, refers, when he says that Bacchylides represented Evenus as roofing a temple with the skulls of the suitors of Marpessa (Bergk, frag. 61).

Σπάρτᾳ ποτ᾽ ἐν [
ξανθᾷ Λακεδα[ιμον
τοιόνδε μέλος κ[
ὅτ᾽ ἄγετο καλλίπα[χυν
5 κόραν θρασυκαρ[δι
Μάρπησσαν ἰο[
φυγὼν θανάτου [

ἀναξίαλος Ποσι[δᾶν
ἵππους τέ οἱ ἰσαν[
10 Πλευρῶν᾽ ἐς εὐκτ[ιμέναν
χρυσάσπιδος υἱο[

[The rest is wanting.]

challenged comparison once more with Pindar by telling the myth of the death of Castor at the hands of Idas, and of its avenging by the thunderbolt of Zeus (Pind. *Nem.* X. 60 ff.).

5. Probably this line should be completed θρασυκάρδιος Ἴδας. The epithet can hardly belong to Marpessa, who already has καλλίπαχυν (or καλλιπάρῃον) and the adjective beginning with *ἰο*—in l. 6.

8. ἀναξίαλος : another of the doubtful compounds in ἀναξι—, of which Bacchylides seems to have been fond.

9. ἰσαν— : perhaps ἰσανέμους.

10. Πλευρῶνα : Pleuron was on the river Evenus, which plays a part in the myth as narrated above by Apollodorus.

FRAGMENTS.

I.

[. . . .]ΑΦΘ[

[. .]ΝΤΡΙΤΆΤΆ˙ΜΕ[

[. .]ΕΡΑ͞ΙΜΙΝωϹΑ[. . . .]Ϲ

[. .]ΥΘΕΝΑΙΟΛΟΠΡ[. .]ΝΟΙ[

5 ΝΑΥϹΙΠΕΝΤΗΚΟΝΤ[.]ϹΥΝ

[.]ΡΗΤωΝΟΜΙΛωΙ

[.]ΙΟϹΕΥΚΛΕΙΟΥΔΕΕ

[.]ΑΤΙΒΑΘΥΖωΝΟΝΚΟΡΑΝ

[.]ΕΞΙΘΕΑΝΔΑΜΑϹΕΝ

10 [.]ΑΙΟΙΛΙΠΕΝΗΜΙϹΥΛΑωΝ

[.]ΝΔΡΑϹΑΡΗΪΦΙΛΟΥϹ

[. .]ϹΙΝΠΟΛΥΚΡΗΜΝΟΝΧΘΟΝΑ

[.]ΕΙΜΑϹΑΠΟΠΛΕωΝῳ[. .]ΤΕϹ

2. ΤΡΙΤΑΤΑ **Δ**, corr. **Δ**¹?   9. Δεξιθέαν] the N is written over a **Δ**.

Frag. 1. Combined by Blass from two pieces of papyrus, and shown (by the evidence of metre) to belong to Ode I. It comes from the column immediately preceding that with which the continuous portion of the papyrus begins. About six lines are lost from the top of the column and nine from the bottom. The passage narrates the marriage of Minos to Dexithea, and the birth therefrom of Euxantius, who, as appears from II. 8, was connected with Ceos—a legend hitherto unknown. Dexithea and Euxantius are just

FRAGMENTS.

The following are the fragments for which it has not been possible to find places in the restored papyrus.

I.

. . .]αφθ[
[ὧ]ν τριτάτᾳ με[τέπειτα]
[ἀμ]έρᾳ Μίνως ἀ[γυιὰ]ς
[ἦλ]υθεν αἰολοπρ[ύμ]νοις
5 ναυσὶ πεντήκοντ[α] σὺν
[Κ]ρητῶν ὁμίλῳ,
[Δ]ιὸς εὐκλείου δὲ ἔ-   στρ.
[κ]ατι βαθύζωνον κόραν
[Δ]εξιθέαν δάμασεν,
10 [κ]αί οἱ λίπεν ἥμισυ λαῶν
[ἄ]νδρας ἀρηϊφίλους.
[οἷ]σιν πολύκρημνον χθόνα
[ν]είμας ἀποπλέων ᾤ[χε]τ᾽ ἐς

mentioned in Apollod. *Bibl.* III. 1. 2, and the scholiast on Apoll. Rhod. I. 186 names Euxantius as father of Miletus, the founder of the town of that name. No connexion between Miletus and Ceos has hitherto been known, but it seems to be traceable through Bacchylides. Miletus claimed a connexion with Pylus, one of its legendary founders being the Pylian Neleus (Strabo, XIV. 633); so also did Metapontum (ib. VI. 264), which Bacchylides claims to have been founded by his ancestors (XI. 120, and note); hence we get an indication of a connexion between Pylus, Miletus, and Ceos, which accounts for the epithet Εὐξαντίς, applied to the latter in II. 8.

O 2

ΚΝѠCCONЇΜЀΡΤΑΝ[. .]ΛΙΝ
15 [.]ΑΣΙΛΕΥCΕΥΡѠΠΙΔ[. .]
[. . .]ΔΕ̣ΚΑΤѠ'Δ'ΕΥΞ[. . .]Ο̣Ν
[. . . . . .]Κ'ΕΥΠΛΟΚ[
[. . . . . . .]ΕΚΥΔΈ[
[. . . . . . .]ΠΡΥΤΑ[
20 [. . . . .]Α̣Ν̣[

2.

]ΑΝΙΟΝѠ̣[
]Ι̣ΝΈΕCΤΡΙΟ̣[
]ΝΦΟΡΕ̣ΫΝ[
]Ο̣Φ̣Ε̣ΥΓ[

3.

]ΠΟΛΛΑ[.]ΔΙ[
]ΟΥΛ: [

4.

]Ι̣ΔΕΘΕѠΝ
]Μ̣ΕΝΟΝΝΥ . [
]ΤΕΚ . [

5.

]ΣΑ̣Ν̣ΡΑ̣Ι[
]. . Ε̣Λ̣ . ΔΕΤ[

16. ΔΕΚΑΤѠ Δ, corr. Δ¹.

Frag. 2. From the top of a column. The restoration is given by the scholiast on Pind. *Ol.* XI. 83, quoting Didymus (Bergk, frag. 41). It does not seem to fit into any of the poems preserved in the present MS.

Frag. 3. From the top of a column.

[Κ]νῶσσον ἱμερτὰν [πό]λιν
15 [β]ασιλεὺς Εὐρωπίδ[ος].   ἀντ.
[τῷ δ]εκάτῳ δ᾿ Εὐξ[άντι]ον
[μηνὶ τέ]κ᾿ εὐπλόκ[αμος]
[κούρα φερ]εκυδέ[α παῖδα]
[. . .] πρύτα[νιν
20 [. . .]αν[

2.

[Ποσειδ]άνιον ὦ[ς
[Μαντ]ινέες τριό[δοντα χαλκοδαιδάλοισιν ἐν
[ἀσπίσι]ν φορεῦν[τες
[. . . . ἀπ]οφευγ[

3.

. . .]πολλὰ[.] δί[
. . .]ουλ . [

4.

. . .]ι δὲ θεῶν
. . .]μενον νί[
. . .]τεκ[

5.

. . .]σαν ῥαί[
. . .] . . . . δετ[

Frag. 4. Ends of lines from the top of a column.

Frag. 5. Two fragments, combined by Blass. Line 5 seems to contain
Bergk's frag. 8, προσφώνει τέ (or προσφωνεῖ τέ, not προσφωνεῖτέ, since
σαίνουσα follows) νιν ἐπὶ νίκαις, quoted by the grammarian Apollonius
Dyscolus, de Pron. 368 a.

]ΑΛΑΚΑΤΟϹ[

]Δ·ΕΠΕΫΝΑΝ̣[

5]Α·ΠΡΟϹΦѠΝΕ[.]ΤΕΝ[

]ϹΑΙΝΟΥϹ·ΟΠΙ

]Ε̣Ν̣ΤΕΡΟΜΑΙ

]ΦᾹ́ΚΕΙΔΫ̆ᾹΙ

]ΕΝῙᾹΙ

10   ]ΕΤ[.]ΠΑΜΠΑ̣[

        ]Α̣Ϲ

        ]ΟΜΟΙ

6.

]Ε̣ΡΙΔΕϹ[

]ΕΝΥΦΑΙ̣[

]ΥϹϊΝΑΚ[

]ΓΆΙᾹϹϊϹΘΜΙ[

5]ΝΕΥΒΟΥΛΟΥ[

]ΒΡΟΝΝΗΡΕ̣[

]ΝΆϹΟΙΟΤ·ΕΥ[

]ᾹΝ·Ε̣Ν . [

7.

]Ι̣ΟΡΑΓѠΝ̣[

]ΤΑΝΛΙΠΑ[

]Ν̣ΑΙϹΕΠΑ[

Frag. 6. Evidently from an Isthmian ode, and referred by Blass to Ode I. In that case the junction between ll. 7, 8 may be restored as νάσοιό τ' Εὐ[ϝ | αντιαδ]ᾶν, and the fragment would begin with l. 4 of a strophe and end with l. 3 of the antistrophe. The contents, so far as they are discernible,

. χρυσ]αλάκατος [
. .]δ' ἐπ' εὐνὰν [
5 . .]α· προσφωνε[ῖ] τέ ν[ιν
. .] σαίνουσ' ὀπὶ
. .]εντ' ἔρομαι
. . ἀμ]φάκει δύᾳ
. .]ενίαι
10 . . .]ετ[ι] πάμπ[αν
. . . . .]ας
. . . .]ομοι

6.

. . .]εριδες [
. .]εννφα[
. .]υς ἵνα κ[
. . .] γαίας Ἰσθμί[ας
5 . . .]ν εὐβούλου . [
. .]βρον Νηρέ[ος
. . νάσοιό τ' εὐ[
. . .]αν· εν . [

7.

. . .]οραγων [
. . .] τὰν λιπα[ρὰν
. . .]ναις ἐπ' ἀ[

would suit the beginning of a poem, and would lead up to the mention of Euxantius in frag. 1.

Frag. 7. The texture of the papyrus resembles that of frag. 12, and is not unlike that of the mutilated col. 13. Hence these fragments may belong to Odes VII or VIII.

]ΙΔΑCΕΛΛᾹ[
5]ΛΥΑΜΠΕΛ[
]ΑΤΟΝΫΜΝ[
]ΗΝΟCΕΝΚ[
]ΠΕΡΑΝΙΠ[
]Π[

8.

]ΡΙΝ[

9.

]ΤΙΟCΚΕΑΡ

10.

]ΚΑC
]ΑΙΤΟΝΑΡΕΙѠ[
]ΠΟΥ·
]ΕΥCѠΝ

11.

]ΥѠΔΕΑΘΕCCΑ[
]ΕΝΓΥΆΛΟΙC·
]ΝΤΕΛΗCΚ[
]Ε[....]ѠΝ

Frag. 8. From the top of a column.
Frag. 9. End of the first line of a column, or else of one much longer than any of those preceding it for a space of some six lines or more.

.   .]ιδας Ἑλλᾶ[

5   .   .   .]λυαμπελ[

.   .   .]ατον ὕμν[ον

.   .   .]ηνος εν κ[

.   .]περάνιπ[

.   .   .]π[

8.

]ριν[

9.

]τιος κέαρ

10.

]κας

]αι τὸν αρειω[

]που·

]ευσων

11.

ε]ὐώδεα Θεσσα[λ

] ἐν γυάλοις·

]ν τέλης κ[

]ε[. . . .]ων

Frag. 10. Ends of lines.

Frag. 11. Evidently from the lost part of Ode XIV, on account of the mention of Thessaly. The metre would suit ll. 4-7 of an epode.

12.

]ΕΧΑΙΡΟΛΑΝ[

]ΕΝΟΝΕΥϹΕΒ[

]ΡΩΙΘΑΝ[. . .]ΙΔ[

]ΙΠΑΤΡΙΔΟϹ·[

5   ]ΝΕΟΚΡΙΤΟ[

]ΆΤΕΚΝΟΝ[

13.

]ΤΟϹ

]ΝΠΥΚ[

]ΓΟΙΚΩ[

]ΑΓΟΡᾹ

5   ]ΜΕΛΙΦΡΟΝΟϹΫ[

]ΕΡᾹΝ

]ΚΑΛΑΝΠΟΛΙΝ

]ΟΙΜΕΝΟΊ

]Ν . ΗΡΟΙϹΑΛΟϹ[

10]ΥΓΑʹϹᾹΕΛ[

14.

]ΛΜΟ[

]ΘΕ . [

]ΔΙΝΕΙ[

Frag. 12. The general appearance of the papyrus and writing is somewhat like that of col. 13.

Frag. 13. This fragment (which has been put together out of two pieces)
and the three next are on papyrus of the same colour and texture, being

12.

. . .]εχαιρολαν[
. . .]ενον εὐσεβ[
. . .]ρῳ θάν[ατον] δ[ὲ
5 . . περ]ὶ πατρίδος [
. . .] νεοκριτο[
. .] ἄτεκνον [

13.

]τος
]ν πυκ[
]γ᾽ οἴκῳ [
] ἀγορᾷ
5   ] μελίφρονος ὕ[πνου
]εραν
] καλὰν πόλιν
]οίμενοί
]ν . ηροις ἁλὸς [
10 a]ὐγαῖς ἀελ[ίου

14.

]λμο[
]θε . [
]δινει[

considerably worn and of dark colour. For μελίφρονος ὕπνου (l. 5), cf. frag. 46 below (Bergk 13).

Frag. 14. The first word may be some part of ὀφθαλμός.

15.

] . ONTO . [
]ΕΓΓΙΝΑΝ[
]ΤΟΝΑΥΤ[
]ΑΛΛΑΙΓΙΝ[
5   ]Δ‘ΕΤΕ[
]ΓΟΝΩΤ[
]ΠΛ[

16.

Col. 1.]ΕΛΕΩΝ   Col. 2. ΤΟΙ . [
        ]ΙΝ   ΚᾹΛ[

17.

]ΡΟΔΙΝΑ[
]ΑΛΟΚΛΕΑ[
]ΠΑ[

18.

]Ν.
]
]Α‘ΝΙΝ
]
]
]Ν

Frag. 15. Line 6 apparently contains a compound of *νῶτον*. The first letter may be a *τ*.

Frag. 16. Ends of two lines and beginnings of the two opposite to them in the next column.

15.

]. οντο . [
]εσσιν ἀν[
]τον αὐτ[ὸν
] ἄλλαισιν [
5   ] δ' ετε[
]γονώτ[
]πλ[

16.

Col. 1.]ελεων   Col. 2. τοι . [
]ιν   κᾱλ[

17.

]ροδινα[
]αλοκλεα[
]πα[

18.

]ν·
]
]αι νιν
]
]
]ν

Frag. 17. From the top of a column or the ends of long lines. The first word may be either ῥοδίναν or πορφυροδίναν (as in IX. 39), and the second appears to be μεγαλοκλέα, an otherwise unknown form parallel to μεγακλέα.

Frag. 18. Ends of lines.

19.

]ΙϹΟΡ

]ΑϹΤΑΛΑΝ[

20.

]ΥϹΈΑ[

]ΑΤ

21.

]Ν

]

]ΑΜΟΥϹΑ̂Ν

]ѠΝ

22.

]ϹΟΘΡΟ[

]ΑΘΟΙ̣[

]ΜΕΓΑ[

]Μ̣ΕϹΑΙ[

5]ΑΜ̣Φ[

23.

]Ρᾼ[

]ΝΠᾹ[

]ΕΛΑΜΠ[

]ΠΟΚΕΥ[

5   ]Π[

Frag. 19. Ends of long lines.
Frag. 20. Probably χρυσέα.
Frag. 21. Two fragments from the ends of long lines.

19.

]ις ορ
]ας ταλαν[

20.

]υσέα [
]απ[

21.

]ν
]
]α Μουσᾶν
]ων

22.

]σοθρο[
]αθοι [
] μεγα[
]μεσαι[
5   ] ἀμφ[

23.

]ρα[
]ν πα[
] ἐλαμπ[
ἀ]ποκευ[θ
5   ]π[

Frag. 22.   The first word appears to be a part of χρυσόθρονος.
Frag. 23.   The papyrus is of the same colour and appearance as col. 17.

24.

]ΑϹΙΝΙΠΠΟΥϚ

25.

]ΑΡ[

]ϹΤΟϹ[

26.

]ΤΡΟϹ

27.

]ΕΙ

]Ν·

28.

]ΑΙ

]

]ΝΟΤΑ[

]ΕΥ[

29.

]ΕΚΑΤΙ

30.

]ΙϹ

31.

]ΑΜ[

]ΛΟ[

32.

]ΟΥ

Frag. 24. From the bottom of a column or the end of a long line. This and the remaining fragments are the merest scraps.

24.
]ασιν ἵππους

25.
]αρ[
]στος [

26.
]τρος

27.
]ει
]ν·

28.
]ᾳ
]
]ν ὅτα[ν
]ευ[

29.
] ἕκατι

30.
]ις

31.
]άμ[
]λο[

32.
]ου

Frag. 29.   From the top of a column or the end of a long line.

P

33·
]ΥΒΡ[

34·
]ΞΑΝΘΥΓΑΤΡΕС[

35·
]ΠΡΟΞΕΝ[

36.
]ΙΝΑΝΒΡΟΤΟ[
]ΛΈωΝ

37·
]ΔΕС · [
]ΑСΒΑСΑ[

38.
]ΙС . . [
]ΜΑΤωΙΒΟΡ[
]ΜΗ[. .]ΝΔ[
]ω[

39·
]ΕΜ[
]ΤΕΙω[

40.
]ΕΝ[
]ΥΝ[
]ω[

Frag. 33. From the top of a column or the end of a long line; apparently part of ὕβρις or its cognates or of βαρύβρομος.

33.
]υβρ[

34.
]ξαν θύγατρες

35.
] προξεν[

36.
]ιναν βροτο[
]λέων

37.
]δεσ . [
]ας βασα[ν

38.
]ισ . . [
]ματῳ βορ[ε
]μη[. .]νδ[
]ω[

39.
]εμ[
]τειω[

40.
]εν[
]υν[
]ω[

Frag. 34.   From the last line of a column, and perhaps the end of it.

P 2

The fragments which follow are the extant quotations of Bacchylides, extracted from Bergk's *Poetae Lyrici Graeci*, ed. 4. Only those which contain the actual words of Bacchylides are given, not mere references to the contents of his poems. Bergk's numbers are added in brackets.

41 [B. 2].

ὄλβιος δ' οὐδεὶς βροτῶν πάντα χρόνον.

42 [B. 3].

παύροισι δὲ θνατῶν τὸν ἄπαντα χρόνον τῷ δαίμονι
δῶκεν
πράσσοντας ἐν καιρῷ πολιοκρόταφον
γῆρας ἱκνεῖσθαι, πρὶν ἐγκύρσαι δύᾳ.

43 [B. 4].

ὡς δ' ἅπαξ εἰπεῖν, φρένα καὶ πυκινὰν κέρδος
ἀνθρώπων βιᾶται.

44 [B. 7].

ὦ Πέλοπος λιπαρᾶς νάσου θεόδματοι πύλαι.

Frag. 41. Stobaeus, *Flor.* XCVIII. 27; attached to the lines printed above as ode V. 160-162.
Frag. 42. Clem. Alex., *Strom.* VI. 745.
Frag. 43. Stobaeus, *Flor.* X. 14, from the Ἐπίνικοι.
Frag. 44. Schol. Pind., *Ol.* XIII. 1.

45 [B. 11].

αἰαῖ τέκος ἁμέτερον,
μεῖζον ἢ πενθεῖν ἐφάνη κακόν, ἀφθέγκτοισιν ἴσον.

46 [B. 13].

τίκτει δέ τε θνατοῖσιν εἰρήνα μεγάλα
πλοῦτον καὶ μελιγλώσσων ἀοιδᾶν ἄνθεα,
δαιδαλέων τ᾿ ἐπὶ βωμῶν θεοῖσιν αἴθεσθαι βοῶν
ξανθᾷ φλογὶ μῆρα τανυτρίχων τε μήλων,
5 γυμνασίων τε νέοις αὐλῶν τε καὶ κώμων μέλειν.
ἐν δὲ σιδαροδέτοις πόρπαξιν αἰθᾶν
ἀραχνᾶν ἱστοὶ πέλονται·
ἔγχεά τε λογχωτὰ ξίφεά τ᾿ ἀμφάκεα δάμναται
εὐρώς·
χαλκεᾶν δ᾿ οὐκ ἔστι σαλπίγγων κτύπος·
10 οὐδὲ συλᾶται μελίφρων ὕπνος ἀπὸ βλεφάρων,
ἁμὸν ὃς θάλπει κέαρ.
συμποσίων δ᾿ ἐρατῶν βρίθοντ᾿ ἀγυιαί, παιδικοί
θ᾿ ὕμνοι φλέγονται.

47 [B. 14].

ἕτερος ἐξ ἑτέρου σοφὸς τό τε πάλαι τό τε νῦν.
οὐδὲ γὰρ ῥᾷστον ἀρρήτων πύλας
ἐξευρεῖν.

Frag. 45. Stobaeus, *Flor.* CXXII. 1, from the Ὕμνοι.
Frag. 46. *Ib.* LV. 3, from the Παιᾶνες. In l. 1 most editors read εἰράνα.
Frag. 47. Clem. Alex., *Strom.* V. 687, from the Παιᾶνες.

48 [B. 19].

εἷς ὅρος, μία δὲ βροτοῖς ἐστὶν εὐτυχίας ὁδός,
θυμὸν εἴ τις ἔχων ἀπενθῆ διατελεῖν δύναται βίον·
ὃς δὲ μυρίαν μενοινὰν ἀμφιπολεῖ φρενί,
τὸ δὲ παρ' ἆμάρ τε καὶ νύκτα μελλόντων χάριν
5 ἐὸν ἰάπτεται κέαρ,
ἀκάρπωτον ἔχει πόνον.

49 [B. 20].

τί γὰρ ἐλαφρὸν ἔτ' ἔστ' ἄπραχθ' ⟨ὧδ'⟩ ὀδυρόμενον δονεῖν
καρδίαν;

50 [B. 21].

πάντεσσι θνατοῖσι δαίμων ἐπέταξε πόνους ἄλ-
λοισιν ἄλλους.

51 [B. 22].

Λυδία μὲν γὰρ λίθος μανύει χρυσόν,
ἀνδρῶν δ' ἀρετὰν σοφίαν τε παγκρατὴς ἐλέγχει
ἀλάθεια.

52 [B. 23].

οὐχ ἕδρας ἔργον οὐδ' ἀμβολᾶς, ἀλλὰ χρυσαίγιδος
Ἰτωνίας
χρὴ παρ' εὐδαίδαλον ναὸν ἐλθόντας ἀβρόν τι
δεῖξαι.

Frag. 48. Stobaeus, *Flor.* CVIII. 26, from the Προσῳδίαι.
Frag. 49. *Ib.* CVIII. 49, from the Προσῳδίαι.
Frag. 50. *Ib.* XCVIII. 25, from the Προσῳδίαι.
Frag. 51. *Ib.* XI. 7, from the Ὑπορχήματα.
Frag. 52. Dion. Hal., *De Compos. Verb.*, c. 25, from the Ὑπορχήματα.

53 [B. 24].

εὖτε τὴν ἀπ᾽ ἀγκύλης ἵησι
τοῖσδε τοῖς νεανίαις
λευκὸν ἀντείνασα πῆχυν.

54 [B. 25].

ἦ καλὸς Θεόκριτος· οὐ μόνος ἀνθρώπων ἐρᾷς.

55 [B. 26].

σὺ δ᾽ ἐν χιτῶνι μούνῳ
παρὰ τὴν φίλην γυναῖκα φεύγεις.

56 [B. 27].

γλυκεῖ᾽ ἀνάγκα
ἐσσυμενᾶν κυλίκων θάλπῃσι θυμόν,
Κύπρις ὥς· ἐλπὶς γὰρ αἰθύσσει φρένας
ἀμμιγνυμένα Διονυσίοισι δώροις,
5 ἀνδράσι θ᾽ ὑψοτάτω πέμπει μερίμνας·
αὐτίχ᾽ ὁ μὲν πόλεων κρήδεμνα λύει,
πᾶσι δ᾽ ἀνθρώποις μοναρχήσειν δοκεῖ·
χρυσῷ δ᾽ ἐλέφαντί τε μαρμαίρουσιν οἶκοι,
πυροφόροι δὲ κατ᾽ αἰγλάεντα ⟨καρπὸν⟩
10 νᾶες ἄγουσιν ἀπ᾽ Αἰγύπτου, μέγιστον
πλοῦτον· ὡς πίνοντος ὁρμαίνει κέαρ.

Frag. 53. Athen. XI. 782 E, from the Ἐρωτικά.
Fragg. 54, 55. Hephaest. 130.
Frag. 56. Athen. II. 39 E. In l. 8 Neue, Bergk, and others read
μαρμαίροισιν.

57 [B. 28].

οὐ βοῶν πάρεστι σώματ᾽, οὔτε χρυσός, οὔτε
πορφύρεοι τάπητες, ἀλλὰ θυμὸς εὐμενὴς
Μοῦσά τε γλυκεῖα καὶ Βοιωτίοισιν ἐν σκύφοισιν
οἶνος ἡδύς.

58 [B. 31].

ὦ Περίκλειτε, τἄλλ᾽ ἀγνοήσειν μὲν οὔ σ᾽ ἔλπομαι.

59 [B. 33].

ἔστα δ᾽ ἐπὶ λάϊνον οὐδόν, τοὶ δὲ θοίνας ἔντυον,
    ὧδέ τ᾽ ἔφα·
αὐτόματοι δ᾽ ἀγαθῶν δαῖτας εὐόχθους ἐπέρχονται
    δίκαιοι
φῶτες.

60 [B. 34].

οἱ μὲν ἀδμᾶτες ἀεικελιᾶν εἰσὶ νόσων καὶ ἄνατοι,
οὐδὲν ἀνθρώποις ἴκελοι.

61 [B. 35].

οὐ γὰρ ὑπόκλοπον φορεῖ
βροτοῖσι φωνάεντα λόγον σοφία.

Frag. 57. Athen. VI. 500 B.
Frag. 58. Hephaest. 76.
Frag. 59. Athen. V. 178 B.
Frag. 60. Clem. Alex., *Strom.* V. 715.
Frag. 61. *Ib. Paedag.* III. 310.

62 [B. 36].

θνατοῖσι δ' οὐκ αὐθαίρετοι
οὔτ' ὄλβος οὔτ' ἄκαμπτος Ἄρης οὔτε πάμφθερσις
στάσις,
ἀλλ' ἐπιχρίμπτει νέφος ἄλλοτ' ἐπ' ἄλλαν
γαῖαν ἁ πάνδωρος αἶσα.

63 [B. 37].

εἰ δὲ λέγει τις ἄλλως, πλατεῖα κέλευθος.

64 [B. 38].

μελαγκευθὲς εἴδωλον ἀνδρὸς Ἰθακησίου.

65 [B. 39].

τὰν ἀχείμαντόν τε Μέμφιν καὶ δονακώδεα Νεῖλον.

66 [B. 40].

Ἑκάτα δᾳδοφόρε Νυκτὸς μελανοκόλπου θύγατερ.

67 [B. 43].

χρυσὸν βροτῶν γνώμαισι μανύει καθαρόν.

Frag. 62. Stobaeus, *Ecl. Phys.* I. 5. 3.
Frag. 63. Plutarch, *Num.* 4. Possibly only the last two words really
come from Bacchylides.
Frag. 64. *Etym. Mag.* 296, 1.
Frag. 65. Athen. I. 20 D.
Frag. 66. Schol. Apoll. Rhod. III. 467.
Frag. 67. Priscian, *Metr. Terent.*, p. 251.

68 [B. 44].

ὀργαὶ μὲν ἀνθρώπων διακεκριμέναι μυρίαι.

69 [B. 45].

πλημμυρὶν πόντου φυγών.

70 [B. 46].

δυσμενέων δ᾽ ἀϊδής.

71 [B. 48].

κούρα Πάλλαντος πολυώνυμε, πότνια Νίκα,
πρόφρων Κραναϊδῶν ἱμερόεντα χορὸν
αἰὲν ἐποπτεύοις, πολέας δ᾽ ἐν ἀθύρμασι Μουσᾶν
Κηΐῳ ἀμφιτίθει Βακχυλίδῃ στεφάνους.

72 [B. 49].

Εὔδημος τὸν νηὸν ἐπ᾽ ἀγροῦ τόνδ᾽ ἀνέθηκεν
τῷ πάντων ἀνέμων πιοτάτῳ Ζεφύρῳ.
εὐξαμένῳ γάρ οἱ ἦλθε βοαθόος, ὄφρα τάχιστα
λικμήσῃ πεπόνων καρπὸν ἀπ᾽ ἀσταχύων.

73 [B. 51].

πυργοκέρατα.

Frag. 68. Zenobius, *Prov.* III. 25.
Frag. 69. *Etym. Mag.* 676, 25.
Frag. 70. Cramer, *Anecd. Oxon.* I. 65, 22.
Frag. 71. *Anth. Pal.* VI. 313.
Frag. 72. *Ib.* VI. 53.
Frag. 73. Apollon., *de Adv.*, Bekk. *An.* II. 596, 14.

The following fragments in Bergk occur in the poems printed above :—

Bergk 1   = V. 50–55.
     2, ll. 1, 2 = V. 160–162.
     6   = V. 37–40.
     8   = frag. 5, l. 5.
     9   = XI. 1, 4–7.
     17   = XVII. 2 (see note).
     29   = XV. 50–56.
     30   = I. 21–23.
     41   = frag. 2.
     42   = XVIII. 2.
     47   = V. 26, 27.
     52   = XIII. 25.
     59   = XV. 7 (see note).
     61   = XX (see introductory note).

INDEX

—✦—

ἅ, III. 10, XVI. 30 (bis).
Ἀβαντιάδας, XI. 40.
Ἄβας, XI. 69.
ἀβροβάτας (proper name, or = Λύδιος), III. 48.
ἀβρόβιος : ἀβροβίων, XVIII. 2.
ἀβρύς : ἀβρύν, fr. 52, 2.
ἀγάθεος : ἀγαθέαν, III. 62 ; ἀγαθέᾳ, V. 41.
ἀγαθός : ἀγαθῶν, fr. 59, 2.
ἀγακλεής : ἀγακλέα, XVI. 12.
ἀγακλειτός : ἀγακλειταῖς, XIII. 57.
ἀγάλλω : ἀγάλλεται, XVI. 6.
ἄγαλμα, I. 46, V. 4, X. 11.
ἀγανόρειος, XIX. 46 (?).
ἀγγελία : ἀγγελίαν, II. 3, XVI. 26 ; person., Ἀγγελία, XVI. 3 (?).
ἄγγελος, V. 19 ; ἄγγελον, XIX. 30.
ἀγέλα : ἀγέλας, XVIII. 10 ; ἀγέλαις, X. 44.
Ἀγέλαος : Ἀγέλαον, V. 117.
ἀγέρωχος : ἀγέρωχοι, V. 35.
Ἀγκαῖος : Ἀγκαῖον, V. 117.
ἀγκύλη : ἀγκύλης, fr. 53, 1.
ἀγλαΐα : ἀγλαΐᾳ, III. 6.
ἀγλαΐζω : ἀγλαΐζέτω, III. 22.
ἀγλαόθρονος : ἀγλαόθρονοι, XVII. 124.
ἀγλαός : ἀγλαάν, V. 154 ; ἀγλαόν, XVII. 61 ; ἀγλαούς, XVII. 2 ; ἀγλαᾶν, XVII. 103.
ἄγναμπτος : ἀγνάμπτων, IX. 73 (?).
ἀγνοέω : ἀγνοήσειν, fr. 58.
ἀγνός : ἁγνόν, X. 29 ; ἁγνοῦ, XI. 25 ; ἁγνᾶς, XV. 54 ; ἁγνάς, XIX. 28 (?).
ἀγορά : ἀγοράν, XV. 43 ; ἀγορᾷ, fr. 13, 4.
ἀγρός : ἀγροῦ, fr. 72, 1.
ἀγρότερος : ἀγροτέρα, V. 123, XI. 37.

ἀγυιά : ἀγυιαί, III. 16, fr. 46, 12 ; ἀγυιάς, IX. 17 (?), XI. 58, fr. 1, 3 ; ἀγυιᾶν, IX. 52.
ἀγχίαλος : ἀγχιάλοισιν, IV. 14.
ἀγχίδομος : ἀγχιδόμοις, XIII. 56 (?). (S.)
ἄγω : ἄγουσιν, fr. 56, 10 ; ἄγον, XV. 37 ; ἄγονται, III. 46 ; ἄγετο, XX. 4 ; ἄγουσα, XVII. 2 ; ἄγοντα, XVIII. 34 ; ἄξοντα, V. 60.
ἀγών : ἀγῶνι, V. 44 ; ἀγώνων, IX. 21.
*ἀδεισιβόας : ἀδεισιβόαν, V. 155 ; ἀ-δεισιβόαι, XI. 61.
ἀδελφεός : ἀδελφεῶν, V. 118.
ἀδίαντος, XVII. 122.
ἄδικος : ἀδίκοισιν, XVIII. 42.
ἀδμάς : ἀδμᾶτες, fr. 60, 1.
ἄδματος or ἄδμητος : ἄδματοι, XI. 84 ; ἀδμήτα, V. 167.
Ἄδραστος : Ἄδραστον, IX. 19.
ἀδύπνοος : ἀδυπνόων, XIII. 40 (?).
ἄεθλον : ἀέθλων, IV. 20 (?), IX. 8 ; ἀέθλοις, VIII. 16, X. 19, XIII. 48 (?), 165.
ἀείδω : ἄεισαν, VI. 6 ; ἀείδειν, IV. 18 ; ἀείδεται, IV. 5 (?).
ἀεικέλιος : ἀεικελιᾶν, fr. 60, 1.
ἀεικελίως, III. 45.
ἀείρω or αἴρω : ἀείρας, III. 36 ; ἄρατο, II. 5.
ἄεκατι, XVIII. 9.
ἀέκων : ἀέκοντα, XVII. 44.
ἀέλιος : see ἅλιος.
ἄελλα : ἄελλαν, X. 22.
*ἀελλοδρόμας : ἀελλοδρόμαν, V. 39.
ἄελπτος : ἄελπτον, III. 29, XIII. 98.
ἀέξω : ἀέξει, XIII. 174 (?) ; ἀέξειν, III. 78 ; and see αὔξω.
*ἀερσίμαχος : ἀερσιμάχους, XIII. 67.

ἄζυξ : ἄζυγα, XVI. 20.
ἀηδών : ἀηδόνος, III. 98.
ἀήτα, XVII. 91.
ἀθαμβής, XV. 58.
'Αθάνα, XIII. 162 ; 'Αθάνας, XV. 2,
  XVII. 7 ; 'Αθάνᾳ, XVI. 21.
'Αθᾶναι : 'Αθάνας, XVIII. 60 ; 'Αθανᾶν,
  XVIII. 1 ; 'Αθάναις, X. 17, XIX. 10.
'Αθαναῖος : 'Αθαναίων, XVII. 92.
ἀθάνατος : ἀθάνατον, X. 11, XIII. 32 ;
  ἀθάνατοι, V. 193 ; ἀθανάτων, V. 86,
  XVI. 4 (?) ; ἀθανάτοισ(ιν), XI. 6, XV.
  45.
ἄθεος : ἀθέων, XI. 109.
ἀθλέω : ἄθλησαν, IX. 12.
ἀθρέω : ἄθρησον, V. 8.
ἄθυρμα, IX. 87 (?) : ἀθυρμάτων, XVIII.
  57 ; ἀθύρμασι, fr. 71, 3.
*ἄθυρσις : ἄθυρσιν, XIII. 60.
αἱ(= εἱ), V. 5, XVII. 64.
αἰαῖ, V. 153, fr. 45, 1.
Αἰακίδας : Αἰακίδαις, XIII. 133.
Αἰακός : Αἰακοῦ, XIII. 150 ; Αἰακῷ,
  XIII. 66.
Αἴας : Αἴαντα, XIII. 71.
Αἴγινα, XIII. 45 ; Αἴγιναν, IX. 55, X.
  35 (?) ; Αἰγίνας, XII. 6.
αἴγλα : αἴγλαν, XIII. 107.
αἰγλάεις : αἰγλάεντα, fr. 56, 9.
Αἴγυπτος : Αἰγύπτου, fr. 56, 10.
'Αΐδας : 'Αΐδα, V. 61.
ἀϊδής, fr. 70.
αἰεί or αἰέν : αἰεί, I. 38, IX. 81 ; αἰέν,
  XIII. 174, XVIII. 43, fr. 71. 3.
αἰετός, III. 19.
αἰθήρ, III. 86 ; αἰθέρα, III. 36, V. 17,
  IX. 35, XVII. 73.
αἰθύς : αἰθᾶν, fr. 46, 6.
Αἴθρα, XVII. 59.
αἰθύσσω : αἰθύσσει, fr. 56, 3.
αἴθω : αἴθεσθαι, fr. 46, 3.
αἴθων, XIII. 17 ; αἴθωνος, V. 124.
αἷμα : αἵματι, XI. 111, XIII. 120 (?).
αἰνέω : αἰνεῖ, XIII. 50 (?) ; αἰνέοι, IX.
  102 ; αἰνείτω, XIII. 168 ; αἰνεῖν, V.
  16, 188.
αἰνός : αἰνά, XVII. 10 (?).
*αἰνόστολος : αἰνοστόλων, XIX. 43.
αἴξ : αἰγῶν, V. 101.
*αἰολόπρυμνος : αἰολοπρύμνοις, fr. 1, 4.
αἰόλος : αἰόλοις, XV. 57.
αἰπεινός : αἰπεινάν, IX. 34.
αἰπύς : αἰπύν, III. 36.
†ἀϊόναξ, XVII. 112.
αἱρέω : εἷλεν, XI. 85 ; αἱρεῦνται, XV. 56.

αἴρω : see ἀείρω.
αἶσα, XIII. 33, fr. 62, 4 ; αἶσαν, X. 32,
  XVII. 27.
ἀΐσσω : ἄϊξαν, XIII. 111 ; ἀΐξον, II. 1 (?).
αἴτιος, XI. 34, XV. 52.
Αἴτνα : Αἴτνας, IV. 14 (?).
Αἰτωλίς : Αἰτωλίδος, VIII. 13.
Αἰτωλός : Αἰτωλοῖς, V. 114.
αἰχματάς : αἰχματάν, XIII. 100.
αἰχμοφόρος : αἰχμοφόροι, XI. 89.
αἰών : αἰῶνα, I. 15 ; αἰῶνι, XIII. 28 (?).
*ἀκαμαντορόας : ἀκαμαντορόαν, V. 180.
ἀκάματος, XIII. 145 (?) ; ἀκαμάτας, V.
  25 : ἀκαμάτοις, XIX. 20.
ἄκαμπτος, fr. 62, 2.
ἀκάρπωτος : ἀκάρπωτον, fr. 48, 6.
ἀκίνητος : ἀκινήτους, V. 200.
ἀκοίτας, X. 9.
ἄκοιτις : ἄκοιτιν, V. 169.
ἄκοιτος : ἄκοιτον, XIX. 23. (S.)
ἀκόλουθος : ἀκόλουθον, XV. 55.
'Ακρίσιος : 'Ακρισίῳ, XI. 66.
ἀκούω : ἄκουσον, XV. 53.
ἄκριτος : ἀκρίτους, X. 46.
ἀκτά : ἀκτάν, XVI. 16.
ἀκτέα : ἀκτέας, IX. 34.
ἄκων : ἄκοντας, XVIII. 49.
ἀλαθεία, XIII. 171 ; ἀλάθεια (or ἀλαθεία),
  fr. 51, 2 ; ἀληθείας (sic), V. 187 ;
  ἀλαθείᾳ, III. 96, VIII. 4, IX. 85.
ἀλαμπής : ἀλαμπέσι, XIII. 142 (?).
ἄλαστος : ἄλαστον, III. 34.
ἀλάτας : ἀλάταν, XVIII. 36.
ἄλγος, XVII. 19.
ἀλέκτωρ, IV. 8.
'Αλεξίδαμος : 'Αλεξίδαμον, XI. 18.
'Αλθαία, V. 120.
ἀλίγκιος : ἀλιγκία, V. 168.
*ἀλιναιέτας : ἀλιναιέται, XVII. 97.
ἄλιξ : ἄλικι, VIII. 7.
ἅλιος or δέλιος : δέλιος, XI. 22 ; ἀλίου,
  III. 80 ; ἀελίου, V. 161, fr. 13, 10 ;
  person., 'Αλίου, XVII. 50.
ἀλκά : ἀλκάν, XIII. 80 (?) ; ἀλκάς, XI.
  126.
ἄλκιμος : ἄλκιμον, V. 146, XVIII. 38 ;
  ἀλκίμων, XVIII. 13.
'Αλκμήνιος, V. 71.
ἀλλά, I. 38, III. 53, 91, V. 103, XI.
  89, 95, XIII. 88, 145, XIV. 16, XV.
  53, XVII. 33, 82, fr. 52, 1 ; 57, 1 ;
  58 ; 62, 3.
ἀλλοδαμία : ἀλλοδαμίαν, XVIII. 37.
ἀλλοῖος : ἀλλοίαν, X. 36 (?), XIV. 7.
ἄλλος, X. 36, XIV. 7 ; ἄλλαν, fr. 62, 3 ;

ἄλλαι, IX. 63; ἄλλους, *fr.* 50;
ἄλλων, I. 19; ἄλλοισ(ιν), V. 127,*fr.*
50; ἄλλαισιν, *fr.* 15, 4.
ἄλλοτε, *fr.* 62, 3.
ἀλλότριος: ἀλλότριον, XV. 60.
ἄλλως, *fr.* 63.
ἄλοχος: ἄλοχον, XVI. 29, XVII. 109;
ἀλόχῳ, III. 33 (?).
ἅλς: ἁλός, V. 25, XVII. 63, 122, *fr.*
13, 9.
ἄλσος, III. 19, XI. 118, XVII. 85.
Ἀλυάττας: Ἀλυάττα, III. 40.
ἀλυκτάζω: ἠλύκταζον, XI. 93.
Ἀλφεός or Ἀλφειός: Ἀλφεόν, V. 38,
181, XI. 26; Ἀλφεοῦ, VI. 3;
Ἀλφειοῦ, VIII. 11, XIII. 160.
ἅμα, III. 91, XIII. 160 (?).
ἀμαιμάκετος: ἀμαιμάκετον, XI. 64.
ἀμαλδύνω: ἀμαλδύνει, XIV. 3.
ἅμαρ, III. 29, *fr.* 48, 4; ἅματι, XI. 23;
ἅματα, V. 113.
ἀμάρυγμα, IX. 36.
ἀμαυρόω: ἀμαυροῦται, XIII. 144.
ἀμάχανος: ἀμαχάνου, I. 33.
ἄμαχος, XVI. 23.
ἀμβολά: ἀμβολᾶς, *fr.* 52, 1.
ἀμβρόσιος: ἀμβροσίων, XIX. 2.
ἄμβροτος: ἀμβρότοιο, XVII. 42.
ἀμείβω: ἀμείψας, XVIII. 16; ἀμειβόμενος, V. 159.
ἀμεμφής: ἀμεμφέα, XVII. 114.
ἀμέρα: ἀμέρας, XIX. 27; ἀμέρᾳ, *fr.*
1, 3.
ἀμέρδω: ἄμερσαν, XI. 36.
ἄμερος: ἀμέρα, XI. 39.
ἀμέτερος: ἀμέτερον, *fr.* 45, 1; ἀμετέρας
(gen. sing.), V. 144, XVIII. 5;
ἀμετέρᾳ, V. 90; ἀμετέρας (acc.
plur.), XII. 3.
*ἀμετρόδικος: ἀμετροδίκοις, XI. 68.
ἄμετρος: ἄμετρον, XVII. 67.
ἀμίαντος, III. 86.
ἀμός: ἀμόν, *fr.* 46, 11.
ἀμπελοτρόφος: ἀμπελοτρόφον, VI. 5.
(S.)
ἀμύσσω: ἀμύσσει, XVIII. 11; ἄμυξεν,
XVII. 19.
ἀμφάκης: ἄμφακες, XI. 87; ἀμφάκεα,
fr. 46, 8; ἀμφάκει, *fr.* 5, 8.
ἀμφί, with acc., IV. 4 (?), X. 33,
XI. 18; with dat., I. 11, VIII. 10 (?),
X. 44, XVII. 105, 124, XVIII. 53.
ἀμφιβάλλω: ἀμφιβάλλει, XVIII. 6;
ἀμφέβαλεν, XVII. 112; βάλωσιν
ἄμφι, XIX. 7.

*ἀμφικύμων: ἀμφικύμονα, XVI. 16.
ἀμφιπολέω: ἀμφιπολεῖ, *fr.* 48, 3.
ἀμφιτίθημι: ἀμφιτίθει, *fr.* 71, 4.
Ἀμφιτρίτα: Ἀμφιτρίταν, XVII. 111.
Ἀμφιτρύων: Ἀμφιτρύανος, V. 156.
Ἀμφιτρυωνιάδας, V. 85; Ἀμφιτρυωνιάδαν, XVI. 15.
ἀμφότερος: ἀμφοτέραισιν, V. 188.
ἀμώμητος: ἀμώμητον, V. 147.
ἄν, I. 42, V. 97, 110, 135, XVII. 41,
XIX. 3; and see κε.
ἀνά: with acc., V. 66; with dat., III.
50.
ἀνάγκα: *fr.* 56, 1; ἀνάγκαν, XI. 72,
XIII. 96; ἀνάγκᾳ, XI. 46.
ἀναδέω: ἀναδησάμενος, X. 16.
ἀνάδημα; see ἄνθημα.
*ἀναιδομάχας: ἀναιδομάχαν, V. 105.
ἀνακάμπτω: ἀνεκάμπτετο, XVII. 82.
ἀνακαρύσσω: ἀγκάρυξαν, X. 27.
ἀνακλαίω: ἀγκλαίσασα, V. 142 (?).
ἀνακομίζω: ἀγκομίσαι, III. 89.
ἀναμίγνυμι: ἀμμιγνυμένα, *fr.* 56, 4.
ἀναμιμνήσκω: ἀνέμνασεν, II. 6.
ἄναξ, III. 39, 76, V. 84, IX. 45, XIII.
115, XVII. 78, XVIII. 2.
*ἀναξίαλος, XX. 8.
*ἀναξιβρόντας, XVII. 66.
*ἀναξίμολπος: ἀναξιμόλπου, VI. 10.
ἀναπάλλω: ἀνέπαλτο, XI. 65.
ἀνάπαυσις: ἀνάπαυσιν, XIX. 36.
ἀναπαύω: ἀμπαύσας, V. 7.
ἀναπτύσσω: ἀναπτύξας, V. 75.
ἀνατείνω: ἄντειναν, XIII. 105; ἀν-
τείναν, XI. 100; ἀντείνασα, *fr.* 53,
3.
ἀνατίθημι: ἀνέθηκε, *fr.* 72, 1.
ἄνατος: ἄνατοι, *fr.* 60, 1.
ἀναφαίνω: ἀναφαίνων, XIII. 43.
ἄνθημα, VIII. 14.
ἄνεμος: V. 65; ἀνέμων, *fr.* 72, 2.
ἀνευθύνω: ἀνευθύνας, X. 51 (?). (S.)
ἀνήρ, III. 10 (?), V. 191, VIII. 8,
XVIII. 7; ἄνδρα, III. 69, X. 48,
XIII. 168, XVIII. 31; ἀνδρός, I. 25,
fr. 64; ἀνδρί, III. 88; ἄνδρας, *fr.* 1.
11; ἀνδρῶν, X. 38, XIII. 156, XIV.
8, 17, XVIII. 40, *fr.* 51, 2; ἀνέρων,
XIII. 163; ἀνδρέσσι(ν), V. 96, XI.
114; ἀνδράσι, *fr.* 56, 5.
ἀνδρόκτονος: ἀνδρόκτονον, XVIII. 23.
ἀνθεμόεις: ἀνθεμόεντι, XVI. 5; ἀνθεμόεντας, XIII. 55.
ἀνθεμώδης: ἀνθεμώδεα, XIX. 39.
ἄνθος: ἄνθεα, III. 94, XIII. 27, XVI. 9,

fr. 46, 2 ; ἀνθέων, XI. 18, XIII. 59 ; ἄνθεσιν, X. 15.
ἄνθρωπος : ἀνθρώπων, I. 23, 31, VIII. 6, IX. 18, X. 48, *fr.* 43 ; 54 ; 68 ; ἀνθρώποισ(ιν), V. 30, VII. 9, X. 12, XIV. 1, XV. 54, *fr.* 56, 7 ; 60, 2 ; incert., IX. 88.
ἀνίκατος : ἀνίκατον, V. 103.
ἀνίσχω : ἀνίσχοντες, XV. 45.
ἄνοπλος : ἄνοπλον, XVIII. 35 (?).
ἀντάω : ἀντάσας, XIII. 94.
Ἀντήνωρ : Ἀντήνορος, XV. 1 (?).
ἀντί, I. 19.
ἀντίθεος : ἀντιθέου, XV. 1 ; ἀντίθεοι, XI. 79.
ἀοιδά : ἀοιδάν, XVIII. 4 ; ἀοιδαί, XIII. 197; ἀοιδᾶν, *fr.* 46, 2 ; ἀοιδαῖς, VI. 14.
ἀολλίζω : ἀόλλιζον, XV. 42.
ἅπαξ, *fr.* 43.
ἅπας : see πᾶς.
ἀπείρων : ἀπείρονα, IX. 30 (?).
ἀπενθής, XIII. 54 (?) ; ἀπενθῆ, *fr.* 48, 2.
ἄπιστος : ἄπιστον, III. 57, XVII. 117.
ἄπλατος : ἀπλάτοιο, V. 62 ; ἀπλάτου, XIII. 18.
ἀπό, I. 29, V. 10, IX. 21, 99 (?), XI. 65, XVII. 55, 103, XVIII. 55, *fr.* 46, 10 ; 53, 1 ; 56, 10 ; 72, 4.
ἀπολαγχάνειν : λαγχάνειν ἄπο, IV. 20.
ἀπόλλυμι : ἀπώλεσεν, XVI. 31.
Ἀπόλλων, III. 29, 58, 76, IV. 2, XIII. 115 ; Ἀπόλλον, XVI. 10.
ἀποπλέω : ἀποπλέων, *fr.* 1, 13.
ἀπόρθητος : ἀπορθήτων, IX. 52.
ἀποσεύω : ἀπεσσύμεναι, XI. 82.
ἀποτρέπω : ἀπέτραπεν, XI. 27.
ἀποφεύγω, *fr.* 2, 4.
ἀποφθίνω : ἀποφθιμένῳ, IX. 79.
ἄπρακτος : ἀπράκταν, X. 8 ; ἄπρακτα, *fr.* 49, 1.
ἅπτω : ἅπτειν, III. 49.
ἀπωθέω : ἀπωσάμενον, V. 189.
ἄρα, XIII. 131, 195.
ἀράχνα : ἀραχνᾶν, *fr.* 46, 7.
ἀργαλέος : ἀργαλέαν, XI. 72.
Ἀργεῖος, I. 4 (?) ; Ἀργεῖον, II. 4 (?) ; Ἀργείων, IX. 11, XV. 5.
ἀργηστάς, V. 67.
ἀργικέραυνος : ἀργικεραύνου, V. 58.
Ἄργος, ὁ : Ἄργον, XIX. 19, 33.
Ἄργος, τό, X. 32, XI. 60, 81, XIX. 15.
ἀρείων, *fr.* 10, 2 ; ἀρείονος, XVIII. 29.
ἀρετά, I. 43, XIII. 143 ; ἀρετάν, I. 22, V. 32, *fr.* 51, 2 ; ἀρετᾶς, III. 90,

XI. 7 ; ἀρεταί, XIV. 8 ; ἀρετᾶν, X. 13.
*ἀρέταιχμος, XVII. 47.
Ἀρήϊος : Ἀρηΐων, XVIII. 57.
ἀρηΐφιλος : ἀρηϊφίλου, V. 166 ; ἀρηΐφιλοι, XV. 50 ; ἀρηϊφίλους, *fr.* I. 11; ἀρηϊφίλοις, XI. 113.
Ἄρης, V. 130, XIII. 113, *fr.* 62, 2 ; Ἄρηος, V. 34, IX. 44.
ἀρίγνωτος, V. 29 ; ἀρίγνωτον, XVII. 57 ; ἀριγνώτοιο, X. 37 ; ἀριγνώτοις, IX. 64.
ἀρίσταρχος : ἀριστάρχου, XIII. 25.
*ἀριστόκαρπος : ἀριστοκάρπου, III. 1.
Ἀριστομένειος : Ἀριστομένειον, VI. 12.
*ἀριστόπατρα, XI. 106.
ἄριστος : ἄριστον, III. 22, XIV. 2 ; ἄριστοι, V. 111.
Ἀρκαδία : Ἀρκαδίαν, XI. 94.
ἅρμα, V. 177.
ἁρμόζω : ἁρμόζει, XIV. 12.
ἁρπαλέαν, XIII. 98.
ἄρρητος : ἀρρήτων, *fr.* 47, 2.
Ἄρτεμις, XI. 37 ; Ἀρτέμιδος, V. 99.
ἀρχά : ἀρχᾶς, XI. 65.
ἀρχαγέτας : ἀρχαγέταν, III. 24.
ἀρχαγός : ἀρχαγόν, V. 179 ; ἀρχαγούς, IX. 51.
ἀρχαῖος : ἀρχαίαν, V. 150.
Ἀρχέμορος : Ἀρχεμόρῳ, IX. 12.
ἄρχω : ἄρχεν, XV. 47.
†ἀσαγεύοντα†, IX. 13.
ἄσπετος : ἄσπετοι, XIX. 34.
ἀσπίς : ἀσπίσιν, *fr.* 2, 3.
ἄσταχυς : ἀσταχύων, *fr.* 72, 4.
ἀστραπά : ἀστραπάν, VIII. 56.
ἀστράπτω : ἄστραψε, XVIII. 71.
ἄστρον : ἄστρων, IX. 28.
ἄστυ, III. 43, XI. 12, 57, XIII. 82 ; ἄστεα, XIII. 155.
*ἀστύθεμις : ἀστύθεμιν, IV. 3.
ἀσφαλής : ἀσφαλεῖ, XIII. 33 ; ἀσφαλέστατον, XIX. 38.
ἀτάρβακτος, V. 139.
*ἀταρβομάχας, XVI. 28.
ἀτάσθαλος : ἀτάσθαλον, XVIII. 24.
ἄτεκνος : ἄτεκνον, *fr.* 12, 7.
ἄτερθε, XVII. 12.
Ἀτρείδας : Ἀτρειδᾶν, XI. 123 ; Ἀτρείδᾳ, XV. 6.
ἀτρέμα, V. 7.
ἀτρόμητος, XIII. 90.
ἄτρυτος : ἄτρυτον, IX. 80 (?) ; ἀτρύτῳ, V. 27.
ἀτύζομαι : ἀτυζόμενοι, XIII. 83.

αὐγά : αὐγάς, XI. 100 ; αὐγαῖς, *fr.* 13, 10.
αὐδάεις, XV. 44.
αὐθαίρετος : αὐθαίρετοι, *fr.* 62, 1.
αὐθιγενής, II. 11.
αὐλά : αὐλᾶς, III. 32.
αὐλός : αὐλῶν, II. 12, X. 54, *fr.* 46, 5.
αὔξω : αὔξουσιν, X. 45 ; αὔξειν, I. 24.
ἄϋπνος : ἄϋπνον, XIX. 23.
αὔρα : αὔραι, XVII. 6.
αὔριον, III. 79.
αὖτε, X. 23 (?).
αὐτίκα, XI. 110, *fr.* 56, 6.
αὖτις, III. 89, XV. 60.
αὐτόματος : αὐτόματοι, *fr.* 59, 2.
Αὐτομήδης : Αὐτομήδει, IX. 25.
αὐτός : αὐτόν, XVIII. 41, *fr.* 15, 3 (?).
αὐτοῦ (ibi), V. 178.
αὐχήν : αὐχένι, II. 7.
Ἀφάρης : Ἀφάρητα, V. 129.
ἄφατος : ἄφατα, XVIII. 18.
ἄφθεγκτος : ἀφθέγκτοισιν, *fr.* 45, 2.
ἄφθιτος : ἄφθιτον, I. 45 (?).
ἀφικνέομαι : ἀφίκετο, XIX. 40.
ἀφνεός, I. 34 ; ἀφνεόν, V. 53 ; ἀφνεοῦ, XVII. 34.
Ἀφροδίτα, XVII. 116.
ἀφροσύνα : ἀφροσύναις, XV. 57.
Ἀχαιός : Ἀχαιῶν, III. 9 (?), XI. 126, XV. 39 ; Ἀχαιοῖς, XI. 114.
ἀχείμαντος : ἀχείμαντον. *fr.* 65.
Ἀχιλλεύς, XIII. 86 ; Ἀχιλλέα, XIII. 68, 101.
ἄχος, XI. 85 ; ἀχέων, XI. 76, XV. 52.
ἀχρεῖος, I. 6 (?) ; ἀχρεῖον, X. 50.
δάς : δοῦς, XVII. 42 ; δοῖ, XIII. 96 ; person., Ἀώς, V. 40.

*βαθυδείελος, I. 1 (?).
βαθύζωνος : βαθύζωνον, *fr.* 1, 8 ; βαθυζώνοιο, XI. 16 ; βαθυζώνοις, V. 9.
βαθύξυλος, XIII. 136.
βαθύπλουτος : βαθύπλουτον, III. 82.
βαθύς, III. 85 ; βαθύν, V. 16, XV. 61 ; βαθείας, XVII. 63.
Βακχυλίδης : Βακχυλίδῃ, *fr.* 71, 4.
βάλλω : ἔβαλλον, III. 51.
βαρυαχής : βαρυαχέας, XVI. 18.
βαρύβρομος : βαρύβρομον, XVII. 76.
βαρυπενθής : βαρυπενθέσιν, XIV. 12.
βαρύς : βαρεῖαν, XVII. 28, 96.
βαρύτλατος, XIV. 4,
βαρύφθογγος : βαρύφθογγον, IX. 9.
βάσανος, *fr.* 37, 2 (?).

βασιλεύς, *fr.* I, 15 ; βασιλεῦ, XVIII. 1 ; βασιλεῖ, XI. 63, XV. 6, 38.
βέλος : βέλη, V. 132.
βία : βίαν, V. 181, XVII. 23, 45 ; βίᾳ, V. 116, XI. 91, XVIII. 10.
βιάω : βιᾶται, XIII. 167, *fr.* 43.
βίος : βίον, *fr.* 48, 2 ; βίῳ, I. 31.
βιοτά : βιοτάν, V. 53.
βλέπω : βλέπεις, XVII. 75 ; βλέποντα, XIX. 19.
βλέφαρον, V. 157 ; βλεφάρῳ, XI. 17 ; βλεφάρων, *fr.* 46, 10.
βληχρός: βληχράν, XIII. 194 ; βληχρᾶς, XI. 65.
βλώσκω : ἔμολεν, XVII. 100 ; μόλε, XVII. 122 ; μόλοι, V. 110 ; μολών, III. 30 (?); μολοῦσα, XIV. 4.
βοά, IX. 68 (?) ; βοάν, IX. 35.
βοαθόος, *fr.* 72, 3 ; βοαθόον, XIII. 70.
βοάω : βοάσε, XVII. 14.
Βοιώτιος : Βοιωτίοισιν, *fr.* 57, 2.
Βοιωτός, V. 191.
Βορέας, XIII. 92 ; Βορέα, V. 46 ; incert., *fr.* 38, 2 (?).
Βορέας (adj.), XVII. 91.
βορήϊος : βορήϊαι, XVII. 6.
βούθυτος : βουθύτοις, III. 15.
βουλά : βουλαῖσι, XI. 121.
βουλεύω : βούλευσεν, V. 139.
βοῦς, XIX. 16 ; βοῦν, XVI. 22 ; βοῦς (acc. plur.), XI. 104 ; βοῶν, V. 102, X. 44, *fr.* 46, 3 ; 57, 1.
βῶπις : βοῶπιν, XI. 99, XVII. 110 (?).
βρίθω: βρίθοντι, *fr.* 46, 12 ; βρίσει, X. 47.
Βρισηΐς : Βρισηΐδος, XIII. 104.
βροτός : βροτῷ, III. 66 ; βροτῶν, I. 14, III. 91, V. 63, 87, 109, 190, 194, IX. 22, 85, XI. 35, XIII. 29, 169, XVII. 32, XVIII. 12, *fr.* 41 ; 67 ; βροτοῖσ(ι), XVII. 118, *fr.* 48, 1 ; 61, 2 ; incert., *fr.* 36.
*Βροτωφελής : βροτωφελέα, XIII. 158.
βρύω : βρύει, III. 15 ; βρύουσι, III. 16 ; βρύουσα, XIII. 146 ; βρύοντα, XIX. 44 (?) ; βρύοντες, VI. 9.
βωμός : βωμόν, X. 30, XI. 41, 110, XIII. 25 ; βωμῶν, *fr.* 46, 3.

γᾶ : γᾶν, XI. 70 ; γᾶς, XV. 63 ; γᾷ, V. 42, VIII. 3, XI. 110.
γαῖα, XIII. 120 ; γαῖαν, *fr.* 62, 4 ; γαίας, V. 24, *fr.* 6, 4 ; γαίᾳ, IX. 38.
γαμβρός : γαμβρῷ, XVII. 50.
γάμος : γάμῳ, XVII. 115.
γάρ, III. 5, 22 (5th word in clause), 51,

83, IV. 4, V. 46, 54, 97, 122, 163
(3rd word), 197, IX. 10 (?), 27, 53,
X. 39, XI. 47, 59, 64, XIII. 17 (?),
142, XVII. 5, 41, 103, XVIII. 12, 43,
fr. 47, 2; 49, 1; 51, 1; 56, 3; 61,
1; 72, 3.
γᾶρυς : γᾶρυν, V. 15; γάρυϊ, XV. 48.
γαρύω, III. 85.
γε, I. 32, V. 4, 55, IX. 25, XI. 23, XIII.
50, XVI. 13.
γέγωνα : γέγωνεν, III. 37.
*γελανόω : γελανώσας, V. 80.
γέμω : γέμουσαν, XVI. 4.
γενεά : γενεάν, XI. 74; γενεᾶς, IX. 49.
γένος, I. 2, XVII. 93.
γεραίρω, XIII. 192; γεραίρει, IV. 3,
VI. 14; ἐγεραίρομεν (?), IV. 13;
γεραίρουσα, II. 13.
γέρας, III. 12, VII. 8, XI. 36, XIX. 14.
γέρων : γέροντα, III. 59.
γενύω : γεύσαντο, IX. 46.
γῆρας, III. 89, *fr.* 42, 3.
γίγας : γίγαντας, XV. 63.
γίγνομαι : γένετο, XIX. 29.
γιγνώσκω : γνῶν, V. 152; γνώσῃ, V. 3.
γλαυκός : γλαυκόν, VIII. 13; γλαυκᾷ,
XI. 29.
γλυκύδωρος : γλυκύδωρε, III. 3, XI. 1;
γλυκύδωρον, V. 4.
γλυκύς : γλυκεῖα, V. 151, *fr.* 56, 1;
57, 2; γλυκεῖαν, II. 12; γλυκύ, I.
37; γλύκιστον, III. 47.
γλῶσσα : γλῶσσαν, V. 196.
γνήσιος : γνησίων, IX. 83.
γνώμα : γνῶμαι, XI. 35; γνώμας, III.
79; γνώμαισι, *fr.* 67.
γνῶμα, X. 51 (?).
γόνος : γόνον, III. 8 (?).
γυάλον : γυάλοις, *fr.* II. 2.
γυιαλκής : γυιαλκέα (acc. sing. masc.),
XII. 8, (neut. plur.), IX. 38.
γυῖον : γυίων, VII. 7 (?), XVII. 104;
γυίοις, XVII. 124.
γυμνάσιον : γυμνασίων, *fr.* 46, 5.
γυνά, V. 139; γυναῖκα, *fr.* 55, 2;
γυναικός, XIII. 103; γυναῖκες, III.
45; γυναικῶν, XI. 112.

*δαδοφόρος : δᾳδοφόρε, *fr.* 66.
Δαϊάνειρα : Δαϊάνειραν, V. 173; Δαϊανείρᾳ, XVI. 24.
δαιδάλεος : δαιδαλέας, V. 140; δαιδαλέαν,
fr. 46, 3.
δαΐζω : δαΐζει, XIII. 93.
δαιμόνιος : δαιμόνιον, XVI. 35.

δαίμων, V. 113, 135, IX. 26, XVI. 23,
XVII. 46, *fr.* 50; δαῖμον, III. 37;
δαίμονι, *fr.* 42, 1 (?); δαίμονες, XVII.
117; δαίμοσι(ν), IX. 84, XIV. 1.
Δαΐπυλος : Δαϊπύλου, V. 145.
δαίς : δαῖτας, *fr.* 59, 2.
δαΐφρων, V. 122, 137.
δάκρυ, XVII. 95.
δακρυόεις, V. 94.
δακρύω : δάκρυσα, V. 153.
Δάλιος : Δάλιε, XVII. 130.
Δαλογενής, III. 58, XI. 15.
δαμάζω : δάμασεν, *fr.* I. 9; δαμασείας,
XVII. 44.
δάμαλις : δάμαλιν, XIX. 24.
δαμασίμβροτος, XIII. 17.
δαμάσιππος : δαμασίππου, III. 23.
*δαμασίχθων : δαμασίχθονι, XVI. 19.
Δαμάτηρ : Δάματρα, III. 2.
δάμνημι : δάμναται, *fr.* 46, 8.
Δαναοί : Δαναοῖς, XIII. 112.
Δαναός : Δαναοῦ, XI. 74.
δάπεδον : δαπέδοις, XI. 25.
δάπτω : δαπτομέναν, XVI. 14.
δάσκιος : δάσκιον, XI. 93.
δάω : ἐδάη, V. 64.
δέ, I. 13, 23, 24, 25, 27, 36, 43, 44, II.
6, 11, III. 9, 17, 29 (?), 31, 35, 39,
47, 49, 75, 86, 87, 88, 92, 94, 96,
V. 6, 14, 17, 22, 27, 36, 42, 68, 71,
74, 76, 84, 89, 91, 93, 104, 111,
113, 121 (?), 124, 132, 149, 151,
152, 153, 170, 187, VI. 10, VII. 8,
VIII. 3, 5, IX. 85, 88, X. 23, 29, 36,
38, 42, 43, 46, XI. 4, 9, 13, 18, 24,
37, 50, 53, 55, 69, 77, 85, 87, 104,
106, 110, 115, XIII. 20, 58, 83 (?),
95, 96, 97, 105, 108, 113, 117,
119 (?), 151, 169, 171, 175, XIV. 3,
7 (?), 8, 18, XV. 37, 44, 45, 57, 61,
XVI. 16, XVII. 11, 13, 14 (?), 16, 17,
28, 46, 48, 58, 64, 67, 71, 76, 78,
81, 86, 89, 90, 91 (?), 92, 97, 106,
107, 124, 128 (bis), XVIII. 18, 31,
47, 49, 54, 56, 57, 60, *fr.* 1, 7, 16;
4, 1; 15, 5; 41; 42, 1; 43, 1; 46,
L, 6, 9, 12; 48, 1, 3, 4; 51, 2; 55,
1; 56, 7, 8, 9; 59, 1 (bis), 2; 62,
1; 63; 70; 71, 3.
δε (enclit.) : πόντονδε, XVII. 94.
δείδω : ἔδεισεν, XVII. 102; δέδοικα,
XVIII. 30.
δείκνυμι : δείξομεν, XVII. 46; δεῖξαι,
fr. 52, 2.
δειλός : δειλοῖσιν, I. 23.

Δεινομένης : Δεινομένευς, III. 7 (MS. -εος), V. 35 ; Δεινομένεος, IV. 13.
δεινός : δεινοῦ, III. 53.
δέκατος : δέκατον, XI. 59 ; δεκάτῳ, fr. 1, 16.
δελφίς : δελφῖνες, XVII. 97.
Δελφός : Δελφοί, III. 21 ; Δελφῶν, XVI. 11.
δέμας, V. 147, IX. 31.
Δεξιθέα : Δεξιθέαν, fr. 1, 9.
*δεξίστρατος : δεξίστρατον, XV. 43.
δέος, V. 84.
δέρκομαι : δέρκεται, XV. 51.
δέσποινα, XI. 117, XIII. 62.
δεῦρο, V. 8.
δέχομαι : ἐδέξατο, VIII. 9 ; δέξατο, XVI. 35, XVII. 85 ; δέκτο, X. 31, XI. 17.
δή, V. 142, 156, XI. 95, XII. 4, XIII. 88, 160.
δῆρις : δῆριν, V. 111.
διά : with acc., III. 61, VI. 4, IX. 30, XIII. 123, XV. 40; with gen., IX. 47, XIII. 19.
διάγω : διάγειν, V. 53.
διαΐσσω : διαΐσσεν, III. 54.
διακρίνω : διακρίνει, IX. 28 ; διακεκριμέναι, fr. 68.
διατελέω : διατελεῖν, fr. 48, 2.
διατρέχω : διέδραμεν, XV. 44.
δίδυμος : διδύμους, III. 78.
δίδωμι : ἔδωκε(ν), IX. 26, XI. 39, XIII. 47 ; δῶκε(ν), IX. 97 (?), XVII. 116, fr. 42, 1 ; δόσαν, XVII. 37 ; δοίητε, IX. 2.
διέπω : διέπουσι, III. 21.
δίζημαι : δίζηνται, I. 39 ; δίζησθαι, XVIII. 60.
δίκα : δίκας, XI. 26, XIII. 12, 169, XVII. 25, XVIII. 42 ; person., Δίκαν, XV. 54.
δίκαιος : δίκαιοι, fr. 59, 2 ; δικαίας (acc. plur.), XI. 123 ; δικαίων, XV. 47 ; δικαίαισι, XIV. 11.
(δίκω) : δικών, XVII. 62.
δινάεις : δινᾶντα, XIII. 131 : δινᾶντος, XIII. 45.
δινέω : δίνασεν, XVII. 18 ; δινεῦντο, XVII. 107.
Διονύσιος : Διονυσίοισι, fr. 56, 4.
Διόνυσος : Διόνυσον, XIX. 50 ; Διωνύσου, IX. 98 (?).
δίς, X. 27, 29, XVII. 2.
δίσκος : δίσκον, IX. 32.
διχόμηνις : διχομήνιδος, IX. 29.

διχοστασία : διχοστασίαις, XI. 67.
διώξιππος : διωξίπποιο, IX. 44, XI. 75.
δνοφερός : δνοφερόν, XVI. 32.
δοιάζω : *δοίαξε, XI. 87.
δοκέω, XVIII. 12 ; δοκεῖ, fr. 56, 7.
δόλιος, XVII. 116.
δολιχαύχην : δολιχαύχενι, XVI. 6.
δολιχός : δολιχάν, XVIII. 16 ; δολιχῷ, XVIII. 45.
δολόεις : δολόεσσα, III. 75 (?).
δόμος : δόμον, III. 49, XVI. 29, XVII. 100 ; δόμους, XVII. 62 ; δόμοις, XVII. 11.
δονακώδης : δονακώδεα, fr. 65.
δόναξ : δόνακος, XIII. 59.
δονέω : δονεῖ, V. 67 ; δονέουσι, I. 41 ; δονεῖν, fr. 49, 1.
δόξα : δόξαν, IX. 1, X. 18, XIII. 28 ; δόξας, X. 37 ; δόξᾳ, XIII. 146.
δορά : δορᾶς, V. 124.
δόρυ, XIII. 87, XVII. 90.
δουλοσύνα : δουλοσύναν, III. 31.
δράκων, IX. 13.
δράω : δρῶν, III. 83.
δρόμος : δρόμῳ, V. 183.
δύα : δύᾳ, fr. 5, 8 ; 42, 3 ; δυᾶν, XV. 46.
δύναμαι : δύναται, fr. 48, 2 ; δύνατο, XIX. 26.
δύναμις : δύναμιν, XV. 59.
δύνασις : δύνασιν, X. 49.
δύο, IV. 17, XVI. 19, XVIII. 46, 49.
δύρομαι : δυρομέναις, III. 35.
δύσλοφος : δύσλοφον, XIII. 13.
δυσμενής, XVIII. 6 ; δυσμενέων, V. 133, fr. 70.
δυσπαίπαλος : δυσπαίπαλα, V. 26.
δύστανος : δυστάνοιο, XI. 102 ; δυστάνων, V. 63.
δῶμα : δώματα, V. 59 ; δώμασι, V. 173.
δῶρον : δῶρα, XVII. 10, 76, 124, XIX. 4 ; δώροις, fr. 56, 4.

ἑβδομήκοντα, II. 9.
Ἕβρος : Ἕβρῳ, XVI. 5.
ἔγγονος : ἔγγονοι, IX. 46.
ἐγγύθεν, XVII. 128.
ἐγκύρω : ἐγκύρσαι, fr. 43, 3.
ἐγχέσπαλος : ἐγχεσπάλου, V. 69.
ἔγχος : ἔγχεα, fr. 46, 8 ; ἐγχέων, IX. 43.
ἐγώ, V. 127, XIII. 188 ; ἐμέ, XVII. 33 ; με, XII. 5 ; ἐμοί, V. 31, 138, XIII. 193, XVI. 2, XIX. 37 ; μοι, V. 151 ; ἅμμι, XVII. 25.
ἕδος, IX. 46.
ἕδρα : ἕδρας, fr. 52, 1.

ἔθειρα: ἔθειραν, V. 29; ἐθείρας, VI. 8, XIII. 164.
ἐθέλω or θέλω: ἐθέλει, I. 24, V. 14; θέλει, XIII. 18; θελήσει, III. 64; ἔθελεν, XI. 73; θέλῃ, V. 135; θέλοιμι, XVII. 41; θέλων, V. 169, XVII. 69.
εἰ, I. 27, V. 190, XI. 27, XII. 4, XIII. 166, 195, XVII. 29, 57, XVIII. 12, fr. 48, 2; 63; and see αἰ and εἴπερ.
εἶδον: εἶδε(ν), V. 40, XI. 22, XVII. 109; ἴδεν, V. 71, XVII. 16; εἴσεαι, XVII. 64; ἰδεῖν, V. 30, XVII. 43; ἰδών, XVII. 72, 101; and see οἶδα.
εἴδωλον, V. 68, fr. 64.
εἴκοσι, XI. 104.
εἰμί (sum): ἐστί(ν), V. 162, 167, XIII. 170, fr. 46, 9; 48, 1; 49, 1; εἰσί, fr. 60, 1; ἦν, XVII. 91 (?), XVIII. 21; ἦσαν, IX. 64; εἴη, X. 12; ἔμμεναι, XVIII. 14; ἔμμεν, V. 144, X. 48, XVIII. 31, 56; ἔσεσθαι, XIII. 24; ἐών, VIII. 8; ἐόντα, IV. 19, XIX. 23; εὖντα, III. 78.
εἶμι (ibo): ἴμεν, XIX. 12.
εἴνεκεν, XIII. 103.
εἶπον: εἶπε(ν), III. 48, 77, V. 86, XVII. 47, 52, 81; εἰπεῖν, IX. 72, fr. 43.
εἴπερ, XVII. 53.
εἰρήνα, fr. 46, 1; εἰρήνᾳ, V. 200, XIII. 156.
εἴρω: *εἴρεν, XVII. 20, 74.
εἷς, fr. 48, 1; μία, ib., XIV. 8; ἕνα, I. 17.
εἰς, XV. 43; see ἐς.
εἴσαντα, V. 110.
εἴτε (or εἶτα), XIX. 29.
ἐκ or ἐξ: ἐκ, V. 15, 82, 132, 141, IX. 35, XI. 36, XIII. 127, XIV. 8, XVII. 24; ἐξ, III. 46, V. 61, XI. 43, XVII. 122, fr. 47, 1.
Ἑκάτα, fr. 66.
ἕκατι, V. 33, VI. 11, X. 15, XI. 9, XVII. 7, fr. 1, 7; 29.
ἐκβάλλω: ἐξέβαλεν, XVIII. 28.
ἔκγονος: ἔκγονον, XVII. 16.
ἐκκαιδέκατος: ἐκκαιδεκάταν, VII. 3.
ἐκπίμπλημι: ἐκπλήσομεν, XVII. 27.
Ἑκτόρεος: Ἑκτορέας (?), XIII. 121.
ἐκτός, X. 52.
Ἕκτωρ: Ἕκτορα, XIII. 76.
ἐλαία: ἐλαίας, VIII. 14; ἐλαίᾳ, XI. 28.
ἔλαιον: ἐλαίῳ, X. 23.
ἐλαύνω, X. 51.

ἐλαφρός: ἐλαφρόν, fr. 49, 1; ἐλαφροῖς, I. 7 (?).
ἐλέφας: ἐλέφαντι, fr. 56, 8.
ἐλέγχω: ἐλέγχει, fr. 51, 2.
*ἑλικοστέφανος, IX. 62.
ἔλλαθι: see ἵλημι.
Ἕλλαν: Ἑλλάνων, III. 12, V. 111, IX. 30; Ἕλλασι(ν), VII. 7, X. 20, XIII. 23, 49; incert., fr. 7, 4.
Ἑλλάς: Ἑλλάδα, III. 63.
ἐλπίς, III. 75, IX. 18, fr. 56, 3; ἐλπίδι, I. 26, X. 40, XIII. 187; ἐλπίσιν, XIII. 124.
ἔλπω: ἔλπομαι, fr. 58.
ἐμβάλλω: ἔμβαλεν, XI. 54.
ἐμός, V. 117; ἐμᾶς, XVII. 64; ἐμοί, XI. 120 (?); ἐμαῖς, XIII. 196.
ἔμπεδον, XIII. 145.
ἐμπίτνω: ἐμπίτνων, X. 24.
ἔμπορος: ἔμπορον, XVIII. 36.
ἐμπρέπω: ἐνέπρεπεν, IX. 27.
ἐν, II. 6, V. 27, 41, 44, 80, 88, 119, 131, 165, 173, 200, VII. 3, VIII. 7, 15, IX. 22, 88, X. 19, 29, XI. 4, 19, 24, 32, 88, XII. 8, XIII. 28, 48, 66, 85, 91, 102, 129, 156, 165, XIV. 12 (?), 15 (?), XV. 53, XVII. 5, 115, 120, XVIII. 23, 45, 49, XIX. 8, 47, XX. 1, fr. 2, 2; 11, 2; 42, 2; 46, 6; 55, 1; 57, 2; 71, 3.
ἐναντίος: ἐναντία, V. 76.
ἐναρίζω: ἐναριζομένων, XIII. 118.
Ἐνδαΐς: Ἐνδαΐδα, XIII. 63.
ἔνδοθεν, XVII. 86.
ἐνδυκέως, V. 112, 125.
ἔνθα, III. 33, V. 63, 107, 127, 182, X. 20 (?), XV. 40, XVI. 17, XIX. 42.
ἔνθεν, XI. 82, 97, 113.
ἐννέα, XVI. 18.
ἐνστάζω: ἐνέσταξεν, XIII. 196 (?).
ἐντυγχάνω: ἐντυχεῖν, XVIII. 44.
ἐντύω: ἔντυον, fr. 59, 1.
ἕξ, V. 113.
ἐξάγω: ἐξαγαγεῖν, XI. 103.
ἐξαιρέω: ἐξείλετο, V. 74.
ἐξαίσιος: ἐξαισίοις, XV. 58.
*ἐξαναρίζω (= ἐξεναρίζω): ἐξαναρίζων, V. 146.
ἐξευρίσκω: ἐξευρεῖν, fr. 47, 3.
ἐξικνέομαι: ἐξίκοντο, XIII. 99.
ἐξόπιν, XVII. 91 (?).
ἔξοχος: ἔξοχον, XIX. 14.
ἑορτά: ἑορταῖς, III. 15.
ἐός: ἐόν, fr. 48, 5.
ἐπαθρέω: ἐπαθρῆσαι, XIII. 194.

ἐπαίσσω: ἐπαίσσων, V. 116.
Ἔπαφος: Ἔπαφον, XIX. 42.
ἐπεί, III. 23, 53, 113, XI. 120, XVI.
    25, XVII. 43, 93, 121, XIX. 39.
ἔπειμι: ἐπιόντα, XVII. 46.
ἔπειτα, V. 74.
ἐπέρχομαι: ἐπέρχονται, fr. 59, 2.
ἐπί: with acc., IX. 41, XIII, 55, 116,
    XVIII. 37, fr. 5, 4; 59, 1; 62, 3;
    with gen., X. 21, XVII. 83, fr. 46,
    3; 72, 1; with dat., V. 83, 90, 133,
    VI. 3, VII. 9, IX. 12, 42, X. 42,
    43, XIII. 72, 160, 170, XIV. 16,
    XVI. 34; incert., fr. 7, 3.
ἐπιβαίνω: ἐπέβαινε, III. 34; ἐπέβασε,
    V. 73.
ἐπιγίγνομαι: ἐπιγινομένοις, IX. 81 (?).
ἐπιδείκνυμι: ἐπεδείξαο, III. 93 (?); ἐπε-
    δείξαμεν, II. 9.
ἐπιδέχομαι: *ἐπιδέγμενοι, XVII. 96.
ἐπίζηλος: ἐπιζήλῳ, V. 52.
ἐπικείρω: ἐπέκειρεν, V. 108.
ἐπικλύω: ἐπέκλυον, XIII. 100.
ἐπικλώθω: ἐπέκλωσεν, V. 143.
ἐπικουρία: ἐπικουρίαν, XVIII. 13.
ἐπιλέγω: ἐπιλεξαμένα, V. 136.
ἐπίμοιρος: ἐπίμοιρον, I. 20.
ἐπίμοχθος, I. 43.
ἐπινίκιον (subst.): ἐπινικίοις, II. 13.
ἐπιπέμπω: ἐπέπεμψε, III. 62.
ἐπισκήπτω: ἐπισκήπτων, V. 42, VIII. 3.
ἐπιστήμα: ἐπιστᾶμαι, X. 38.
ἐπιτάσσω: ἐπέταξε, fr. 50.
ἐπιτίθημι: ἐπέθηκεν, XVII. 113.
ἐπίφρων: ἐπίφρονα, XVI. 25.
ἐπιχθόνιος: ἐπιχθονίων, IV. 15, V. 5,
    54; ἐπιχθονίοις, V. 96, X. 14.
ἐπιχρίμπτω: ἐπιχρίμπτει, fr. 62, 3.
ἐπιχώριος: ἐπιχωρίαν, XIII. 59 (?).
ἔπομαι: ἕπεται, I. 32; ἕσπεο, XI. 115.
ἐποπτεύω: ἐποπτεύοις, fr. 71, 3.
ἔπος: ἔπει, IX. 2.
ἑπτά, XVII. 2.
ἑπτάπυλος: ἑπταπύλοισι, XIX. 47.
ἐραννός: ἐραννόν, XVII. 42.
ἐρατός: ἐρατᾷ, XVII. 129; ἐρατῶν, XI.
    43, fr. 46, 12; ἐρατοῖσιν, XVII.
    110.
ἐρατύω: ἐράτυεν, XVII. 12.
*ἐρατώνυμος, XVII. 31.
ἐράω: ἐρᾷς, fr. 54.
ἔργμα: ἔργματι, XIV. 17.
ἔργον, IX. 82, fr. 52, 1; ἔργα, XVIII.
    18; ἔργοισι(ν), X. 43, XIII. 170.
ἔρδω: ἔρδων, I. 25, V. 36; ἔρδοντα,

XIV. 18, XVIII. 43; ἐργμένον, XIII.
    174; ἐρχθέντος, XIII. 32.
ἐρείπω: ἤρειπον, XI. 68.
*ἐρειψιπύλας: ἐρειψιπύλαν, V. 56.
ἐρειψίτοιχος: ἐρειψιτοίχοις, XIII. 134(?).
ἐρεμνός: ἐρεμνόν, XVII. 116.
ἐρέπτω: ἐρέπτειν, IV. 16; ἐρέψωνται,
    IX. 24; ἐρεφθείς, XIII. 37.
ἐρεύθω: ἔρευθε, XIII. 119.
Ἐρίβοια, XVII. 14 (?); Ἐριβοίας, XIII.
    69.
ἐριβρύχας, V. 116.
ἐρίζω: ἐρίζει, I. 30.
ἐρικυδής: ἐρικυδέα, XIII. 157.
*ἐρισταλκής: ἐρισταλκές, VII. 7.
ἐρισφάραγος: ἐρισφαράγου, V. 20.
ἔρνος, V. 87.
ἔρομαι, fr. 5, 7.
ἐρύκω: *ἐρύκεν (infin.), XVII. 41.
ἔρχομαι: ἤλυθεν, fr. 1, 4 (?); ἦλθε(ν),
    IX. 41, XVIII. 16, fr. 72, 3; ἔλθῃ,
    XVII. 28; ἐρχομένων, XVI. 33; ἐλ-
    θόντα, XII. 7; ἐλθόντες, XI. 78;
    ἐλθόντας, fr. 52, 2.
ἔρως: ἐρώτων, IX. 73.
ἐς, II. 2, III. 29 (?), 35, 59, 62, V.
    12, 61, 106, IX. 17, 20, 34, XI.
    48, 55, 72, XII. 4, XIII. 110, XV.
    61, XVII. 62, 73, 76, XX. 10, fr. 1,
    13; εἰς, XV. 43.
ἐσεῖδον: ἐσιδόντες, XIII. 106.
ἐσθλός: ἐσθλόν, V. 129; ἐσθλοί, V.
    198; ἐσθλούς, XIV. 3 (?); ἐσθλῶν,
    X. 47, XVII. 132.
ἐστία: ἑστίαν, IV. 14.
ἔσχατος: ἔσχατα, IX. 41.
ἔσω, XVII. 22.
ἕτερος, X. 42, fr. 47, 1; ἑτέρου, fr. 47,
    1; ἑτέραν, XVII. 89.
ἔτι, III. 31, IV. 1, V. 174, XI. 47, fr.
    49, 1.
ἔτος, XI. 59; ἔτεα, III. 81.
ἐτύμως, XIII. 195.
εὖ, I. 13, 25, III. 94, V. 36, 78, 190,
    IX. 72, XIII. 32, XIV. 1, 18.
*εὐαίνετος: εὐαίνετε, XIX. 11.
εὔανδρος: εὐάνδρους, IX. 17.
Εὔβοια: Εὔβοιαν, X. 33.
εὔβουλος: εὔβουλος, XV. 37; εὐβούλου, fr. 6, 5;
    εὐβούλων, X. 27.
*εὔγυιος: εὐγυίαν, XI. 10.
εὐδαίδαλος: εὐδαίδαλον, XVII. 88, fr.
    52, 2.
εὐδαιμονία: εὐδαιμονίας, V. 186.
εὐδαίμων, V. 55, XIV. 9 (?).

Εὔδημος, fr. 72, 1.
εὔδματος : εὔδματον, IX. 54.
εὔδοξος, VII. 9 ; εὔδοξον, XIV. 22 ;
εὐδόξων, IX. 21.
*εὐεγχής, XIII. 114.
εὐειδής : εὐειδέος, XIII. 69.
εὐεργεσία : εὐεργεσιᾶν, I. 19.
εὐθαλής : εὐθαλές, IX. 5.
εὐθύδικος : εὐθύδικον, V. 6.
εὐθυμία : εὐθυμίᾳ, XVII. 125.
εὐθύνω : εὔθυνε, XII. 2.
εὐκλεής : εὐκλεᾶ, V. 196.
εὔκλεια : εὐκλείας, I. 46 ; εὐκλείᾳ, XIII.
150.
εὐκλεΐζω : εὐκλεΐξας, VI. 16.
*εὔκλειος : εὐκλείου, fr. 1, 7.
εὐκτίμενος : εὐκτιμέναν, V. 149, XI.
122, XV. 10, XX. 10.
ἐΰκτιτος : ἐΰκτίτων, III. 46.
*εὐμαρέω : εὐμαρεῖν, I. 37.
εὐμαρέως, V. 195.
εὐμενής, fr. 57, 1.
εὔμοιρος : εὔμοιρε, V. 1.
εὐνά : εὐνάν, fr. 5, 4.
*εὐναής, IX. 42.
εὐνομία : εὐνομίᾳ, XIII. 153 ; person.,
Εὐνομιάς, XV. 55.
Εὐξαντίς, II. 8.
Εὐξάντιος : Εὐξάντιον, fr. 1, 16 (?).
εὔοχθος : εὐόχθους, fr. 59, 2.
εὔπακτος : εὐπάκτων, XVII. 82.
εὔπεπλος : εὔπεπλοι, XI. 42 ; εὐπέπλοισι, XV. 49.
εὐπλόκαμος, fr. 1. 17 ; εὐπλοκάμοις,
III. 34.
εὐποίητος : εὐποίητον, V. 177.
εὔπρυμνος : εὐπρύμνοις, XIII. 117.
εὔπυργος : ἐΰπύργους, V. 184.
εὑρίσκω : εὑρήσει, XI. 124.
*εὐρυάναξ : εὐρυάνακτος, V. 19.
εὐρυβίας, XVI. 31 ; εὐρυβίαν, V. 104 ;
εὐρυβία, XI. 52.
*εὐρυδίνας : εὐρυδίναν, III. 7, V. 38.
εὐρυνεφής : εὐρυνεφεῖ, XVI. 17. (S.)
εὐρύς : εὐρεῖαν, XV. 40 ; εὐρείας, IX.
47 ; εὐρείαις, X. 17.
εὐρυσθενής : εὐρυσθενέος, XIX. 17.
εὐρύχορος : εὐρύχορον, X. 31.
Εὐρωπίς : Εὐρωπίδος, fr. 1, 15.
εὑρώς, fr. 46, 8.
εὐσέβεια : εὐσέβειαν, III. 61.
εὐσεβής : εὐσεβέων, XIII. 155.
εὖτε, I. 45, III. 25, XIII. 85, fr. 53, 1.
εὔτυκος : εὔτυκον, IX. 4, XVIII. 50.
εὐτυχία : εὐτυχίας, fr. 48, 1.

εὔυδρος : εὔυδρον, XI. 119.
εὐφεγγής, IX. 29 ; εὐφεγγέας, XIX. 26.
εὐφραίνω : εὔφραινε, III. 83.
εὐφροσύνα, III. 87, X. 53 ; εὐφροσύναι,
XI. 12.
εὐχά : εὐχάν, XVII. 67 ; εὐχᾶς, XVII.
65 ; εὐχάς, VIII. 12.
εὔχομαι : εὔχοντο, XV. 46 ; εὐχομένου,
XI. 107 ; εὐξαμένῳ, fr. 72, 3.
εὐώδης : εὐώδεα, fr. 11, 1.
ἐφάμερος : ἐφάμερον, III. 73.
ἐφίημι : ἐφίησι, XIII. 15.
ἐφίστημι : ἐπιστάσας, III. 55.
ἐχθρός : ἐχθρά, III. 47 ; ἔχθιστος, III.
52.
Ἔχιδνα : Ἐχίδνας, V. 62.
ἔχω : ἔχει, I. 29, XI. 124, XIV. 7, fr.
48, 6 ; ἔχουσιν, III. 63 ; ἔσχεν, V.
104, XIII. 73, XVIII. 27, 41 ; ἔχειν,
I. 22, XVIII. 48 ; ἕξειν, XIII. 130 ;
ἔχων, fr. 48, 2 ; ἔχοντα, XVIII. 32.

ζάθεος : ζαθέαν, II. 7 ; ζαθέας, V. 10 ;
ζαθέοις, XI. 24.
ζεύγνυμι : ζεύξασα, XI. 46.
Ζεύς, III. 55, V. 200, XI. 73, XV. 51,
XVII. 68 ; Ζεῦ, VIII. 10, XVII. 53 ;
Ζηνός, III. 11, 26, V. 20, IX. 5, X.
29 ; Ζηνί, XI. 5, XVI. 18 ; Δία, V.
178 ; Διός, III. 70, V. 58, 79, VI. 1,
XI. 9 (?), 52, XIII. 25, XVI. 28, XVII.
20, 30, 75, 86, XIX. 17, 30 (?), fr.
1, 7.
Ζέφυρος : Ζεφύρου, V. 28 ; Ζεφύρῳ, fr.
72, 2.
ζωά : ζωάν, III. 82 ; ζωᾶς, V. 144.
ζώω : ζώη, I. 42 ; ζώειν, I. 29.

ἤ, IV. 18, V. 87, IX. 36, X. 39, 41, XI.
34 (bis), XIII. 124 (or ἦ), 136 (or
ἦ), XVIII. 8, 11, 35, XIX. 35, fr.
45, 2.
ἦ, V. 89, 165, XIII. 21, 46, XVIII. 5,
41, XIX. 33 (or ἤ), fr. 54.
ᾗ (' where '), V. 9 (?).
ἥβα : ἥβαν, III. 90, V. 154.
ἤδη, XI. 59, XIII. 163.
ἡδύς, fr. 57, 2 ; ἡδείᾳ, XVI. 7.
ἤθεος : ἤθεοι, XVII. 128 : ἠθέων, XVII.
43, 93.
ᾐών : ᾐόνων, XVI. 8.
ἡμίθεος : ἡμίθεοι, IX. 10, XI. 62 ;
ἡμιθέοις, XIII. 122.
ἥμισυ, fr. 1, 10.
ἠπιόφρων : ἠπιόφρον, XIII. 45.

Ἥρα, V. 89, IX. 8, XI. 44, XIX. 22;
Ἥραν, XI. 107.
ἦρα (prepositional), XI. 21.
Ἡρακλῆς: Ἡρακλεῖ, IX. 9.
ἥρως, V. 71, XV. 37, XVII. 47, 73, 94;
ἥρως (voc.), XVII. 23; ἥρω, IX. 56,
XIII. 71; ἥρωες, XI. 81.
Ἡσίοδος, V. 192.
ἦτορ, XVII. 50 (?).
ἠΰδενδρος: ἠΰδενδρον, XVII. 80.
ἠΰτε, XIII. 54.

θαητός, XI. 14, XIII. 82.
θάλασσα: θάλασσαν, XIII. 148;
θαλάσσας, XIII. 116.
θάλεια: θάλειαν, III. 89.
θαλία: θαλίας, XIII. 154; θαλίαις,
XIV. 15.
θάλλω: θάλλουσιν, V. 198; τέθαλεν,
X. 40; θάλλουσα, XV. 58.
θάλπω: θάλπει, fr. 46, 11; θάλπῃσι,
fr. 56, 2.
θαμβέω: θάμβησεν, V. 84.
θάνατος: θάνατον, V. 134, XX. 7, fr.
12, 3 (?); θανάτοιο, XIII. 30.
θάπτω; θάπτομεν, V. 115.
(θάπω): τάφον, XVII. 48.
θαρσέω: θαρσεῖ, V. 21.
θάρσος, XVII. 50 (?).
θαῦμα, XVII. 123.
θαυμάζω: θαυμασθείς, I. 14.
θαυμαστός, V. 71; θαυμαστύν, IX. 31.
θεά, V. 103; θεᾶς, XI. 49, XVII. 9.
Θεανώ, XV. 7.
θεάτηρ: θεατήρων, X. 23. (S.)
θεῖος, IX. 4.
*θελημός: θελημόν, XVII. 85.
*θελξιεπής: θελξιεπεῖ, XV. 48.
θέλω: see ἐθέλω.
θεμερόφρων: θεμερόφρονος, XVI. 3 (?).
θέμις, III. 88; person., Θέμιτος, XV,
55.
θεόδματος: θεόδματον, XII. 7, XIII.
130; θεόδματοι, fr. 44; θεοδμάτους,
XI. 58.
θεόδοτος: θεοδότους, VIII. 12.
Θεόκριτος, fr. 54.
θεόπομπος: θεόπομπον, XVII. 132.
θεός, V. 36, 50, XI. 34, XIV. 18, XVIII.
41; θεύν, III. 21 (bis); θεοί, IX. 50;
θεούς, I. 25; θεῶν, III. 38, 57, V. 95,
179, IX. 63, XI. 121, XVII. 24, 100,
124, fr. 4, 1; θεοῖσ(ιν), IV. 18, XIII.
105, XV. 14, 45, fr. 46, 3.
θεοτίματος: θεοτίματον, IX. 98.

θεότιμος: θεότιμον, XI. 12.
θεοφιλής: θεοφιλές, XI. 60.
θεράπων: V. 14.
θερμός, X. 22.
Θερμώδων: Θερμώδοντος, IX. 43.
*θερσοεπής, XIII. 166.
θεσπέσιος: θεσπεσίῳ, XIII. 75.
Θεσσαλία: Θεσσαλίαν, fr. 11, 1 (?).
Θεσσαλός: Θεσσαλάν, XVIII, 54.
Θέστιος: Θεστίου, V. 137.
θευπροπία: θευπροπίαν, X. 41.
Θήβα, X. 30; Θήβας, IX. 54.
Θῆβαι: Θήβας, IX. 20.
θηροσκόπος, XI. 107.
Θησεύς, XVII. 16; Θησεῦ, XVII. 74;
Θησέα, XVII. 2, 99.
θιγγάνω: θίγεν, XVII. 12.
θίς: θῖνα, XIII. 116.
θνάσκω: θάνῃ, I. 45; θανεῖν, III. 47;
θνάσκοντες, XIII. 133.
θνατός, I. 28; θνατόν, III. 78; θνατῶν,
III, 61 (?), XVIII. 21, XIX. 45 (?), fr.
42, 1; θνατοῖσ(ιν), I. 38, III. 51, 93,
V. 160, X. 52, XI. 7, XIII. 12, XV. 52,
fr. 46, 1; 50; 62, 1.
θοίνα: θοίνας, fr. 59, 1.
θοός: θοάν, XVII. 55; θοούς, V. 129;
θοάς, III. 3.
θοῶς, XV. 59, XVII. 98.
θράσος: θράσει, XVII. 62; and see θάρσος.
θράσσω: θράσσον, XIII. 84.
θρασυκάρδιος, XX. 5; θρασυκάρδιον, XIII.
73.
θρασυμέμνων: θρασυμέμνονος, V. 69.
θρασυμήδης: θρασυμήδεα, XVI. 15.
θρασύς: θρασύν, XVIII. 39.
*θρασύχειρος or θρασύχειρ, II. 4.
θροέω: θρόησε, III. 9.
θρώσκω: θόρεν, XVII. 94; θρώσκουσα,
XIII. 57.
θυγάτηρ, V. 124, XVII. 34; θύγατερ,
VII. 1, XIII. 44, fr. 66; θύγατρα,
XI. 99 (?); θύγατρες, XI. 84, fr. 34;
θυγατρῶν, V. 167, IX. 50; θυγατράσι,
III. 35.
θυμάρμενος: θυμάρμενον, XVII. 71.
θυμός, I. 5, XVII. 82, fr. 57, 1; θυμόν,
I. 41, III. 83, V. 80, X. 45, XIII. 187,
XVII. 23 (?), fr. 48, 2; 56, 2.
θυσία: θυσίαισι, V. 101.
θύω: θύσω, XI. 104; *θύεν (infin.), XVI.
18.

ἰαίνω: ἰαίνει, XIII. 187; ἰανθείς, XVII.
131.

ἰάπτω : ἰάπτεται, *fr.* 48, 5.
ἰατορία : ἰατορίᾳ, I. 11 (?).
Ἰάων : Ἰαόνων, XVII. 3.
Ἴδα : Ἴδας, V. 66.
Ἴδας, XVII. 30.
*ἱδρώεις : ἱδρώεντα, XIII. 24.
ἱερός : ἱεράν, II. 2, X. 34 ; ἱερᾶν, XVIII. 1 ; ἱερά (subst.), III. 15.
Ἱέρων, III. 64, 92 ; Ἱέρωνα, IV. 3, V. 16 ; Ἱέρωνος, III. 4 ; Ἱέρωνι, V. 49, 185, 197.
ἴζω : ἔσσαν, XI. 120 (?).
ἵημι : ἵησι, *fr.* 53, 1 ; ἵεται, V. 48 ; ἵετο, XVII. 90 ; ἱεῖσαι, XI. 56.
Ἰθακήσιος : Ἰθακησίου, *fr.* 64.
ἰθύς : ἰθεῖαν, XV. 54.
ἱκάνω : ἵκανεν, XI. 96.
ἴκελος : ἴκελοι, *fr.* 60, 2.
ἱκνέομαι : ἵκετο, IX. 39, XVI. 16 ; ἱκνεῖσθαι, *fr.* 42, 3 ; ἱκέσθαι, XI. 30.
ἴκρια : ἰκρίων, XVII. 83.
ἵκω : ἷξον, XIII. 116.
ἵλεως : ἵλεῳ, XI. 15.
ἵλημι : ἔλλαθι, XI. 8.
Ἴλιον : Ἰλίου, XIII. 82.
ἱμείρω : ἱμείρει, I. 34.
*ἱμεράμπυξ : ἱμεράμπυκος, XVII. 9.
*ἱμερόγυιος : ἱμερογυίου, XIII. 104.
ἱμερόεις : ἱμερόεν, XI. 118 ; ἱμερόεντα, *fr.* 71, 2.
ἱμερτός : ἱμερτάν, *fr.* I. 14.
ἵνα (‘that’), X. 11, *fr.* 6, 3.
ἵνα (‘where’), XI. 79.
Ἴναχος : Ἰνάχου, XIX. 18.
ἰοβλέφαρος : ἰοβλέφαροι, XIX. 5 ; ἰοβλεφάρων, IX. 3.
Ἰόλα : Ἰόλαν, XVI. 27.
ἰός : ἰόν, V. 75.
*ἰόπλοκος : ἰόπλοκον, IX. 72 ; ἰόπλοκοι, XVII. 37.
ἰοστέφανος : ἰοστέφανον, III. 2 ; ἰοστεφάνου, XIII. 89 ; ἰοστεφάνων, V. 4.
ἱππευτάς : ἱππευταί, XIII. 127.
ἵππιος : ἵππιον, XIX. 15 ; ἱππίου, XVII. 99.
ἱππόβοτος : ἱππόβοτον, XI. 80.
*ἱπποδίνητος : ἱπποδινήταν, V. 2.
ἵππος : ἵππον, XIV. 22 ; ἵππους, III. 4, XX. 9, *fr.* 24 ; ἵππων, IV. 6, V. 44.
ἱπποτρόφος : ἱπποτρόφον, XI. 114.
*ἵππωκυς : ἱππώκεος, XI. 101.
ἰσάνεμος : ἰσανέμους, XX. 9 (?).
Ἰσθμιονίκας : Ἰσθμιονίκαν, X. 26.
Ἰσθμιόνικος : Ἰσθμιόνικον, I. 18.
Ἴσθμιος : Ἰσθμίαν, XVIII. 17, *fr.* 6, 4.

Ἰσθμός : Ἰσθμόν, VIII. 2 ; Ἰσθμοῦ, II. 7.
ἰσόθεος : ἰσοθέων, XIII. 123.
ἴσος, V. 46 ; ἴσον, I. 34, *fr.* 45, 2.
ἵστημι : ἵσταν, XI. 112 ; ἔστα, *fr.* 59. 1 ; στᾶσον, V. 177 ; στασάμεθα. V. 112 ; στᾶθι, V. 80 ; σταθείς, XIII. 72, XVII. 84 ; σταθέντων, III. 18.
ἱστίον, XIII. 98.
ἱστός : ἱστοί, *fr.* 46, 7.
ἵστωρ : ἵστορες, IX. 44.
ἰσχυρός : ἰσχυρόν, XVIII. 38.
ἰσχύς : ἰσχύν, XIII. 42 ; ἰσχύι, V. 22, XVIII. 20.
ἴσχω : ἴσχουσι, V. 24 ; ἴσχε, XVII. 23 ; *ἴσχεν (infin.), XVII. 88.
Ἰτωνία : Ἰτωνίας, *fr.* 52, 1.
Ἴφικλος : Ἴφικλον, V. 128.
Ἰώ, XIX. 41.
Ἴωνες : Ἰάνων, XVIII. 2.

Κάδμος, XIX. 48.
κάδος : καδέων, XIX. 36.
καθαρός : καθαρόν, *fr.* 67.
καί, I. 21, 23, III. 23, 48, 97, V. 31, 56 (?), 78, 97, 102, 159, 182, 194, VI. 7, VII. 1, 7, 10, VIII. 2, 10, IX. 4, 19, 33, 79, X. 9, 44, 49, 50, XI. 7, 10, 12, 24, 58, 66, 75, 91, 112, 113, XII. 4, XIII. 30, 34, 50, 65, 148, 149, 188, XIV. 14 (?), 18, 23, XV. 55, 57, 62, XVII. 25, 29, 33, 58, XVIII. 14, 15, 38, 39, 50, 53, 58, XIX. 5, 33, 46, 51, *fr.* 1, 10 ; 43 ; 46, 2, 5 ; 48, 4 ; 57, 2 ; 60, 1 ; 65.
καιρός : καιρῷ, *fr.* 42, 2.
καίω : καῖε, V. 140.
κακομάχανος : κακομάχανοι, XVIII. 8.
κακόποτμος, V. 138.
κακός : κακόν, *fr.* 45, 2 ; κακῷ, XVIII. 44.
καλέω : καλεῖ, II. 11 ; καλῶν, III. 96 ; κέκληται, VII. 9.
καλλίζωνος, V. 89.
καλλικέρας : καλλικέραν, XIX. 24.
Καλλιόπα, V. 176 ; Καλλιόπας, XIX. 13.
καλλίπαχυς : καλλίπαχυν, XX. 4 (?).
*καλλιρόας : καλλιρόαν, XI. 26, 96.
καλλίχορος : καλλίχορον, V. 106 ; καλλιχόρῳ, XI. 32.
καλός, *fr.* 54 ; καλόν, IX. 82, 101 ; καλάν, *fr.* 13, 7 ; καλῶν, II. 6, V. 51 ; κάλλιστος, XIV. 17 ; κάλλιστον,

IX. 86, X. 47, XI. 79; κάλλιστα, III. 93.
Καλυδών: Καλυδῶνα, V. 106.
καλυκοστέφανος: καλυκοστεφάνου, V. 98; καλυκοστεφάνους, XI. 108.
κάλυμμα, XVI. 32, XVII. 38.
καλύπτω: καλύψῃ, XIII. 31.
καλῶς, XIII. 173.
κάμνω: κάμον, XI. 77; κάμοι, V. 36.
κάμπτω: κάμψεν, X. 26 (?).
καναχά, XIV. 15; καναχάν, II. 12.
κάπρος: κάπρον, V. 105.
καρδία: καρδίαν, XVII. 18, fr. 49, 2; and see κραδία.
καρπός: καρπόν, fr. 56, 9 (?); 72, 4.
καρτερόθυμος, V. 130.
καρτερός: καρτεράν, XVIII. 27; καρτερᾷ, XI. 46.
καρτερόχειρ, I. 3.
κάρτος, V. 114.
κᾶρυξ, XVIII. 17; κάρυκες, XV. 40.
καρύσσω: καρύξοντι, XIII. 198.
καρχαρόδους: καρχαρόδοντα, V. 60.
Κάσα: Κάσαν, XI. 119.
κασιγνήτα: κασιγνήτας, X. 9.
κασίγνητος: κασιγνήτοις, XI. 65.
Κασταλία: Κασταλίας, III. 20.
κατά: with acc., IX. 46 (?), X. 32, XI. 93, 94, XIII. 147, XVII. 80, 87, XIX. 26, fr. 56, 9; with gen., XVII. 94.
κατακτείνω: κατέκτανον, V. 128; κατέκτανεν, XVIII. 25.
καταναίω: κατένασσε, III. 60, XI. 41.
κατανεύω: κατένευσε, XVII. 25.
καταπέφνω: κατέπεφνεν, V. 115.
*καταχραίνω: κατέχρανεν, V. 44.
κατέχω: κάτεχε, XVII. 28.
κατορθόω: κατορθωθεῖσα, XIV. 6.
κε or κεν, IV. 13, V. 169, XI. 30 (?), XIII. 195, XVII. 64.
κέαρ, I. 27, XVII. 8, 87, 108, fr. 9; 46, 11; 48, 5; 56, 11.
κεδνός: κεδνά, XVII. 29; κεδνᾷ, III. 33; κεδνῶν, V. 118.
κεῖθι, IX. 10 (?), XIII. 22 (?)
κεῖμαι: κεῖται, IX. 84, XV. 53.
κεῖνος: κεῖνα (fem. sing.), XV. 62; κεῖνον, V. 90; κεῖνο, V. 164; κείνῳ, XI. 23; κείναν, IX. 21.
κελαδέω: κελαδοῦσι, XI. 11 (?); κελαδῆσαν, XVI. 12; κελαδῆσαι, XIV. 21.
κελάδω: κελάδοντος, IX. 65.

κέλευθος, V. 31, XIX. 1, fr. 63; κέλευθον, IX. 47, X. 36, XI. 26, XVIII. 17; κελεύθου, V. 196.
κελεύω: κέλευσε(ν), III. 48, XVII. 87, XIX. 21.
κέλομαι, XVII. 40.
Κέος: Κέον, II. 2, VI. 5, 16.
*κεραυνεγχής: κεραυνεγχές, VIII. 10.
κέρδος, fr. 43; κερδέων, III. 84.
Κερκυών: Κερκυόνος, XVIII. 26.
κεφαλά: κεφαλάν, X. 16; κεφαλᾷ, V. 91.
Κήιος: Κηία, XIX. 11; Κηίας, III. 98; Κήϊῳ, fr. 71, 4; Κηίων, III. 69 (?), XVII. 130.
Κήναιος: Κηναίῳ, XVI. 17.
κιγχάνω: κιχεῖν, I. 39, XV. 53; κιχήσας, V. 148.
κικλήσκω: κίκλησκε, XI. 99.
κινέω: ἐκείνησεν, X. 10.
Κίρρα: Κίρρας, XI. 20.
κίω: κίον, XI. 48.
κλάδος: κλάδον, IX. 33.
κλάζω: ἔκλαγεν, XVII. 128, XVIII. 3; ἔκλαγον, III. 49.
κλεεννός or κλεινός: κλεεννός, V. 182; κλεεννάν, V. 12; κλεεννῷ, II. 6; κλεεννάς, VIII. 6 (?); κλεινός, V. 13; κλεινόν, XIX. 9; κλεινᾷ, XI. 78; κλεινοί, IX. 22; κλεινοῖς, VIII. 16.
Κλειώ, XIII. 195; Κλειοῖ, III. 3, XII. 2.
Κλεοπτόλεμος: Κλεοπτολέμῳ, XIV. 19.
κλέος, IX. 40 (?), XIII. 32, XVII. 80.
κλέω: κλέομεν, XVI. 13.
κλισία: κλισίῃσιν, XIII. 102.
κλονέω: κλονέων, XIII. 85.
Κλύμενος: Κλύμενον, V. 145.
κλυτός: κλυτάν, XVII. 73; κλυτόν, XI. 80; κλυτᾶς, XVII. 7; κλυτάς, XVII. 101.
κλυτότοξος, I. 9 (?).
κλύω: ἔκλυε, XI. 106; κλύε, XVII. 67; κλύῃ, XVII. 64.
κνίζω: κνίσεν, XVII. 8.
Κνώσιος or Κνώσσιος: Κνώσιον, XVII. 120; Κνωσίων, XVII. 39.
Κνώσσος: Κνώσσον, fr. 1, 14.
κοινόω: κοινώσας, XV. 49.
κόμα: κόμαν, IX. 24; κόμαισι, XVII. 113.
κομπάζω: κομπάσομαι, VIII. 4.
κόνις, V. 44.
κορυφά: κορυφαί, V. 24.

κορώνα : κορώνας, V. 73.
κοσμέω : ἐκόσμησε (?), VII. 11 ; κοσμῆσαι, XII. 7.
κόσμος : κόσμον, III. 95, XVII. 63.
κόρα or κούρα : κούρα, V. 104, 137, XI. 9, *fr.* 1, 18 (?) ; 71, 1 ; κούραν, III. 2 ; κοῦραι, IX. 44, XI. 42, XVII. 125 ; κούρας, XI. 109 ; κούραις, III. 60 ; κόρα, XVII. 32, XIX. 18 ; κόραν, XX. 5, *fr.* 1, 8 ; κόρᾳ, XVI. 20 ; κόρας, XVII. 103.
Κουρής : Κουρῆσι, V. 126.
κοῦρος : κούρους, XVII. 3
κοῦφος : κοῦφα, XIII. 56 ; κουφόταται, I. 40.
κραδία : κραδίαν, XI. 85, XVIII. 11 ; and see καρδία.
κραίνω : κραίνων, XIII. 12.
Κραναΐδαι : Κραναϊδῶν, *fr.* 71, 2.
κράς : κρατός, XVIII. 51.
κραταιός : κραταιοῦ, XVIII. 18.
κρατερός : κρατερόν, XVIII. 40 ; κρατεράν, XIII. 110 ; κρατερᾶς, XI. 20 ; κρατερᾷ, V. 21.
κρατέω : κρατεῦσαν, VI. 7 ; κρατήσας, VI. 15.
Κρεμμυών : Κρεμμυῶνος, XVIII. 24.
Κρέουσα : Κρεούσας, XVIII. 15.
κρέων : κρέουσαν, III. 1.
κρήδεμνον : κρήδεμνα, *fr.* 56, 6.
Κρής : Κρητῶν, *fr.* 1, 6.
Κρητικός : Κρητικόν, XVII. 4.
κρίνω : κρίνεις, XI. 6 ; κρίνει, V. 131 ; κρινεῖ, XVII. 46 ; κρίνειν, VII. 6.
κριτός : κριτοί, IX. 11.
Κροῖσος : Κροῖσον, III. 28.
Κρονίδας, I. 17, XI. 73, XVII. 77 ; Κρονίδαν, V. 178 ; Κρονίδα, X. 29, XVIII. 21.
Κρόνιος, XVII. 65.
κρόταφος : κρόταφον, XVII. 30.
κρύπτω : κρύπτειν, III. 14 ; κρυφθεῖσα, XIII. 144.
κτείνω : ἔκτανεν, V. 89 ; κτανεῖν, XIX. 31.
κτίζω : κτίζειν, XI. 72.
κτύπος, *fr.* 46, 9.
*κυανανθής : κυανανθεῖ, XIII. 91.
κυάνεος : κυάνεον, XIII. 31.
κυανοπλόκαμος : κυανοπλοκάμου, V. 33, IX. 53 ; κυανοπλόκαμοι, XI. 83.
κυανόπρῳρα, XVII. 1.
κυανῶπις : κυανώπιδας, XIII. 127.
κυβερνάω : κυβερνᾷς, XVII. 22 ; κυβερνᾷ, XIII. 152 ; κυβερνᾶται, XIV. 10.

κυβερνήτας, XII. 1 ; κυβερνήταν, V. 47.
κῦδος, I. 22, VI. 3, X. 17.
κυδρός : κυδροτέρᾳ, I. 26.
κύκλος : κύκλον, IX. 30.
Κύκλαψ : Κύκλωπες, XI. 77.
κύκνος : κύκνῳ, XVI. 6.
κύλιξ : κυλίκων, *fr.* 56, 2.
κῦμα : κύματα, V. 26 ; κύμασιν, XIII. 92.
κυνέα : κυνέαν, XVIII. 50.
Κύπρις, *fr.* 56, 3 ; Κύπριδος, V. 175, XVII. 10.
κυρέω : κυρῆσαι, III. 8.
κύων : κύνα, V. 60.
Κωκυτός : Κωκυτοῦ, V. 64.
κῶμος : κῶμοι, XI. 12 ; κώμων, XIII. 41, *fr.* 46, 5.
Κῶς : Κῶν, III. 71.

λαγχάνω : ἔλαχεν, I. 28, 42 ; λάχε, VI. 2 ; λέλογχεν, XIII. 154 ; λάχῃσι, XIX. 3 ; λαχών, I. 13, III. 11 ; λαχοῖσαν, XIX. 13 ; λαχόντας, XI. 70 ; λελογχώς, X. 39.
λάϊνος : λάϊνον, *fr.* 59, 1.
λαῖς : λαῖδος, XVI. 17.
λαιψηρός : λαιψηρῶν, VII. 6.
Λάκαινα : Λάκαιναν, XVIII. 50.
Λακεδαιμόνιος, XX. 2 (?).
Λάμνιος : Λαμνίαν, XVIII. 55.
λαμπρός : λαμπρόν, III. 54.
λάμπω : λάμπει, III. 17, VIII. 5 ; λάμπε, XVII. 104, 123 : λαμπόμενον, V. 72.
Λάμπων, XIII. 193 ; Λάμπωνος, XIII. 35.
λανθάνω : λαθεῖν, XIX. 27.
Λαομέδαν : Λαομέδοντος, XIII. 109.
λαός, III. 9 (?) ; λαῷ, XIII. 198 ; λαούς, XI. 67 ; λαῶν, IX. 35, XI. 117, *fr.* 1, 10.
λαοφόνος : λαοφόνον, XIII. 87.
λάρναξ : λάρνακος, V. 141.
Λατοίδας, III. 39.
Λατώ : Λατοῦς, V. 124, XI. 16, 98.
Λάχων, VI. 1.
λάω : *λῶσιν, XVII. 118.
λέγω : λέγει, XVIII. 18, 32, 47, *fr.* 63 ; λέγουσιν, V. 57 ; λέγειν, V. 164.
λείπω : λείπει, I. 45 ; ἔλειπον, XIII. 83 ; λίπον, V. 172 ; λίπεν, *fr.* 1, 10 ; λιπεῖν, XVI. 13 ; λιπών, I. 16 ; λιποῦσα, XIX. 15 ; λιπόντες, II. 8, XI. 60, 81, XIII. 108 ; λιποῦσαι, XI. 57 ; λείπεται, IX. 87, XIII. 31.
λεπτόθριξ : λεπτότριχα, V. 28.

*λεπτόπρυμνος: λεπτόπρυμνον, XVII.
119.
λευκός: λευκόν, fr. 53, 3; λευκᾶν, XVII.
13.
λευκώλενος, IX. 7, XVII. 54; λευκώλενε,
V. 176; λευκώλενον, XVI. 28; λευκωλένου, V. 99.
λέχος: λέχει, IX. 56 (?), XVII. 30.
λέων: λέοντα, IX. 9; λέοντος, I. 4;
λέοντι, XIII. 14.
λῃστάς: λῃσταί, XVIII. 8.
λήγω: λῆξεν, XIII. 89, 95.
*λιγυκλαγγής: λιγυκλαγγῆ, V. 73;
λιγυκλαγγεῖς, XIV. 14.
λιγύφθογγος: λιγύφθογγον, X. 10;
λιγύφθογγοι, V. 23.
λικμάω: λικμήσῃ, fr. 72, 4.
λίθος, fr. 51, 1.
λιπαρόζωνος: λιπαροζώνων, IX. 49.
λιπαρός: λιπαρά, VII. 1; λιπαρόν, XVI.
29; λιπαράν, V. 169, XI. 38, fr. 7,
2; λιπαρᾶς, fr. 44; λιπαρῶν, I. 19.
λίσσομαι: λίσσοντο, XI. 69; λισσόμενος, V. 100.
λόγος, XV. 44; λόγον, fr. 61, 2; λόγων,
XV. 47.
λογχωτός: λογχωτά, fr. 46, 8.
Λοξίας, XIII. 115.
Λοῦσος: Λοῦσον, XI. 96.
Λυγκεύς: Λυγκέος, XI. 75.
λυγρός: λυγραῖς, XI. 68.
Λυδία: Λυδίας, III. 24.
Λύδιος: Λυδία, fr. 51, 1.
Λύκιος: Λυκίων, XIII. 114.
Λυκόρμας: Λυκόρμᾳ, XVI. 34.
λύσσα: λύσσας, XI. 102.
*Λυταῖος: Λυταίου, XVIII. 21.
λύω: λύει, fr. 56, 6; ἔλυσεν, I. 15,
XIII. 80.

Μαῖα: Μαίας, XIX. 25.
μαίνομαι: μαίνοιτο, XIII. 86.
μάκαρ: μακάρων, XI. 121.
μακρός: μακράν, X. 51.
Μαλέα, III. 72.
μάν, I. 43, XIII. 149.
μανία: μανιᾶν, XI. 109.
Μαντινεύς: Μαντινέες, fr. 2, 2.
μανύω: μανύει, fr. 51, 1; 67; μανῦον,
X. 14.
μαρμαίρω: μαρμαίρουσιν, fr. 56, 8.
μαρμαρυγά: μαρμαρυγαῖς, III. 17.
μάρναμαι: μαρνάμεθα, V. 125; μάρ-
ναντο, XIII. 118.
Μάρπησσα: Μάρπησσαν, XX. 6.

ματεύω: ματεύει, X. 35.
μάτηρ, V. 138; ματρί, III. 50.
μάτρως: μάτρωας, V. 129.
μάχα: μάχαν, XIII. 84; μάχας, I. 6,
XVIII. 59; μάχαις, XI. 68, XIV. 13.
μεγάθυμος, XIII. 162.
*μεγαίνητος: μεγαίνητε, III. 64;
μεγαινήτους, I. 16.
*μεγαλοκλεής: μεγαλοκλέα, fr. 17,
2 (?).
μεγαλοσθενής: μεγαλοσθενές (voc.),
XVII. 52.
*μεγαλοῦχος: μεγαλοῦχον, XVII. 23.
μέγαρον, XVII. 101; μεγάρων, III. 46;
μεγάροις, V. 119, 165.
μέγας: μεγάλα, fr. 46, 1; μέγαν,
XVII. 98; μεγάλαν, X. 49, XIII. 46;
μέγα, XIII. 122 (?); μεγάλου, V.
79; μεγάλας, V. 24; μεγάλων, I.
35, XV. 52; μεγάλαισιν, XIII. 124;
μεῖζον, fr. 45, 2; μέγιστον, I. 21;
III. 19, IX. 55 (?), fr. 56, 10;
μεγίσταν, XIX. 45; μεγίστου, VI.
1; μέγιστα, III. 61.
μεγασθενής, XVII. 67.
*μεγιστοάνασσα, XIX. 21.
*μεγιστοπάτωρ: V. 199.
μεδέων, XVII. 66 (?).
μειλίχιος: μειλιχίοις, XI. 90.
μείρομαι: εἱμάρθαι, XIV. 1.
*μελαγκευθής: μελαγκευθές, III. 55 (?),
fr. 64.
μέλαθρον: μελάθρων, XI. 44.
*μελαμφαρής: μελαμφαρεΐ, III. 13.
μελάμφυλλος: μελαμφύλλου, XV. 33.
*μελανόκολπος: μελανοκόλπου, fr. 66.
Μέλας, II. 4 (?).
μέλας: μέλαινα, XIII. 120; μέλαν,
XVII. 17.
Μελέαγρος, V. 93; Μελεάγρου, V. 77,
171.
μελέτα: μελέταν, XIII. 158.
μελίγλωσσος: μελιγλώσσου, III. 97;
μελιγλώσσαν, fr. 46, 2.
μέλισσα: μέλισσαν, X. 10.
μελίφρων, fr. 46, 10; μελίφρονος, fr.
13, 5.
μέλλω: μέλλει, V. 164; ἔμελλε, III.
30; μέλλε, XVI. 19; μέλλον, XIII.
131; μέλλον (part.), IX. 96, X. 45;
μέλλοντος, IX. 14; μελλόντων, fr.
48, 4.
μέλος, XX. 3; μελέων, XIX. 2.
μέλπω: μέλπουσι, XIII. 61; μέλπετε
(imperat.), XIII. 157.

μέλω : μέλει, V. 92 ; μέλειν, fr. 46, 5.
Μέμφις : Μέμφιν, fr. 65.
μέν, I. 2, III. 15, 68, 85, 90, V. 3, 37,
  144, X. 47, XIII. 81, 170, XIV. 1,
  XVII. 1, 24, 75, XIX. 37, fr. 51, 1 ;
  56, 6 ; 58 ; 60, 1 ; 68.
Μένανδρος : Μενάνδρου, XIII. 159.
μενέκτυπος : μενέκτυπον, XVII. 1.
Μενέλαος, XV. 48.
μενεπτόλεμος, XVII. 73 ; μενεπτολέμου,
  V. 170 ; μενεπτολέμοις, V. 126.
μενοινά : μενοινάν, fr. 48, 3.
μένος, III. 54 (?).
μέριμνα, III. 57, XI. 86, XIX. 11 ; μέριμναι, I. 41, XIX. 34 ; μερίμνας, fr. 56,
  5 ; μεριμνᾶν, V. 7.
Μέροψ : Μέροπος, III. 71 (or Μεροπίς).
μέσος : μέσῳ, XV. 53.
μετά, with dat., V. 30 ; with gen., XI.
  123.
Μεταπόντιον, XI. 10, 116.
μεταπρέπω : μετέπρεπεν, V. 68.
μετέπειτα, fr. 1, 2 (?).
μή : III. 68, V. 36, 81, 160, XI. 27,
  XIII. 166, XVIII. 43.
μήδομαι : μήσεται, XVIII. 42 ; ἐμήσατο,
  XVI. 30 ; μησάμενον, IV. 16.
μηλόβοτος : μηλοβότους, V. 66.
*μηλοδαίκτας : μηλοδαίκταν, IX. 6.
μηλοθύτας : μηλοθύταν, VIII. 1.
μῆλον : μῆλα, V. 109 ; μήλων, XI. 111,
  XVIII. 9, fr. 46, 4.
μηλοτρόφος : μηλοτρόφον, XI. 95.
μήν : μηνός, VII. 2 (?) ; μηνί, fr. 1,
  17 (?) ; μῆνας, XI. 93.
μῆρα, fr. 46, 4.
μήτε, V. 161.
μῆτις : μῆτιν, XVI. 25, XVII. 29, 52.
μίγνυμι : μιχθεῖσα, XIII. 66 ; μιγεῖσα,
  XVII. 31.
μικρός : μείων, I. 35.
μιμνάσκω : μεμνᾶσθαι, XVIII. 58.
μίμνω : μίμνειν, III. 31 ; μίμνοντα,
  XIII. 102.
μιν, XI. 111.
μίνυνθα, V. 151.
μινύθω : μινύθει, III. 90.
Μίνως, fr. 1, 3 ; Μίνωϊ, XVII. 8 ; Μίνωϊ,
  XVII. 68.
μίτρα : μίτραισιν, XIII. 163.
μοῖρα : (' share '), μοῖραν, IV. 20, V. 51 ;
  (' fate '), μοῖρα, V. 121, 143, IX. 15,
  XVII. 24, 89.
μοναρχέω : μοναρχήσειν, fr. 56, 7.
μόνος or μοῦνος : μόνος, fr. 54 ; μόνον,

XVIII. 35 ; μόνους, XVIII. 46 ;
  μοῦνον, III. 80, IV. 15, V. 156 ;
  μούνῳ, fr. 55, 1.
*μουνοπάλα : μουνοπάλαν, XII. 8.
Μοῦσα or Μοῖσα : Μοῦσα, II. 11, III.
  92, XV. 47, fr. 57, 2 ; Μουσᾶν, V.
  193, IX. 3, 87 (?), X. 11, XIX. 4, fr.
  21, 3 ; 71, 3 ; Μοισᾶν, V. 4.
μῦθος : μῦθον, XV. 39 ; μύθοισι, XI. 90.
μύριος : μυρία, V. 31, IX. 48, XIX. 1 ;
  μυρίαν, fr. 48, 3 ; μυρίαι, X. 38, XIV.
  8 (?), fr. 68 ; μυρίας, XI. 126
  μυρίων, III. 41, XIII. 163.
μύρω : μυρομένοις, V. 163.
μυχός : μυχοῖς, IV. 14.
μῶμος, XIII. 169.

ναίω : ναίεις, XI. 116 ; ναῖον, XI. 61,
  80 ; ναίειν, IX. 99.
ναός or νηός : ναόν, XVI. 12, fr. 52, 2 ;
  ναοῦ, III. 19 ; νηόν, fr. 72, 1.
νάπα : νάπαις, XVIII. 23.
νασιώτας : νασιώταν, X. 10 (?).
νᾶσος : νᾶσον, II. 8, X. 35, XII. 6, XIII.
  42, 149 ; νάσοιο, fr. 6, 7 ; νάσου, V.
  11, fr. 44.
ναυβάτης : ναυβάται, XVII. 48.
ναῦς, XVII. 1 ; νᾶα, XVII. 89, 119 ;
  νᾶες, fr. 56, 10 ; νᾶας, XIII. 74 ;
  νέας, XIII. 128 ; ναυσί, XIII. 117,
  fr. 1, 5.
νεανίας : νεανίαι, VI. 9 ; νεανίαις, fr.
  53, 2.
νεβρός, XIII. 54.
νεῖκος, XI. 64.
Νεῖλος : Νεῖλον, XIX. 40, fr. 65 ;
  Νείλου, IX. 41.
Νεμέα : Νεμέαν, VIII. 2 ; Νεμέᾳ, IX.
  22, 82 (?), X. 29, XII. 8, XIII. 34.
Νεμεαῖος : Νεμεαίου, IX. 4.
νέμω : νείμῃς, VII. 8 ; νείμας, fr. 1,
  13 ; νέμονται, X. 33.
*νεόκριτος, fr. 12, 6.
*νεόκροτος : νεόκροτον, V. 48.
νεόκτιτος : νεοκτίτῳ, XVII. 126.
νέος : νέον, XVIII. 3, 16 ; νέοι, XIII.
  157, XVII. 129 ; νέων, XI. 11, XVIII.
  14 ; νέοις, fr. 46, 5.
Νέσσος : Νέσσου, XVI. 35.
νευρά : νευράν, V. 73.
νέφος, III. 55, XIII. 31, fr. 63, 3.
νῆις : νῆιν, V. 174.
Νηρεύς : Νηρῆος, XVII. 102 (?); Νηρέος,
  fr. 6, 6.

Νηρηίς: Νηρῆδος, XIII. 90; Νηρηίδες, XVII. 38.

νίκα, IX. 67 (?); νίκαν, II. 5, V. 49, IX. 82, XI. 39, XIII. 157; νίκας (gen. sing.), VI. 11, VII. 9, X. 52; νίκᾳ, III. 5; νίκας (acc. plur.), VIII. 9; person., Νίκα, XI. 1, XII. 5, *fr.* 71, 1; Νίκας, V. 33, X. 15.

*νίκασπις: νικάσπιδες, IX. 10.

νικάω: νικᾶν, XIII. 172; νικάσας, V. 183; νικάσαντα, V. 40; νικάσαντι, IX. 25.

νιν: (sing.), III. 92, V. 24, 43, 78, 159, IX. 26, X. 27, 31, XI. 15, 22, 86, 89, XIII. 197, XV. 57, XVI. 31, XVII. 84, 112, XVIII. 35, XIX. 27, 42; (plur.) IX. 15; (incert.) *fr.* 5, 5; 18, 3.

νίπτω: νιψάμενος, XI. 97.

νόημα, XI. 54.

νόος: νόον, V. 95; νόῳ, IV. 9; V. 8.

νόσος or νοῦσος: νόσων, *fr.* 60, 1; νούσων, I. 32.

νόσφιν, I. 32.

νότος: νότου, XIII. 97.

νῦν, V. 4, 31, VI. 10, IX. 25, X. 9; XI. 10, 37, XII. 3, XIV. 20, XVII. 55, *fr.* 47, 1.

νυν (enclit.), XIX. 8.

νύξ: νύκτα, *fr.* 48, 4; νυκτός, IX. 29, XIII. 94, 142 (?); νύκτας, XIX. 28; person., Νυκτός, VII. 2, *fr.* 66.

νωμάω: νωμᾶται, V. 26.

*ξανθοδερκής, IX. 12.

ξανθόθριξ: ξανθότριχα, V. 37.

ξανθός: ξανθάν, III. 56, IX. 24, X. 15; ξανθᾶς, XI. 51, XIII. 103; ξανθᾷ, V. 92, XX. 2, *fr.* 46, 4.

ξενία: ξενίαν, XIII. 191.

ξένος or ξεῖνος: ξένος, V. 11; ξείνα, XI. 85; ξείναν, I. 12; ξείνοισι, XII. 5.

ξεστός: ξεστούς, XVIII. 49.

ξίφος, XVIII. 48; ξίφεα, *fr.* 46, 8.

ξουθός: ξουθαῖσι, V. 17.

ξύλινος: ξύλινον, III. 49.

ξυνίς: ξυνόν, X. 12.

ὁ, ἡ, τό: demonstr., ὁ, XVII. 71, *fr.* 56, 6; ἁ, XV. 59 (or relat.); τόν, V. 71, 93, 170, XI. 85; τάν, V. 169; τοῦ, XI. 106; τῷ, V. 76, 111, XVII. 81; τᾷ, XI. 40 (?); τοί, V. 149, *fr.* 59, 1; οἱ, X. 43, *fr.* 60, 1; ταί, XIII. 58; τά, V. 91; τούς, V. 121; τάς,

XI. 43; τῶν, XIII. 67; ταῖσιν, V. 68, XI. 53. Article, ὁ, I. 25, 34, 35, III. 17, 28, 51, 76, 87, IV. 2, V. 183, 199, XIII. 172, XVII. 66; ἁ, IX. 7, XIII. 161, 171, XV. 57, *fr.* 62, 4; τό, I. 36, IX. 96, X. 45, 47, XIII. 50, 173, XVII. 62 (?), *fr.* 47, 1 (bis); 48, 4; τόν, V. 180, X. 50, XI. 71, XVIII. 19, XIX. 49, *fr.* 42, 1; 72, 1; τάν, III. 25, XVIII. 26, *fr.* 7, 2; 65; τήν, *fr.* 53, 1; 55, 2; τῷ, XVIII. 45, *fr.* 42, 1; 72, 2; αἱ, IX. 63; τά, I. 38, III. 47, XVII. 46, *fr.* 58; τῶν, V. 4, XVI. 32, XVIII. 2; τᾶν, XVIII. 1; τοῖς, *fr.* 53, 2; ταῖς, XIX. 9. Relative, τόν, V. 142, IX. 12, XVII. 115; τάν, XIII. 160, 193, 195; τοῦ, IX. 40; τᾷ, XIII. 188; ταί, IX. 42; τούς, V. 199; τῶν, I. 17, XIII. 34, 135; τοῖσιν, V. 135.

*ὀβριμοδερκής: ὀβριμοδερκεῖ, XVI. 20.

*ὀβριμόσπορος: ὀβριμοσπόρου, XIX. 32.

ὅδε: τόδε, V. 160, IX. 82; τόνδε, I. 42, XVII. 60, *fr.* 72, 1; τάδε, IV. 15, V. 163, 191, XVII. 74; τοῖσδε, *fr.* 53, 2.

ὁδός, *fr.* 48, 1; ὁδόν, XVII. 89, XIX. 13; ὁδοῦ, X. 52.

ὀδούς: ὀδόντι, V. 108.

ὀδύρομαι: ὀδυρόμενον, *fr.* 49, 1.

Ὀδυσσεύς: Ὀδυσσεῖ, XV. 5.

ὅθεν, XIX. 46.

ὅθι, IX. 6.

οἶδα, X. 49; οἶδε, III. 13, IX. 53; εἰδώς, V. 78, X. 42.

οἰκεῖος: οἰκείων, I. 29.

οἰκέω: οἰκεῦσι, IX. 43.

οἰκίζω: ᾤκισσαν, IX. 51.

Ὀϊκλείδας, IX. 16.

οἶκος: οἴκῳ, *fr.* 13, 3; οἴκοι, *fr.* 56, 8.

οἰκτείρω: οἰκτείροντα, V. 158.

Οἰνείδας: Οἰνείδαις, X. 18.

Οἰνεύς, V. 97; Οἰνέος, V. 120; Οἰνῆος, V. 166.

οἶνος, *fr.* 57, 2.

οἶος: οἶον, XVI. 30; οἵαν, XIII. 13; οἷα, V. 66, XVIII. 36; οἵαισιν, XVII. 120.

ὀϊστός: ὀϊστόν, V. 82.

Οἰχαλία: Οἰχαλίαν, XVI. 14.

οἰχνέω: οἰχνεῖς, X. 1 (?).

οἴχομαι: ᾤχετο, *fr.* 1, 13.

ὄλβιος, V. 50, *fr.* 41; ὄλβιον, III. 8; ὀλβίαν, XII. 4; ὀλβίου, XVII. 102; ὀλβίων, XV. 56; ὀλβίαις, XIX. 10.

ὄλβος, fr. 62, 2; ὄλβον, III. 22; ὄλβου, III. 92.
ὄλεθρος: ὄλεθρον, V. 139.
*ὀλιγοσθενέω: ὀλιγοσθενέων, V. 152.
ὁλκάς: ὁλκάδα, XVI. 2 (?).
ὄλλυμι: ὤλεσε, V. 121; ὤλεσσεν, XV. 63.
ὀλολύζω: ὠλόλυξαν, XVII. 127.
ὀλοός: ὀλοά, V. 121.
Ὀλυμπία: Ὀλυμπία, VI. 6, VII. 3.
*Ὀλυμπιοδρόμος: Ὀλυμπιοδρόμους, III. 3.
Ὀλυμπιονίκης: Ὀλυμπιονίκας, IV. 17.
Ὀλύμπιος: Ὀλύμπιον, V. 179.
Ὄλυμπος: Ὀλύμπῳ, XI. 4.
ὁμαρτέω: ὁμαρτεῖν, XVIII. 46.
ὁμιλέω: ὁμιλεῖ, I. 23.
ὅμιλος: ὅμιλον, X. 24; ὁμίλῳ, fr. 1, 6.
ὄμμα, XVII. 18; ὀμμάτων, XVII. 95, XVIII. 54; ὄμμασι, XIX. 19.
ὀμφά, XIV. 13.
ὀμφαλός: ὀμφαλόν, IV. 4 (?).
ὄπα, XVIII. 30.
ὀπάζω: ὤπασεν, XV. 60; ὄπαζε, XVII. 132.
ὀπίσσω, XIII. 20.
ὅπλον: ὅπλοισι, XVIII. 33.
ὁπλότερος: ὁπλότερον, XI. 71.
ὁππότε, XIII. 77.
ὀξύς: ὀξεῖαν, XIII. 84.
ὁράω: ὄψεαι, III. 79.
ὀργά: ὀργαί, fr. 68.
ὀρέγω: ὄρεξεν, V. 114.
ὀρθόδικος: ὀρθοδίκου, XI. 9, XIV. 23.
ὀρθός: ὀρθᾶς, XI. 27.
ὀρθόω: ὀρθοῖ, XIV. 18 (?).
ὀρθῶς, I. 44, V. 6.
ὀρίνω: ὠρείνατο, XIII. 79.
ὅριον: ὅρια, XVIII. 6.
ὁρμά: ὁρμάν, X. 20, XIII. 123.
ὁρμαίνω: ὁρμαίνει, fr. 56, 11; ὁρμαίνοντα, XIII. 73.
ὁρμάω: ὁρμᾷ, XVIII. 41.
ὄρνις: ὄρνιχες, V. 22.
ὄρνυμι: ὦρσαν, XIII. 112; ὄρνυε, XVII. 76: ὀρνύμενον, V. 45; ὀρνύμενοι, XV. 41.
ὄρος, XI. 55.
ὄρος, fr. 48, 1; ὅρον, V. 144.
ὀρούω: ὄρουσε, XVII. 84.
*ὀρσίαλος: ὀρσιάλῳ, XVI. 19.
*ὀρσιβάκχας: ὀρσιβάκχαν, XIX. 49.
*ὀρσίμαχος: ὀρσιμάχου, XV. 3.
ὄρχος: ὄρχους, V. 108.

ὅς (relative), V. 11, XIV. 23, XV. 51, XVIII. 20, XIX. 3, fr. 46, 11; 48, 3; ἅ, IX. 19, X. 50, XIII. 64, XVII. 112, XIX. 49; ὅν, V. 193; ἅν, X. 37; ᾧ, VII. 8; οἵ, IX. 23, X. 33, 34, XIII. 81; οὕς, V. 115; ἅς, IX. 50; οἷσιν, fr. 1, 12.
ὅς (possessive): ὅν, V. 47; ᾗ, XVI. 6.
ὅσιος: ὅσιον, XVII. 21; ὅσια, III. 83.
ὅσος or ὅσσος: ὅσσον, I. 42; ὅσσα, VI. 4, X. 15; ὅσοι, III. 63; ὅσα, II. 6.
ὅσπερ: ἅπερ, XIX. 38 (?).
ὅστε, XIII. 72, XVIII. 39 (?).
ὅστις, III. 67 (?), V. 110, XI. 124; ὅντινα, I. 40; ὅ τι, III. 57, V. 164, XVII. 24, 117; ᾧ τινι, V. 50.
ὅταν, XIII. 30, XVII. 27, fr. 28, 3.
ὅτε, XI. 95, XIII. 88, XVI. 34, XIX. 19, 50, XX. 4.
ὅτι, III. 61, 79, 81, VI. 15, XVI. 27.
ὀτρύνω: ὤτρυνε, IX. 35, XIII. 113.
οὐ, οὐκ, οὐχ: I. 8, III. 30, 88, 90, 95, V. 24, 43, 53, 84, 122, 129, 136, 162, IX. 15, 53, XI. 22, XIII. 17 (?), 142, XIV. 12 (?), XV. 52, XVII. 41, 81, XVIII. 43, fr. 46, 9; 52, 1; 54; 57, 1; 58; 61, 1; 62, 1.
οὗ, 3rd pers. pron.: οἱ, dative, I. 17, XI. 110, XVII. 18, 37, 115, XVIII. 46, XX. 9, fr. 1, 10; 72, 3.
οὐδέ, V. 25, XIV. 15 (?), XIX. 25, fr. 46, 10; 47, 2; 52, 1.
οὐδείς, fr. 41; οὐδέν, I. 37, III. 57, XVII. 118, fr. 60, 2.
οὐδός: οὐδόν, fr. 59, 1.
οὐκέτι, XVII. 11, 21.
*οὔλιος: οὔλιον, XVIII. 53.
οὖλος: οὔλαις, XVII. 113.
οὖν, XIX. 29, 37.
Οὐρανία: Οὐρανίας, V. 13, VI. 11, XVI. 3 (?).
οὐρανός: οὐρανοῦ, XVII. 55.
οὔριος: οὐρία, XIII. 97.
οὖρος: οὖρον, XVII. 87.
οὔτε, XIX. 26, 28, fr. 57, 1 (bis); 62, 2 (ter).
οὔτις, III. 63, VIII. 6.
οὗτος: τοῦτο, III. 83; τοῦτον, XVIII. 31; ταῦτα, V. 136, XVIII. 30; τούτων, XVIII. 39.
ὀφθαλμός: ὀφθαλμοῖσιν, X. 7.
ὄφρα, XVIII. 42, fr. 72, 3.
ὀφρύς: ὀφρύων, XVII. 17.

ὄχθα : ὄχθαισιν, VIII. 11.
ὄψ : ὀπί, XVI. 7 (?), XVII. 129, fr. 5, 6.

παγκρατής, XI. 44, XVII. 24, fr. 51, 2.
παγκράτιον : παγκρατίου, XIII. 23.
πάγνυμι : πᾶξαι, XI. 88.
πάγξενος : παγξένῳ, XI. 28.
παιανίζω : *παιάνιξαν, XVII. 129.
παιδικός : παιδικοί, fr. 46, 12.
παῖς, VIII. 8; παῖ, X. 47; XIII. 62;
  παῖδα, V. 146, 156, XI. 14, 32,
  XIII. 70, XVIII. 56, XIX. 41; παιδί,
  XVII. 70; παῖδες, V. 36, XV. 56;
  παῖδας, I. 15, XI. 69, XV. 63;
  παίδεσσι, XV. 39; παισί, X. 42.
Πακτωλός, III. 45.
πάλα : πάλας, IX. 36, XI. 21.
πάλαι, fr. 47, 1.
παλαίστρα : παλαίστραν, XVIII. 26.
πάλιν, IX. 16, XVII. 81.
παλίντροπος : παλίντροπον, XI. 54.
Πάλλας : Πάλλαντος, fr. 71, 1.
Παλλάς : Παλλάδος, XV. 3; Παλλάδι,
  V. 92.
παμμαχία : παμμαχιᾶν, XIII. 43 (?).
πάμπαν, fr. 5, 10.
*πάμφθερσις, fr. 62, 2.
πανδαμάτωρ, XIII. 172.
πανδερκής : πανδερκέα, XVII. 70.
Πανδίων : Πανδίονος, XVII. 15, XVIII.
  15.
πάνδωρος, fr. 62, 4.
Πανέλλανες : Πανελλάνων, XIII. 165.
*πανθαλής, XIII. 196; πανθαλέων, XIII.
  36.
Πανθοίδας : Πανθοΐδα, I. 9 (?), II. 14.
*πάννικος : παννίκοιο, XI. 21.
παντᾷ, V. 31, IX. 48, XV. 44.
παντοδαπός : παντοδαπῶν, IV. 19.
πάντοθεν, XIX. 20.
παντοῖος : παντοίαισι, XIII. 16.
παρά : with acc., III. 6, IV. 14, V. 38,
  IX. 39, X. 29, XI. 26, 119, XIII. 25,
  XVI. 12, XVII. 119, XIX. 39, fr. 48,
  4; 52, 2; 55, 2; with gen., III. 11,
  XIV. 10 (πάρ), XVI. 35, XIX. 3, 13;
  with dat., III. 20, V. 64, IX. 84,
  XIII. 117, XIV. 1.
παραπλήξ : παραπλῆγι, XI. 45.
παρατρέπω : παρατρέψαι, V. 95.
παράφρων : see πάρφρων.
πάρεδρος : παρέδρου, XI. 51.
πάρειμι : πάρεστι(ν), III. 67, XIX. 1,
  fr. 57, 1.

παρηΐς : παρηΐδων, XVII. 13.
παρθενικά : παρθενικᾶς, XVII. 11.
παρθένιος : παρθενίᾳ, XI. 47.
παρθένος : παρθένῳ, XVI. 21; παρθένοι,
  III. 50, XIII. 61.
παρίημι : παρέντα, III. 88 (?).
παρίστημι : παρισταμένα, XI. 5.
πάροιθε(ν), III. 19, VI. 4.
πάρος, XII. 4.
πάρφρων : πάρφρονος, XI. 103.
πᾶς or ἅπας : πᾶν, VIII. 5, XVII.
  93 (?); πᾶσαν, IX. 40; παντί, I.
  30, XIII. 198; ἅπαντα, XV. 51, fr.
  42, 1; πάντα, V. 55, XV. 38, XVIII.
  45, fr. 41; πάντων, I. 36, XVII.
  66, fr. 72, 2; πάντεσσι(ν), XIII.
  48, 170, XVII. 123, fr. 50; πᾶσι(ν),
  XV. 54, fr. 56, 7.
πασιφανής, XIII. 143.
πασσυδίᾳ, XIII. 108.
πατήρ, V. 101, XI. 2, 96, XV. 37,
  XVII. 78; πάτερ, XVII. 53; πατέρα,
  XI. 51; πατρός, XVII. 62, 99, 109.
πάτριος : πατρίων, I. 7.
πατρίς : πατρίδος, fr. 12, 4.
πατρῷος : πατρῷαν, XIII. 41.
παῦρος : παύροισ(ι), IX. 95 (?), XIII.
  29, fr. 42, 1; παυροτέρων, I. 36.
παύω : παύσει, XIII. 12; παῦσεν, V.
  98, XI. 108; παῦσαι, XI. 76; παύσασθαι, XV. 46.
πεδίον, XIII. 110; πεδίῳ, XI. 19, XIII.
  85.
*πεδοιχνέω : πεδοιχνεῖν, XVI. 9.
πέδον, IX. 5.
πείθω : πεῖθε, IX. 16; πιθοῦσα, XI.
  107; πείθομαι, V. 195.
πεισίμβροτος : πεισίμβροτον, IX. 2.
πέλαγος, XVII. 4, 77.
πελάζω : πέλασσεν, XI. 33; πελάσσων,
  IX. 38 (?); πλαθεῖσα, XVII. 35.
Πελλάνα : Πελλάναν, X. 33 (?).
Πέλοψ : Πέλοπος, V. 181, VIII. 15,
  XI. 25, fr. 44.
πέλω : ἔπλετο, I. 3; πέλονται, X. 38,
  fr. 46, 7.
πέμπω : πέμπει, V. 11, XV. 61, fr. 56,
  5; πέμψει, V. 91; πέμπεν, IX. 20;
  ἐπεμψεν, XVI. 2; πέμποι, XVI. 29;
  πέμπειν, V. 197; πέμψαι, III. 66.
πενθέω : πενθεῖν, fr. 42, 2.
πενία : πενίας, I. 33.
πενταέθλος : πενταέθλοισιν, IX. 27.
πέντε, I. 15.
πεντήκοντα, III. 81, VII. 2, fr. 1, 5.

πέπων : πεπόνων, *fr.* 72, 4.
πέρθω : πέρσαν, XI. 122.
περί : with gen., v. 124 ; with dat.,
XIII. 22, XVIII. 47; incert., VIII. 12.
Περίκλειτος : Περίκλειτε, *fr.* 58.
περικλειτός : περικλειτοί, XI. 81 ; περικλειτῶν, IX. 8 ; περικλειτοῖσ(ιν), v.
120, X. 19.
Περσείδας, XIII. 15.
Πέρσης : Περσῶν, III. 27.
πέταλον, v. 186.
πετάννυμι : πέτασεν, XVII. 72.
Πετραῖος : Πετραίου, XIV. 20.
Πηλείδας, XIII. 77.
Πηλεύς : Πηλέα, XIII. 64.
πῆχυς : πῆχυν, *fr.* 53, 3.
πιαίνω : πιαίνεται, III. 68.
Πιερίδες, XIX. 35 ; Πιερίδων, XIX. 3.
πινυτός : πινυτᾶς, XV. 55.
πίνω : πίνοντος, *fr.* 56, 11.
πῖος : πιοτάτῳ, *fr.* 72, 2.
πίπτω : ἔπεσον, XI. 20; πεσεῖν, XI. 72 ;
πεσόντα, XI. 23.
Πίσα : Πίσαν, v. 182.
πίσυνος, v. 21, XIII. 188.
Πιτθεύς : Πιτθέος, XVII. 34.
πίτνω : πίτνον, XVII. 6.
πιφαύσκω, v. 42 ; πιφαύσκοι, IX. 81.
πλάξιππος, v. 97 ; πλαξίππῳ, IX. 20 (?).
πλάσσω : πλᾶξεν, XI. 86.
πλατύς : πλατεῖα, *fr.* 63.
Πλεισθενίδας, XV. 48.
*πλείσταρχος : πλείσταρχον, III. 12.
Πλευρών : Πλευρῶνα, v. 151, XX. 10.
πλείων or πλέων : πλείονα, III. 65 ;
πλέονας, VIII. 8 (?).
πλημυρέω : πλημυρῶν, v. 107.
πλημ(μ)υρίς : πλημμυρίν, *fr.* 69.
πλόκος : πλόκον, XVII. 114.
πλοῦτος, I. 22 ; πλοῦτον, III. 13, XV.
59, *fr.* 46, 2 ; 56, 11 ; πλούτου, X.
49 ; πλούτῳ, XI. 51.
πνέω, X. 22 (or compound) ; πνέων, v.
153 ; πνέουσα, XVII. 91.
πνοά : πνοαῖσιν, v. 28.
ποδάνεμος : ποδάνεμον, VI. 13.
ποδάρκης : ποδάρκεα, XIX. 30.
πόθεν, XVIII. 31.
ποιέω : ποιήσατο, III. 33 (?).
ποῖος : ποίᾳ, v. 88.
ποικίλος : ποικίλον, X. 43 ; ποικίλαις,
XI. 33.
ποιμήν : ποιμένων, XVIII. 9.
*πολέμαιγις : πολεμαίγιδος, XVII. 7.
πολέμαρχος : πολέμαρχε, XVII. 39.

πολεμήϊος : πολεμηϊαν, XVIII. 4 : πολεμηϊοις, XVIII. 3.
πόλεμος : πολέμοιο, XIII. 88 ; πολέμου,
XVIII. 58 ; πολέμῳ, v. 131.
πολιοκρόταφος : πολιοκρόταφον, *fr.*
42, 2.
πολιός : πολιόν, III. 88.
πόλις : πόλιν, IV. 2, v. 12, 150, IX. 54,
66, 98, XI. 114, 122, XII. 7, XIII.
38, 130, 152, XV. 41, *fr.* 1, 14 ; 13,
7 ; πόλει, XI. 78 ; πόλεων, *fr.* 56, 6.
πολυδάκρυος : πολυδάκρυον, III. 30 (?).
πολύδακρυς : πολύδακρυν, XVI. 24.
πολύζηλος : πολυζήλῳ, XI. 63.
πολυζήλωτος, VII. 10 ; πολυζήλωτε, IX.
45 ; πολυζήλωτον, I. 46 (?), X. 48.
πολυήρατος : πολυηράτοις, XIX. 9.
πολυκρατής : πολυκρατές, IX. 15.
πολύκρημνος : πολύκρημνον, *fr.* 1, 12.
πολύκριθος : πολύκριθον, XI. 70.
πολυλήϊος : πολυλήϊον, v. 34 (?).
πολύλλιστος : πολύλλιστον, XI. 41.
Πολυνείκης : Πολυνείκεϊ, IX. 20.
Πολυπήμων : Πολυπήμονος, XVIII. 27.
πολύπλαγκτος : πολυπλάγκταν, XIII.
148 ; πολύπλαγκτοι, XI. 35.
πολύς : πολύ, XI. 50 ; πολλάν, XVIII.
34 ; πολέες, XI. 17 ; πολέας, *fr.* 71,
3 ; πολέων, v. 100 ; πολλῶν, X. 48 ;
πόλλοις, I. 14, v. 127 ; and see
πλείων.
πολύστονος : πολύστονον, XVII. 40.
*πολύφαντος : πολύφαντον, XIII. 28.
πολύχρυσος : πολυχρύσῳ, XI. 4.
πολυώνυμος : πολυώνυμε, *fr.* 71, 1.
πόνος : πόνον, XIII. 23, *fr.* 48, 6 ;
πόνους, *fr.* 50.
πόντιος : πόντιον, XVII. 84 ; ποντίῳ,
XVII. 35.
πόντος, XVII. 128 ; πόντον, XIII. 96,
XVII. 94 ; πόντου, III. 86, *fr.* 69 ;
πόντῳ, XIII. 92.
Πορθαονίδας : Πορθαονίδα, v. 70.
πόρος : πόρῳ, IX. 42.
πόρπαξ : πόρπαξιν, *fr.* 46, 6.
πορσύνω : ἐπόρσυνε, XVII. 89.
πορτιτρόφος : πορτιτρόφον, XI. 30.
πορφύρεος : πορφυρέαν, XVII. 112 ;
πορφύρεον, XVIII. 52 ; πορφύρεοι, *fr.*
57, 1.
*πορφυροδίνας : πορφυροδίναν, IX. 39.
πορφυρόζωνος : πορφυροζώνοιο, XI. 49.
(πόρω) : ἔπορεν, v. 51 ; πεπρωμέναν,
III. 25, XVII. 26.
Ποσειδᾶν, XVII. 79, XX. 8 ; Ποσειδᾶνος,

Χ. 19, ΧΙV. 20; Ποσειδᾶνι, ΧVII. 36, 59.
Ποσειδάνιος: Ποσειδάνιον, *fr.* 2, I.
ποταίνιος: ποταινίαν, ΧVII. 51.
ποταμός: ποταμοῦ, ΙΧ. 65, ΧΙΙΙ. 44; ποταμῷ, ΧVI. 34; ποταμῶν, ΙΧ. 45.
ποτέ, Ι. 5, ΙΙΙ. 23, VI. 6, ΧΙ. 40, ΧΙΙ. 4, ΧΙΙΙ. 21, ΧVII. 115, ΧΧ. I.
πότερος: πότερα, ΧVIII. 33.
ποτί : see πρός.
πότμος: πότμον, V. 158.
πότνια, ΧΙΙ. 5, *fr.* 71, I.
ποῦ, ΙΙΙ. 38, 39.
που, V. 91.
ποῦς: ποδῶν, VII. 6, Χ. 20; πόδεσσι, VI. 2, ΧΙΙΙ. 53; ποσσί(ν), Ι. 7, V. 183, ΧVII. 108; ποσίν, ΧVIII. 17.
πρᾶξις, V. 163.
πράσσω: πράσσοι, V. 190; πράσσοντας, *fr.* 42, 2; πράξαντι, ΙΙΙ. 94.
πρέπω: πρέπει, ΧΙΧ. 12.
πρεσβύτατος: πρεσβύτατον, VII. 8.
Πρίαμος: Πριάμοιο, ΧΙ. 120; Πριάμῳ, ΧV. 38.
πρίν, ΧΙ. 72, ΧΙΙΙ. 81, ΧVI. 13, *fr.* 42, 3.
πρόγονος: πρόγονοι, ΧΙ. 119.
πρόδομος: προδόμοις, VI. 14.
προίημι: προίει, V. 81.
Προῖτος: Προίτου, ΧΙ. 45, 83; Προίτῳ, ΧΙ. 66.
πρόκειμαι: πρόκειται, ΧΙV. 9.
Προκόπτας, ΧVIII. 28.
προλείπω: προλείπων, V. 154.
προπάροιθε(ν), ΙΙΙ. 32, V. 148.
προπέμπω: πρόπεμπε (imperat.), ΧVII. 55; προπέμπων, ΙΧ. 34.
πρόπολος, V. 192.
πρός or ποτί : with acc., V. 45, 149, ΧΙ. 96 (ποτί), 100, ΧVI. 29 (ποτί); with dat., ΙΧ. 38 (?), ΧΙ. 23.
προσεῖδον: προσιδεῖν, V. 161.
προσεῖπον: προσεῖπεν, V. 78.
προσεννέπω: προσήνεπεν, ΧV. 9.
πρόσθε, ΙΙΙ. 47, ΧVII. 45.
πρόσπολος, ΧV. 2.
πρόσφημι: προσέφα, V. 93, 171.
προσφωνέω: προσφωνεῖ, *fr.* 5, 5.
πρότερος: πρότερον, ΧΙΙΙ. 131; προτέρων, V. 43.
προφαίνω: προὔφηνας, Χ. 20 (?); προφάνῃ, V. 77.
προφανής, ΙΙΙ. 51.
προφάτας, ΙΧ. 3; προφάται, Χ. 28.
προφέρω: προφέρειν, ΧΙ. 51.

πρόφρων, *fr.* 71, 2.
προχοά: προχοαῖσι, VI. 3.
πρύμνα: πρύμνᾳ, ΧΙΙΙ. 72.
πρύτανις: πρύτανιν, ΧΙΧ. 43 (?), *fr.* I, 19 (?).
*πρώθηβος: πρώθηβον, ΧVIII. 57.
πρών : πρῶνας, V. 67.
πρῶτος, ΧV. 47; πρῶτον, ΙΧ. 9; πρώτοις, Ι. 30; πρώτιστον, ΙΧ. 11 (?).
πτάσσω : πτάσσοντι, V. 22.
πτέρυξ : πτερύγεσσι, V. 18.
Πυθέας: Πυθέα, ΧΙΙΙ. 158.
Πυθιόνικος, ΙV. 5; Πυθιόνικον, ΧΙ. 13.
Πύθιος: Πύθιε, ΧVI. 10.
πυθμήν: πυθμένες, V. 198.
Πυθώ, ΙΙΙ, 62.
Πυθών: Πυθῶνα, VIII. 1; Πυθῶνι, V. 41.
πυκινός: πυκινάν, *fr.* 43.
πύλα : πύλαι, *fr.* 44; πύλας, *fr.* 47, 2.
πύματος : πύματον, V. 153.
πυνθάνομαι: πύθετο, ΧVI. 26.
πύξ, VI. 7.
πῦρ: πυρός, ΙΙΙ. 54, ΧVII. 105; πυρί, ΧΙΙΙ. 75, ΧVI. 14.
πυρά : πυράν, ΙΙΙ. 31.
*πυργοκέρας: πυργοκέρατα, *fr.* 73.
πύργος : πύργων, V. 148.
πυργόω : πυργωθέντα, ΙΙΙ. 13.
*πυριέθειρα : πυριέθειραν, ΧVII. 56.
πυροφόρος : πυροφόροι, *fr.* 56, 9.
Πυρρίχος : Πυρρίχου, ΧΙV. 22.
πυρσός: πυρσόν, ΧΙΙΙ. 49.
*πυρσοχαίτας: πυρσοχαίτου, ΧVIII. 51.
πω, V. 43, 122.
πῶλος : πῶλον, V. 39.
πῶμα, V. 76.

ῥά, V. 165, ΧΙΧ. 33.
ῥάδιος : ῥάδιον, ΧVIII. 43; ῥᾷστον, *fr.* 47, 2.
ῥέεθρον : ῥεέθροις, ΙΙΙ. 20, V. 64.
ῥέπω : ῥέπει, ΧVII. 25.
ῥιπά : ῥιπᾷ, V. 46.
ῥιπτέω : ῥιπτῶν, ΙΧ. 32.
ῥοά : ῥοαῖς, ΧΙΙΙ. 160.
ῥοδοδάκτυλος, ΧΙΧ. 18.
ῥοδόεις : ῥοδόεντι, ΧVI. 34.
ῥόδον : ῥόδοις, ΧVII. 116.
ῥοδόπαχυς : ῥοδόπαχυν, ΧΙΙΙ. 63 (?).

σαίνω : σαίνει, Ι. 27; σαίνουσα, *fr.* 5, 6.
σακεσφόρος : σακεσφόρον, ΧΙΙΙ. 71.
σάλπιγξ, ΧVIII. 4; σαλπίγγων, *fr.* 46, 9.
σᾶμα, ΙΧ. 14, ΧVII. 57.

R

σαμαίνω : σάμαινεν, XV. 38.
σαόφρων, XIII. 153.
σάπω : σάπεται, III. 87.
Σάρδιες, III. 27.
σαφής : σαφῆ, XVII. 75.
σβέννυμι : σβέννυεν, III. 56.
σεισίχθων : σεισίχθονος, XVIII. 22 ;.
    σεισίχθονι, XVII. 58.
σείω : σείων, XIII. 87.
σελάνα, IX. 29.
σέλας, XVII. 104.
Σεμέλα : Σεμέλαν, XIX. 48.
*σεμνοδότειρα, II. 1.
σεμνός : σεμνά, XIII. 162 ; σεμνάν, XVII.
    110 (?) ; σεμνοῦ, XI. 52 ; σεμνᾶς, V.
    99.
σεύω : σεύοντι, XVIII. 10 ; ἔσσευε, V.
    104 ; σεύοντο, III. 5 (?) ; ἐσσυμενᾶν,
    fr. 56, 2.
σθένος, VII. 7, XVIII. 40 ; σθένει, V. 107,
    IX. 37 (?), XVII. 90 (?).
σιδαρόδετος : σιδαροδέτοις, fr. 46, 6.
Σικελία : Σικελίας, III. 1.
Σικυών, X. 32 (?).
Σίνις : Σίνιν, XVIII. 20.
σιωπά, III. 95.
Σκάμανδρος : Σκάμανδρον, XIII. 132.
σκᾶπτρον, III. 70.
Σκίρων : Σκίρωνα, XVIII. 25.
σκοπέω : σκοπεῖς, III. 74.
σκότος : σκότῳ, III. 14.
σκύφος : σκύφοισιν, fr. 57, 2.
σμερδαλέος : σμερδαλέαν, XI. 56.
σός : σόν, XIII. 50, XVI. 12 ; σᾶς, IX.
    49 ; σῶν, IX. 45 ; and see τεός.
σοφία, fr. 61, 2 ; σοφίαν, fr. 51, 2.
σοφός, X. 39 (?), XII. 1, fr. 47, 1 ;
    σοφόν, XIII. 168.
Σπάρτα : Σπάρτᾳ, XX. 1.
στάδιον, VI. 7, 15 ; σταδίου, X. 21.
στάσις, fr. 62, 2.
στείχω : στείχει, IX. 47 ; στείχειν, X.
    17, XVIII. 36.
στέρνον : στέρνοισ(ι), XI. 88, XVIII.
    53.
στέφανος : στεφάνῳ, IX. 23 ; στέφανοι,
    XI. 19 ; στεφάνους, fr. 71, 4 ;
    στεφάνων, I. 20, III. 8 ; στεφά-
    νοισ(ιν), II. 10, IV. 16, VI. 8, XIII.
    22, 36 ; incert., XIX. 51.
στεφανόω : ἐστεφάνωσεν, XIII. 164 ;
    στεφανωσάμενον, XI. 29 ; στεφανωσά-
    μεναι, XIII. 58.
στῆθος : στηθέων, V. 15 ; στήθεσσι,
    XI. 54.

στίλβω : στίλβειν, XVIII. 55.
στολά : στολάν, XVIII. 32.
στορέννυμι : στόρεσεν, XIII. 96.
στραταγέτας, XVIII. 7 ; στραταγέταν,
    XVII. 121.
στραταγός : στραταγέ, V. 2.
στρατιά : στρατιάν, XVIII. 34.
στρατός : στρατῷ, III. 27.
στρέφω : ἐστρέφθη, XIII. 19 (?).
στρωφάω : στραφᾶται, XIII. 147.
στυγερός : στυγεράν, V. 111 ; στυγερῶν,
    XI. 76.
σύ, III. 92, VII. 8, XIII. 34, XVII.
    28 (?), 44, 76, fr. 55, 1 ; σέ, VI. 10,
    XVII. 29, 39, 58, XIX. 12, fr. 58 ;
    σέθεν, XI. 9 ; σέο, III. 65 ; σοί, V.
    168, XI. 2, XVII. 54 ; τοί, XI. 104,
    118, XVII. 78, XVIII. 11 ; τίν,
    XVIII. 14.
συλάω : συλᾶται, fr. 46, 10.
συμπόσιον : συμποσίων, fr. 46, 12.
συμφορά, XIV. 3.
σύν, II. 10, III. 5, 6, 33, 34, 60, 96,
    V. 8 (?), 9, 28, 52, 127, VIII. 4, IX.
    51, 85, 103, XI. 23, 63, 115, 125,
    XIII. 33, 56, 95, 150, 169, XV. 13,
    XVII. 125, XVIII. 33, fr. 1, 5.
συνετός : συνετά, III. 85.
συνεχέως, V. 113.
σύνοικος : σύνοικον, XV. 56.
Συρακόσιος : Συρακοσίαν, IV. 1 ; Συρα-
    κοσίων, V. 1.
Συράκουσαι : Συρακούσσας, V. 184.
σῦς, V. 116 ; σῦν, XVIII. 23.
σφάζω : σφάξε, V. 109.
σφέτερος : σφέτερον, XI. 50 ; σφετέρας,
    III. 36.
σφῦρα : σφῦραν, XVIII. 28.
σχάζω : ἔσχασεν, XVII. 121.
σχέτλιος : σχέτλιον, XVII. 19.
σῶμα, XVII. 62 ; σώματος, XIII. 19 ;
    σώματι, III. 91 ; σώματα, IX. 38, fr.
    57, 1.

ταινία : ταινίαι, XVII. 107.
τάκω : τᾶξεν, XVII. 86 (?).
Ταλαιονίδας : Ταλαιονίδαν, IX. 19.
τάλαντον, XVII. 25.
ταλαπενθής : ταλαπενθέα, XVI. 26 ;
    ταλαπενθέος, V. 157.
τάλας, fr. 19, 2 ; τάλαινα, XVI. 30.
τάμνω : τάμνε, XVII. 4 ; τάμνων, V. 17.
τανίσφυρος : τανισφύρου, V. 59 ; τανι-
    σφύροις, III. 60.

τανίφυλλος : τανίφυλλον, XI. 55.
τανύθριξ : τανυτρίχων, *fr.* 46, 4.
τάπης : τάπητες, *fr.* 57, I.
ταρφύς : ταρφέων, XIII. 53.
ταῦρος : ταύρους, XVI. 18.
ταῦσιος : ταῦσιον, V. 81.
τάφον : see (θάπω).
τάχα, V. 89.
τάχος, VII. 6 (?).
ταχύς : ταχύν, XIII. 68 ; ταχεῖαν, X.
  20 ; ταχείαις, V. 18 ; τάχιστα, *fr.*
  72, 3.
τε, I. 7 (?), 8, 11, 12, 14, 19, 29, 33,
  34, 35, III. 2, 3, 6, 33, 34, 50, 71,
  79, IV. 3, 17, V. 33, 34, 41, 51, 52,
  65, 80 (bis), 86, 101, 109, 117,
  129, 134, 140, 178, 180, 181, VI. 7,
  VII. 1, 6 (?), VIII. 1, 2, 8, IX. 3, 4,
  42, 63, 104, X. 18, 30, 32, 33, 34,
  44, XI. 7, 12, 66, 67, 68, 73, 86, 90,
  94, 111, 118, XII. 8, XIII. 63, 67 (?),
  68, 69, 80, 91, 96, 112, 114, 116,
  129, 147 (?), 153, 154, 155, 157,
  158 (?), 160, 163, 172, 191, XIV.
  20, 22, 23, XV. 6, 39, 59, XVI. 19,
  20, 32, XVII. 2, 8, 18, 20, 37, 50,
  51, 52, 68, 71, 74, 84, 87, 95, 100,
  109, 113, 125, XVIII. 19, 23, 24, 26,
  27, 32, 35, 38, 53, 58, XIX. 5, 45,
  XX. 9, *fr.* 5, 5 ; 6, 7 ; 46, 1, 3, 4,
  5 (bis), 8 (bis), 10 ; 47, 1 (bis) ;
  48, 4 ; 51, 2 ; 56, 5, 8 ; 57, 2 ; 59,
  1 ; 65.
τέγγω : τέγξαι, V. 157.
τεῖχος, XI. 77 ; τείχεα, XIII. 109.
τέκνον : τέκνα, XI. 102.
τέκος, VI. 13, XVIII. 22, *fr.* 45, 1.
Τελαμών : Τελαμῶνα, XIII. 65.
τελειόω : τελειοῦσαι, III. 26.
τέλεος : τελέους, XI. 92.
τελευτά : τελευτάς, X. 46.
τελευταῖος : τελευταίας, IX. 36.
τελευτάω : τελευταθεῖσα, I. 44.
τελέω : τελεῖς, III. 82 ; τελεῖ, XVII.
  78 ; τέλεσσον, VIII. 11 (?); τελεῖν,
  V. 164 ; τελεῖται, XVIII. 30, 45.
τέλος, V. 45, XI. 6.
τέμενος, XI. 48, 110, XIV. 21.
τεός : τεάν, X. 13, XVII. 21.
τέρας, XVI. 35, XVII. 72.
τέρπω : τέρπον, XVII. 107 ; τερπόμενος, XVI. 7.
*τερψιεπής : τερψιεπεῖς, XIII. 197.
τερψίμβροτος : τερψιμβρότων, XIII.
  39.

τέρψις, I. 31.
τεῦχος : τεύχεσι, V. 72.
τεύχω : τεύχει, III. 58 ; τεῦχον, XI.
  110.
τέχνα : τέχναις, XI. 33, XIII. 16.
τηλαυγής : τηλαυγέι, XVII. 5.
τίθημι : τίθησι, X. 50 (?) ; θῆκας, X.
  18 ; θῆκεν, I. 19 ; ἔθηκαν, III. 7 ;
  θέμεν, XVII. 70 ; θείμαν, V. 169.
τίκτω : τίκτει, X. 46, *fr.* 46, 1 ; ἔτικτεν,
  XIII. 64 (?); τίκτε, XIX. 50 ; τέκε(ν),
  V. 119, IX. 56, XVII. 30, 35, 54, *fr.*
  1, 17 (?).
τιμά : τιμάν, X. 39, XIII. 47, XIV. 6,
  XVII. 69, XIX. 7 ; τιμᾷ, I. 12 (?).
τιμάω : τιμᾷ, XIII. 150; τίμασεν, XIII.
  161 ; τιμῶν, XI. 74.
Τιρύνθιος : Τιρύνθιον, XI. 57.
Τίρυνς : Τίρυνθα, XI. 71.
τίς, V. 86, 89, IX. 53, XV. 47 ; τί, I.
  42, IV. 18, X. 51, XVIII. 3, II, *fr.*
  49, 1 ; τίνα, XVIII. 31, 32.
τις (enclitic), III. 21, 97, V. 5, 54,
  162, 165, 190, X. 37, XI. 27, XIII.
  51, XVIII. 5, *fr.* 48, 2 ; 63 ; τι, XIX.
  9, *fr.* 52, 2 ; τινά, X. 41, XIII. 13,
  24, 166, 190, XVII. 43 ; τινί, XVIII.
  12.
τιταίνω : τιταίνει, X. 43.
τιτύσκω : τιτύσκων, V. 49. (S.)
τλάμων, V. 153 ; τλάμονες, XIII.
  124 (?).
τόθεν, V. 197.
τόθι, III. 7 (?), 19, XVII. 101.
τοί, I. 30, V. 84, XIII. 46.
τοῖος, IX. 30.
τοιόσδε : τοιόνδε, XX. 3 ; τοιῷδε, IX.
  37 (?).
τοιοῦτος : τοιοῦτον, V. 87.
τοξόκλυτος, XI. 39.
τόξον, X. 43.
τόσος : τόσα, I. 9, III. 48, XVI. 11,
  XVII. 47 (?).
τότε, III. 58, V. 143, 156, IX. 19, XVI.
  23, XIX. 31 (?).
τραχύς : τραχύν, V. 82.
τρέφω : τρέφει, III. 92, XIII. 29 ;
  θρέψεν, V. 88, IX. 7.
τρέω : τρέσσαν, XVII. 92.
τριέτης : τριέτει, IX. 23.
τρίοδους : τριόδοντα, *fr.* 2, 2.
τρίπους : τριπόδων, III. 18.
τρισευδαίμων, III. 10.
τρισκαίδεκα, XI. 92.
τρίτατος : τριτάτᾳ, *fr.* I, 2.

τρίτος : τρίτον, IV. 4.
Τροία : Τροίας, IX. 46.
Τροιζήνιος : Τροιζηνία, XVII. 58.
τροχοειδής : τροχοειδέα, IX. 32.
Τρώς : Τρῶες, XIII. 100, XV. 50;
    Τρώων, XV. 42.
τυγχάνω : τεύξεται, X. 38; τύχον, V.
    144; τυχών, XIII. 34, XVIII. 29;
    τυχόν, IX. 83; τυχόντες, XV. 12.
τυφλός : τυφλά, V. 132.
τύχα, X. 47; τύχαν, XVII. 132; τύχᾳ,
    V. 52, XI. 115; τύχαις, IX. 51.
τῷ ('therefore'), XVII. 39.
τώς, V. 31.

ὕβρις, XV. 59; ὕβριν, XVII. 41; ὕβριος,
    XIII. 11.
ὑγίεια : ὑγιείας, I. 27.
ὑγρός : ὑγροῖσι, XVII. 108.
ὕδωρ, III. 86.
υἱός, XI. 15, XIII. 90 (?), XVI. 28,
    XVII. 86, XIX. 26, XX. 11 (?); υἱέ,
    V. 79, XIII. 35, XVII. 20, XVII. 15;
    υἱόν, II. 14, IV. 13, V. 62; υἱῷ, III.
    77 (?).
ὕλα : ὕλαν, XI. 93.
ὑμέτερος : ὑμετέραν, V. 11, 32.
ὑμνέω : ὑμνεῦσι, XI. 13; ὑμνήσει, III.
    97; ὕμνει, III. 3; ὕμνησον, V. 179;
    ὑμνεῖν, V. 33, IX. 6; ὑμνέων, VIII.
    2; ὑμνῶν (or ὕμνων), XIII. 190.
*ὑμνοάνασσα, XII. 1.
ὕμνος, VI. 11; ὕμνον, V. 10, IX. 78, fr.
    7, 6; ὕμνοι, fr. 46, 12; ὕμνους, IV.
    10; ὕμνων, IX. 83, XVI. 4; ὕμνοισιν,
    XIX. 8.
ὕπερ, XVIII. 51.
ὑπεράφανος : ὑπεράφανον, XVII. 49.
ὑπέρβιος : ὑπέρβιε, III. 37 (?); ὑπέρ-
    βιον, XIII. 42, XVIII. 19.
Ὑπερβόρεος : Ὑπερβορέους, III. 59.
ὑπέρθυμος : ὑπέρθυμον, XIII. 70; ὑπερ-
    θύμῳ, IX. 37 (?).
ὑπέροπλος, IX. 13.
ὑπέροχος : ὑπέροχον, XVII. 68; ὑπερόχῳ,
    III. 5, XIX. 44.
ὑπέρτατος : ὑπέρτατον, III. 84, XI. 36,
    XVII. 79.
ὑπερφίαλος : ὑπερφίαλον, XIII. 125;
    ὑπερφίαλοι, XI. 78; ὑπερφιάλους, XV.
    62.
ὕπνος, fr. 46, 10; ὕπνου, fr. 13, 5.
ὑπό or ὑπαί : with acc., XVII. 30;
    with gen., V. 43, X. 48, XIII. 106

(ὑπαί), 121, XVII. 17; with dat., III.
    17, XIII. 92, 133.
ὑπόκλοπος : ὑπόκλοπον, fr. 61, 1.
ὑσμίνα : ὑσμίναν, XIII. 111.
ὕστερος : ὕστερον, X. 53 (?), XVI. 33.
ὑφαίνω : ὕφαινε, XVII. 51; ὕφανεν,
    XVI. 24; ὕφαινε (imperat.), XIX. 8;
    ὕφανας, V. 9.
ὑφαιρέω : ὑφαιρεῖ, IX. 18.
*ἰψαυχάς, XIII. 51 (?).
*ὑψιάγυιος : ὑψιάγυιαν, XIII. 38.
*ὑψιδαίδαλτος : ὑψιδαιδάλτων, III. 18.
*ὑψίδειρος : ὑψιδείρου, IV. 4.
ὑψίζυγος, I. 18, XI. 3.
ὑψικέρας : ὑψικέραν, XVI. 22.
ὑψιμέδων, XV. 51.
ὑψίνοος : ὑψινόου, XIII. 11.
ὑψίπυλος : ὑψιπύλου, IX. 46.
ὑψιφανής : ὑψιφανῆ, XIV. 5.
ὑψοῦ, V. 18, IX. 84; *ὑψοτάτω, fr. 56,
    5.

φαεσίμβροτος : φαεσιμβρότῳ, XIII. 95.
φαίδιμος : φαιδίμοισι, XVIII. 47.
φαίνω, XIII. 191; φαῖνε, IX. 31;
    (ἐ)φάνη, XVII. 119, fr. 45, 2;
    φαίνων, XIII. 50.
Φάϊσκος : Φαΐσκου, XI. 14.
φάλαγξ : φάλαγγας, XV. 42.
φαμί, I. 21, XIII. 211; φασίν, V. 155;
    φάσω, I. 21, XI. 24; ἔφα, fr. 59,
    1; φάτο, V. 84; πέφαται, X. 52.
φάος, III. 80, V. 61, XVII. 43; φάη,
    IX. 28.
φαρέτρα : φαρέτρας, V. 76.
φᾶρος, X. 24; φάρεϊ, XVII. 5.
φάσγανον, XI. 87, XIII. 21 (?).
φάσκω : φάσκον, XI. 50.
φάτις, IX. 48.
φέγγος, III. 91, V. 162.
(φένω) : πέφνεν, IX. 13; ἔπεφνεν,
    XVIII. 19.
Φέρης : Φέρητος, III. 77.
*φερεκυδής : φερεκυδέα, XIII. 149, fr.
    1, 18 (?).
Φερένικος, V. 184; Φερένικον, V. 37.
φερεστέφανος : φερεστέφανοι, XIX. 6.
φέριστος : φέριστον, V. 160.
Φερσεφόνα : Φερσεφόνας, V. 59.
φέρτερος : φέρτερον, IV. 18.
φέρτατος, XVIII. 20; φέρτατον, V. 118,
    VI. 2, XVII. 33; φερτάταν, XIX. 12;
    φερτάτου, XVII. 20, XIX. 17.
φέρω : φέρει, III. 95, V. 134; φέρον,

XVII. 97; ἔνεγκε, XVII. 63; φέρων,
III. 59, V. 185; φέρουσα, II. 3, XIX.
41; φέροντες, XIII. III.
φεῦ, XVII. 119.
φεύγω: φεύγεις, *fr.* 55, 2; φεῦγε, XIX.
16; φεῦγον, V. 150, XI. 55, 84, 94;
φεύγοντα, I. 38; φυγών, XX. 7, *fr.*
69.
φήμα: φήμαν, V. 194; person., Φήμα,
II. 1, X. 1 (?).
φθέγγομαι: φθέγξατο, XV. 49; φθέγγου,
XVIII. 12.
φθίνω: φθιμένων, V. 83.
φθόνος, XIII. 167, XVI. 31; φθόνον, V.
188; φθόνῳ, III. 68.
φθόρος: φθόρον, XV. 61.
φιλάγλαος: φιλάγλαον, XIII. 191 (?);
φιλαγλάους, XVIII. 60.
φιλάνωρ: φιλάνορι, I. 12.
φιλέω: φιλεῖ, IV. 1, XIII. 171.
φίλιππος: φίλιππον, III. 69.
φιλόξεινος: φιλοξείνου, XIV. 23; φιλοξείνῳ, V. 49.
φιλοξενία: φιλοξενίας, III. 16.
φίλος: φίλον, II. 14, IV. 19, V. 131;
φίλαν, XVII. 109; φίλην, *fr.* 55, 2;
φίλῳ, XVII. 69; φίλα, III. 47; φίλας,
III. 50.
φιλοστέφανος: φιλοστεφάνῳ, XIII. 151.
φιτρός: φιτρόν, V. 142.
φλέγω: φλέγονται, *fr.* 46, 12.
Φλιοῦς: Φλιοῦντα, IX. 4.
φλόξ: φλόγα, III. 56 (?), XVIII. 56;
φλογί, *fr.* 46, 4.
φοβέω: ἐφόβησε, XI. 43.
φόβος: φόβον, XIII. 112; φόβῳ, V.
23.
Φοῖβος: Φοίβου, III. 20.
φοῖβος: φοίβαν, XIII. 106.
φοινικόθριξ: φοινικότριχας, XI. 105. (S.)
*φοινικοκράδεμνος: φοινικοκραδέμνοιο,
XI. 97; φοινικοκραδέμνοις, XIII.
189 (?).
φοινικόνωτος: φοινικονώτων, V. 102.
Φοῖνιξ: Φοίνικος, XVII. 31.
φοῖνιξ: φοίνισσαν, XVIII. 56.
Φοίνισσα, XVII. 54.
φοινίσσω: φοινίξειν, XIII. 132.
φοιτάω: φοιτᾷ, V. 133.
φόνος: φόνου, IX. 14; φόναν, III. 52.
φορέω: φορεῖ, *fr.* 61, 1; φορεῦντες, *fr.*
2, 3.
φόρμιγξ: φόρμιγγος, XIV. 13.
φραδά: φραδαῖσι, XIX. 17.
φρήν: φρένα, V. 6, XVI. 7, XVII. 131, *fr.*

43; φρενί, *fr.* 48, 3; φρένας, I. 24, XI.
45, 124, XII. 3, *fr.* 56, 3; φρενῶν,
XVII. 22; φρένεσσιν, XIV. 11.
*φρενοάρης: φρενοάραις, XVII. 118.
φρονέω: φρονέοντι, III. 85.
φροντίς: φροντίσι, XVII. 120.
Φρύγιος: Φρυγίου, VIII. 15.
φυά: φυάν, V. 168.
φυλάσσω: φυλάσσει, V. 200 (?), XIII.
156; φύλαξε, III. 29; *φυλάσσειν
(infin.), XIX. 25; φυλάσσων, V. 47.
φύλλον: φύλλα, V. 65.
φυτεύω: φύτευσε(ν), XVII. 59, 68;
φύτευσαν, XIX. 35 (?).
φύω: ἔφυ, V. 55; φῦναι, V. 160.
φωνά: φωνάν, XI. 56.
φωνάεις: φωνάεντα, *fr.* 61, 2.
φωνέω: φώνασεν, V. 191.
φώς: φῶτα, XVI. 15; φωτός, V. 158,
XVIII. 19, 30; φῶτε, XVIII. 46;
φῶτες, *fr.* 59, 3; φωτῶν, XIII. 119.

χαίτα: χαίταν, XI. 28, XIII. 37; χαίταις, XVII. 105.
χαλεπός: χαλεπόν, V. 95.
χάλκασπις: χαλκάσπιδες, XI. 62.
*χαλκεόκρανος: χαλκεόκρανον, V. 74.
*χαλκεόκτυπος: χαλκεοκτύπου, XVIII.
59.
χάλκεος: χαλκεᾶν, *fr.* 46, 9.
*χαλκεόστερνος: χαλκεοστέρνου, V. 34.
χαλκοδαίδαλος: χαλκοδαιδάλοισιν, *fr.*
2, 2.
χαλκοθώραξ: χαλκοθώρακα, XVII. 14;
χαλκοθωράκων, XI. 123.
χαλκόκτυπος, XIV. 16 (?).
*χαλκοκώδων, XVIII. 3.
χαλκός, XIII. 18 (?).
*χαλκοτειχής: χαλκοτειχέος, III. 32.
χάος: χάει, V. 27.
χάρις, III. 38; χάριν, III. 97, IX. 97,
XIV. 19, *fr.* 48, 4; χάριν (prep.),
V. 187; person., Χάριτες, IX. 1, XIX.
6; Χαρίτων, I. 13, X. 28 (?), 39;
Χαρίτεσσι, V. 9; Χάρισσιν, XV. 49.
χαριτώνυμος: χαριτώνυμον, II. 2.
χάρμα, X. 13.
χειμών: χειμῶνος, XIII. 107.
χείρ: χέρα, VIII. 3; χεῖρα, XIII. 16,
XVII. 11; χειρός, IX. 35, XIII.
121 (?), XIV. 10, XVII. 61; χεῖρε,
XVII. 72 (?); χέρας, III. 35, XIII.
105, XV. 45; χεῖρας, III. 50, XI. 100;
χειρῶν, V. 82, 132, XI. 36, 91, XVII.

45; χέρεσσι, XVIII. 49; χερσίν, V. 189.
χέρσος: χέρσον, XIII. 99.
χέω: χέον, XVII. 96; χέων, V. 15.
χθών: χθόνα, IX. 40, XVII. 80, fr. 1, 12; χθονός, IV. 4, XVIII. 5; χθονί, V. 88, XI. 32.
χιτών: χιτῶνα, XVIII. 52; χιτῶνι, fr. 55, 1.
χλαμύς: χλαμύδα, XVIII. 54.
χλωραύχην: χλωραύχενα, V. 172.
χόλος: χόλον, V. 99, 104, 123.
χολόω: χολώσατο, XVII. 50; χολωσαμένα, XI. 53.
χορός: χορόν, fr. 71, 2; χορῷ, XVII. 107; χοροί, XIV. 14, XVI. 11; χορούς, XI. 112; χορῶν, XIX. 51; χοροῖσι, XVII. 130.
χραίνω: χραῖνον, XI. 111.
χρέος, VIII. 5.
χρή, III. 78, V. 164, 187 (?), X. 56, XIV. 20, fr. 52, 2.
χρηστός: χρηστόν, X. 51.
χρόνος, IX. 80, XIII. 173; χρόνον, I. 42, fr. 41; 42, 1; χρόνῳ, VIII. 7, XI. 120, 125, XVIII. 45; person., Χρόνου, VII. 1.
χρύσαιγις: χρυσαίγιδος, fr. 52, 1.
χρυσαλάκατος, XI. 38, fr. 5, 3 (?); χρυσαλάκατοι, IX. 1.
χρυσάμπυξ: χρυσάμπυκος, V. 13.
χρυσάορος, III. 28 (?).
χρυσάρματος, XIII. 161.
χρύσασπις: χρυσάσπιδος, XX. 11.
*χρυσεόπλοκος: χρυσεόπλοκοι, XVII. 106.

χρύσεος: χρυσέα, XI. 117, XIX. 16; χρυσέαν, XVI. 2; χρύσεον, XVII. 36, 60; χρυσέας, V. 174, XV. 4; χρυσέᾳ, X. 40.
*χρυσεόσκαπτρος, IX. 100.
χρυσοδίνας, III. 44 (?).
χρυσόθρονος, fr. 22, 1 (?).
χρυσοκόμας, IV. 2.
*χρυσόπᾱχυς, V. 40.
χρυσόπεπλος, XIX. 22.
χρυσός, III. 17, 87, fr. 57, 1; χρυσόν, III. 65, fr. 51, 1; 67; χρυσῷ, fr. 56, 8.
χρώς: χρόα, XI. 97.
χώρα: χώρᾳ, V. 80.

ψεῦδος: ψεύδεσσι, XV. 57.
ψυχά, V. 77, 151, 171; ψυχᾷ, XI. 48; ψυχάς, V. 64; ψυχαῖσ(ιν), V. 83, 133.

ὦ, II. 1 (?), III. 64, VI. 13, VII. 1, VIII. 10, IX. 1, 15, 45, XI. 116, XIII. 44, 157, XV. 50, XVIII. 15, fr. 44; 58.
ὧδε, XVIII. 39; fr. 49, 1 (?); 59, 1.
ὠκύμορος: ὠκύμορον, V. 141.
ὠκύπομπος: ὠκύπομπον, XVII. 90.
ὠκύπους: ὠκυπόδων, IV. 6.
ὠμηστάς: ὠμηστᾷ, XIII. 13.
ὦμος: ὤμοις, XVIII. 47.
ὡς ('so'), V. 84, XIII. 100, XVII. 81, fr. 56, 11.
ὡς ('as'), IX. 27, XIII. 91, fr. 2, 1; 43; 56, 3; ('when'), V. 71.
ὡσεί, XII. 1.
ὥστε, XVII. 105.